CW00919626

Frank Penny

&

The Well of Darkness

THE FRANK PENNY BOOKS

Frank Penny

&

The Well of Darkness

Jeremy Elson

First published in 2022 by Oddsocks Puddles Publishing

The moral right of the author has been asserted.

Cover image copyright © Glyn Bateman

ISBN 978-1-7396613-0-4

All rights reserved. No part of this book may be reproduced,
stored in a retrieval system, or transmitted in any form, or by
any means, electronic, mechanical, photocopying, recording or
otherwise, without prior written permission from the publisher.

A catalogue record of this book is available
from the British Library.

Any resemblance to persons fictional or real,
living or dead, is purely coincidental.

Thanks M

In memory of Philip Jones – the castle of bygone hopes lives on.

Before

The Wildfire

She'd pretend to be asleep. Every night. Every endless night, while her nerves burned. And her mother would sit or lie next to her on whatever bed she found herself in this time, her gentle fingers ghosting through her untethered hair, thinking she was dreaming with the carefree abandon of all young girls.

She'd feel the comfort of her fingertips; tender, unhurried, the very opposite of the lives they led. Then the warmth of her tears and the hard edge of concealed sobs, caught in her throat, in a shallow attempt to keep them inside in case her daughter should hear.

She heard them all. Enough weeping to fill two lifetimes.

So she'd pretend, just another easy lie for a young girl, not understanding just how out of reach sleep really was. But she did it for her mother, to absorb her mother's pain, the depth of which she would never understand.

She'd stay for an hour, sometimes more, until her father beckoned her away from the bedside, her warm lips brushing her cheek.

Every night. Every endless night. Pretending. Her mother's tears stretching her wakefulness into the early hours.

Sometimes she'd sit at the top of the stairs and listen to her parent's hushed conversations, their whispers muddling her young mind, her world, her complicated world that young girls should never have to inhabit.

'I won't let it curse her like it's cursed me,' her mother whispered, concern pitiful and heavy on her fractured voice. 'Not my child.'

She had never understood, not back then and not now, now

that she was older. Exclusion had been her constant companion. But she knew, as all children do, that a curse was not a thing to be welcomed, not in her house, not in her short life.

Her mother would fret endlessly about the smallest things, about everything, about nothing, and rarely went out, preferring to confine herself to the house where she'd prowl the floor like a caged animal, constantly chewing her fingernails, pulling at the edge of the curtains. Her only respite when she played her lyre. Even then, there was nothing remotely joyous in the melodies which strung themselves throughout the house like songs from tortured souls, so she'd go out or confine herself to her room with silent pleas for them to stop.

They moved from house to house, never stopping in one place long enough for her to make any friends, the way that normal children do. At first it all seemed like a great adventure, new places, new worlds, a different town, different country but their lives always beating to the same unbearable, nervous rhythm.

But as she got older and able to think and act for herself, the constant changes became increasingly difficult to bear.

The clashes with her mother increased in regularity and in venom. Arguments that shed tears, her mother's tears. Her face clouded by ghosts, her body burdened as if her spirit had been broken by a weight that she was never fit to carry, never letting go of the reason why. The distance between them began to grow like a twisting vine, pushing slowly and unnoticed until they were strangers in the same house; she would sit in her own room, her own world, her escape, and dream of a life when she was old enough, away from her suffocating mother. Alone. Free. Happy.

So she waited, and pretended to be asleep.

Then *she* burst into her world. Like a wayward meteor. Full of colour and laughter.

A chance meeting by the lake where she lived and she was completely hooked. She was everything she'd ever wanted to be, the image she'd tried so desperately hard to see in the mirror day after day but always failed; the life she'd led in her head for as long as she could remember. Anti-establishment, unafraid, hopelessly carefree with a beauty beyond her teenage dreams. Becky wasn't *like* wildfire – she *was* wildfire. Completely untamed. Completely feral. Completely without boundaries. No more than a few days in her company and rebellion bit her hard; sending her beyond the margins of unruly, the confines of the years spilling out in a new found confidence on the heels of the young maverick that had entered her life, uninvited. They immediately became best friends, completely inseparable; tearing up the neighbourhood like unruly twins with no thought or heed of the consequences.

Becky taught her. Skills and secrets no one else could possibly have imagined or understood. But she did, as if something had lay buried beneath her skin waiting to be discovered by this gorgeous rebel. They grew together; the perfect couple and, for the first time, she began to create a thin but sweet layer of normality as the blank pages of her life story began to fill with the vivid colour it had always lacked. Until now.

And her adolescent fire was lit. She felt her skin spark and her blood ignite just at the thought of being with her. The way she played with her wild blonde hair, slow and sultry, twisting it around her fingers as she spoke; the way she teased her tongue between her teeth when she smiled; the way she'd throw her head back and laugh with unedited abandon and the way she moved her small, slender figure like a the stem of a lily in the breeze.

When they weren't together her stomach churned, tightening at their separation, restless for the nights to end so she could consume herself with her newly-discovered treasure once more.

The days together seemed without end, time spent walking around the lake, swimming naked in the cold water, touching the goose-bumps on each other's young skin, feeling the warm ache of desire amidst the long, cold, innocent touch. The deep long look in her eyes that spoke a thousand words of how she felt.

The first kiss had set her alight, turning her bones to ice and fire at the same time; lasting for a lifetime but over too soon. Unfamiliar, yet like she'd known it forever and all the time she kept wondering how long the dream would last. They'd lay on Becky's bed in the tiny cottage by the lake, gazing into the aching depths each other's eyes and swore to each other that nothing would tear them apart. Ever.

And Becky's mother wasn't like her own; the short, hardy woman whose gruff curses easily concealed her kindness let them do just as they pleased, with a freedom even her dreams couldn't begin to conjure. She would always vouch for them, when the authorities came knocking, on the occasions when they weren't caught and hauled back home where her own mother would show her usual lack of understanding.

But this time her family stayed. Maybe it was because her mother saw a new colour in her daughter. A spark of starlight about which she could never ask and although her mother remained anxious, the summer passed in the kind of idyllic freedom she'd always believed was reserved for others.

But then the winds changed.

As the days darkened, so did her mother. She could sense the change at home, in her mother's behaviour. Sense the unsettling atmosphere, the familiar signposts and the pathway to which they pointed. The increase in the cleaning, the lack of melody through the house from her mother's playing, more standing at the window watching as the invisible spectre that forever followed them neared, threatening to call.

The day had been soft and green, spent by the shimmering crystal of the lake, the fading early autumn sun keeping them from the eyes of the world. They laid down their unbreakable bond, writing it, encircling it with a magical heart, believing it could never be broken. She'd kept one half, Becky the other, two parts of the same token, understood by those who knew the true meaning of their love. She would keep it always, its touch reminding her of what it was like to be so alive in the arms of another. But Becky's perfection left her unprepared as she skipped through the front door, to be confronted by her father packing their things into the worn and scuffed cases that told the story of a life drifting on the wind. Her life.

She took the stairs two at a time, finding her mother in her bedroom. She stood in the door and felt the anger on her skin. She could barely make eye contact, but her mother didn't stop, stalking her room to pack her clothes, making no attempt at tidiness, the drawers left open and hanging.

'I'm not going.' She could taste the bitterness in her words. Her mother's haunted eyes just looked through her, to the unpacked clothes in the drawer and kept on. 'Didn't you hear me? I'm not going.'

'You don't have a choice, we have to.'

'Where are we going?' Her question met with silence. 'Why? Why do we have to move all the time?' Her mother's weary, lifeless eyes stopped on her.

'You wouldn't understand; you're —'

She snapped, her voice high, wielded like a razor. 'What? What am I? Still a child?' Her mother's face tensed. 'Only because you still treat me like one,' she shrieked. 'I'm nearly sixteen.'

'I said...'

'I heard what you said.' She felt her blood start to simmer, her fists clench at her sides. 'What's this all about, Mum. What are you so *afraid* of?' She pinned her eyes on her mother. A stare that wished her dead. Her mother flinched but still refused to share the burden she carried. Only the sound of heavy breathing fractured the silence. Her mother went for the door, but still she blocked the way.

'I don't want to go. I have a life here now, a friend. My first real friend.'

'I'm sorry, but we leave in the morning, it's too dangerous here.'

Her emotions boiled over. 'I hate you. I wish you were dead.' No regrets at her words, designed to more than wound. 'I'll stay. Stay with Becky. I'd do anything for her and she'd do anything for me.'

Her mother stopped, looked lost in her thoughts but, before she could answer, the pile of clothes was knocked from her arms and

11

the doorway emptied.

She'd fled the house. Desperate tears swept down her face as she ran, ran all the way to the little cottage by the lake, to the only person who truly understood her.

She pressed herself into her arms. Her last evening breathing in Becky's beauty; her golden braids and blue eyes sparkling in the moonlight. She couldn't bring herself to look into them, couldn't bear that her mother would tear her from her salvation as if she were ripping at her heart, but that's how she felt. In Becky she had been rescued but now, lying next to her on the warm grass by the lake, perhaps for the last time, she felt truly alone.

'You're troubled,' Becky said. An observation rather than a question. Her eyes burned as she forced a smile; tears ran hot and fast down her pale cheeks and her resolute emotional wall, unerring throughout her childhood, crumbled under Becky's sweet smile. There was no judgement, no questions as she held her and kissed the tears from her face, each a reminder of what she was going to lose. She told her everything – of the unknown reason for her mother's torment, how her feelings crushed in from both sides at the thought of being prised from the girl she'd found and loved; the pity she felt for a life on the run and how she could rip her mother's throat out at the same time for taking her away from the only whisper of happiness she'd known. As she listened, Becky stroked her face so gently she could barely feel it, yet it set her alight.

'I wish she was dead,' she said. 'Dead. So I could stay here, with you.'

Becky paused, then ran her fingertips over the worried lines of her brow, over her cheeks and breathed the words gently.

'You know I'd do anything for you,' she said, her warm breath moistening her ear, the barest touch of her lips sending a single hot shiver through her.

'I know,' she said, her words barely audible over the slight ripple of breeze on the water. Becky sat up and held her head between her hands, turning her face towards her, locking her eyes with a hard intensity that made her freeze, made her feel a little frightened without knowing why.

'No, you don't understand.' Despite the sweet smile, Becky's voice was suddenly serious. 'I mean it. *Anything.*'

1

THE RAGE

Frank pushed the heels of his hands into his eyes and tried to slow his breathing; tried to hollow out the dark anger in his head, tried to make it bleed quickly from him. The glass jar lay smashed against the wall, the spilled liquid on the floorboards leaching like a dark phantom towards him. He got to his feet and paced the small bedroom, grabbing at his hair, then dumping himself down on the bed again, the sliver of early morning light that the curtains let through ran down his face; an angry scar.

The vile image he'd just thrust away started to hunt him; a restless beast, snarling at his heels. He was unable to think, unable to breathe, unable to believe that Blackburn's clever formula had revealed he was the son of Dagmar Dag. Relentless hot emotion surged through him, unabated; pitching him sideways and he could never imagine it stopping.

He jumped to his feet again, hesitating before punching the wall, feeling unusual comfort in the pain. He punched again, letting out the shout that brewed in his lungs. And again, then leaned his head against the wall, knocking his forehead gently, eyes tight shut to will away the horror. Still the image taunted him, wouldn't leave, wouldn't let itself be unseen. He licked at the grazed knuckle, sucking on the sweetness as he bled.

He caught his reflection in the mirror. He stared, focused; unfocused. The face was familiar but in the few minutes that had lain waste to his existence he didn't recognise himself, didn't know who he was anymore. Rage ran hot under his skin, bending his mind in different directions. They lied; they were all liars. And his dad was the greatest liar of them all.

Despite the hour he was tired to his guts. A heavy consuming tiredness that clung to his skull and fogged his mind. The pressure inside his head was unbearable. He needed air, something to cleanse him. He needed to get out but, more than anything, he needed someone who could make sense of all of this, who could give him answers he couldn't hope to find by himself, who could tell him this wasn't happening, to stop his young life disintegrating before his eyes before it was too late. But there was only one person who could tell him but, at that moment, he could never imagine setting eyes on him again, so deep and red was his rage.

He grabbed his bag and headed downstairs, taking two steps at a time, thunder in every thud of his feet. Knox would be arriving soon, tasked with taking him back to Smithwood. He wouldn't go. Not for all the gold in Byeland.

He was relieved to find that Polly was in the shop at the front, preparing for opening but Maddy sat at the table with another girl, doing a jigsaw. Both looked up as he rushed into the room; Maddy's reluctant smile and the smear of freckles on the other girl's face looked back at him. Neither spoke.

'Can you tell your mum I'm going to stay at my gran's for a bit,' he said, hoisting his bag further on to his shoulder and turning towards the back entrance, flexing his hand against the pain.

'But aren't you going home today?'

Frank looked at Maddy and had to stop the anger in him biting at her. 'No,' he said. 'I'm not,' before turning and heading out.

'But what about Mr Knox...'

But Frank had gone, out into the street, into the warmth of the mid-morning, determination in his steps, trying to clear the thick fog of confusion that wouldn't leave him.

The side streets around Murgatroid square were quiet, although had they been as crammed as they were during the week of the festival, Frank wouldn't have noticed. He stopped. People passed unnoticed as he wondered what he was going to do. He wasn't sure he wanted to go to his gran's, he wasn't certain where he was headed, he just felt like he was falling, not knowing when he was going to hit the ground. He began to wander aimlessly through the streets of Rhaeder; familiar, yet he felt like a stranger, a stranger in his own life peering helplessly in at the shambles, at the aftermath of the disaster yet to be picked through.

He walked up Iron Lane and stopped at the edge of the marble plaza, looking over to the academy and the great stone vulture that kept guard. Just looking at the place made him boil, simmering hatred for the place that had brought him into contact with the Simbrian, with Dagmar, with everything he now despised. He grabbed a small rock from the ground and headed across the plaza and, once within reach of the huge statue he hurled it with as much venom as he could muster. It bounce off the underside of the vulture with little more than a faint thud. It was laughing at him, they were all laughing at him. Well, he didn't need them and they could all go to hell.

2

THE LOVE LETTER

The view across the lake began to take the edge off his anger. The gentle hills that ascended on either side were soft and green and flecked with pink and purple from the heather, reflected perfectly across the water's rippled surface. He sat, arms folded across his knees and felt the cool of the breeze that blew down the valley, caressing his face, a soothing balm that brought some calm away from the confines of the town. His eye was drawn to the flitting of a dragonfly as it skimmed the water. Everything looked just as it should, but everything was different.

'Frank?' He turned; his gran stood at her back door, her squinting eyes fixed on him. He turned his head towards her, gave her the briefest of looks and turned back to the lake, unsurprised at the brusque footsteps that followed, approaching him from behind. 'I thought you were going home today?'

'Well, I decided to stay for a bit.' He didn't look at her, but could sense her stare on him. He imagined the shrug in her shoulders as she turned and headed back to the cottage.

'I'll get you some cake,' she said.

Frank stayed looking across the water. He stood, picking up a handful of large stones scattered at his feet. He threw the first one in, then another, harder, more venom in the recoil of his arm. Then the next, until he'd thrown them all and he could hear the blood pumping in his ears and his short breath through his nose. He closed his eyes, tried to relax and stop the gradual fraying of his emotions, then headed into the cottage.

His gran had some limewater and fruit cake on the table, as if

17

she knew he'd come in, given time. If she'd seen him trying to bust the lake with the rocks she didn't say anything and he found the quiet of her kitchen calming. None of this was her fault, so he tried to push the events of the morning from his mind.

'I see Phanderas has gone then.' He couldn't have missed the huge black stag, even if his mind wasn't entirely focused. His gran nodded as she stood at the sink, carelessly bashing some empty dishes as she washed them up.

'Got himself up and off to unwanted island yesterday,' she said. 'Best place for him and Menetti will look after him, although I was getting used to having him around the place.' She turned and grabbed a tea-towel. 'Something on your mind?' She didn't look at him or break the rhythm of her voice. Frank just took a bite of cake. Iris didn't appear concerned about his lack of response, instead, she grabbed a crust of bread and, stepping to the back door, threw it out into the early afternoon sun where Ingozi lay against the outside wall. She paused, her eyes staring to the lake, before turning to him.

'You know, your dad'll be worried if you don't go home,' she said. Frank felt himself tense. 'If you've got a problem with him, you'd best talk it over.' He avoided her old weather-beaten eyes, giving her all the confirmation she needed. She let out a breath through her nose. 'Never mind. Anyway, I've got something interesting for you. I found something that belonged to your mother.'

With a seamless flick of her unusual conversation skills, she veered Frank to the nearest side-street and down the road of a completely different subject, whether by design or not Frank couldn't really tell as she carried her diminutive frame through into the living room.

Frank stuffed some more cake into his mouth and followed her in to see her reaching for a small box on a shelf. She sat in her old wooden chair and placed the box in her lap. She looked at it, holding it still in her hands with unusual care like it might disintegrate if she dropped it. She rubbed the tips of her fingers over the polished wooden lid which was inlaid and patterned with orange and black intertwining circles. Her fingers followed the pattern with just the faintest of sounds, like a whisper on a still night.

'These are the letters your dad wrote to your mum.' She didn't look up. Frank stared at the box, thoughts of Dagmar slipping silently, unnoticed, from his thoughts. 'I found them the other day when I was clearing out one of my bedroom cupboards. I've not read very many, just a few to know what they are. Not really a mother's place to read her daughter's personal things. I'd never look at her diary when she was a teenager. It's important for kids to have their secrets; I'm sure it's the same with you.' She raised her eyes, then held the box out to Frank.

He took it gently, embracing it as he would an injured bird. The corners of the lid were worn and scuffed, faded with wear, from his mother's touch. He lifted the lid up an inch, peering through the thin gap into the dark interior. The dull, fusty scent of aged paper rose in the air, making him sniff. He flipped the box open, breathing in the heartache of a stash of treasure he never imagined he'd get to see. The underside of the lid was lined with patterned paper the shade of daffodils.

He looked at the top piece of paper; scruffy black ink, smudged in places, filled the page. Blots, large and small punctuated the spidered lettering that slanted to the right. Unmistakeably his dad's handwriting; he recognised it immediately and was instantly brushed with both the tender shiver of fondness and the crimson burn of resentment. He lifted it from the box and scanned it quickly, turning it over. The letter was a single sheet, written on one side, the other blank. The letter started with "My sweetheart Becky" and was signed with a simple letter "L", together with a small, badly drawn heart.

His grandmother looked on in awkward silence.

'Do you mind if I take these outside?' said Frank.

'I think that would be for the best, Frank,' she said with a thick slice of relief. 'No good having your grandmother looking over your shoulder when any fool should know these are best read on your own. I hope they'll show you how much they meant to each other. Go on. It's a lovely day. You take your time, Frank; come back when you're ready, I'm not going anywhere.'

Frank put the letter back in the box and closed the lid. Given what he'd just found out, his gran's timing could have been better. Nevertheless, he gave his gran a fond, thankful smile and went outside into the sunshine and over to the lakeside, sitting on his favourite fishing spot.

The day glowed warm and pleasant, the heat wave during the festival had waned and there was a slight, comforting breeze that picked at his hair. Ingozi followed Frank out and plonked himself clumsily on the warm flat rock next to Frank, looking out from under his saggy black brow. Frank put the box down on the rocks beside him. He leaned down and brushed the surface of the water, feeling its cooling balm. A small fish rose to kiss his fingers, then darted to the depths.

He sat for a few minutes, gearing himself up before the inevitable foray into the contents of the box. His long breaths told him he wasn't sure he was ready to see the most intimate jottings from his dad. His dad? He wasn't sure he even knew what that meant anymore.

Frank looked down to the box, catching Ingozi's eye.

'What are you looking at?' The dog raised its eyes. Frank huffed and picked the box up, flipping the lid open, running his fingers along the edge of the yellow lining paper before lifting the pile of letters out.

There were about two dozen in all. Frank read each one, taking his time to draw in the most personal words of his teenaged father. The passion within them stirred something in Frank, the depth of feeling his dad had for his mum was undeniable. And she'd kept them all, she hadn't discarded them like they were just the jottings of a love-struck young man. Each one was carefully folded and placed inside the box away from the prying eyes of her mother. The final one was short:

Becky,

Please don't go.

If you do, I don't know what I'll do. The thought of not seeing you again is tearing me apart.

I know you don't love him.

Please stay. Please.

L

There it was, with a palpable sense of pleading. He didn't need to stretch his mind too far to know what it was about, where his mum was going, and who she was going to. Frank re-read and re-read, felt himself wrestling with his thoughts, wondering what their relationship was really like, what had happened to drive her across the border and into the arms of Dagmar. The letter made it seem very real.

He grasped the lid and went to shut the box but, as he did, he caught his thumbnail under the patterned paper, cursing to himself as it tore slightly. He swore again; the box had survived for years with his gran but ten minutes with him and he'd already damaged something beyond precious.

He pushed the paper back up, hoping it would stick back to the lid but it was no good. He'd have to fix it. He gave it a close inspection, checking the damage and trying to console himself that he'd be able to repair it when he noticed something unusual between the lining and the lid; the corner of a slip of paper nestled innocently in the opening he'd carelessly created.

He turned the box up and gave it a slight shake to move the trapped piece of paper forward. After a few further gentle shakes, the corner of the trapped paper protruded slightly from the gap in the lining, enough for him to tease it between his thumb and forefinger. He pulled at it gently, but it was immediately apparent it was too big to fit through. With no other option, he gave a sigh and carefully tore the lining paper along the edge and eased out the hidden sheet. He paused for a moment, staring at the single folded sheet of paper clasped tightly between his thumb and forefinger, wondering why his mum might have kept it hidden, then slowly opened it up.

He wasn't sure what he would find but, as he unfolded it, he realised it was just another handwritten letter. He thought it might have just got stuck inside the lid lining and had stayed there ever since, long forgotten amongst its paper companions – but the lining had been sealed.

Frank shrugged and was about to place it back in the box with the others when he realised there was something different about it. The handwriting – it wasn't his dad's, it was written in a different hand. This time, the script was neat and upright, vaguely familiar although he couldn't recall exactly where, or if, he'd come across it before. And there was something else. Although the message appeared complete, the page had been torn in half, the bottom section missing. He read:

> *Becky*
>
> *My first love*
>
> *You are my breath, my blood, my bones.*
>
> *Our bond will not break.*
>
> *Whenever we are apart, we shall never be.*
>
> *The hand of the earth and the breath of the wind both bear witness to this solemn vow.*
>
> *As I am you and you are me.*
>
> *Forever, without end.*

He absorbed the prose, the words a thing of beauty, the bare passion and emotion, a window into the soul of whoever wrote them. He couldn't imagine writing something so simple yet so intricate to anyone, not even Libby. He noticed how the ends of the y's looped in an unusual way and the i's were topped with small circles rather than dots. It looked like the work of a talented artist.

Encircling the writing was a large, hand-drawn red heart, incomplete where the paper had been torn in two across the centre of the page. Frank prised the lid lining open to see if the other half had got stuck inside, he shook it with a couple of sharp jolts. Without the paper packing the inside of the thin compartment, something else moved inside the lid; not paper, something small but solid, heavier. He shook it some more until a small, coin sized object fell from the box, bounced on his lap and sank in the shallows of the lakeside with a hollow splash, sending ripples out across the surface of the water.

Frank bent down quickly as the tiny waves cleared and dipped his hand into the cool water, feeling its bite, grabbing the object as it lay, blurred and innocent, under the water. He pulled it out and opened his hand, familiarity jolting him as he looked down on the black disc, edged in gold – a Dahke pass. Exactly like the one Dagmar had given him in Kzarlac weeks before, the strange permit that would allow unrestricted and unquestioned access and travel in and across Kzarlac to anyone who produced it.

He rubbed his thumb across the wet surface, feeling the relief of the scorpion image on one side, then turned it over. The token bore the number one – the first Dahke pass? Was that right? Whatever he thought, this vanished any doubt he might have had that his mum had been to Kzarlac. There was simply no other way she would have come to possess it. A potent symbol of her past, of his past and he suddenly felt a separation from his dad, a wide chasm that he might find impossible to bridge and, despite the words, both spoken and unspoken in his letters to his mum, the rage started to bubble beneath his skin. However much he tried not to think about it, he felt the pull of his new-found connection to Kzarlac and the lure of the Simbrian and Dagmar's promise of bounty beyond his wildest dreams.

Dagmar, the image he couldn't dispel. Telling him time and time again through his ruthlessness that his dad was a coward, that Frank didn't really know him and now the feeling burned as bright as the orange streak in his hair. Dagmar was right, he didn't really know anything.

He inspected the scorpion symbol, his mind taking him back

to the chamber where he'd witnessed the awesome power first-hand and wondered if the signposts in his short life pointed in one direction, to Alsha Kar, Dagmar and the Simbrian.

He shook himself back to the present, cursing through his teeth, clenching his fists against his disbelief that he could even conjure such black thoughts. He couldn't believe how far down the winding slope into darkness he'd just travelled. Cursing again, he thrust the letter and Dahke pass into his pocket, flipped the lid of the box shut and headed back up to the cottage.

'Find out anything you didn't know,' said Iris.

Frank kept quiet as he handed the box back to her, but caught the furrows on her ancient brow as he dumped himself onto the sofa. He remembered that she'd told him his mother had never visited Kzarlac. Did she know but kept it from him, to protect him? He felt just a hint of distrust which he quickly brushed away as he held up the torn letter he'd discovered in the lid of the box. He looked at it, then to his gran.

'Gran, do you recognise the writing on this letter?' He held it out for her and she took it in her arthritic fingers.

She screwed up her eyes and held the letter as far away from her riven old face as her arms would allow. She shook her head.

'Like I've said to you before, Frank, you kids need your secrets. Looks like your mum had hers.'

That would be the understatement of the century, thought Frank.

3

THE MAP

Frank stayed a few days at his gran's, penning a short note to his dad, telling him he'd decided to stay in Rhaeder so he didn't need to be concerned and appear at Polly's unannounced, each word forced from the end of his pencil.

Iris made him feel welcome and made a fuss of him, but his restlessness persisted and he could tell she knew there was something eating at him. But she didn't pry, just asking here and there if he was alright and leaving him to his own thoughts, on which he stewed.

He heard her mumble something about moody teenagers when he became particularly grumpy one evening but he dismissed the occasional thought that he should tell her and decided to head back to Rhaeder to see if time spent with Libby might lift his mood, but even the thought of being entwined with her failed to relieve him of the constant shadow that rested easily over him.

Polly was pleased to see him back as was Maddy, who seemed to have become more attached to the freckle-faced girl Frank had seen her with the day he'd stormed out.

'I told Mr Knox you'd decided to stay on a bit,' said Polly as she wiped down the kitchen worktops. 'He's a strange one, that man. I felt sorry for him so I offered him an iced bun. You should have seen the look on his face, Frank. It was as if I'd asked him out on a date.' She whooped at her own words and went back to her cleaning. At least she had dragged a smile from him. He went for the door, determined to go and see Libby; for her to kiss the shade from him.

'Oh, Frank,' said Maddy. 'This arrived for you yesterday.' She leaned across the table and picked up an envelope, glancing at the writing on the front as she handed it to him.

Frank immediately recognised Gabby's awful writing. He breathed in and closed his eyes. In all the confusion that surrounded him, he felt a twinge of something good for the first time in days, the warm touch of the familiar, of those who understood him. He wrestled with his thoughts and decided to leave Libby until later.

He took the letter upstairs, closing the door to his bedroom before jumping on his bed and carefully sliding his finger under the flap. After the time spent at his gran's, he thought he might be a little weary of reading letters, but he hoped this one would pick him up a little. He pulled the letter out, unfolded the paper and smiled as he read.

> *Dear Frank,*
>
> *I hope you are okay and your chat with Spargo revealed what we needed to know. Sorry we couldn't all stick around to find out.*
>
> *Has our little book revealed anything interesting, now that we know Spargo is the next guardian? I hope it has.*
>
> *It's good to be home, although mum keeps nagging me to protect my academy stuff with something called thief's spite so no one nicks it. I keep telling her I'd prefer if they did, then I wouldn't have to go anymore – ha ha!*
>
> *Anya thinks she's right, but we all know about her lack of forecasting ability.*
>
> *I can't believe we'll be back in a week or so, but at least the summer was fun.*
>
> *See you soon, Frankie and don't go getting into any trouble, not before we get back.*
>
> *Miss you*
>
> *Gabby xxx*

Frank turned the letter over in his hands and felt a smile tug at his mouth. Gabby's words had instantly lifted his permanent daze. He smiled at the thought of her mum pestering her, an image he didn't find hard to conjure and was certain Gabby, like most sixteen year olds, would resist anything she was told to do. And Anya *was* probably the most unreliable forecaster Excelsus had ever let through its doors and they now knew that her abilities were in the art of unarmed combat rather than in telling the future. So much for Excelsus.

Even so, he was warmed by the letter and felt strangely pleased that Gabby missed him, trying not to read anything into the three kisses she'd put at the foot of her note. He wondered whether he should respond and tell her about what had happened since they went their separate ways, but what exactly would he say? "Hello Gabby, hope your summer is going well. By the way, I thought you should know that Dagmar's my dad."

No, he wasn't going to tell them. He wasn't going to tell anyone.

He sighed, picturing Gabby's dark hair and the variety of unique metalwork that adorned her face. He pictured Libby, her teasing smile, the shine of her auburn hair and the emerald of her eyes that swallowed him up and felt a hard wrench of guilt. Nothing was easy.

He re-read the letter. He'd forgotten all about their book, the strange pages that revealed, one by one, clues to the guardians of the Simbrian.

He put the letter down on his bedside table and pulled open the small drawer. The book sat together with the short metal skewer that the unfortunate Sapphire Hark had given him before her enchanted hideout in the middle of Alsha Kar had been raided by Dagmar. Then there was the powder-white, lace-edged handkerchief that had been the property of the troubled Edwina Chetto that he'd used to dab her unsettled brow before he had fled her bedroom in her grand house. Both were barbed and painful reminders of what he had endured during their few days in Kzarlac, of the people he'd encountered and the horrible price they'd paid for their part in keeping the world a safer place. They'd ultimately failed, no thanks to Frank and the others. He owed it to them not to do the same.

He turned the book over in his hands. In the hands of Wordsworth Hums it had looked almost new. Now it bore the battle scars of their two year quest. The leather cover, once a clean, pale purple, was scuffed and worn and looked fit for the dustbin. Flicking the pages open, Frank stopped at the image of the peacock feather, the picture that marked his dad as one of the guardians of the Simbrian. His breath stuttered as his eyes froze. Liar. He felt the heat rising in his blood.

He turned the page, hoping the book would lead them on, that it would reveal the next symbol that represented the sixth guardian. His heart sank. It was blank, but he wasn't surprised — Spargo wasn't the one they were looking for. He knew that now and it likely meant that he'd have to see his dad if they wanted the book to reveal what they needed. The thought jabbed him. Two left to reveal, thought Frank, knowing that Dagmar only needed to find one. Was Dagmar's missing guardian his dad? The one Dagmar sought? He contemplated the implications of his own question. He didn't know. Didn't care.

With a long sigh, he rippled the remaining pages with an indifferent flick of his thumb. He knew what he would find. The chalk-white paper was flecked with blots, stains and an odd collection of shapes and symbols that, so far, meant nothing to him or his friends. They knew it was meant to be some kind of enchanted text, Gabby's mum had confirmed that, but the whole thing was still a complete mystery.

He could feel his interest beginning to drip from him as he turned to the final few pages when his attention was caught by something staring out at him from inside the back cover. He let the page drop open and felt himself sit up and take notice as he found himself staring at the intricate detail of a hand-drawn map.

4

THE HAND

He studied it, intoxicated by how beautifully sketched and coloured it was. It appeared to show an area of woodland, the size of which was difficult to gauge, extending across the page to the blue of the sea to an unbroken chain of high, sheer cliffs. A bold, dark line ran across the middle of the trees, snaking from one edge of the page to the other, dividing the woodland in two. The trees under the line were a sharp shade of green, while above it they were shaded in dark grey. The word *Irundi* was inked in amongst the ashen trees with an arrow pointing to a picture of a circular turret. At the bottom of the page the words *'beware the queen of the forest'* had been written in an assured hand.

Frank shook his head, wondering if his eyes were deceiving him. He also knew the map had never been there previously. Or did he? During their quest, they'd only ever looked beyond the page of the symbol that represented the guardian they'd just discovered. Now he thought about it, neither he nor the others had really looked through the whole of the book since soon after they'd met Hums just over a year ago.

They'd not bothered because of the blots and lines that were indecipherable and they hadn't seen the need. They'd just concentrated on the first few pages and the symbols that marked the guardians. So the map he now stared at could have been there for months, hidden from view, perhaps giving them an important clue of some kind.

Frank's eyes wandered over the small page, checking he wasn't missing anything. He knew finding the map was one thing, knowing what it showed or what it meant would be another task, one he wasn't in the mood for. Why whoever wrote the thing couldn't just tell them what they wanted to know in short, simple sentences or just place the map in a more obvious place pinched him with annoyance, putting an extra spark to his temper.

He let out a long, vexed breath which is when he noticed an unusual image on the opposite page. If he hadn't been studying the map so closely he would have missed it, it was so faint, white on white but he could just make out an outline of a hand, the fingers splayed slightly.

He held the image closer, then rubbed his fingertips gently across the picture, wondering if it had some other quality not visible to the naked eye. Nothing. Another long and peeved breath left his nostrils but, then, he noticed the outline change slightly. It glowed, ever so slightly, but he was certain it had. He slowly traced the outline with the tip of his index finger, trapped in concentration before the edges of the hand shimmered once more. He hadn't imagined it and it felt like the page was calling to him.

On impulse, Frank placed his palm flat on the page, pressing it gently, his hand wholly within the glowing outline. Instantly the image flamed, taking Frank completely off guard and unprepared for the sudden acute stinging pain that burned through his palm, up his arm and scattered into his chest. His breathing faltered in shock and he immediately went to pull his hand from the page, but it stuck hard. The paper held it fast, grabbed him unwillingly, his hand adhered to the surface as a wave of shocks ran up his arm in hot pulses.

Then, as quickly as it had started, it stopped. He ripped his hand away, expecting the flesh to be torn from his fingers, and threw the book across the room where it thumped the door and fell to the floor, the map ripped from the back of the book where he'd been holding it. Grabbing his wrist, he turned his palm towards him, fingers splayed and tense, the agony still hot on his skin.

Shock replaced pain as he looked at the unusual symbol that

was burnt into his palm. The outline pulsed and glowed slick black back at him, raising itself from his flesh; he sat transfixed, unable to tear his eyes away from the elaborate array of concentric circles centred around what looked like a letter K. He let the fingers from his right hand travel across the image, feeling its indelible mark in sharp relief, an unwanted magical brand that held his gaze captive. Then the image began to dull, fade. The clear, defined, raised outline paled, blurring and seeping away at the edges and drifting back into the white of his hand before the whole thing just disappeared before his astonished eyes.

Frank turned his hand over and back again but the image was gone. The palm of his hand, aflame with the sting of a dozen trapped hornets not a minute earlier, looked like nothing had happened to it; there was no sign of the enchanted assault he'd just been subjected to.

He got up from his bed, walked the few steps to the door and stood over the book which had landed cover-side up. He poked at it with his toe, then pushed it over with his foot and took a step back. The pages lolled open and lay there, benign. He bent down and picked it up, careful not to touch the outline of the hand a second time then sat back on the bed; he'd forgotten to breathe and exhaled loudly.

An inexplicable urge to place his hand back on the page surged through him. His caution left him and, with a deep breath he thrust his palm back onto the page and felt his whole body tense, awaiting the pain that had consumed him moments earlier. Nothing happened. He looked at his palm again; the strange symbol wasn't there.

Frank slumped onto the bed. A tired river coursed through him. If he were to shut his eyes he was sure he'd never find the energy to open them again.

This whole journey had already cost him enough, cost him his happy home life, his carefree teenage spirit and his identity. He snapped the book shut, opened the drawer of his bedside table and threw it in, slamming it shut with as much contempt as he could muster, along with any lingering interest in his search for the remaining two guardians.

5

THE DISCLOSURE

Frank curled himself up on his bed, nursing his simmering temper. The ripped-out map stared up at him from his bedroom floor, mocking him. He stared back, trying to decide what he should do. The others weren't going to be back for a few weeks and he definitely wasn't going home. He craved the welcoming arms of Libby, the one person who knew nothing about their quest, who could draw his mind away from anything with her sensual lips and warm embrace.

He drew in a sharp breath and got to his feet, grabbing the map, resisting the sudden urge to shred it into small pieces. Instead, he took a good look at it again, willing it to combust, before shoving it in his trouser pocket and heading downstairs. He poured himself a glass of water and gulped a few mouthfuls. The house was quiet. Maddy and her friend had disappeared, leaving half-empty glasses on the dining room table.

Polly burst in, her round face like a pale cherry.

'Oh my goodness, it's so busy out there today,' she said, drawing the back of her hand across her forehead.

'Can I give you a hand?' He hoped she wouldn't need one, relieved when she waved him away.

'Don't worry yourself, handsome,' said Polly. 'You get off and see that young lady of yours.' Frank nodded, as if Polly had read his mind.

Polly was right. As Frank opened the through-door to the teashop, the sound of blended conversations, each undiscernible, jabbed and poked at the air. A sea of relaxed and smiling faces greeted him, each one engaged in its own private chatter. Amused tones and shades of laughter consumed the small café. Raised hands signalled Polly over and Frank saw Maddy helping at the counter, her pale cheeks flushed with the lunchtime rush. He hesitated, knowing he should help; perhaps it would take his mind off of things, although he was sure Libby would do a better job of that.

Polly looked over and caught his eye, flicking her head in the direction of the teashop door, silently telling him to go. Frank dipped his head in acknowledgement and made his way through the litter of tables. He grasped the door handle and was about to open it, to escape the crowd and head to Libby's on the north side of town, when someone caught his attention.

The boyish figure of Spyro Spargo sat at the table, legs outstretched, propped up on a chair and crossed at the ankles, hands clasped in his lap. He smiled at Frank, his gold tooth gleaming through his tanned face. Spargo appeared to have carved out a space by the window and had it all to himself.

'At last,' he said. 'I was going to send out a search party, Frank.' He uncrossed his legs, lowering them before pushing the empty chair round in Frank's direction with an outstretched foot. 'Why don't you have a seat?' It was an instruction rather than a polite invitation.

'Spyro?' said Frank. He looked around for signs of anyone looking their way but no one appeared bothered by the presence of the head of the Alphaen in the corner, not even Polly. Frank let go of the door and took an exploratory step over. 'What are you doing here?'

Spargo grinned. 'The sausage rolls are the best in town, why else would I be here?' He flicked a hand to the crumbs on his empty plate, catching Frank's sarcastic smile and chuckling. 'Oh, and then I was chatting to your old friend Atticus Blackburn, who seems very fond of you, by the way.' Frank stiffened at the mention of Blackburn's name, knowing instantly that Spargo hadn't dropped his name into the conversation without reason. 'He was telling me a thing or two about you.' His eyes widened. He had Frank's attention. 'We had a bit of a laugh about you thinking you were on the trail of old Ludlow Hums —'

'He told you about that?' A snap in his voice.

'Of course, couldn't get him off the subject once he'd started and, of course, he was telling me all about the unlockable drawer episode.'

Frank would have liked to have forced even a weak smile but felt Spargo's interest in him and his friends botched tracking of the guardians of the Simbrian begin to eat at him. Frank thought he'd previously steered him away from the subject but now he knew that was a foolish notion; the head of the Alphaen might project the casual air of the uninterested but that was how he lulled people into his confidence, people like Blackburn who would sit and talk for hours about almost anything. He could easily imagine him spilling a flurry of anecdotes about Frank as Spargo, overflowing with charisma, drew him in like a spider reels in a silken thread.

He shouldn't be surprised that Spargo had been doing some digging, doing all he could to uncover what lay beneath the object of his interest. Even though Frank liked Spargo, he felt himself close his eyes and added him to his growing list of problems.

Spargo beckoned Frank closer with a jerk of his head, adjusting himself in the chair. Frank didn't move, drawing another grin from Spargo's youthful face.

'I know that you know,' he said, a terrifyingly open question that had Frank reaching for all of the answers he could think of. There were a hundred things Frank knew that others didn't. Which one was Spargo talking about? Which one did Spargo know about? Frank could have kept quiet but, knowing Spargo was the master of silence, a sound which preyed on his willpower and could draw out a quick response to ease the discomfort, he decided against it.

'Know what?' he said, guarded. Spargo brushed some imaginary dust from his trousers. Taking a moment before his big reveal.

'That your dad was a guardian of the Simbrian.'

He didn't bother to lower his voice, not that anyone was paying the slightest bit of attention to the otherwise normal encounter at the front of the shop and however big a disclosure Frank had expected, he was nearly knocked off his feet by the weight of Spargo's words even though he tossed them at Frank like confetti. He stood there, thoroughly dumbstruck as Spargo let his disclosure sink in before continuing.

'Yes, Frank. I know too, obviously.' He rolled his eyes, a nonchalant gesture, and looked on as Frank struggled to put words to his shock. 'I knew as soon as you spoke to me about the peacock feather on your dad's old sword. It took me a moment, but I could tell you had found the connection between the feather and the guardianship; you just happened to think it was me.' Spargo casually inspected the back of his hand. 'An easy mistake, of course, seeing as I have the sword.' He looked up. 'How did you make the connection in the first place? I'm intrigued. To everyone else, it's just a peacock feather cast in gold on a sword hilt; but to you...you knew.' He offered the chair to Frank again with an open palm. Frank sat. He could feel his breathing becoming erratic under Spargo's charismatic eyes.

'I'm not sure I want to tell you,' he said, immediately disappointed in his lame answer which, he thought, revealed more than he wanted. Spargo nodded like he'd been expecting it.

'Of course. Why would you?' He leaned forward, bracing his elbows on his knees. 'We live in dangerous times, Frank. There are men and women who just want to set the world alight and watch it burn.' Spargo rubbed the stubble on his chin. 'We think that Byeland and the territories beyond will soon come under a new threat from Kzarlac. That that threat may be more imminent than you think and, when it comes, no one will be in a position to stop it.'

Frank tried his best to keep his face neutral. He knew Spargo's words held credibility, he knew Dagmar only needed one more part to realise his dream of re-creating the Simbrian. Power that would have him and his forces marching through the Longshadow Mountains and sweeping away all before them. It was just a matter of time. Perhaps Spargo knew.

'How do you know about my Dad?'

'Because he told me.'

'Then as long as he keeps it safe.' Frank noticed a slight change in Spargo's expression which made him pause. 'Why aren't you out there protecting him? I've never once seen any interest in him from you or the Alphaen all the time I was at the farm. You'd think you'd send a guard or something.' Frank could taste a rising anger in his words. There was Spargo, playing his casual playboy role with well-worn indifference while his dad was in immediate danger. 'Call yourself his friend?' Spargo held his hand up.

'Oh, I'm afraid it's too late for that, Frank. You see, I wasn't the only one who knew.' Spargo locked eyes with Frank who realised he had been expertly manoeuvred towards Spargo's punchline. 'Dagmar knew, too.'

The words grabbed Frank by the throat. An icy shiver shook him into a mild, inner panic as an unpalatable realisation of what lay behind Spargo's words as they began to sink in. Spargo continued. 'Dagmar already has Lawrence's fragment of the Simbrian.'

Frank started to shake his head. He hadn't needed Spargo to tell him. Although disbelief filled the void, he knew Spargo was telling the truth. His dad wasn't the last hope against the tyranny of Etamin, the one who could protect his country against attack, stop Kzarlac wielding the almighty power that Dagmar was assembling.

'Perhaps I should tell you a bit more?' Spargo searched Frank's face but Frank could tell that Spargo wasn't expecting a one-sided conversation. He wanted to bargain, a trade of information. Already beaten up and scarred by the revelation that his dad was not only a guardian, but wasn't his dad at all, Frank wasn't sure he was ready to take any more. He got up; Spargo raised his eyebrows and shrugged his shoulders as Frank looked toward the door.

'In your own time, Frank,' he said, sensing Frank was bringing this short encounter to an end. 'I can wait. But not too long.' Spargo's face was the picture of indifference, irking Frank even more. If he was expecting to have things his own way and use what he knew to drag information out of Frank's reluctant mouth, he could think again. Frank turned and left.

6

THE STREET CORNER

It was just something else to contend with. That's what he told himself as he headed through the town, Spargo's words still in his ears. Words solely designed to get Frank to open up, to tell him what he knew, to trust him with the information that would help keep Byeland safe. Well, he wasn't going to get it. Frank thrust his hands deep into his pockets and pictured himself punching the smug smile off Spargo's face.

His strides lengthened as he approached the town square, determined to put as much distance between him and the Alphaen chief. Still, he felt Spargo's spectre at his back, trying to dig deeper under his skin and succeeding.

Rhaeder was a big town, but not big enough to avoid the reach of the Alphaen, however many ways Frank tried to think about how.

His head still echoed with Spargo's voice as he entered the square, his eyes on the road. He stopped, looking up and across to the Council building which looked right back at him. Frank felt himself grind his teeth as he stood, surveying those just going about their usual business, wishing he could do the same. He drew in a few deep breaths, ignoring the odd looks he received from a couple of passers-by and turned towards the north of the town when something caught his eye across the other side of square, towards the lane that led to Laskie's. He had to check himself and stood for a moment making sure he wasn't mistaken.

Libby stood on the corner talking to an older boy. Even at this distance, Frank noticed how she flicked her hair and laughed when he spoke, bumping him with a playful fist. Frank, backed into a doorway, placing a pillar of the portico between him and the square as a shield. He watched as the boy pretended to be injured, Libby adopting a coy pose as the boy, tall and striking, feasted on her auburn hair and green eyes. A deep wave of emerald jealousy careered through him, anchoring him to the pathway as he watched his girlfriend in the midst of some obvious and shameless flirting.

Although the minutes were probably mere seconds, Frank stood watching what looked like clear sexual sparring until the boy leaned in, wrapped his arms around her and gave Libby a kiss on the lips. Frank's insides burned, a crimson mist descended over him, igniting his frayed rage as Libby laughed; laughter that he thought was just reserved for him, between them, not to be shared with others. With a brief flick of his hand, the boy turned and headed across the square, deep confident strides to where Frank was standing. Frank looked down as he approached, then he was past him, whistling as he went. Frank felt the burn of his jealous stare follow, feeling his top lip curl in the boy's wake. His stomach dropped. He looked back to the street corner where he'd just witnessed his girlfriend openly flirting with someone else, but Libby had disappeared too, along with his one reason to stay in Rhaeder.

Frank couldn't move, eyes latched onto the empty path. He cursed; and again, then turned and kicked the expensively painted door to the offices where he stood, rattling it in its frame, wondering if his life could actually get any worse.

He stalked out of the doorway, barging into a woman who shot a profanity him, but he didn't look round. He went to the middle of the square and flung himself down on one of the benches and swore, thumping his fist down on the seat. He looked around, taking in the familiar setting, knowing he couldn't stay in the town. Not with the probability that Spargo's cheery but expectant face appearing at Polly's again and at every street corner. And street corners were not at the top of his best places to visit after what he'd just witnessed. He sat, stewing in his own anger, with no idea what he should do.

He felt the town pushing in on him, so much so that for the

next few days he confined himself to his room and only ventured downstairs at meal times. He assumed Polly just took it as normal adolescent behaviour but he knew he couldn't keep it up. He was used to being outdoors, not stuck in and not living in fear of bumping into anyone. The others would be returning for the start of term in a week but that seemed a long way off. He knew Libby wouldn't call in. He was meant to be back at home and she appeared to have taken advantage of his absence.

He lay on his bed, flicking through a magazine with disinterest, before throwing it down on the bedcovers and folding his arms across his chest, eyes unfocused on the ceiling. He glanced at his bedside table, at the letter from Gabby and picked it up. His eyes travelled over her handwriting, imagining her in her small house in Crossways and what she might be up to away from all the things that made Rhaeder feel like the last place he wanted to be, and made his decision.

7

THE WELCOME

The transport came to an abrupt halt along the dusty main street of the village. The driver looked down from his seat as Frank jumped to the ground and shut the carriage door behind him. He gave the driver a nod of thanks, the warm evening shadows masking his face, and made his way towards the shattered backstreets of Crossways. The two elderly women who had been his travelling companions peered at him as he went. Neither had spoken a word to him on the day's journey to Gabby and Anya's home village and Frank had been grateful for their silence, preferring to wrap himself up in his own thoughts and watch the world wind its innocent way across his eyes.

He'd tried to cleave the unforgiving thoughts from his mind but whatever he had tried had ended in predictable failure, hauling him back into the broken landscape of his life. His dad, Dagmar, Libby, the Simbrian. His world turned upside-down in a week and the whole thing had left him unable to shake the feelings of exhaustion or dampen his ill-temper. Even when he started trying to frame how he was going to tell his friends what he now knew, words failed him and he felt the pressure build in his head. He couldn't imagine Gabby's reaction when he revealed he was the heir of Dagmar Dag, her homeland's conqueror or that his dad had been a guardian, one of the seven they sought.

Whichever way he cut it, no explanation worked. He couldn't tell them, wouldn't tell them. He wouldn't tell anyone.

He felt his shoulders sag as he stood outside the worn and scuffed wooden door of the Asaro's tiny ramshackle terraced house.

Back in his bedroom, turning up unannounced at Gabby's seemed like a good idea but now he was here it felt like a stupid one. He couldn't imagine why anyone would want to see him, especially given the dark mood that he wore like a favourite cloak.

Drawing in a long breath he knocked loudly and waited. Familiar voices and laughter on the other side made him feel even worse about his decision to come before the door opened and he was greeted by Gabby's surprised face. She did a double-take, her brows knitting.

'Frank?'

Anya appeared at her shoulder.

'Hello Frank, what are you doing here?'

Frank shrugged and pulled his bag further onto his shoulder. Any thoughts about what he was going to say evaporated in the late afternoon and he found he couldn't get the words past his lips. Thankfully, Gabby stepped to the side and ushered him in before turning to Anya.

'You'd better get going,' said Gabby as Anya crossed the threshold into the street. They exchanged a look. 'Perhaps I will see you tomorrow after all.' She raised her eyebrows. Anya smiled at Frank.

'Sorry I can't stay and catch up, Frank. Lana's going off tomorrow to goodness knows where, so we've got a family thing going on tonight. Can't get out of it, unfortunately.'

Frank tried to smile back, but as Anya turned to go he remembered what she had told them about her sister, Lana, when they'd first met. She was an Excelsus graduate and an explorer.

'Hang on a sec, Anya' said Frank, reaching into his pocket and pulling out the piece of paper which contained the map as Gabby and Anya exchanged more looks. He handed it to Anya. 'Can you show this to your sister; see what she makes of it?'

Anya took the paper from Frank and shrugged. 'Sure.'

She turned to go.

'Come round as early as you like,' said Gabby as Anya hurried down the street. She shut the door and turned to Frank. She folded her arms and he watched her long lashes as she blinked. Her silence demanded an explanation but all he offered was a weak smile.

'Why aren't you at home?' said Gabby. She looked him up and down.

'I thought I'd come and see you.' It was true, as far as it went.

'Just you, then?' she said, a mischievous lilt on her tongue. 'You haven't brought what's-her-face along?' Frank felt himself bristle, his head momentarily dragging up an unwanted image.

'She'll be here tomorrow,' said Frank, trying to keep a straight face. Gabby gave a forced smile at his attempted humour and stood looking at him. He felt himself warm under her gaze. 'Can I stay?'

'You know we'll be going back to Rhaeder in a few days?'

Frank didn't have an answer, perhaps he might have been a bit too quick in his decision to come. Perhaps he hadn't been thinking straight and his befuddled mind had reaped the wrong choices. His head filled with sadness, sadness for his own situation and Gabby appeared to notice the sorrow in his eyes.

'Come on,' she said, taking him by the hand. 'Let's go and ask Mum.'

He shouldn't have expected anything other than the welcome the Asaros gave him. Warmer than the summer sun and just as cheerful, Gabby's family treated him like one of their own, stretching their food to allow the extra place he'd created at the table. Gabby had hardly had to say anything and her mum was so pleased to see him.

Of course he could stay, said Helen, although he'd have to make do with the sofa. But, after the days and weeks since he'd last seen Gabby, it was like he'd stepped through the door of another world, one where no one knew what he'd discovered, one where he could simply forget anything had ever happened.

Through supper Gabby's dad, Andre, did his usual cajoling of Gabby joking that he was going to fix magnets to the front door so that she wouldn't be able to leave the house with her usual array of heavy metal jewellery and piercings while her sister, Elena, kept herself to herself. The meal was followed by a bout of hearty singing from the whole family, who laughed when they got the words wrong or hit the wrong notes. It was a reminder of what he didn't have, of the life he'd led before his world took a different turn. Even so, Frank was aware of the shackles of his anger and frustration beginning to fall away and as his weariness finally took hold of him, he felt better than he had in a while.

The house eventually headed to bed. Gabby brought Frank some blankets and a pillow before they said their goodnights and he listened as his hosts made their way upstairs, leaving him to a silence that had him retreating into his problems once more.

He sat on the floor of the living room, his back to the window, his knees drawn up to his chest and dropped his head. The ink-black night, still and quiet, was perforated by glistening stars, none of which, he thought, shone for him. He looked up and stared at the closed door, behind which Gabby and her close-knit family slept soundly, happily, together. They could count on each other, be there to support in hard times, to draw the pain from each other with a simple hug and sing with abandon. His mind wandered back to Smithwood, to his simple and quiet life on the farm. His dad, aunt Rachel, Phoebe and Brigg. Memories of a happier time swept him up and embraced him until he gripped his fingers to his temples, put his hands over his eyes and started to weep.

8

THIEF'S SPITE

Frank woke from a deep, satisfying and dreamless sleep, fighting the squint in his eyes as bright sunlight spilled through a gap in the curtains, like a welcome, friend into the living room, warming his face as he lay on the sofa. Despite his temporary bed barely allowing him to stretch his legs out, he felt surprisingly well rested, even though sleep had failed to shake the lead weight in his head. He swung himself round and bent himself forward, his elbows rested on his knees, rubbing his eyes with his fists. He yawned deeply, shaking the remaining tiredness from his bones, finding an unfamiliar but much-needed comfort in being alone in the small, simple room.

Looking up, he realised he wasn't by himself. Wilkins, Gabby's mum's large black cat and familiar stared back at him from the pile of clothes he'd carefully folded and placed on the small coffee table the previous evening. He was sure it hadn't been there when he went to bed. He thought, perhaps, Helen had let the cat in, maybe to keep an eye on him, noting his sombre mood.

He went to get up, letting the warm woollen blanket fall from his tired body when he suddenly remembered that Helen could see through the cat's eyes and quickly grabbed it back to cover himself once more. The cat just blinked back at him and tucked its front legs under itself before commencing a doze.

He had no sense of the time but was aware of voices from the hallway beyond the door, wondering if that was what had dragged him from his sleep. Laughing. Young laughing. He pulled together his concentration and realised that Gabby was talking to someone at the front door. He squeezed the heels of his hands into his eyes, moistening them and clearing any remaining blur of the early morning as he strained to listen. Just muffled voices, intimate, punctuated with Gabby's laughing.

He heard her say goodbye, followed by the click of the front door as she shut it. Frank went to the window and peeled a wider gap between the curtains, just enough to see a teenage boy pass and head away from the house. Frank took in the shoulder length blond hair, tanned skin and strong jawline. The spring in his step and smiling face didn't go unnoticed. He stood there for a moment, wondering when he'd last heard Gabby laugh like that. The last time he'd made her laugh like that? He couldn't remember.

He sighed, closed his eyes and shook his head before turning his attention back to the slumbering cat, who seemed to sense Frank's intentions and looked at him through slitted eyes. He managed to slide his hands under the feline enough to lift the cat up and place it gently on the dented cushions of the sofa, thinking the waning body heat from his night's rest would make a fine alternative and cosy sleeping place for a cat but, with typical fickleness, Wilkins stood, instantly awake and leapt to the door, pawing at the frame to be let out. The cat waited patiently while Frank quickly dressed, then, as Frank opened the door, shot through like an evil spirit was on its tail.

Frank's weary gaze followed the cat as, tail in the air, it padded quickly and quietly down the short hallway and into the kitchen at the back of the house. He closed his eyes and felt his chest stretch tight as he drew in a long breath and waited. He wasn't sure why he hesitated. Despite sharing the evening with Gabby's family, perhaps he knew he wasn't entirely ready for people, to be in anyone's company and wondered again if coming to Crossways had been too impulsive. He wasn't ready to tell anyone about his dad, about him being a guardian. If only that had been the only thing he wasn't ready to talk about.

He steadied himself for a minute or two, then followed in Wilkins's wake.

Gabby sat at the kitchen table, her hair hung over her shoulder, pulled back in a braid that could barely keep her wild locks contained. Frank glanced at the objects on the table in front of her — an open bottle of gin, a bowl of what looked to be sugar and an empty glass. A pink rose lay on the table next to the glass.

'Bit early for that,' he said, making her spin round as he entered the room, a broad smile illuminating her face, the sparkle in her eyes illuminating *him* as he felt a fraction of his worries fall away.

'Thought you were going to sleep in all day.' She turned back to the table. 'Mum's gone up to the farm to get some supplies. We've all had to go around on tip-toes because Mum was afraid we'd wake you.' Frank nodded and stared vacantly through the table. 'Looks like you needed it.' He noticed the unasked question in her voice and her badly hidden worry. Frank pretended to yawn and forced a smile although he doubted he'd throw Gabby off the scent. She still looked at him, opened her mouth but, after a pause, closed it.

'Looks interesting?' Frank jerked his head to the table. Gabby gave him a look and shrugged.

'Just mixing up some thief's spite,' she said. 'Mum makes me put it on anything valuable – which is nothing.' She gave Frank a goofy look. 'But since we left Prismia she's become a bit neurotic about it. You know what parents are like.' Frank didn't respond. 'She wants me to put some on my tabix even though I keep telling her I don't mind if someone nicks it.'

Frank watched as she ran her hands down the length of her braid. 'There's some tea in the pot.' She twitched her head towards the worktop. Frank poured himself a mug and slid himself into a chair alongside Gabby, who pushed her bangles up her arms before reaching for the bottle of gin.

'I heard you at the door,' he ventured. Gabby kept her eyes off him, arranging the objects on the table.

'Sorry if I woke you,' she said.

'Sounded like you were having a bit of a laugh.'

Gabby stretched her arms, arching her back, her hands feeling behind her neck, searching for the clasp that held her academy

47

necklace in place.

'Oh, that's just Leo.' Frank tried to keep his look as disinterested as possible, but his silence spoke for him. 'We've known each other for ages.' She paused as her fingers finally managed to release the clasp. 'We used to hang out together before I went to the academy.' She placed the tabix on the table next to the gin bottle. 'He's really sweet and I think he quite likes me.' Her voice was light as she broke into a smile meant for herself. A smile of secret thoughts, sweet abandoned thoughts. Frank felt the muscles in his face harden.

'So what does it do?' he said, steering himself down a different path as he flicked his finger at the objects on the table, his head wrestling with the image of the good-looking boy who he'd seen walking away from Gabby's house.

'This? It's meant to stop someone stealing whatever's coated in it,' she said, pouring a good measure of gin into the glass. Frank watched as the clear liquid glugged through the neck of the bottle. She kept pouring until the glass was three-quarters full. She took the rose, gently holding the stem as if it might break, picked off two or three petals from the flower, and dropped them carelessly into the gin-filled glass. 'You mix this lot together,' she said, taking the sugar-like substance and gently pouring it in. 'Mum made the powder. Apparently it's quite easy, although I've not seen her do it.' As she spoke the mixture began to froth up, tiny delicate bubbles of dusty pink rose to the top of the glass; the foul odour of rotten eggs spread up and into the room, making Frank recoil. 'Oh, sorry, ignore the smell.'

Frank looked at Gabby, her eyes, the colour of freshly tilled soil, deep in concentration, the gentle curve of her exposed neck, taught and flawless, a small scar behind her ear and the smoothness of her skin. She caught his stare.

'You okay?'

'Yeah.' Frank looked back at the concoction she was assembling, trying not to breathe in the stench that had swamped the kitchen. The liquid in the glass had now turned to a thick pink foam. Gabby picked the tabix from the table and dunked it in the foam, making a few up and down movements to make sure the whole thing was coated, then lifted it back out and plonked it on the table. The coating of foam quickly disappeared and the tabix sat there looking a bit more bright and sparkly, but otherwise no different. Gabby picked up the glass and headed to the sink.

'I'd better get rid of this before I choke my guts up,' she said, tipping the bright bubbling contents down the plughole. Frank picked up the tabix and gave it a short inspection which revealed nothing out of the ordinary.

'So this works...how?'

'Like I said, it catches anyone who steals your stuff.'

'Yeah, but how?'

Gabby looked into the empty glass, then back to Frank and started laughing, her girlish giggle breathed light into the small kitchen and Frank felt himself smile, feeling that, this time, it was reserved for him.

'Do you know, I'm not sure.' She put the back of her hand to her mouth to stop herself laughing. 'Mum makes me put it on my stuff, but nothing's ever been nicked, so I've not found out. I even put some on our book when I brought it home the first time. Anya kept going on about how she thought someone was going to steal it; such is our friend's forecasting ability, so I did it just to keep her quiet. But now that Chetto boy knows, perhaps it was a good idea.'

'I thought we'd agreed Oliver is one of the good guys,' said Frank.

Gabby flashed him a cheeky grin, but said nothing. She picked up the package with the spite powder in it and took it over to the corner cupboard. Frank rose from his chair and joined Gabby as she pulled the doors open, his eyes scanning the bottles, jars and other containers like a child in a sweet shop. Nothing was labelled; nothing indicated what was in each. Her mother's stores, the ingredients she used for her sorcery.

Helen was such an insignificant and slight looking woman, but the power stoppered in each and every one of the containers sent a shiver through Frank, wondering what she held back, what she might be capable of, what she daren't unleash on the world. Whether she kept her own daughter a whisker away from conjuring fire or unleashing a plague, like his gran, who used her abilities for good, not to brutalise or kill. He wondered if Helen had the power in this innocent-looking cupboard to smite a whole city. His hand went to a small frosted bottle shaped like a leaf on the top shelf but Gabby quickly smacked it away.

'Hands off,' she said. She glanced sideways at Frank, an impish grin on her face. 'No touching.'

Their eyes met, Frank felt his face close to hers and he found himself looking at her soft lips but quickly pushed away the flutter in his stomach before making a grab for a small, round, rusty and battered tin from the bottom of the cupboard. Gabby made a grab for him, hooking her soft hands onto his wrist but he was too quick and he backed away as she shot him an unforgiving look.

The sound of a number of small objects rolling around noisily, inside, made Frank shake the tin, then hold it steady to open it. Gabby looked over, her brow creasing, her eyes fixing on Frank's hands. Frank looked back, shrugged and opened the tin. Inside, a dozen pea-sized spheres, the colour of mustard, looked back at him. Each one with a thin blue stripe circling the middle; except one bead was as clear and cold as a fresh raindrop. He picked one out, surprised how its weight pushed down on his palm, and gave it a slight squeeze. It was as hard as granite, with no give in it at all. He put it back in the tin and tried it with another as Gabby looked on.

'What are they?' said Gabby.

'Why are you asking me?' said Frank. 'I thought you knew everything your mum had in here.'

Gabby held out her hand and Frank passed the tin to her.

'I thought I did, but I've not seen these before.'

'Well, they were tucked away in the corner. Perhaps your mum's forgotten about them.'

Gabby moved the tin from side to side, watching as the little balls ran circuits around the inside, their motion laboured, inhibited by their weight. They were as unusual in their movement as they were ordinary in appearance.

'Careful with those.' Helen's bright voice caught them by surprise. She stood right behind them, amusement dancing from the usual dullness in her eyes. Helen reached over and took the container from Gabby. She looked in, carefully counting the beads with her eyes and giving herself the slightest of nods.

'What are they?' said Gabby.

'These are time beads,' said Helen matter-of-factly. Frank passed her the tin lid.

'Time beads?' said Gabby, screwing her nose up. 'That sounds interesting, why don't I know about them?'

Helen moved the tin from side to side, watching as the off-yellow spheres lolled languidly inside. She glanced to the cupboard, frowning.

'I forgot I had them.' She sat, picking up one of the spheres and smiling like it was a forgotten childhood toy as she rolled it between her thumb and forefinger. Her expression clouded slightly. 'I remember when I got these.' She looked up. 'I bought them at a market in Anetra when I was about your age. I remember wanting to collect as many interesting and unusual trinkets and knick-knacks as I could, anything to quench my appetite for tricks and spells and the flea market there was a wellspring of weird stuff.' She charmed them with her soft reminiscing so much that Frank felt the tension in his bones unwind further. 'I'm sure the woman who sold them to me was a witch.' A shudder. 'And she was virtually giving them away.' She held the bead in the flat of her hand. 'I thought they looked really interesting and when she told me what they did I thought they might be useful but I subsequently found out they're not that good or very useful for anything if you've only got a handful; like these. I think she saw a naïve young woman captivated by the world and decided to take advantage of her and sold me what turned out to be a useless tin of old rubbish.' Helen blinked indifferently into the tin as the kitchen fell silent.

'What do they do?' said Frank.

Helen's smile wrinkled her cheeks.

'They make time stand still.'

9

TIME BEADS

Helen uttered the words so softly that Frank thought he must have misheard. He'd been so taken in by her short story and her claim that the small balls not being of any use, he was expecting her to throw the tin in the bin. But the mention of their ability to make time stand still instantly had Frank and Gabby gripped.

'How can that *not* be useful,' said Gabby. She made a grab for the tin but Helen's anticipation was sharp, holding it out of range. She chuckled, her plain face a raft of lines. She lifted a finger to her daughter's curiosity.

'I can see you scheming already, Gabriella and, no you can't have them. Like I said, they're not much use so don't go thinking these are the gateway to eternal youth or immortality. That's what the witch told me and I was foolish enough to believe her.'

Gabby screwed her nose up, her eyes still glued on the tin.

'Like I would, Mum.'

Helen raised her eyebrows at her daughter.

'So, how do they work?' said Frank. He leaned forward, bumping shoulders with Gabby, feeling her lean into him as his co-conspirator against her mum.

'I'll show you if you like.' Helen looked at the excitement etched across their faces.

'Are you kidding?' said Gabby.

'It's just the effect only covers a very small area. If you could get a small piece of ice from the cold store, sweetheart.'

Frank sat next to Helen as Gabby headed out of the back door and into the small, shabby yard that hemmed the back of the house

53

in, returning with a chunk of ice which she cradled in the palm of her hand.

Frank's eyes widened as Helen took the ice cube from Gabby and placed it on the table. Gabby slid herself back into the chair next to Frank as her mother picked out six of the time beads, gently placing them in the palm of her hand, her wrist taut against their weight. She inspected each one closely before carefully placing all but one of them in a circle on the table around the ice. She held the final bead – the clear bead - between her thumb and forefinger. She twitched her nose.

'Now the tricky bit.'

Helen stared rigidly at the final bead; a picture of deep concentration as she held it six inches above the centre of the circle she'd just made with the others. Her hand hovered over the middle of the ice. Frank wasn't sure what he was looking at, but the flutter of anticipation rose in his stomach as he looked on. Helen held the bead there for a moment, then let go. As her fingers parted, the tiny sphere fell to the table with a thick slap, followed by a frustrated huff as she picked the errant bead up again.

'I can never get this right,' she said with an irritated shake of her head. 'When I first got these, it took me about fifty attempts the first time. I'd have thought the old woman was telling me a load of old nonsense had she not given me a demonstration before I bought them, Needless to say, she did it first time whereas I was so frustrated I chucked them across the room and cried and I never got the knack so, in the end I just put them back in the tin and forgot about them.' As she spoke, she let her hand hang over the ice again. Frank watched on, hypnotised by the strange ritual she was conducting until, after what seemed like minutes and a lot of long exhaling, Helen let go of the bead and, to Frank and Gabby's astonishment, it sat floating in the air, rotating on an invisible cushion.

'Goodness,' said Helen, a breath escaping her as if she'd been holding it underwater. 'That's the quickest I've done that. I thought we'd be here half the morning.' She sat back and folded her arms, a satisfied smile on her pale face. 'You see, not a particularly interesting or great result.' Frank looked on, not exactly sure what he was meant to be looking at.

'So what's going on?' said Gabby, her face scrunched in her familiar unimpressed expression. Helen leaned forward again, her index finger outstretched, making a small circular motion around the clear bead, taking care not to touch it as it hovered over the kitchen table.

'The top bead forms a connection with the others. You see?' She drew a number of invisible lines with her hand, connecting the clear bead with those on the table around the ice. 'The space enclosed within the beads is where time has now stopped.'

'You're kidding me,' said Gabby.

'You know I never kid about anything, sweetheart,' said Helen, soft and calm. 'But there's a bit more going on than you might think. To the naked eye, what you can see still follows real time. Keep watching.' They watched in silence as the warmth from the corner stove and the cosy heat in the room started to slowly and gradually melt the ice until it had dissolved into a small pool of water on the table. Helen didn't take her eyes off Gabby and Frank. 'You see, it's melted, just like it should. But...' She broke into a smile as child-like mischief uncharacteristically filled her eyes. She looked at Frank with a sparkle. 'Why don't you take the bead away, Frank?'

'Which one?'

'The top one, dummy,' said Gabby, making a face.

She reached over and plucked the clear bead from its position in the air before Frank could react. Instantly, the ice, cold and frosted, appeared back on the table, exactly as it had been when Helen put it there. Untouched, unmelted, unmoved. Gabby gasped, wide-eyed, her fingertips touching the top of the cube. She looked at the cool wetness on her fingertips, then to Frank with an open mouth.

'You see,' said Helen. 'What you see isn't always what it seems. Whatever is within the field created by the time beads is stood still as long as the field remains intact. Remove the top bead, the field collapses and it starts time again. Simple and very alluring at first sight but, as I said, not much use.' Helen pushed her forefinger against the ice, sliding it across the table, leaving a glistening trail as it began to dissolve.

'But surely that could be really useful,' said Gabby. Helen looked up.

'For what, exactly? As you can see, the size of the area is so very small and anything has to be contained in it forever for it not to age. You can't pick it up and move it around; the field would collapse.'

'Perhaps you could have an immortal gerbil as a pet,' said Frank, barely able to contain his laughter. Gabby gave him a frosty look, then laughed with him, her dimpled cheeks igniting something inside him.

'I've never found anything I need to use them for,' said Helen, picking the beads up. 'If you want to hide something, you're much better using the shield charm I showed you.' She dropped them, one by one, back into the tin, the kitchen filling with the clacking of metal as they hit. She placed the lid back on, stood and went to the cupboard. 'There,' she said. 'I think they can go back in corner where they belong.'

10

THE VISITOR

Before Helen shut the time beads away, she took a large bottle of clear liquid from one of the shelves in her cupboard and placed it on the table, turning to Frank and Gabby.

'Now, I'm really behind. I've dinner to prepare and I've not even begun to make the tonic I promised Mr Johns and he'll be here any minute.'

Frank noticed Gabby shiver and screw up her face.

As Helen spoke a sharp knock on the front door echoed through the tiny house. Helen's shoulders dropped, she loosed a long breath and looked at the clock.

'That'll be him now,' she said, shaking her head and wiping her hands on a tea towel. 'Can you let him in, please, sweetheart.'

Gabby shivered again and grabbed Frank by the wrist.

'Sorry, Mum,' she said, leading Frank out of the kitchen and down the hallway. 'Frank and I need to have a chat,' she called back, yanking Frank into the living room and shutting the door, leaving Helen in her wake. Frank heard her mum's footsteps approaching the front door and went to speak, only to have Gabby hush him up with a glare and a raised hand. Their silence was followed by the sound of the front door opening.

'Hello, Mr Johns.' Helen's kind voice carried easily into the house. 'Come on in.'

Frank stood back as footsteps receded to the kitchen and waited for an explanation.

'Millington Johns,' she said with a hush, a frown creasing her face as she looked at the closed door. 'I can't *stand* him, gives me the right creeps.' She shivered again and wrapped her arms around herself. 'I'm surprised he's even come here; I don't think anyone's ever seen him outside his own house.'

'What, so he's a bit of a recluse?'

'Not just a bit.'

'So what's your mum doing with him?'

Gabby shrugged, tightening her embrace.

'She does a bit of healing here and there, nothing like Excelsus standards, but she's learned a bit of simple stuff, so I think she's helping him out with something. I can imagine what he's got. Yuk. Weirdo.'

Frank barely held down his laughter, earning him a solid glare. He'd missed Gabby. Blunt as a stone and sharp as a razor all at the same time.

'So, what, are we going to stay in here until he's left?'

She nodded stiffly, as if anything else would have been unthinkable. Frank sat on the sofa as someone rapped hard on the window. Anya's face appeared with a glowing smile. Gabby tensed.

'I'll let her in,' said Frank.

'No,' hissed Gabby. 'Don't go out there, you'll bump into him. You'll probably catch whatever he's got.'

Frank shook his head but went to the door, opened it and stepped through into the hallway with an unfounded but peculiar feeling of wariness on the heels of Gabby's comments. There was no one there. Voices travelled from the kitchen as Frank snapped the front door open and let Anya in.

'Hi, Frank. Gabby got you answering the door already?' She pushed her glasses back on her nose and looked past Frank and down the hallway.

'Don't ask.'

Anya propped herself against the hallway wall and, as she eased her boots off, she said:

'Oh, just in case I forget, which I probably will, Lana said the map looks like it's of the silent forest.'

Frank was about to ask the obvious question when footsteps from the kitchen drew his attention to the far end of the hall where Helen appeared with a middle-aged man. The man, bald-headed with a week's growth of stubble on his chin, followed her towards the front door where Frank and Anya stood, his heavy eyes flitting from them to the floor. He wore a thick, grey jumper which hid his broad shoulders. His hands gripped an old flat cap which he twisted like he was wringing out an old flannel.

'Hello Anya,' said Helen. She turned to Frank. 'Where's Gabriella?' Frank looked at the half-open door into the living room where Gabby stood, unseen, holding a finger to her lips, pleading silently with her eyes for Frank not to give her away.

'I think she's gone upstairs to get something,' he said, moving to one side as Helen ushered her guest to the door, the slight aroma of eucalyptus hung in his wake. Helen turned from Frank and looked at the man who already had his hand on the doorknob in apparent eagerness to be out on the street.

'I'll drop it round later, Mr Johns,' she said.

The man grunted and lifted his unshaven chin, avoiding any eye contact with Frank or Anya. He quickly had the door open and was gone like a ghost on the wind, closing the door silently behind him. Gabby pushed the living room door open with a long exhaling, peering round the corner at the closed door. She sniffed the air and turned her nose up.

'I thought you were upstairs,' said Helen, looking at her daughter, then back to Frank. Frank held his palms up.

'Thanks, Frank,' said Gabby, jerking her head to indicate that Frank and Anya should follow her back into the living room. Helen put her hands on her hips and huffed, her look at her daughter a mixture of fire and ice.

'There's nothing wrong with him, Gabriella,' she said, aiming a rare scowl revealing where Gabby got that particular characteristic from. 'He's just a bit misunderstood, that's all.'

'If by misunderstood, you mean weird, then I agree,' said

Gabby. Frank pushed down the laugh that had quickly risen in his throat.

'I thought I'd brought you up to be a bit more considerate,' said Helen with a hint of disappointment. 'Give him a bit of leeway.'

'I think he needs me to give him a personality before leeway.' She snorted at her own joke, but Frank felt Helen bristle.

'Okay, I think that's enough.' Gabby rolled her eyes and clamped her teeth together behind her lips but didn't push. Helen's scowl deepened. 'Just for that, you can take his tonic round to him when I've made it. I'll see to it now.'

'Mum! Please don't make...'

Helen started back to the kitchen.

'I've a lot to do, so you'll be helping me out. I'll only be ten minutes.' She turned and met Gabby's sulky face. 'Don't think about going anywhere with Frank and Anya.' She raised a finger. 'And maybe it'll teach you to be a bit kinder.' She disappeared into the kitchen, unaware of the face Gabby made to her back. Frank and Anya could hardly hide their amusement.

'What?' shot Gabby.

'I'd say that didn't go too well,' said Anya. 'Enjoy your visit to Mr Johns's house.' But a grin broke across Gabby's face.

'I've got a better idea,' she said. 'You two can come with me.'

Millington Johns

Millington Johns lived on the dusty outskirts of Crossways, across the road from a small brewery, away from people, away from life. Gabby dragged her feet as they headed across the village, explaining to Frank that the miserable old man had a reputation for being excessively and unbearably irritable with the temper of a tired and hungry bear with constant toothache and he didn't care much for having people clogging up his life. Anya nodded as Gabby spoke, unable to hide her amusement at the detailed and colourful description that Gabby painted as they approached the edge of the village, the heavy but wonderful smell of mashing grains and boiling wort guiding them.

He lived alone, presumably by choice, and fit the definition of a recluse with ease. Gabby explained that her mum had run a few errands for him and, despite his elusiveness and irascibility, he had been one of the more welcoming and accepting of the small number of Prismian refugees that had settled in the village.

Despite her natural aversion to him, Gabby said he'd always been kind to Elly and her, even though he gave her the creeps but since the previous winter his health had deteriorated, prompting him to withdraw further into his own company, away from irksome people.

Helen, though, wasn't put off and provided him with medicine in exchange for a selection of fruit and vegetables from his apparently well-tended and abundant garden.

The detached stone cottage was the last on the road heading west out of Crossways. Solitary, bitter and unwelcoming. The small front garden was bare and unfenced. The ground was just bare earth – no grass, no plants. As Frank looked at the house he noticed that all the windows had metal grilles firmly mortared into the surrounding brickwork on both levels and all the curtains were pulled across, leaving only a small gap at each opening. The hairs on his neck moved as they stood at the end of the short pathway that led to the front door. It appeared more fortress than house.

'See what I mean,' said Gabby, her lip twitching as they made their way up to the sturdy wooden door that separated its occupant from the outside world, severing him from the society he appeared to naturally shun.

She paused in front of the door. The thick, bare piece of oak had no knocker, no bell. Just a small spy-hole connected the inside to the outdoors. Gabby turned to the others. 'Promise you won't run off if I knock.'

'You talk like he's some sort of serial killer,' said Frank.

He took a step to the door and rapped hard, stepping away from the unseen, lurking eye on the other side of the threshold. Silence. The three of them exchanged glances, waiting. Nothing severed the eerie quiet until Gabby clicked her tongue.

'Oh, well,' she sighed with a large dose of mock disappointment. 'Looks like our local mister creepy-crawly is out. Maybe he's visiting his favourite colony of rats, or something.'

She screwed her foot into the ground and turned to go when she was halted by the thrum and clank of heavy bolts being thrown back on the other side of the door. They all took a wary step back as the door glided open on silent hinges, revealing the sullen and bald-headed figure of Millington Johns. He took in the faces of his three unexpected visitors. No sign of emotion on his face as he scratched at the back of his neck.

'What?' Short, gruff and uninviting. Gabby appeared to shiver, but put her hand in her pocket and produced the bottle of tonic her mum had given her, holding it out and giving it a slight wave at the end of her fingertips. Johns jerked his head.

'Why don't you come in,' he growled, barely making eye contact, his tone brimming with tetchiness and suspicion. Gabby looked like she'd just been asked to feed Wilkins to a crocodile.

'We can't stay,' said Gabby. 'Mum gave...' but Johns had turned and was already heading towards the back of the house.

'Make sure you shut the door,' he said without looking back. They watched as he disappeared through a door at the end of the hallway. Gabby's shoulders sagged, her arm still extended. She looked at Frank and Anya, her eyes full of annoyance.

'Weirdo,' she muttered. 'Why don't I just leave this here?' She glanced down at the doorstep.

Frank wasn't sure what to do. He certainly hadn't expected to be invited in, but Johns had asked them like they didn't have a choice so, with a glance at Gabby's uncertain face, he headed into the house, a long exhaling at his back as the others followed.

Frank had no idea what to expect inside but as he made his way slowly down the hallway, carpeted in dull red, he was surprised at how spotless it was. The walls were punctuated by hand-drawn, unframed pictures of a variety of unusual looking symbols. The scent of tea-tree oil lit the air. Frank paused to look on the curious, interlocking geometric shapes, some struck through with harsh swipes of a wide brush. He looked at Anya who shrugged. Gabby just screwed up her nose.

'Protective runes,' she said. 'At least that's something I learned at Excelsus. And from that misery, Lanks.'

The door at the end of the hall opened into a well-proportioned kitchen at the back of the house. The back door was open and Johns was nowhere to be seen. Windows opened the view onto an impressive vegetable garden. Immaculate and well-tended, the journey into the late summer revealed canes weighty with beans, beds of chard and lettuce and plants heavy with ripe raspberries, all planted in perfect rows. Johns certainly kept himself busy in his isolation.

Once again, Frank noticed the bars on the windows and more of the same unusual symbols drawn on large scraps of paper pinned to the door frames. The room was orderly and sparkled like it had just been cleaned. Something about it reminded him of Knox. A good sized table, oozing beeswax and lavender, occupied the middle of the floor and a copper kettle steamed lazily on the range but it was the maps on the wall that grabbed Frank's attention.

Every available wall space was covered with charts and pictures. From mountain ranges to vast oceans, strange foreign lands with thick forests, wastelands of ice and angry volcanic islands. All drew Frank in with their own special spell. He stared with boyish intrigue, his interest in their owner rising a notch.

But it was the largest map that drew him in. One entire wall was covered in a huge map of Byeland and Kzarlac. Frank slowly scanned the whole thing, taking in Crossways and Rhaeder. The ghastly border town of Garrim, nestled in the fist of the Longshadow Mountains sent ice down his spine. His gaze wandered to Alsha Kar, dredging up his recent memories. An image of Etamin Dahke burned before his eyes, quickening his breath before he snapped himself away, his eyes coming to rest on the village of Smithwood, his home. He thought of his dad and felt the flame of his temper.

A sound at the back door brought him back to the room as Johns stepped through, carrying a fretted wooden box filled with a range of assorted fruit and vegetables. Gabby instantly took a step back as he placed it on the table before shutting the door and turning the key. He took a small bowl of fresh raspberries from the box, putting it on the table nearer the three students, then took a step back.

'Here, take these,' he said to Gabby. 'Tell your mum I should have more later in the week if she needs anything.' He was abrupt, his voice clipped but polite. Gabby gave an unconvincing nod.

'Thanks,' she just about managed, her eyes dancing over the produce but avoiding Johns's look.

'You're very kind,' said Anya.

'Nonsense.' He looked at Gabby, who inspected her shoes. 'You've all been through enough; giving away food that I don't need is the least I can do.' He gave a curt wave towards his garden.

'I've plenty.' He flicked a finger at the table. 'Help yourself to the raspberries.'

Anya stepped forward and took the bowl, offering them to the others. Frank grabbed a small handful while Gabby refused with a raise of her palm, her face searching for something contagious in the small, pink fruit.

Johns coughed. A deep, throaty sound echoed through the room as he covered his mouth with his fist. Remembering she was still holding the bottle of tonic, Gabby held it out, before putting it on the table, next to the box of vegetables.

Johns nodded.

'Thank your mother for me, please,' he said, his cold façade melting a little. He coughed again, tensing his fist against his mouth, drawing Frank's eyes to the white scars, dozens of them, lining the back of his hands, criss-crossing his knuckles and tanned skin in a painful, randomly cut fretwork. Some were broad, some barely a hair's breadth and, even though they looked like they were made some time ago, Frank found himself wincing. Johns lowered his hand, looking at Frank through sharp eyes. He glanced down to the patchwork of lines, then to Frank who felt like he'd inadvertently intruded into something private. Johns slowly rubbed the back of one hand with the palm of the other. A firm, slow motion.

'We all bear our scars,' he growled, looking back up, the shadows around his eyes accentuating the cold expression that sent another shiver down the middle of Frank's back. 'Some of us on the outside, but all of us on the inside.'

'We should be going,' said Gabby, stepping forward to take the box from the table. 'I'll tell...'

'Why have you got those odd symbols all over your house?' said Frank, moving a step towards the table. Johns backed off, maintaining his distance, his senses peaked. He narrowed his eyes, lines marking the corners and his narrow forehead, and turned his nose up, looking slowly and deliberately to the door. 'And the bars on the windows?'

'Burglars?' added Anya. Johns gave a low throaty laugh under his breath, making himself cough once more.

'Burglars,' he chuckled, more to himself than to them. 'That's right.' He reached across the table, casting them a guarded look before taking the bottle of tonic. He inspected the contents through the glass as it rested in his beaten hand. He looked at Gabby. 'Your mother's a kind woman.'

He turned his back to them, opening a cupboard and placing the bottle of tonic on a shelf. He squared the front to match the other jars and containers within, all arranged in height order. He took a sideways step to the sink and proceeded to wash his hands, soaping them to a thick lather and rinsing them in long convoluted strokes of his palms. He shook off the wet residue and grabbed a towel.

Gabby shuffled her feet and cleared her throat with a pointed look at Frank and Anya. He noticed her twitching her head towards Johns's front door and open her mouth, presumably with a nice excuse for them to exit when Johns said:

'You have an interest in the silent forest?'

1 2

THE WARNING

A wave of hush swept through the room. Gabby stopped her exaggerated head-flicking and Frank stared at Johns's broad back. He hadn't remembered Johns being in the hallway when Anya had told them back at Gabby's house.

Johns stared out of the kitchen window, inspecting his garden, drumming his fingers expectantly on the worktop. None of them spoke.

He turned, his stubbled face expressionless, hollow, unmoving. His hands massaged his scars. His eyes asked the question.

'Do you know it?' said Anya, her smile, full of sweetness, thawing the frosty Johns just a bit. He puckered his lips. 'My sister's an explorer —'

'I know.' His face hardened.

'She said...' Her voice trailed off. Johns caught the sideways glance to Gabby and Frank.

'What did she say about it?' Abrupt, like he found his own words too valuable to waste.

'What can you tell us about it?' said Frank.

'I thought it was me who just asked a question.' Still no hint of softness behind his deep-set eyes.

Frank pulled out the map from his pocket. He hesitated, not bothering to look at Gabby or Anya for support, before unfolding the piece of paper and flattening it on the table. He pushed it in Johns's direction and took a step back. Johns's permanently v-shaped eyebrows raised a little, his eyes dipped to the image and back to Frank.

'Where d'you get that?' He continued the ritual of rubbing his knuckles, his eyes shifting around the room. He stepped to the back door and pushed the handle down. It didn't shift; locked. He pressed on the pictures, the symbols with the flat of his palms before stepping back.

Frank didn't answer, but felt his throat bob under Johns's stare.

'I asked where you got that.' Frank looked at the map then back to Johns, but refused him an answer. 'You'd be best staying as far from the forest as you can,' said Johns. Frank felt a flutter in his chest. Johns knew something. *Knew* something. Now his thoughts of a quick getaway quickly turned on their head. He sensed it in the others.

'So, it's a real place, then?' said Gabby.

Wordless, Johns took a step to the table, not looking remotely comfortable at closing the gap between him and Frank.

'Do you know where this is?' said Frank, dipping his chin to the map.

Johns sniffed indifference, flexing his broad shoulders and rotating his neck. He reached into his breast pocket, produced a small pair of spectacles and perched them on the end of his nose, his eyes flitting from the table to the three teenagers standing on the other side. He slid the small piece of paper towards him, gripped it by the top right-hand corner and held the map at arms-length, narrowing his eyes. He screwed up his mouth, his unwavering gaze dancing over the image as he looked over to the large map on the wall behind Frank. Silently, his gaze shifted from his hands to the wall, and again.

'It says something about Irundi,' said Frank. He went to lean in, to point at the map in Johns's hands, but Johns backed away.

'I can read,' he snarled, the muscles in his face flexing. He held the map up. 'Where did you get this?' he asked again, the natural tension in his voice spreading across the room.

'I'm afraid I can't tell you that.' Johns looked him over for a moment, then nodded, whether in acknowledgment or approval,

Frank couldn't tell.

'But you know where it is,' said Anya, her soft tone a soothing balm on the prickly air.

'Uh-huh,' he mused. He placed the map back on the table and slid it an inch towards Frank. 'Irundi. Not heard of it?' Frank shook his head. Johns nodded slightly, biting at the inside of his mouth. 'I've come across the term a few times over the years. Nearly as mysterious as me, Irundi.' The scored lines on his gruff old face creased into as much of a smile as it dared. His eyes focused on the large map on the wall, once more.

'What is it?' asked Frank. Johns's eyes became momentarily unfocused.

'Some say there is an ancient clearing in the forest where the light can never reach.' His voice was level and steady. Another glance over Frank's shoulder. 'Not even at the height of summer, in the grip of the hottest day. Where all the land around bathes peacefully in the radiance of the sun, Irundi remains as dark as a badger's mask like a living, breathing patch of tortured evil. Immovable, impenetrable. As cold and dark as the eyes of the dead. If you believe that sort of thing.' He looked at Frank. 'Which I don't. I've no time for fairy stories.' He narrowed his eyes. 'There are tales of folk disappearing into its shadow and never returning. Since the time of Kester.' If he was trying to scare them, Frank felt he was going in the right direction. 'Then there's the stories of the flesh-eating woodland sentinels.' Johns looked on as their faces paled and dropped before letting out a single loud, sharp laugh that caught in his throat.

'You're joking, right?' said Frank, who thought a dark, solitary place in the middle of the woods sounded like the sort place Millington Johns would find himself completely at home. He didn't think Johns looked like the sort of man who knew his way around a joke, but still couldn't be certain whether he was just toying with them for his own amusement. Johns sniffed, wiping his nose on his fingers.

'I've heard it referred to as the spring of secrets, which seems rather stupid if you can't see the damn thing or, worse still, if you're never seen again.' Hs face darkened. 'No secret's worth risking your neck for, you'd do well remembering that.' He looked at the map once more before Frank picked it up. 'Of course, it's a load of old rubbish, like all that stuff they teach you lot over in Rhaeder.'

'So you've never been to have a look,' said Gabby.

'You obviously weren't listening to me. I've seen plenty of similar maps.' He nodded at the paper in Frank's hand. 'All drawn by schoolchildren, all showing the whereabouts of a stash of gold or a bejewelled crown guarded by a dragon or something worse. If I believed all the stuff I saw I'd never set foot outside my front door.' As if he did that, anyway, thought Frank. 'Like I said, all a load of old rubbish. So stay away.'

Johns coughed and rubbed his belly like it was a delicate bowl of glass, a grimace brushing his face. He looked at Gabby.

'Thank your mum for the tonic.'

'I will.' Her tone now warm. 'And she'll be really pleased with the veg. Are you sure you can spare it?'

Johns waved his hand in a dismissive gesture.

'Well, you've have had a tough time. Your family more than most.' His gruff tone mellowed. 'I understand what that's like.'

***

'Nothing unusual about him, then,' said Frank as they walked up Johns's garden path, turning to look back at the house, watching for a twitch of the curtains.

'See what I mean?' said Gabby.

'He knew his stuff, though,' said Frank. Gabby stopped as they turned onto the road.

'And you believe him?'

Frank frowned and looked at the piece of paper in his hands. There had been nothing about Johns that gave him the impression he was lying. Yes, he came across as eccentric, but the clarity in his eyes as he told them about Irundi, the strain in his voice, the stillness in him, was completely compelling.

'It was something he said,' said Frank. 'Stay away.' He stopped. 'Stay away from something that doesn't exist?' He shook his head. 'This came from our book.' Frank waved the map in front of him. 'I think we should check it out, don't you?'

'I think so,' said Anya. 'Although we shouldn't tell Cas about the flesh-eating woodland sentinels.'

Gabby grabbed the map from Frank and studied it. Looking at the others she said:

'But he didn't tell us where it is, and I'm not going back in there to ask him.' She handed it back the Frank.

'I thought he was quite nice to you,' said Anya, dipping her head to the box of fruit and vegetables she was carrying. Gabby sniffed.

'Well, you can go back and ask Mr Creepy if you want to,' she said. 'I'm going home.' She wrapped her arms around herself and turned to go.

'There's no need,' said Frank. Gabby stopped.

'No need what?'

'No need to go back. Because I think I know exactly where the silent forest is.'

13

THE WRITING

He'd seen it on the map; a small hatched area of forest nestling in the larger area of woodland to the north of Rhaeder. Confirmed by Johns's eyes each and every time they fixed on the wall. The map of Byeland was so large there was no mistaking where his unforgiving gaze had landed a number of times, an innocent reflex every time he mentioned Irundi. He explained this to the others, although Johns's description didn't exactly hold an ounce of excitement for a trip to the forest. But Johns knew there was something there. How, was another question, one they were never going to ask.

***

The academy term didn't start for another week, but they agreed they'd head back early so they could spend a few days investigating what the map and Johns had told them and take a short trip up to the area of thick woodland a few miles to the North of Rhaeder, along the coast.

From the area Frank had seen marked on the map, he couldn't believe it would take them more than a couple of hours exploring the terrain; they'd be there and back in a day with, hopefully, the puzzle of the map and what it actually meant solved.

They wrote to Cas, asking him to meet them back in Rhaeder, explaining what they'd discovered and arranged transport the following day. Helen didn't appear to mind and was quite pleased that Gabby seemed more enthusiastic about returning to her studies, Frank and Anya conveniently forgetting to tell her the real reason.

Frank woke, pulling the covers up over his head, encasing

himself in darkness. He'd not slept well. Images of Johns's haunting description of their next destination and the thought of running into Spargo kept any rest from him. He couldn't shake his encounter with the head of the Alphaen from his mind. He knew about his dad's connection to all of this while Frank just had to make it up in his head. He had much more information about it than Frank would ever uncover unless he had the raging argument that was a constant thorn in his thoughts. Like it or not, he made the decision to seek Spargo out and find out more, regardless of what he might uncover, to try and make sense of the circular conversations he kept having in his head. Conversations that went nowhere.

He also kept replaying the images of Libby, as well as Gabby's laughed conversation with the boy from Crossways, earning him a restless few hours before dawn and a descent back into his troubled life.

Frank hauled himself up and willed himself into wakefulness, trying to focus on something positive but failing miserably. As he put the rest of his clothes in his bag and wandered to the kitchen, he felt the now familiar heavy weight of misery settle on his mood and he knew he would come across withdrawn or disagreeable the instant he laid eyes on Gabby.

He entered the kitchen where Gabby and Helen were animated in their discussion, Gabby's rebellious face trained on her mother. It was the envelope in Helen's hand that caught his eye and which appeared to be the subject of their exchange.

'Why would you want to do that?' said Gabby, making to snatch the envelope out of her mum's hand. Helen was too quick and held it away, out of Gabby's reach. Helen looked at Frank, careful not to take her attention from Gabby.

'Morning, Frank,' she said. She turned back to Gabby. 'We'll discuss this later.'

Gabby let out a loud huff and pouted. Turning to Frank, she said:

'Mum's threatening to have my Excelsus letter framed.'

'It's not a threat, Gabriella,' said Helen. 'I thought it would be nice to show your achievement. That's all.' Helen handed the envelope to Gabby, who grabbed it like it was about to disappear. 'There's no need to get all difficult about it.'

'I'm not being difficult.' Gabby growled the words through her teeth. 'I just don't see the point. No one's going to be interested and I don't want to see the name Aurora Moonhunter each time I come into the house thank you very much.' She turned to Frank. 'Tell me you don't have your letter on the wall back at the farm.' Frank shook his head, reluctant to get himself dragged into what seemed like a particularly insignificant and petty quarrel. His head was occupied with other things. Gabby braced her hands on her hips and looked back to Helen. 'You see, normal people don't have their children's letters framed.' She pulled the letter out of the envelope and opened it up. 'Dear Miss Asaro...' she read in a mocking and superior tone. 'I bet they're all the same standard drivel.' She handed it to Frank, discarding the envelope on the kitchen table. 'Recognise it?'

'Okay, that's enough,' said Helen. 'We'll discuss it when you can be sensible about it.'

'I am being sensible. You're the one who's being ridiculous.'

Frank could sense that Gabby wasn't going to back down but, then, neither was her mother who was doing a good job of keeping herself calm in the face of her sparky and challenging daughter. He dipped his eyes to the letter, his mind wandering back to St Barnabus school in Smithwood where he'd first read his own in Oliver Jelly's office; when his life was normal, before any of this started.

He looked back at the envelope, recalled the fabulous lettering, written in beautiful azure ink, which had first caught his attention; how important it made him feel. He stared for a moment before an uneasy feeling started to work its way into his stomach – something about the envelope. No, not the envelope; not that – something else, something there but just beyond his grasp. Something wasn't quite right. He felt Gabby's eyes on him.

'You've got that look on your face,' she said.

'Hm?'

'That look. The one you have when you're trying to work something out.'

'I wasn't aware I had a look of any sort.'

'You do. I know you. What's up?'

He shrugged. Gabby watched him with interest as Frank picked the envelope up and turned it over in his hands. Time hung for a moment as his mind thumbed through his thoughts, searching, discarding. His eyes scanned the copperplate lettering. No, not that. With a final look he placed the envelope back on the table and turned his attention to the letter, carefully examining the words. That was it. There was something about the words. He read the letter. It was the same as his, but...

Then he had it. He knew. He knew precisely what troubled him; what was out of place, yet he couldn't believe what he was thinking, what he was seeing. It wasn't possible. Not possible, yet he knew. He tried to remain calm, his gaze not leaving the single sheet of paper as his mind stopped him. He stood, paralysed by his certainty, of what it confirmed. He could still feel Gabby's steady eyes on him as he slowly re-read. And there it was, yet it couldn't be. The unusual curl of the y's and the uniquely crafted circles above each letter i made his skin flare and his breathing stop.

'It's nothing,' he said, placing the letter on the table while wondering how Aurora Moonhunter's handwriting could *exactly* match that on the mysterious love note he'd found hidden in the lining of his mum's small wooden box back at his grandmother's.

14

THE CONFRONTATION

Frank receded into silence for the journey back to Rhaeder. Both Gabby and Anya were with him, but he had no appetite for talking. He hoped they'd just put it down to adolescent moodiness – perhaps it was. He'd made some poor excuse to Gabby about his reaction to the letter, saying it brought back a mixture of memories – good and bad – through a forced smile. It wasn't altogether untrue but he found it hard to believe he'd had to add something else to his growing list of things that didn't make any sense. As if he didn't have enough to consume him without the thought of Moonhunter being another player in his family's unfolding mess.

His young mind wasn't adequately prepared for any of this. He could feel himself teetering on the edge of control as his thoughts boiled. He'd had enough of Moonhunter's evasiveness. She'd been as slippery as an eel ever since he'd first met her. Well, she wasn't getting out of this one; it was time to take control before it took control of him.

He was thankful that the transport to Rhaeder left when it did, meaning Gabby and her mum had to postpone their argument so they could get out of the door and meet Anya. It meant no one would notice the look on his face or sense him withdrawing into his own head until they were on their way, but as Gabby and Anya failed in their attempts to draw him into conversation, he knew that would only be temporary and he could tell by her sideways looks that Gabby was already feeling short tempered with his sulkiness. He didn't blame her, but he didn't care.

The transport made good time and reached the town in the honeyed sunshine of the mid-afternoon. Frank's journey had been consumed with thoughts of Moonhunter. Nothing else. He gave a cursory goodbye to the others, trying his best to appear slightly more cheery but noticing the spread of annoyance on Gabby's face. They agreed to meet up at the town's north arch the next day before going their separate ways.

Frank made a direct line for the academy. He had no way of knowing if Moonhunter would be there, but his insides were so tight he didn't care. He'd wait all day and night if he had to. His mind raced hard; whatever her connection to his family, he was going to find out and he wouldn't leave without an answer.

The walk from the town square, up Iron lane to the academy and the great stone vulture was one he'd made hundreds of times; even so, it seemed to take twice as long as normal for him to arrive at the bridge and head into the depths of the west wing and Moonhunter's office.

Excelsus was empty. With every stride Frank's boots seemed to thunder on the polished stone floor, echoing through the wood-panelled walls and down towards the small atrium where the painted eye on Moonhunter's office door would be waiting, watching. He stopped in the middle of the floor, adjusting his bag so he could access the small side pocket where he'd put the letter after leaving his gran's. He pulled out the torn love note and ran his weary eyes over it in anticipation, readying himself.

The door faded away as he approached, allowing him access to her office. He gulped bravery, fingering his locket, and entered. Moonhunter was sitting at her desk and looked up as he strode in. For a moment his confidence left him as her alluring gaze fixed on his.

'Hello Frank. I wasn't expecting you back.' Her calm smile would normally draw him in, relax him, but not this time. He didn't answer as he made his way purposefully across the room and thrust his hand at her before dropping the half-sheet of paper in the middle of her desk. Star hissed. Moonhunter didn't flinch. Calm as a sleeping serpent, her eyes silently questioned Frank who stiffened slightly. She shrugged, then looked down to the paper.

All Frank could hear was the sound of his own breath and the pulse in his neck as his heart rate ramped up. The voice in his head was shouting at her, screaming for her to tell him how she knew his mum.

Slowly, Moonhunter let her left hand wander to the sheet of paper. She slid it slowly around on the desktop, the shifting of paper on wood the only sound. She let the tips of her polished nails dance on it.

'What is this?' she said behind her indifferent smile, soothing Frank's nerves and quelling his anticipation. He said nothing, but simply nodded at the letter, demanding with his eyes that she pick it up and look at it. With a degree of caution he'd not seen in her before, she slid her thumb into the fold and opened it up, the writing drawing her attention. Her eyes wandered over the page but her expression remained completely neutral. She looked at Frank and shrugged again.

'I'm not sure I understand,' she said, looking back at the letter before folding it and placing her scarlet nails on the top. She tapped a slow rhythm. Frank felt himself fluster.

'The writing,' he said. 'It's yours.' He could feel the tightness of his breath but was determined to see this through, to see how she tried to twist her way out of this. She couldn't, he wouldn't let her.

'The writing? I don't —'

'Please don't play games with me.' Frank surprised himself with the assertiveness in his voice. 'The letter's in your handwriting.' He nodded again to the paper under Moonhunter's tapping hand. She opened it up once more and looked back down at it. A slow blink. Her face gave absolutely nothing away.

'Are you sure, Frank?' She was entirely composed and unerringly rich in her tone. 'Anyone might have written it. I agree that it's similar to mine, but that would be a coincidence.' She paused. 'Where did you get it?'

Frank felt himself swallow hard. He could feel his confidence, brimming on the way to her office, start its slow retreat, although he felt there was something odd in her question. Not in her tone, or the way she asked, but that she'd asked it at all.

He couldn't have got it wrong, could he? Ever since he'd seen Gabby's Excelsus invitation at her house in Crossways he was completely sure that it and the letter that Moonhunter drummed upon were penned by the same person but, now he stood in the face of the unflappable principal, the heavy seeds of doubt began to bear fruit. As bubble bursting went, this was a terrifically large one. He was sure Moonhunter was about to conjure a large hole to swallow him up.

Frank shook his head as uncertainty clawed at him. He could feel the heat rising within him. He wasn't wrong but... Now all he wanted to do was get away. He was on the verge of turning, to make his way out of her office at a quicker pace than that with which he'd arrived until Moonhunter's fingers twitched, pulling the piece of paper towards her in what looked like an involuntary reflex. He noticed her jaw tighten, making him reconsider – he was right. He knew he was right yet Moonhunter, with her calm mastery, made him doubt himself.

Their eyes locked and Frank saw a flicker of something he couldn't quite put his finger on, a faraway look, glassy and cheerless, like someone had loosed a single drop of lead into her eyes.

The room shivered. Had this woman been involved with his mum? If so, she wouldn't have seen her for at least fifteen years. She might be able to conceal her feelings from an old torn letter, but from a picture... Quickly, he grabbed the thin silver chain that hung around his neck and lifted the locket over his head, Moonhunter's eyes tracked him, followed his movements the way her cat silently hunted. With fumbling fingers he pulled at the catch, prising the delicate metal casing apart, taking a long look at the portrait of his mother before placing it face-down on the desk with as much gentleness as he could muster. He thought he saw Moonhunter's expression tense as she looked down, then back to Frank.

'Go on,' he said with a slight jerk of his chin. 'Take a look.'

Moonhunter's eyes lingered on the locket, a muscle in her jaw flexed. She was still impossible to read. The moments passed for what seemed like forever; still she looked down. Deliberating. Slow breaths. Silence swung like a lead pendulum between them. She reached with her flawless painted fingernails and touched the ornament, gently pulling it towards her, sliding it silently over the polished oak of her desk, her fingers lightly stroking the fretwork casing. Star watched it like a mouse.

'What is this, Frank?' she said, her tone light. She looked back up at him, the light from the window playing on her soft cheekbones and her slight smile, now looking forced.

'Take a look,' he repeated. 'Please.'

Unhurried, she took the locket between her thumb and index finger and slowly turned it over, the sunlight glinting off the metal case cast delicate dabs of yellow over her desk.

Frank watched as Moonhunter's eyes fixed on the picture inside. She appeared not to see anything unusual at first, like it was simply an image of an unknown woman; but then she looked closer. And closer still. Her hand went to her mouth. For a moment she froze, staring, disbelieving. Her usual calm and neutral splendour crumbled as hot tears welled in her eyes, tumbling down her shocked face.

She let out a choked gasp, holding back what appeared to be a deep flood of emotion; Frank could feel her fighting it, could see the slight tremors in her hand, working their way across the whole of her body. Moonhunter tensed, swallowing hard in her fight to keep control. Whatever reaction he thought he'd get, it certainly wasn't this. He looked on as Moonhunter let out a sob, biting her knuckle in an attempt to quell the seething emotion the locket had laid upon her.

'Becky,' she whispered.

15

The Confirmation

The word hung between them, pealing like a struck bell. Shock slackened her face. Tears fell in hot streaks faster than she could wipe them from her cheeks. She tried to blink them away then lifted her clouded eyes up from the locket. He marked every tick and flicker. Her eyes danced across Frank's face; she'd seen him a hundred times before but now she regarded him as if for the first time. Frank felt a hot shiver pass down his spine. Hearing his mother's unfamiliar name on her tongue snapped something loose in him.

'No.' The cold granite in her voice caught Frank by surprise as Moonhunter stood, shaking her head, the grind from the chair legs filling his ears. 'You *can't* be. You can't be...Becky's son.' Her voice trailed off to a whisper of disbelief. She bit her knuckle again. 'Tell me it's not true,' she said, her voice trembling, shaken hard by an earthquake of emotion as Frank looked on in disbelief, knowing that he was right. She had known his mother and now a thousand questions littered his brain, pushing on the inside of his head but in the moment he couldn't find one to ask the enigmatic Moonhunter who now stood in suspended silence.

With the principal still fixed on the locket, he quickly decided that now wasn't the time to engage in a deep discussion of the past; a discussion that could wait until he could clear his mind; *if* he could clear his mind. He couldn't be sure what might happen if he stayed and it was obvious from Moonhunter's reaction that something raw, something untamed still cut her inside.

Snatching up the locket from her hand, Frank gave the principal a bewildered look of his own before turning and leaving her office.

He strode out of the building, overflowing with confusion. He stopped in the middle of the plaza; a few wagons pulled past him and on into the town, one had to swerve, narrowly missing crushing him under its heavy load. The driver stopped and threw a string of curses but Frank barely heard him and, at that moment, he wouldn't have cared if he'd been mangled in the spokes or dragged through the streets. Nothing was capable of dousing the fire in his head. In fact, he thought it would never clear.

He stood staring at his feet, trying to find his focus, to make sense of things, replaying the last twenty minutes second by second, over and over but it was no good. Nothing fitted together. Then all he could picture was Moonhunter's shattered eyes against her paling skin and that she shared his utter astonishment of how they were somehow bound together. But that didn't even take a single step to answering the one question that throbbed in his head and she may never give it to him, the answer to the question of how she'd come to write half of a love letter to his mum.

16

THE PUNCH

Frank climbed the steps in front of the gothic portico of the Council building and pushed at the door. The spartan, functional foyer, dressed for the blandness of business was an echo of jabbing voices and buzzing with Council officials and visitors talking noisily around the uninviting space.

Frank passed them like they weren't there, striding up to the raised reception desk to the rear, the meeting with Moonhunter still fresh and playing in his mind. He barged shoulders with a short man who growled at him but Frank kept his spinning head down and headed straight on, ignoring the pointed words aimed at his back.

'Can I help you?' The sharp voice of Mrs Frost, the vulture-like receptionist whose gauntlet they had run before, lanced him. Frank drew in a short, irritated breath and felt the red rise in his bones. He knew his decision to come straight here after his unsatisfactory trip to the academy was the wrong one, but any straight thinking had just been bent at right-angles and as he looked at the harsh features of the officious woman he could feel himself spoiling for something unruly.

'I need to talk to Spyro.'

Mrs Frost peered at him over her glasses, looking like she'd swallowed something unpleasant.

'If you mean commander Spargo, then I'm afraid he's a very busy man. You'll have to make an appointment.' She sniffed and looked back at the papers on her desk.

'He'll want to see me,' said Frank, cold impatience beginning in his voice. She appeared to sense it and regarded him again, a thin, superior smile spreading across her face.

'And why would he want to see a boy like you?'

Frank flared at her tone.

'None of your damn business.' He immediately wanted to punch her glasses off. He fixed her with a falcon-like stare which she returned, an invitation for confrontation. She beat a rhythm on the table with her pencil.

'If you take that attit—'

'Just *get* him.' Frank wasn't sure how far he raised his voice, but the whole foyer descended into instant quiet, each of the dozen or so faces ditching their own conversations and turning to see what was starting to boil up at the far end of the room. Mrs Frost twitched her nose, her eyes shifted sideways at the security who guard appeared behind her, standing a few yards back in silent observation.

'Will you kindly remove this impudent young lout,' she said, not taking her eyes off Frank.

The guard nodded and stepped forward, his large hands making a grab for Frank's arm. Frank shrugged him off, batting the guard's arm away and took a step back. The silence in the lobby clotted some more. The guard, stocky and shaven-headed, drew in a long breath, his expression turning to fire, looking like his long, bored days spent pacing around the insipid entrance had put him in the mood to finally do someone some damage. He reached for Frank, again.

'Get your hands off me.' Frank gave the hefty guard a heftier shove, knocking him off balance. He looked back at Mrs Frost. 'I need to see Spyro,' he repeated with restrained calm, knowing that it wasn't going to get him anywhere as the security guard stepped forward again, making a grab for Frank's collar.

He wasn't sure what came over him but as the guard toppled back, blood pouring from his nose, he realised too late that he'd thrown an instinctive punch. Frank splayed the fingers of his right hand, wincing at where his knuckles had connected to the man's face, looking at the spray of red across his hand and fingers. Then everything slowed as he felt himself being pushed to the ground, at least two people were on him, pinning him to the dry, hard stone floor and tying his hands behind his back. He felt hands grip him painfully underneath the armpits before he was hauled back to his feet and dragged away like a common drunkard.

17

THE CELL

Time twitched by at a snail's pace in the small cell deep within the Council offices. Frank sat, knees pulled to his chest, inspecting his hand, feeling the hard bed of stone underneath the thin sacking, stuffed with straw that served as a rudimentary mattress.

His scuffed knuckles were already beginning to bruise and he flexed his back against the pain from the knee that had pinned him to the ground seconds after he'd lamped the security guard. He should feel sorry, feel he'd let himself down but all he felt was anger, that he'd do it again if he could. Even now, in his cold isolated incarceration he had trouble finding the threads of his own sanity to keep himself from boiling over.

He folded his arms across his chest and looked from one side to the other. The cell was an eight foot square hole of complete misery. Steel bars separated his confinement from two others, one on either side which, thankfully, were empty, reserved for drunks and vagrants and petty criminals. People like him. Small, barred windows above head height let in sunlight from the street above.

Over the threshold of his prison door a short corridor ran to a hefty wooden door which had been closed and locked as soon as Frank had been thrown in. The sound of the heavy key turning in the lock followed by the guards receding footsteps the last thing he'd heard from within. The hush was unbearable. He'd occasionally hear a muted voice from the window, whispering taunts of liberty but the outside world seemed a long way away. He sat. He stewed.

The molten red inside him began to subside as the minutes slowed. He could feel himself simmering, sitting in the large, stinking cow-pat of his own misery, but he wasn't sure he cared. What would they do to him? He'd hit a Council security guard, an unforgivable crime. Perhaps they'd get his dad to come and get him; in which case he'd rather stay where he was, where nothing else would trouble him. If keeping him here was meant to give him time to reflect on his actions and show signs of atonement, they could all stuff it. Being locked up was the least of his worries.

More time limped past, the light outside the small windows began to fade. Frank pressed the heels of his hands into his eyes as he heard the lock to the main door open with a heavy clunk that echoed through the thick air around the cell bars. First, a guard appeared, then, into the corridor strode Spyro Spargo, wearing his full Alphaen uniform, casting a different, more serious and official look to the casual playboy that Frank had encountered before.

He nodded to the guard to leave and stepped in front of Frank's tiny cell, looking through the bars.

Then he laughed. Frank couldn't believe it, but the head of the Alphaen actually laughed at him as he stared though the bars like he was a zoo attraction. Frank felt his anger start to rise again.

'Piss off, Spyro,' said Frank, which only made Spargo laugh louder. Despite Spargo's customary charismatic smile Frank wanted to rip his throat out. 'Glad to see you find it funny.' He could feel the subtle violence in his voice.

'Hilarious,' said Spargo, unable to wipe the familiar grin off his face. Frank looked away. 'Oh don't worry Frank, I spent a night or two in here when I was your age.' Frank looked back, his eyebrows raised, Spargo's comment, cool and calm, extinguishing some of the anger inside him. 'What, think you're the first youngster to get himself into a spot of bother?' Spargo shook his head and clicked his tongue. 'Teenagers,' he tutted. 'The last time the guards hauled me down here I was so drunk I spent a whole day and night in this very cell sobering up. Jeez, I was a filthy mess. Puked my guts up all over the place.' He laughed again, this time at himself. 'They'd caught me urinating over the door of the Council offices. I couldn't remember a thing, but there you go. Not a story to tell my grandchildren.' He chuckled and Frank felt the shackles of his confinement shift a little. 'Or perhaps it is.'

'Thanks for the story, but have you come to get me out of here, or what?'

Spargo pursed his lips.

'Punching a Council guard is pretty serious, Frank.'

'Well he asked for it.' Spargo's eyes widened, his smile an indication that he was, for some reason, impressed. Frank shrugged at the silence. He wasn't sorry.

'You can't just go around doing stuff like that.' Spargo's tone turned serious. 'Whatever's eating you, you need to sort it out another way.' Frank took a deep breath in and exhaled long and loud. Spargo could think what he liked, he wasn't living Frank's life, he had no idea what he was going through. No one did. His life sucked, it was the worst life of anyone he knew. 'I'm sure I could pull the odd string or two for the son of my old mate.'

'Don't bother,' said Frank. 'Really.' Spargo hesitated.

'Maybe we should have a chat first.' He held up a small bunch of keys and gave them a shake. Frank glanced quickly at the sound, then to the boyish grin on Spargo's golden face.

'It's your fault, anyway' said Frank. Spargo raised an eyebrow. 'If you weren't so important I wouldn't be in here.'

Spargo let out a laugh.

'Is that right,' he said. 'And I guess it was my fists doing the work too, eh?'

Frank attempted a smile but was sure he was unsuccessful.

'What do you want to talk about?'

'In my office.' Spargo jerked his head to the door that spelled a degree of freedom. Frank hauled himself onto his tired feet, prompting Spargo to lower his hand and insert the key. He turned the key in the lock and stepped to one side, ushering Frank out.

18

The Golden Intake

Spargo's office was understated. Situated in a quiet corner of the upper floor of the office building it had a view on to the narrow streets to the rear of the town square. The northerly aspect, small windows and the height of the surrounding buildings outside gave it a permanent feeling of dusk, despite the bright salmon walls. The room was awash with the fresh fragrance of citrus and rosewater. Brightly painted wooden furniture lined the walls and a scarlet rug covered the floor, offsetting the pinkish paint perfectly. A huge map of Byeland and the neighbouring territories was spread across a wall, reminding him of Johns's kitchen.

Frank stood at a large bookcase, inspecting the leather-bound spines of the books, feigning interest. Spargo had left him there while he attended to some business. Behind the small desk, Spargo's sword hung in its sheath and belt from a hook on the wall, the peacock-shaped pommel gleaming at him. His dad's old sword, the symbol of his heritage clearly visible. The symbol that marked his dad out as a guardian. Frank felt himself tense, the sword gripping him, thoughts flashed through his mind of him brandishing it at his dad's throat. The image lingered.

The spell was broken when the door opened and Spargo walked in holding a small silver tray on which stood two cups of tea together with half a dozen chocolate cookies.

'Polly tells me these are your favourite,' he said, placing it down on his desk.

Frank had forgotten the last time he had eaten anything and felt the tap of hunger on the inside of his stomach. He also registered

Spargo's comment, lightly thrown, designed to reveal that he'd been dipping into Frank's life, to show something of the game he was playing, moving in the shadows, or in plain sight, sweeping up the threads of Frank and the others quest, casually drawing in the strands he knew existed. Building the picture.

Frank felt himself beaten, mere moves away from check-mate with a far more talented player. It was more than just an uneven match.

Spargo sat and waved his hand at the chairs on the other side of his desk. They sat.

'So, Frank. What was so important that you felt you had to break someone's nose for?' Spargo chuckled to himself, his pristine white teeth sparkled. Frank fumbled for a cookie, drawing up the questions and conversation he'd rehearsed in his head and took a deep breath.

'I need to ask you something about my Dad; about his part of the Simbrian.'

Spargo cocked his head to one side and nodded.

'Fire away, as long as you don't feel you need to punch it out of me.'

Frank let Spargo's continued attempts at humour fall flat to the ground.

'How do you know he doesn't have it any more?'

Spargo's good-natured grin faded. He sat back and regarded the teenager for a moment. Frank felt his shoulders twitch.

'It's a long story, Frank. I'm not sure it's mine to tell.' Frank exhaled. He knew exactly whose story it was, but Spargo could stuff it if he thought he was going to ask his dad. 'You know, I should let him know that you've been in a spot of bother.'

'Do what you like,' said Frank. 'I don't care what he thinks.' He saw the shift in Spargo's eyes. 'My dad's not going to tell me.'

'Have you asked him?' The raise of an eyebrow. Spargo didn't need to ask Frank the question but, even so, an image of Frank's next conversation with his dad flashed through his mind. It wouldn't be about the Simbrian. If he ever had another conversation.

'I don't think he's my favourite person at the moment.' Spargo raised an eyebrow again, flashed his teeth and nodded.

'I fell out plenty of times with my dad when I was your age. Whatever it is, you'll soon get over it.'

Frank shrugged. He wouldn't, whatever anyone told him, whatever Spargo thought of his dad, or what he thought he knew. Spargo might know about his dad being a guardian, but Frank tensed at what Spargo didn't know, the darkness that ran in his blood, the truth that no one knew but him.

'The Simbrian would have been passed to me, eventually.' Frank felt a stab of emotion. That wasn't true. He wasn't the next in line. No Penny blood flowed through his veins and nothing he could do would ever change that, but he banked on Spargo not knowing. Spargo nodded. 'So, you see, I'd like to know what happened without having to bring it up with my dad.'

Spargo scratched the back of his neck and looked out of the window. The receding sun cast a dark shadow across his smooth cheeks. Frank waited. After a moment, Spargo took a sip of tea and a mouthful of cookie and said:

'Back when we were at Excelsus, we were part of a little club, a secret society; although I'm sure it wasn't all that secret.' He kept his eyes fixed on the outside. With a few selected words he immediately had Frank's attention. An image of Wordsworth Hums passed through Frank's mind, of the old man telling him and the others how Dagmar was a member of some underground club when he was at the academy. With Spargo?

'When you say "we"?'

Spargo chewed the inside of his mouth.

'The golden intake. There was me and Lawrence, Dagmar and Simeon Peth, your uncle.' The mention of his strange uncle's name caught Frank off guard. The four names seemed the most unlikely of bed-fellows but even though Frank's mind started to pick at the reasons why, he knew his head wasn't thinking straight enough to understand the connections from years ago.

'Just the four of you?' was all he could think of saying.

'Just the four of us; oh, and the person who ran it, of course.'

'Who was that?'

'Hector Baggus.'

'The principal?'

'One and the same, Frank. I think he had the knack of identifying which of his students were a bit more capable than the others. He even saw through my complete lack of effort and thought I had something to offer. Remember, Frank, Excelsus never makes mistakes. He used to allow us to involve ourselves in areas outside the usual curriculum, talk about the kinds of things that we were really interested in and that involved the darker elements of our country's history. Then, one day, Dagmar brought up the subject of the Simbrian.' Frank's eyes opened wide, Spargo fixed him with a searching look and let the comment hang. 'I remember Baggus being miserably vague on the subject at the start, but Dagmar wouldn't let it drop. Session after session he'd want to talk about nothing else – a right terrier down a rabbit hole. I don't know where he got his information but Baggus couldn't shake him off the subject.'

'Wouldn't his dad have told him?'

'No, Dagmar's father died when he was young and he was drawn closer to the Dahkes. I reckon the younger Etamin started feeding him some details once he got his place here. I wasn't sure at the time if it was just idle interest but, looking back, I would say that Etamin created the spark that lit his obsession. Then your dad met your mum and the group kind of split up.' Spargo caught the question in Frank's face. 'That's right, Lawrence began an obsession all of his own.' Frank's mind flashed back to Moonhunter's office, to the letter.

'Did you know her before they met?'

Spargo shook his head. 'No, Lawrence met her while he was out riding one day. I think her horse had gone lame and he just happened to be passing. He helped her back home and the rest, as they say, is the rest.' Spargo shot Frank a grin. 'He adored your mum. True, raw love. But...there was something about her, Becky. She was...different.'

'Different?'

Spargo hesitated, searching for the words. Frank waited, wondering if Spargo's hesitation was deliberate.

'Wild, unleashed.' His eyes sparkled, searching Frank's face. 'Dangerous.' It was an odd choice of words. 'Don't think I'm speaking out of turn, Frank. That's just how I saw her; how a lot of people saw her.'

'Is that how my dad saw her?' It was an obvious question.

'No.' Spargo's response was quick. He appeared to sense it and let out a chuckle under his breath. 'What I mean is that when you're as smitten as Lawrence was, it can be difficult to see anything other than what you want to see. Lawrence is a good man, Frank, but I wasn't sure he and Becky were suited. I think Dagmar sensed it too.' Frank felt himself bristle at Spargo's comment. He wasn't there to talk about his parent's relationship, nor did he care for Spargo's opinions and he could feel the conversation meandering off the subject. Frank was wary, Spargo had previously demonstrated his mastery at drawing out information and he had no idea which blind alley he might be being led down.

'You were talking about Dagmar's interest in the Simbrian,' he said. Spargo eyed Frank for a moment. 'Did he know? Did Dagmar manage to steal my Dad's part of the Simbrian?' The clear stepping stones to his conclusion. Spargo's silence egged him on. 'That's why they fell out. Dagmar told me...' Frank bit his tongue, but noticed the glint in Spargo's eyes, like he'd just triggered the trap he'd been leading Frank into.

'You met him, then?' Frank's look gave him away but Spargo shook his head. 'Don't worry, Frank. It was obvious when you brought back the black stag that you'd been up close and personal with him. So what did Dagmar tell you?'

Frank gave an inward shake of his head as he tossed around the thought of telling Spargo anything but, with a long breath:

'Dagmar told me he and my dad had been best friends, but they had a falling out.' Frank didn't have to put too many pieces of the simple puzzle together to understand what had sliced them apart, but Spargo gave a shake of his head.

'You're right in that they were best friends and you'd think that would be the case. Kzarlac's biggest bandit, the one with the Simbrian obsession does over his best mate to further his own ambition. Sounds about right, eh but, no, that's not how it went.' Frank looked on. Spargo's unravelling tale had him bewitched. 'They were best friends until Becky came along.'

Frank didn't get what Spargo was talking about.

'But if Dagmar didn't steal it, how does he have it?'

'Well, given what I've just told you about our small club, maybe it's a bit more obvious?' Frank shook his head. Spargo's tanned brow creased. 'Ever wondered why Lawrence hates your uncle Simeon so much?'

It all began to fit. A seamless puzzle; you just had to draw the lines in the right place and make the connections which were obvious to those involved. Through the medium of the golden intake's most capable members, Simeon had uncovered Frank and his family's legacy and used it to strengthen his bonds with Kzarlac.

Frank had never heard anyone speak a word in his defence or say anything even slightly flattering or kind about him. The building blocks of the plan his weasel of an uncle must have hatched, refined and executed started to fall one by one around Frank's feet. No wonder Simeon had got close to and even ended up marrying his aunt Rachel. How much closer could he actually have managed to get to the Penny family in order to steal what wasn't his.

In that moment he felt like the woeful Edwina Chetto, her life wilfully plundered with immoral cruelty for the fragment of the Simbrian; ruined by the greed of her husband. And so it was with Simeon.

'I suppose that's why he's never spoken about it?' said Frank, wondering if his dad felt either embarrassed at losing it to someone like Simeon or just wanted to forget the whole thing. Certainly time hadn't even begun to close the chasm of animosity between them. But Spargo shook his head again.

'No, that's not the case,' he said, bracing his forearms on his thighs and clasping his slender fingers together. 'What you have to understand, Frank, is that the Simbrian's power is meant to be truly fearsome; overwhelming even. There are many facets to it, most of them unknown and likely to stay that way. One of them is the curse that is bound to the guardians. If a guardian has been relieved of their fragment, either by force or voluntarily, they cannot openly talk about it. Only if they are asked directly by another can they safely discuss it otherwise the curse will inflict a great degeneration of the mind on the individual, designed to keep the secret. And, given so few people even know of the Simbrian, it's unlikely that would ever happen.'

Again, Frank thought back to his uncomfortable encounter with Edwina Chetto, Oliver's poor bedridden and wretched mother who lived out her existence as a prisoner of her own mind, her recurring and frantic delusions keeping her chained to her bed in their grand house in Nimiz without any hope of peace or escape. The curse Spargo had just revealed had, without doubt, embedded itself in her soul.

'So,' Spargo continued. 'The fact of the matter is your dad couldn't talk about it, not even with you, once Simeon stole it and gave it to Dagmar, although he probably didn't want to. That's what Lawrence is like, he keep things inside.' Frank felt his skin prickle. Tell me something I don't know, he thought. 'But he only does that to protect those he loves.'

Frank huffed and Spargo caught the sneer on Frank's face. 'Maybe you should ask him about it. There are always two sides to a story, Frank.'

19

THE WOODLAND

One night at the Black Feather was one too many as far as Frank was concerned. Sitting in miserable isolation just off the main road from Rhaeder towards the border with the Kontox territories, set back so it wouldn't bother travellers, dark as a coal scuttle and just as uninviting, the inn was the sort of place that you'd normally take one look at and decide very quickly not to enquire any further.

But Frank, Gabby, Cas and Anya didn't have the luxury of choice. The wild, late summer storm that served as their travelling companion had since swept through, but their arrival at the inn the previous evening was greeted with a maiming wind and rain that spat from the sky in great chunks, meaning any thoughts of camping at the edge of the forest were washed away with the dirt and debris and they were forced to seek shelter. The angry clouds, the colour of an oil slick, darkened the building beyond unwelcoming. The front door and weather-beaten shutters chattered uncontrollably against the ferocity of the storm.

The landlady couldn't have been less interested in them as she brought them scant plates of boiled salted pork, unsalted over-boiled vegetables and a pitcher of weak and watery ale. The room they rented had two double beds, covered in damp sheets that reeked of mildew and pillows barely filled with millet, making Frank yearn to be back in his cell in Rhaeder. They had to ask twice for the landlady to light the fire while the storm hammered its fist on the windows until the small hours.

A bad night's sleep was the last thing Frank needed. He'd started waking before dawn, head stuffed with angry thoughts of his dad, of Moonhunter, of Leo, of his uncle Simeon and more and fatigue clawed at his sore eyes and ran through his body. Exactly what he didn't need as they set off toward the thick tree line which lay a hundred yards behind the inn.

He was grateful that Spargo had been called to an important meeting the previous day and had simply shown him the door, allowing him into the freedom of the streets even though his mind held him prisoner. Back at Polly's he'd not got much rest before meeting up with the others in the morning, delaying their trip until later in the day because of the weather, which dipped his mood even more.

Frank had deliberately set his distance from the others during their slow progress as they made their way north. He could tell they knew, that he kept himself apart – both mentally and physically, keeping himself a few yards ahead, enough to shut them out of the twists his life had taken, that showed no sign of unravelling. He hoped a short foray into the forest might be just the thing he needed to distract him, just to take his mind away from his troubles. But they noticed.

Welcome sunlight drifted down on them in milky amber shafts, warming them and injecting its gentle spirit into their steps as they reached the row of mature sycamores, the gatekeepers of the forest, stopping to gather their thoughts.

'What are we looking for?' said Cas, peering into the light that found a path through the canopy and between the trees.

Frank shrugged. He didn't know, he just knew there was something unusual here, somewhere beyond what they could see. He'd wanted to release Tweedy, to send her up an on to scout the forest, to save them the time and effort but, in the melee of his meeting with Moonhunter and punching the Council guard, he'd let it slip his mind.

Anya's face was taut, carefully scanning the woodland, very different to Cas who hadn't looked particularly enthusiastic when he'd arrived in Rhaeder to be told all they knew about the map, their encounter with Johns and the need to find something in the silent forest.

'I guess we'll know when we find it,' said Anya, her words slightly distant. 'I can't sense anything.' She looked round, the sun lighting her olive skin. 'I know I'm a rubbish seer, but I can normally sense something but here...nothing.'

Frank wasn't concerned. He'd grown up more or less living in the woodland around the farm. Being hemmed in by nature didn't worry him, familiar as he was with the quiet sounds and rhythm of what the forest offered. Even so, this felt different. He could sense the edge to their venture, to what lay beyond the trees and, thus far, nothing connected to the Simbrian had gone particularly well. There was something in there, buried deep in the woods, away from the distractions of civilisation.

Johns knew. How he'd known was a mystery but Frank felt his imagination playing tricks on him as he looked into the trees. Johns's brief description had initially found him excited and curious but now they were here, the cautionary colour of his gruff and solitary voice kept his senses alert.

He pulled the map out of his pocket and inspected it for the hundredth time. West, that's was all it told him. West into the forest, towards the sea, towards the strange turret symbol inked into the map that had led them here. If only he could clear his head, shake off the simmering but the others still regarded him as if he'd been possessed by an angry, miserable and unapproachable spirit.

It was Gabby who took the first steps into the trees, silently urging the others to follow. Anya adjusted her glasses and headed after her. Frank noticed Cas's shoulders hunch and watched as his friend swallowed, his eyes catching Frank's.

'Come on,' said Frank. 'The sooner we get in, the sooner we get out.'

Frank brought up the rear, tracking Gabby as she strode ahead in silence. Frank watched the way she turned her head left and right, then up into the lower branches of the trees, the natural movements of someone who had learned to be alert to danger. Instincts forged both from their years of brushing up against the evil of Kzarlac, and from her life as a Prismian refugee.

The treetops were rich with cool shades of green. The dense foliage still allowed the watery shades of morning light through, pitching shadows across their path but not slowing their progress. The undergrowth was thin, nothing to impede them as they headed in the general direction of their unknown destination. The forest swallowed them up, wrapping its arms around them and gathering them up into its bosom. Birdsong rose and fell to the rhythm of their footsteps, discarded twigs and branches snapping under their feet, testament to the dry summer that had left its mark across Byeland, untouched by the previous day's downpour.

Deeper into the trees they headed going at pace, jogging and weaving further, keeping the sun to their left, the welcome shade keeping the sweat at bay. Despite no discernible pathway, the space between the tree trunks provided easy access into the forest. By the way Johns had talked about the place, Frank had expected them to find ghouls and demons lurking in the dark corners behind every large oak or birch. But there was absolutely nothing unusual about it. Nothing exceptional.

Then Gabby came to a stuttering halt. Frank, maybe twenty yards behind, slowed but could see she stood staring hard at the ground, her head turning from side to side. The others quickly caught up with her, Cas puffing out his cheeks and bracing his hands on his knees.

'What's up,' said Frank, placing his hand on the back of Anya's shoulder as she stood next to Gabby, both girls silent. She didn't look up, keeping her concentrated stare on the woodland floor.

'This is odd,' she said. 'Don't you think?'

20

THE SILENT FOREST

The deep fissure ran left and right as far as they could see, through the undergrowth and out of sight like a badly infected wound. The colour of the deepest midnight. It was no more than three feet wide along its entire length, but the forest had retreated further, away from the narrow chasm in the ground, exposing a sickly, unnatural void through the trees. Jagged, silvery rock edged the precipice, glinting in the apricot light, lying exposed and threatening to bite at their feet. Gabby took a tentative pace forward and looked down between the gnarled edges.

'Strange,' she said to herself, unable to avert her eyes from the abnormal crevice. She turned and shrugged. 'It goes pretty deep. I can't see the bottom.'

Frank stepped over and peered into the gap. Darkness stared back at him, masking the deep as well as the feeling that something unknown lurked out of sight, an unseen demon set to jump up and snap them out of the air should they defy the warning signs and cross. The caustic smell of ash and charred vegetation rose in his nostrils.

Frank looked across to the other side. Something tugged against his instincts to turn and go back, something further in the forest. A group of rooks burst from the trees and rose, heading away, back to the road, deep-throated calls thrown their way as a warning.

'We need to go that way,' he said, jerking his chin, not looking at the others. He breathed deeply and stepped across the divide, stopping and looking into the tangle of trees before him. The air turned a degree lower. Frank felt it as he turned around. Shivered.

'Coming?' Anya sprung over, followed by Gabby. Cas stood, hands on hips. He shook his head slightly.

'Why do I think this is a bad idea?' he said.

'Because we never have any good ideas?' said Frank.

The woods were bare and thick, thicker than any Frank had been in before. He'd been brought up around nature, learned not to fear its presence. This felt different. Completely different. Fear; dark oppressive fear hung between the boughs of the trees, and remaining thoughts of goodness or kindness immediately leached away from him.

What limited light they could make out struggled to make its way through the desolate branches above and the thin layer of mist that swam over the forest floor. The rough bark of the trees looked like the crawling fingers of the undead. But that wasn't what bothered Frank — it was the quiet, the thick unnerving quiet, that Frank felt most disturbing.

Woodlands always ran to their own rhythm, to their own sound; subtle birdsong, delicate rustling of leaves, the creak of a bough in the breeze but, for reasons he couldn't understand, not this one. The place to which they had been brought by their mysterious map had had its soul completely ripped out, like nature didn't want to be there and much of it had made its escape and found itself a more welcoming place to live and breathe many years ago. It swam of death, and cold – like the longest winter night.

Frank turned to Anya.

'Keep your wits about you,' he said.

He looked between the trees; as much as he tried he couldn't convince himself of anything other than there was something waiting for them there.

Gabby took a few steps forward and stared into the bleakness.

'Any ideas which way,' she said. 'And don't say back the way we came, Cas.' Her eyes stayed fixed on the woodland, her jaw tight, face harrowed.

'I guess it's onward.' Frank looked at Anya; she nodded back, her face determined. With a deep breath, he made his way past

Gabby and into the black maw of the forest.

There was none of the comfort of the sweet smell of chestnut and pine or earthy, heady feel of dry loam underfoot. There was none of that; the stark lack of life or anything to move the senses troubled Frank. It was like the forest had died a slow agonising death and the trees had given up on any chance of salvation.

There was no clear pathway. Dying fronds of bracken, brown and decaying were being reclaimed by the forest floor. The sun was trying, not hard enough, to cleave the darkness. Up above, Frank could just see it attempting to disentangle itself from the dead branches at the top of the tree canopy.

They moved on in single file, all that the terrain would allow. Gabby bought up the rear, allowing Cas the comfort of knowing that nothing would accost him from behind. Anya's eyes were wide and alert. Frank kept glancing round at her, hoping any seeing ability she possessed would at least give them a hint of a chance of knowing something was about to happen, before it happened. That she would alert them before the tiger struck.

He stopped to check his bearings, the others close by, not spread out like before, their progress slowing to an anxious walk. He felt the tightness in his throat, in his bones, unable the shake the feeling he should stop, turn and bolt like a hare.

Further through the trees they walked. Cautious. Fear creeping along with them, an unwelcome companion. The sound of their boots scuffing the forest floor seemed louder than it should; stale, dead air pushing into their lungs. Frank could feel his chest thumping and the heat of adrenalin in his blood as the forest closed around them like a clenched fist. The quiet, the bleak oppressive and unending quiet started to prey on Frank, began to panic him. He could feel it infecting the others, see it on their faces and hear it on their breath. Frank stopped. For no reason his skin erupted into goose bumps, the hairs on his arms stood up.

A sudden shrill whistle struck them still, froze them with inner dread and had them staring hawk-like into the dark. Their eyes darted quickly to each other, enough to see the terror looking back, then back into the midnight of the trees. Frank's skin flared again. He hadn't imagined it. *They* hadn't imagined it. It was the first thing they had heard since they'd crossed the rift and entered the woods on this side and it had them all fretting like new-born lambs at the scent of the fox.

A second whistle scythed through the air. Closer. Clutching at their backs. No one spoke, each of them caught with an instant primal instinct of survival, the quick blade of fear cutting them all hard. Frank tried to focus through the trees, trying to detect the slightest hint of movement, trying to decipher the direction from where the noise had come. There was a faint rustling behind them, or had they imagined it? Then again, this time to the side.

They backed into each other, forming a small circle, turning slowly, their collective terror binding them tight. Waiting; waiting for something to happen, for whatever monster was stalking them to show itself from the jaws of the trees. The seconds passed; leaden ticks of the clock. Nothing happened. The wait stretched out, testing them. Minutes ticked by. They hadn't imagined it, but the forest stilled and beckoned them on.

They moved forward. Wordless. Treading as silently as they could, focusing all their attention on listening; listening to the darkness, to the hushed beast that they were convinced was now tracking them as they pushed on through the undergrowth with no idea where they were going or how long it was going to take them to get there. Still the trees kept the sunlight out, barely a few strands of grey were allowed through, hindering their progress, cutting any chance of the speed that Frank craved. He stopped and turned to the others with the intention of giving them as much reassurance as he could conjure; saw the taut looks on the three faces, ashen, eyes wide with the nerves he, too, felt.

As he opened his mouth to speak, the undergrowth parted and, with a blur of green and brown, something burst from the trees and grabbed him by the throat.

21

BALAL

It was on him before he had time to think, before he had time to react. A blur and he was on the floor, face down. Something pressed against his back. Instinctively, he pushed his hands into the ground and turned himself over, whatever had ambushed him was dislodged, thrown off and Frank scrambled to his feet, crouched, looking at the others.

Gabby looked back at him, her tawny eyes quickly trying to decipher what had just happened when she went down, grappled by another small shape that lanced itself from the trees with a shriek. She landed with a heavy thud, air exiting her lungs with a high pitched squeal.

Cas turned to run but his escape was blocked by another figure. He backed himself against a tree as, down from the low branches, gripping the trunk like a spider grips a wall, dropped a large, human-like figure brandishing a long staff, one end tipped with a deadly-looking two-pronged fork, the tines of which extended eighteen inches from the shaft.

The figure, death on its face, drew back its arm and threw its weapon with uncompromising venom towards Cas. Such was the ferocity that it cut the air with the deadly hiss, Cas let out a shout as the fork, aimed at his throat, pinned him hard to the tree, the sharp points embedding themselves deep in the wood, either side of his neck. The shaft shuddered, then was still.

Anya quickly stepped forward, drawing the creature's attention. It hissed, but didn't move. Anya crouched as she came within an arms-length, poised and balanced as if ready for its violent reaction.

She grabbed the assailant by the arm, dodging the first blow, the huge fist, strands of her hair snapping. She made to throw it to the ground but the creature was so damn fast Frank could barely register its movements. If Anya thought she could side-step a second time she was badly wrong. He could only look on as it rammed its palm into Anya's face, sweeping its leg through hers as it did, sending her down to the ground with fluid ease, knocking her glasses off.

The creature was on her, pressing down on Anya's shoulder before delivering a hard punch to her face and hauling her violently onto her feet by the hair, the cold steel of a dagger instantly at her throat. Blood dripped in a thick stream from Anya's nose as she fought for breath, her eyes glassy.

Frank looked around, his attacker had backed off at the appearance of the huge form, but it crouched, ready to spring on him again. It was much smaller than he had first thought and he could barely make it out against the forest. It blended into the background, so much that Frank had to move his head to the side to keep it in view against the weave of greens and browns.

He quickly shot a look back to Gabby, seeing two more of the small woodland creatures holding spears to her abdomen as she lay prone while the faint rustle in the undergrowth confirmed there were more encircling them.

But it wasn't them that dried his throat. He could see how the small creatures waited. Still and focused. Alert to the next instruction, spoken or unspoken, from the natural leader that grasped Anya like she was a toy doll.

The large creature – not human or beast – lifted its head and sniffed deeply. It moved its solid neck around as it drew in the fetid woodland air. Frank watched on; it wasn't the action of something breathing in their scent, it was the feral instinct of something else, of something taking in what they *were*.

With its fist still balled in Anya's hair, it growled like a rabid dog at the prone figure of Gabby as she tried her best not to shift under the deadly weapons aimed at her vital organs. A long snort followed, then long, deep looks at Cas and Frank. Brutal and meaningful looks that spoke of what was to come, that said only one thing – you're all going to die.

'Intruders,' said the figure, a female, plain and matter-of-fact, shifting her grip on Anya's hair, making her gasp under her breath. Frank simply stared in response. Dark, pitiless eyes looked back. Every inch of her was corded with muscle; broad chest and heavy, bursting biceps, her entire body a dark, earthy mix of woodland colours. She drew back her lips in a ferocious snarl, exposing a set of hideous pointed fangs as long and slender as a bear's claws. Silvery and deadly, enough to scare the living shit out of anything. Saliva dripped in a fast flurry from the uncompromising points. 'Balal does not like intruders,' she said, sucking on its drool.

Frank looked sideways at the smaller woodland creatures that stood back, eyes darting from their captives to their leader, guarded, awaiting their next command. One or two chattered in an unfamiliar tongue.

'All in good time,' chuckled their captor, with a short nod. 'The Sapirai will dine well tonight.'

Cas's eyes opened as far as they could. He gripped the shaft of the fork, letting out a series of grunts as he tried to pull it from the tree in a series of panicked, unsuccessful jerks. Balal threw Anya to the floor and walked over to him, her impressive frame drumming the woodland floor. Frank watched the fluid movement of something at ease in its natural habitat, the enormous thigh muscles and rippling calves as Balal drew close to Cas's face.

'All in good time.' A long black tongue snaked from between her lethal jaws, finding Cas's taught cheek, drawing in his flavour. Cas let out a whimper and pushed against Balal's powerful, unmoving torso.

Frank recognised they had little time. That whatever this foul creature was, she looked like she and those that served her were intent on consuming them – either where they stood or somewhere deeper in the forest, to feast on them later; rage and recklessness overtook his intense fear.

Without thinking, he quickly stooped and grabbed a heavy branch that lay at his feet. One of the smaller creatures pounced but he wielded it quickly at its oncoming form, connecting hard with a savage crack, sending it to the side in a squealing mass, crimson arching in the air and over his shirt and face. Before he turned he knew what was going to happen and braced himself.

Balal let out a long, cold sneer and bared her teeth. Dagger in hand she launched at him. Frank had no time to gather himself or get himself out of the way as Balal ploughed into him with the full force of her hard bulk, knocking him clean off his feet onto his back, his breath exiting in a loud grunt. He felt the crack of his ribs as pain reared in his chest where she connected.

At once he could feel her immense strength weighing on him. He struggled hard, knowing his life depended on it, as Balal made an easy shift of her weight to pin him to the ground, settling into a position to make the strike that would end his life. His brain kept telling him that death was moments away, in a dark, bleak forest at the hands of an indescribable monster and he fought any impulse to yield. Somehow he managed to summon the strength to get in a brutal kick to her side, sending her reeling back, kicking up dirt from the forest floor but she was quickly on her feet, snarling, face contorted with delirious rage, dagger gripped tightly.

He propped himself up on his right hand, looking into her black, soulless eyes, absorbing the unrestrained look that told him she was going to kill him right there. She took a step forward, blade raised as Frank held up his left hand, palm facing away from him in a futile attempt to stop the inevitable. He heard Balal's guttural intake of breath as she prepared to launch at him and strike the fatal blow. He turned his face away, feeling his hand burn with the intensity of a raging bushfire, like it had been sliced off, the first of many such cuts that signalled the beginning of the slow, agonising death she was determined to enjoy. He knew that once she had butchered him, savoured the spilling of his blood, she would inflict the same punishment on the others. So he waited for the next blow. Waited.

But, then, nothing.

No muscular frame of the woodland creature descended on him, no dagger pierced his torso, no terrifying victory cry as she ended his life. Nothing. He turned his head and peered through his splayed fingers, through slitted eyes. Balal was standing still, staring through his hand, chest heaving. Only the sound of her short growling breaths punctured the air.

Frank lowered his hand as Balal licked the blade of her dagger and placed it back in its sheath. She crossed her formidable arms across her chest, sinews flexing easily.

'You must excuse my impertinence,' she said, her voice low. Frank struggled to his feet, his nerves kicking him. The smaller woodland creatures encircled them, clenching and unclenching their fists. Small bows were slung across their backs. 'I am at your service,' Balal continued with a slight, slow bow of her oversized head, her eyes not leaving his.

'W...w...what?' said Frank.

'You were about to slit his throat,' said Gabby.

Balal pursed her lips and spat out a noise. One of the creatures pinning Gabby down pushed the end of its spear further into the skin of her abdomen, making her squeal.

'The queen of the forest is commanded not to harm he who bears the Qine mark, sorcerer.' Once more she gave the slightest of bows, reluctant. Frank shook his head.

'The Qine mark?'

Balal nodded towards his hand. Frank turned it toward him and looked at his blood-stained palm. There was nothing there. He looked back at Balal.

'It was there,' she said. 'On your palm. Lucky for you I saw it, whiteskin.'

The fierce burning he had felt must have had nothing to do with the fight. Instinctively, Frank knew that his hand had scorched him in exactly the same way it had when he'd placed it against the page of the book back in his room, when it had branded him and left an invisible mark, a mark that must have shown itself the instant Balal prepared to slice him into pieces.

'You saw the mark on my hand?'

Balal nodded and continued to inspect him, the way a cat inspects a cornered mouse.

'And my friends,' said Frank. 'You won't harm my friends?'

'If that is your desire.'

'Tell her it's your desire,' shot Cas, his face still a portrait of fear.

Frank nodded. Balal walked over to Cas and, with a grip of controlled and easy power, pulled the spear out of the tree trunk. She stared into Cas's terrified face with a smile, drawing close. Intimidating. A muscle tightened on her jaw.

'Although if the thief doesn't keep his dirty little hands to himself, then Balal might have to relieve him of them.' Cas stood rigid against the tree as Balal strode back to Frank, her large bare feet silent on the forest floor. 'And you; you think you can defeat Balal with your bare hands?' she said to Anya. But Anya didn't seem to notice. She still breathed heavily from her moments in the hands of the beast. She dabbed at her face, the stream of blood now clotting and drying as she winced at her own touch. Balal licked her lips and let out a low growling chuckle.

Balal's Sapirai, her band of wood folk, muttered to each other at her words, their hands still clutching their weapons, not giving an inch or allowing Frank to stay his heightened sense of alert. Whatever privileges the mark on his hand had brought them, this was still their territory. They were bound to the forest's natural contours, undoubtedly danced to the rhythm of the seasons from the delicate shoots of new growth in the spring to the dead hollows of winter. They weren't just natives, permanent occupiers of the woodland. They *were* the woodland.

22

THE REQUEST

Frank didn't believe in ghosts or faeries or fae creatures. Johns had laughed at his own mention of woodland sentinels, but he'd been right. Some legends are truer than others – that's what Excelsus had taught him. This was one of those truer ones and Johns had warned them off coming. Perhaps he really had known. Not that they would have ever listened to the sour old man from the prison of his house back in Crossways.

But these creatures were right out of a horror story. Adept in their terrain, confident in their ability to fight off the toughest and meanest of foes, anyone that tried to lay claim to their home. He found he couldn't divert his attention from their leader as Balal, only a stride away, ran her black tongue over her rapier-like teeth.

'How can Balal help you, bearer of the Qine?' she said, eyes on Frank, making him feel like he was still less than a breath away from being skewered on the end of her spear.

The Sapirai murmured to each other. He took a deep breath. Still wary. Balal flexed her immense shoulders, her joints popping. Her broad biceps and forearms as massive as the tree trunks that surrounded them. Her skin wasn't just green and brown, but cloudy greys and murky shades of black, marred all over by thick scars, so many they could have been the stripes of a jungle cat. Not the marks of a victim or the beaten. That much was obvious. No, these were the trophies of a survivor, a warrior, someone who had earned the right to wear them in her climb to the head of her people, to serve as reminders to anyone who thought of her as weak or afraid. She was neither of those.

She waited patiently for him to speak, her nose still twitching in the stale air, still breathing them in. Her fangs shone, breath reeking of rotten flesh.

'Irundi,' he said, his words breathy. 'Have you heard of Irundi?' He fumbled in his pocket for the Elemental Ball. Balal's eyes were drawn.

'Your magic won't work here,' she said, a delicious smile cracking on her brutal face.

'Do you know it?' said Gabby.

Balal's head recoiled, her terrifying stare penetrating Gabby who still lay on the ground.

'The strange looking sorcerer would do well to keep her silence with Balal,' she said with the natural menace that ran through her entire being, screwing her face up at Gabby, her long fingers tensing in the shaft of her weapon. She looked back at Frank. 'Irundi. Where only the lost and the forgotten dwell. If it is your wish, then Balal will show you what you seek.'

Frank nodded.

'Yes, if you know where it is.'

Balal threw back her head and laughed. An unnatural, evil sound.

'There is not a single inch of the forest that is unknown to me, young whiteskin. Balal has been queen of the silent forest for more years than you could count. I know all the trees, their names, their desires. There is nothing within my kingdom that goes unnoticed to Balal.'

Balal sniffed and flicked her head at the Sapirai. There was a high-pitched muttering as they formed a cordon around the four students and awaited their next command. She eyed Frank, who shifted on his heels.

'Are you sure, whiteskin?' she asked. 'It is not for Balal to question why you seek Irundi, but disappointment is all you will find.' Frank held her soulless gaze but said nothing. 'Very well. I am commanded to show you.'

Dense scrub stung their heels as Balal and her Sapirai, moving as one, wove with the fluid grace of a leopard through the forest. The trees were oppressively dense, pushing against the glimmers of light that were knotted in the branches above, tightening around them like a snare. Sycamore, oak and birch all blocked them, never showing them a clear path, keeping them guessing about the right way, trying to throw them off the scent, away from their target – except they were in the thrall of the queen of the forest.

Balal bucked and snaked at the head of the line, Frank and the others struggled to keep up, even though she appeared to sense exactly where they were while not looking back, running just fast enough, allowing them not to fall too far behind. Her warriors flanked them, two bringing up the rear, moving silently, hurdling the twisted roots with ease, alert and in tune with their surroundings. Frank hadn't had time to be worried as they plunged headlong through the trees.

He trusted his instincts; Balal could have gutted him on the spot; had probably wanted to, intended to, but hadn't. As he watched her broad back career easily through the woods he wouldn't have had her down as a creature of honour, but he also felt the natural world that she and her band of savages inhabited ran to its own code.

He hoped he was right and they weren't being steered towards their butchering blocks deep in the pitch dark of the forest where no one would ever find them.

On they tore, the undergrowth thickening, brambles skinning their ankles, low branches whipping their faces, constantly wondering when a rest would come. There was no let-up in pace from the Sapirai and Frank only had the vaguest notion they'd been tracking for nearly an hour when, in an instant, the dark of the forest stopped. Bright autumnal sunlight cast a spectrum of greens and yellows in front of them as Balal led them to the brink of a huge circular clearing two hundred yards or more across.

An unusual ring of dead grass circled the edge, clinging to the ground just by the tree line and Frank noticed how Balal had stepped up to it, but was careful not to overstep. She stopped and swept the area slowly and carefully, her eyes sharp. She raised her head and inhaled deeply, her broad chest expanding as she closed her eyes and breathed in the shape and tone of the air.

Her followers looked edgy. Some grabbed their bows off their backs while others shifted in the shadows of the undergrowth, as far from the circle as their leader allowed. Balal shifted on her feet and gave a snort. For the first time Frank detected an element of uncertainty around their guide. A silent moment passed before Balal turned, not stepping into the open, remaining in the familiar shadow of the trees. Her bulk cast a formidable silhouette.

'This, whiteskin,' she said, 'is Irundi. I hope you are suitably unimpressed and disappointed, like Balal said you would be. Here is where you and I part company.' She looked to the Sapirai and spoke a few harsh words.

Frank nodded. He wasn't sure if he should express any thanks – thanks for not ripping Anya's head off, thanks for not skewering Cas like a catfish, thanks for not serving them up as a fine woodland banquet.

Balal lowered her gaze, snake eyes not leaving Frank's face for a second. 'I can sense that we are destined to meet again.' She look round at the others, unpleasantness on her face. 'And the woods are difficult to find your way out of if you don't know what you're doing. He who bears the mark of Kester will need safe passage out of the forest. If, indeed, you return.' She lifted her head and took a look back across the wide clearing, an evil smile tugging the corners of her mouth.

The Sapirai grinned and eyed each other and, with a shift of the wind, followed their queen back into the night of the woods, disappearing quickly from sight, melting easily and silently into their landscape, leaving the four teenagers completely alone.

23

The Clearing

It took them more than a few silent minutes to drag themselves back from the dark place to where their experience with Balal had taken them. Frank looked on in silence at the fractured faces of the others, all of them taking in deep breaths to cure their burning lungs after the long dash through the woods in the hands of the band of woodland thugs. The same stale air that followed them through the forest still breathed at the edge of the clearing.

Frank took his water bottle from his bag and took a long draw, feeling himself revive slightly as he swallowed, letting it spill onto his cheeks and run down his neck. He offered it to Anya who cupped her hands, rubbing the water Frank poured into them over her face, clearing the mess of red before drinking from the bottle.

They'd had no right to survive their encounter with the Sapirai, that was the unspoken message that spread itself into the void between them. Of all the episodes they'd gone through, this was the closest they'd come to watching each other die. Frank felt himself go hot as he looked at his friends, wondering how much more of this they could put themselves through and whether it was really worth the cost.

They stood close to each other. Frank felt the glimmer of security in their bond, hoping the others felt it too, but he felt the flush of confusion as he surveyed the scene before him. They all stared in silence across the wide landscape of devastation, captured within the large circular arena in the middle of the thick woodland.

The ruins of what looked like had once been a large building lay strewn around the ground. Great chunks of blue-grey rock and masonry, some reaching forty feet to the sky, lay idly and randomly as if knocked into petrified waste by the stamp of a giant's well-aimed heel then scattered by hand. Centuries of erosion and decay had poked and prodded at the mess like the dying embers of a fire long ago extinguished, dulled by the wind and rain of the passing years. The shattered remains extended to the distant trees on the other side.

To their right, hugging the trees, the remnants of a tower, a high curved wall of decaying stonework, rose up from the splinters below, the skeleton of something once grand and majestic stared back at them, sad in its cold, perishing demise. The last traces of a stone spiral staircase clung vigorously to the inside of what had once been the inner wall of the tower, reaching to the rotting beams of what must have been the turret's upper floor, but was now just a gut-churning fifty foot drop to the battered ground. The last steps hung askew, looking ready to drop, but gripping on in a final desperate attempt to remain part of the structure.

'Well let's just say I'm not exactly overcome with excitement,' said Cas. 'Looks like a great number of armies got here first. And they came with a wrecking ball.'

'Or a dragon,' said Anya, picking at the last remnants of blood that still caked her upper lip, a bruise beginning to blacken her cheek.

'Now, dragons I don't believe in,' said Gabby as she strode into the open and began to pick her way through the patchwork of broken stones.

'I didn't believe in murderous little woodland folk until an hour ago,' said Cas, scouring the tree line. 'Not that Balal was particularly little.'

Gabby stopped, placing her hands on her hips and turned to Frank. 'What are we looking for?'

Frank shrugged and shook his head as he surveyed the carnage. He knew there had to be something here, something significant although he couldn't say it with any certainty or self-belief.

They'd been through enough to realise that the map, like all the things that had appeared to them in their book, had some meaning, that it had led them here, to a fabled spot in the middle of a woodland that wasn't meant to exist. His mind started to turn things over as he took a few steps to the outer ring of angular, lifeless and cold rubble.

Nothing moved amongst the mass of bindweed and dying vegetation that gripped firmly to the stone, hugging tightly and pinning it prisoner to the ground. Frank stopped and looked around, he watched as Gabby moved further into the middle of the clearing, shifting smaller chunks of rubble with a push of her foot, occasionally stooping to pick up the odd stone.

He considered the troubled look on Balal's face, how the woodland monster hadn't stepped even an inch into the open sunlight. She was the queen of the forest, but not of this place, of that he was certain.

Cas took a wary step after Frank, moving cautiously into the clearing as Anya headed over to inspect the shaky-looking remains of the tower.

'There's nothing here, so let's just head back, shall we?' he said.

Gabby's head popped up from behind a hunk of the pewter rock.

'Nothing here?' she called. 'Take a look around, dummy. There's something here alright.'

'Well, there used to be. But whatever it was has been completely levelled, probably by something big and terrifying that's lurking somewhere in there.' He pointed to the trees. 'I vote we leave.' He thrust his hand into the air. 'Anyone else?' The others looked at each other, then at Cas who lowered his hand and slumped his shoulders.

'Look, Cas,' said Frank, barely hiding his instant frustration at Cas's immediate and predictable whingeing. 'Let's just have a look around. It won't take long.' He continued to pick his way to the centre of the wreckage, towards Gabby while Cas kept glancing back into the trees, his hands in his pockets, looking like he wanted to be anywhere else.

The day ticked slowly into the afternoon as, cautiously and

carefully they covered the whole area. By the time the sun had begun its descent from the clouds, a thick silence had fastened itself to them, broken only by the occasional gust that picked at the treetops and Frank's desire to continue, the sharp prickles of irritation starting under his skin. Gabby and Anya looked just as fed up, just about managing half-hearted prods at the loose stones, arms folded across their chests.

Frank looked over to Cas. Darkness shrouded the area behind him as the thick woodland loomed at his shoulders. He felt a shiver shoot through him as he scoured the trees, unable to shake the feeling that they were being watched, that the souls of a thousand evil spirits lay in wait for them just over the tree line, ready to devour them. The whole place stood bereft of any warmth and he daren't even consider why a monster like Balal sniffed at the clearing as if something even more unearthly than her was buried under the ancient rubble that lay strewn at their feet.

'Cas is right. I don't think there's anything here, Frank,' said Gabby, kicking at a tuft of grass. 'Waste of time.'

'Told you,' said Cas, stamping his heel into the ground, the glare of a petulant child on his face.

Frank couldn't believe that the map had led them here, just to find a ruin of a ruin. They knew the book wasn't that old and if the actual building was here when the book was written, he couldn't believe nature would have wreaked such carnage in just a few years, it just wasn't possible. It was obvious that whatever had been here had been rocked to its foundations a very, very long time ago. He rubbed the back of his neck and looked at the ground. Nothing made any sense.

24

THE TOWER

He picked his way over to the tree line to where the round tower stood, its skeletal remains now more reminiscent of something unfinished, unloved and forgotten than its once impressive structure. He stood at the foot of the stone steps and looked up. Damp moss clung like foul limpets to the decay; grey stone, turned green with time and slime, loomed over him, bearing inwards, threatening to tumble down on top of him, daring him to ascend. Ancient ivy had invaded the mortar, weakening what was left of the building, waiting to push it on to whoever was stupid enough to climb up. It taunted Frank to mount the first step.

His eyes travelled over each tread. They were cut into the wall and, now he was close up, looked sturdy enough, although it was difficult to tell. A few had already broken free and fallen, leaving gaps in the ascent to the top and those right at the very height of the winding stonework hung askew. He'd have to be stupid to think he would be able to make it to the top. But there had to be something here; of that he was sure and his instincts backed him up. He felt someone at his shoulder.

'Do you want me to go,' said Anya, looking upward. 'I'm probably the nimblest of us all.' She look at Frank, adjusting her glasses. 'What do you think?'

'I'm not sure what you're hoping to find, mate,' said Cas.

'Me neither,' said Frank, sensing an edge of annoyance in his own voice.

'This place looks like it's been a wreckage for centuries. And it looks a bit dangerous up there,' said Anya.

Frank nodded.

'Okay,' he said. 'I'll go up and see if there's anything interesting. If not, we'll leave it to the lovely Balal and her band of ugly wood creatures. Agreed?'

Cas shrugged, giving Frank a tight look. Frank looked across the clearing where Gabby was still rummaging around in the tangle of weeds and masonry. The whole thing was beginning to get under his skin, plucking at his anger.

Puffing out his cheeks, he pressed his foot on the first step, feeling its cold, dead form under the sole of his boot, but at least it felt secure. Danger or not, he wasn't afraid; he didn't really care. He just wished he could stop the rising irritation that tied itself to his insides once more.

As he thought, it was solid and unyielding and bore his weight like a circus strong-man. Slowly he made his way up the staircase, conscious of the damp, slippery moss, wary that the next step could set itself loose and send him tumbling to the ground which became ever distant with each careful tread. He glanced down. Gabby had joined the others at the foot of the wasted stairs and stood looking up. He took a brief look at the others watching him in anxious silence, willing him safely to the top with their eyes.

Higher and higher he took himself. About half way up, two consecutive steps had been sheared off, leaving a pair of ugly granite stumps protruding from the wall with just enough left for him to edge his foot onto. He looked down through the gap, then up to the following step. He could probably jump it, but decided to use the rough stumps as stepping stones.

His tentative boot pressed hard into the remnants of the step, using its rigidity as a springboard upward but he misjudged it and, as he went to propel himself to the next tread his boot slipped, sending him down with a churn of his stomach, making him reach out to the wall, to thin air. The fall was twenty feet or more to the broken fragments of tower below; as his stomach entered his mouth he thrust out a hand, quickly finding wet stone as the cold and moss spat him back. Down he went with a frightening jolt, just managing to find the protruding stone that had been his nemesis a moment earlier and clung on, his feet swinging beneath him. His throat tightened.

'Frank!' hollered Gabby.

Her cry echoed around the clearing as Frank struggled to pull himself up. He could feel his fingers slipping slowly across the damp stone as his strength started to desert him. The cold granite started to rob his fingertips of feeling, panic grasping at his throat. He was going to fall. One hand slipped off the rock, leaving him dangling moments away from a drop which, at the very least, would break his legs. A cry stuck in his throat as he felt his grip failing. Then, despite his desperate attempt to hang on, his fingers gave up their grip.

A hand grabbed his wrist as he headed down, jolting him from the brink. Gabby held him tight. In his frantic effort to keep himself from falling he'd not noticed her coming up the staircase, without a thought for her own safety on the unforgiving slime that coated the stones. With her help, he yanked himself up and pressed himself against the wall; his face close to hers, feeling her sharp breaths warming his face. For a moment they locked eyes.

'How about I save you, this time?' she said.

25

THE REALISATION

Frank could feel his legs shaking. He regulated his breathing and took another terrified look down from the steps, feeling that any sense of calm was beyond his reach. Gabby put her hand on his arm which made his fear subside. A fraction of a second and she'd have missed him and he'd either be dead or seriously injured, deep in the dark of a strange forest, surrounded by unseen creatures with little hope of walking out.

'We should head down,' said Gabby. Her gentle voice soothing him. He looked up to where the steps headed.

'No,' he said. 'Not until we've go to the top.' He looked at her. 'You coming?'

Gabby drew in a deep breath and shook her head at him. She flicked her head in the direction of the platform ahead, indicating he should move on.

Together they made their way from each step to the next. Frank was relieved to see the higher steps were drier and virtually moss free. Perhaps being away from the damp undergrowth of the forest floor and open to the sky had done the trick, but he was still wary that any one of them might be loose as the ancient set of stones drew him on, each one testing his courage while the wind threw an occasional gust at them, scattered clouds keeping the sun at bay. He and Gabby kept themselves pressed tightly to the wall, scaling it like a pair of frightened lizards, trying not to think about the steadily increasing and mind-numbing height and the certainty of death if they fell.

Finally, Frank reached the wider area which must once have formed the top platform of the original turret, open to the sky. He tried to ignore the continuous quiver in his thighs as he grasped the remnants of the stone wall that had once surrounded the thick wooden floor, trying to secure himself to the structure in any way he could. He noticed Gabby did the same. They were fifty feet up with barely a few square yards of old, dry rotting boards to keep them safe. Frank didn't want to think about how they were going to get back down.

They looked down to the vast clearing, at the devastation they'd been picking through. A film of mist had begun to form and hung in the air above their heads. From their new vantage point they could clearly see how the once impressive building had crumbled, spreading itself across the eastern end of the clearing in a grey, forlorn mess. Even at this height the tower sat below the top of the tree canopy, nestled securely out of sight. Beyond there was nothing to see, nothing but dark forest which spread out for miles like a tangle of matted fibres. Frank sighed and looked down at the rotting floor. One of the old timbers stretched ten feet out, otherwise there was little room for manoeuvre.

The sun strayed in and out from behind the clouds, making Frank shield his eyes as a cold gust of autumn wind picked at them as if playing some mischievous game.

He looked back across to the tops of the trees on the far side of the clearing, wondering what they were doing here, stuck in a strange uninhabited clearing in the middle of a lifeless but fearsome forest ruled by the unimaginable terror of Balal and the Sapirai. Why had he thought it a good idea to come here? And why hadn't one of the others stopped him, had a different view than his?

He closed his eyes and wished himself back in Rhaeder, back with Libby, hoping that his absence hadn't somehow sent her further into the arms of another. He fought his anger, fought to control it rising to the surface where it would be the creator or accomplice of more bad decisions. It had all been a huge mistake. Once again, no one knew where they were and they'd just wasted their time, risked their lives for a stupid pile of old rock.

That was it; there was nothing else here. He cursed loudly then banged his heel back into the stonework of the tattered old wall, feeling the stones move. He felt himself clench his fists, squeezing his eyes shut, muttering an obscenity under his breath at the folly of their situation.

The sun warmed his tired face as it revealed itself once more between the gathering clouds. He stared aimlessly out from the derelict, abandoned turret, whispering curses to himself to try and quell his anger, to try and make sense of the whole thing, just staring into nothing.

Then he saw it.

Only for the merest fraction of a second, but he saw it — a tell-tale glint in the sun, but there was no mistaking it. He let go of the wall and stood on the edge of a splintered floorboard staring, unbelieving, but there it was, again. He hadn't imagined it. He felt a run of ice down his spine and all at once the whole scene of devastation that he looked on below made complete sense.

26

THE JUMP

If he'd blinked, he'd have missed it. But, as the glint of sunlight escaped from the clouded sky and descended on the small clearing, he saw it again – a tiny transparent orb suspended in the sky no further than twelve feet from where he and Gabby stood, and maybe a foot higher in the air.

He fixed on the point, making sure he wasn't imagining it, that it wouldn't disappear, then another shaft of light picked at the small sphere as it sat in mid-air, cushioned by the thin mist that coated the old building like a shawl of gossamer. He hadn't imagined it. He tugged hard at Gabby's sleeve and pointed to where he was looking, his hand trembling slightly.

'See it?' said Frank.

Gabby squinted, shook her head and screwed her face up in concentration, her dark hair twisted and battered by the crisp, damp wind.

'There,' he said as the ball revealed itself, once more, in the welcome sunlight.

Gabby shrugged then, as the clouds finally created enough space for the sun to warm their frightened faces, she gasped. She stared like the prey stares at the cat, then looked back at Frank.

'You're absolutely kidding me,' she said. She looked wide-eyed at him. 'It's...it's...a time bead.'

Frank nodded, struck dumb by his excitement; not knowing what to say. Whatever he thought about their journey into the silent forest, he hadn't thought this; and it changed everything.

'But, this means...'Gabby's face became puzzled.

'That, if this is the same as your mum's, there's —'

'Something hidden. Underneath.'

Frank nodded. Something hidden, something suspended in time, something no one would or should ever be able to find. But they had, with a cart-load of luck and perseverance.

'What do you think it is?' said Gabby.

Frank looked back down the dilapidated steps, at the shell of a building and its labyrinth of ruins heaped on the ground below.

'It's this,' he said, waving his arm in an arc as he looked down. 'It must be this but...' he looked at Gabby, '...not this. It must be the actual building, from back in time when the bead was set. It's here, or under here.'

As he said it he thought it just sounded absurd but, from Helen's kitchen demonstration, he and Gabby knew it was possible. Still, he couldn't even begin to imagine what they were dealing with, or what they would find once they removed the bead; *if* they could remove it.

Remove the bead? He looked back into the air then edged his way to the brink of the wooden platform. His breath came fast. Don't look down. He stared ahead, picking out the bead once more, barely visible against the brightening sky when he felt a tug on his shirt.

'Careful, Frank,' said Gabby.

He snatched his shirt back, ignoring her, feeling the pin-pricks of irritation. He fixed his eyes back on the bead, then looked down at his feet, feeling the acute tremble in his knees as he caught the distance from his toes to the ground. It was a *long* way down. It didn't matter which way he looked at it or how long he thought about it, he already knew the bead was out of reach. He balled his fists, pressing his fingernails into his palms. Nothing was ever easy.

'We can't just leave it,' he said, not looking round. Even as he thought, the anger he felt tightened itself against his bones. He wished he'd followed his instinct and released Tweedy when he had the chance. She'd just pluck the bead out of the air at his command, but now they were stuck, knowing that even if they threw stones at it for the rest of the week, it would remain firmly fixed, irritating them like a nettle.

'It's too far away,' said Gabby.

'*I can see that,*' said Frank with all the short-tempered tetchiness of a spoiled child.

Gabby tightened her lips, folded her arms and pressed herself back against the wall, as far away from Frank as their situation would allow. He turned, saw the familiar dark of thunderclouds forming in her eyes as a dense silence filled the small gap between them. Frank tried to push his frustration to the edge of his mind. He closed his eyes and took in a deep breath through his nose. He clenched his fists again. He knew Gabby didn't deserve his sharp edge, but he wasn't about to apologise.

'Everything alright up there?' Cas's voice cut through from below and Frank opened his eyes.

'Yeah,' he said. 'Just give me a minute.' He turned to Gabby. 'Any suggestions?'

Somehow he couldn't bring any softness to his voice. Gabby just shrugged and glared. Her frown and pout told him all he needed to know – you sort it out. Frank looked down at the rotting floor, scuffing the sole of his boot across the thick timbers as he tried to think.

He looked at Gabby, estrangement in her eyes, then to the wall that she leaned against. He was drawn to the curvature of the stones. Barely a quarter of the wall was intact; deep gouges in the brickwork where the failing mortar had long left, the rest cracked and crumbling. Frank's eyes followed the line of the circular tower, mentally tracing the imaginary line of the former turret out into the void. Gabby watched him as he slowly turned around, facing back across the clearing, pinpointing the position of the small bead, then down to the floor, studying its distance.

Grey clouds gathered once more and a cool wind blew in from the surrounding treetops. He hoped he was right. Knew he'd only have one shot at it; knew the resentment that festered in his body was getting the better of his judgement and willed it to the side-lines.

'What are you doing?' said Gabby, shifting uncomfortably. Frank detected a low note of concern. He looked down to Cas and Anya.

'Stand back,' he shouted and without a second thought for anyone around him he backed himself against the wall, took what little run up there was and launched himself into the bleak air.

27

IRUNDI

He felt the tension in his calves bite him as his feet left the decaying floorboards. Not once did he take his eyes off the tiny orb, he fixed on it like a falcon bearing down on its prey. He hoped his instincts were right, hoped he'd gauged the dimensions of the turret top without error. Everything happened in slow-motion. He felt his heart ripping up his throat as he lifted himself into the air, heard the muffled shriek from Gabby, his name being shouted from below.

He was quickly upon it, unerring in his determination not to miss. He could sense the strain on his outstretched fingers against the wind, closing them rapidly around the small, transparent bead, dragging it out of the sky, pressing his fingernails as far into his palm as his pain threshold would allow, all the time his eyes alert with the bracing fear that he would be wrong.

Before he'd made his decision to jump he knew he'd fall within a second. As he pulled the bead out of the sky he looked down, arms flailing, a flashing glimpse of the scene of devastation, wondering upon which hunk of rock his body would be smashed. He couldn't close his eyes, even if he had wanted to and he wasn't sure he even cared if he fell. The tops of the trees across the clearing stayed suspended as he felt himself drop; a drop that might be the last thing he would ever experience in his young life but, at that moment, he didn't care.

Then it happened.

The first thing he knew about it was when his fall was broken by strong, sturdy timbers, then the instant sear of pain as his face connected hard with the blunt stone of the newly revealed wall where there had been none. He felt the impact burn through his shoulder and ribs as he hit hard; the sting of the skin on his cheek being ripped open, the familiar taste of blood spreading across the inside of his mouth as his teeth punctured his tongue.

The hard, smooth blockwork brought him to an abrupt halt, crumpling his body in an unceremonious heap and leaving him momentarily dazed. He heard himself exhale loudly and curse against the pain as he brought his hand up to his face, then ran his fingers over his tongue, checking the damage, the long gouge along his cheekbone, knowing that his face would be a blot of bruising in the coming days. He rolled himself onto his back, staring unfocused at the sky, then a rush of footsteps turned his head. Gabby knelt beside him, her hand gently on his head.

'What did you just *do*?' she said.

Frank just groaned, pinching his aching forehead between his thumb and fingers. Propping himself up on his elbows, he looked back to where he'd taken his run-up just moments before, to the tumbledown wall and rotten floor that had been there as he stood deciding what to do.

It was all gone, replaced by bright grey stone, with its pristine pointing, as though it had only been laid the day before. The rough floor had been replaced by new timbers, sanded smooth and gleaming with a fine sheen as if they had just been polished. A heavy iron pull-ring was embedded into a trapdoor in the surface where they'd been standing.

'Who'd have thought it?' The words struggled out of his winded body. He gave Gabby as much of a smile as he could muster only to have it return with anger. 'What?' Silence. 'I was right. It's here isn't it?' He pushed himself up on his knees with a struggle, deep dull pain pushing his teeth together, and peered over the turret wall, staring in disbelief at what stood before him.

Below stood a small castle. A small stone box of a keep sat neatly on the edge of the clearing with the newly- formed turret attached to one corner, rising majestically from the main building. The keep was roofed in dark grey slate, its shallow pitch rising to a point in the middle on which a flagpole stood. A small flag flapped lazily in the breeze. Vast, pristine gardens – lush manicured lawns and large scattered flower beds stretched to the west, butting up against the trees while a scattering of outbuildings – large and small but equally unspoiled — lay in the grounds beyond.

He was brought back to his senses by Gabby raining a couple of weighty blows around his head.

'Don't you ever do anything like that to me again,' she snapped as Frank raised his arms to shield himself.

'What do you —'

'I don't know what's going on with you, Frank, but you don't just jump off a fifty foot building without letting people know, especially me. Okay?'

She glowered at him. Whatever answer he was going to use to justify his actions, it caught in his throat as he looked into her eyes noticing her anger turn to concern and instantly he felt foolish.

'Okay,' he said, nodding his head as the quiet word escaped.

Gabby reached up and touched his cheek, the tenderness in her fingertips closing his eyes. He sucked in a breath over his teeth at the sting of the wound. For a brief moment she cupped his face in her palm, before reaching into her pocket and producing her healing stone.

'Here,' she said.

In a moment, she'd uttered a short incantation but the rip in his skin didn't close. If anything, it burned with a greater fury as Gabby stood back with the stone in the palm of her hand, resignation on her face. Balal had been clear – their magic didn't work here.

'It'll bruise quite nicely. Try explaining that one to what's-her-face.'

Frank smiled.

'I'll tell her you hit me.'

'Good, she'll believe that and if only you knew how nearly true that is.' She cocked her head at him before standing and looking over the turret wall. Cas and Anya stood at the side of the clearing, staring around the building that, moments ago, had lain before them in ruins. Cas looked up as Gabby appeared above them.

'That's unbelievable,' he shouted.

'Wait there,' she shouted back. 'We're coming down.'

She glanced down at Frank.

'Come on, we shouldn't split up. Who knows what we're going to find here?'

She held out her hand, which Frank grabbed and hauled himself up, wincing at the pain that shot across his battered ribs and picking at the rip in the elbow of his shirt. He puffed out his cheeks and looked down at Cas and Anya, giving them a quick thumbs-up before brushing himself down and heading over to the hatch in the floor. He pulled at the heavy iron ring and the hatch swung up easily revealing the stone staircase which disappeared into a spiral below. Gabby stepped forward and went to go through the opening.

'Sorry,' Frank muttered, barely audible as it wisped across to Gabby as she stood at the top of the steps. She stopped, flashed him a glare and disappeared down into the turret without response.

28

THE CAPTURE

They hurried down the newly-revealed steps. The staircase was lit at intervals by arched, latticed windows, antique and sparkling. On each floor, a heavy oak door, sparkling with varnish and held by heavy iron hinges, led inside, drawing Frank's eye. Gabby had disappeared, keeping well ahead of him. As he rounded to stairs at the bottom of the tower, he found her drawing two heavy bolts back across a heavy iron-clad door before pulling it open and heading out into the light without looking back.

They gathered on the edge of the clearing, staring back toward the building that had appeared from the noxious forest air. The whole, vast area had changed in the instant Frank had brought down the bead. It was alive. The trees looked greener and happier to be there; the sound of birdsong and the abrasive 'kaa' of crows breathed life into the glade which before had exuded such a bleakness and sense of dread that they couldn't believe it was the same place.

From the ground, the small fortification was as impressive as it was unexpected. Its ancient square keep looked down on them. Neatly hewn hunks of rock in light and dark shades of grey set evenly and proficiently atop one another bore not even a slight resemblance to the withering mass of forlorn boulders that they had stumbled upon when they first entered the clearing. The walls gleamed with the sparks of silica and mica as if the whole edifice had been polished. The building was unerringly square, with the one round tower in the corner. No lichen or moss bothered the stonework.

Leaded windows punctuated the walls with regularity over the three floors and the flag still swung lazily from the pole at the centre in the shelter of the tall surrounding trees.

The castle didn't appear to have any fortifications – no arrow slits or thick, impenetrable entranceway with a foreboding portcullis of any sort. No scars of survival. Not built as a fortress or designed to outlast endless enemy attacks or sieges. It was more stately residence than defence. Not that it looked warm and welcoming. Just intimidating, imposing, unforgiving. Kept hidden for a reason; hidden beyond the wit of anyone who came looking, literally buried in the bottomless vaults of time, away from the prying eyes of both the outside world and the foul spirits that haunted the forest.

'So now we've found it, I guess there's only one thing left to do,' said Gabby, breaking from the others and striding alone across the grassed edge of the clearing towards the heavy doors set into the west face of the castle. Cas looked at Frank's face and winced, but said nothing. He and Anya followed Gabby, leaving Frank standing by himself. He watched the others, softly patting the mess on his cheek, still aching in his ribs and feeling like he wanted to be somewhere else, somewhere by himself. Uncovering the hidden castle hadn't made him feel the slightest bit happier, not that he'd expected it to. He thrust his hands into his pockets and, with a quick look into the woods, followed.

Up close, they could breathe in the craftsmanship of the tower. The stonemasons who slaved and toiled in its making had left an example of their artistry beyond compare yet one that no one would ever set eyes upon. The grassed area around the walls was as green as limes and manicured to perfection. Across the huge clearing, spread with a careful hand, a range of outbuildings, large and small, were scattered around the inside and the perimeter, making it impossible to see the extent of area from the ground.

As they approached the large pair of rectangular oak doors, studded with bronze, Frank breathed in the sweet scent of beeswax, a reminder of his kitchen table at home making his shoulders drop and his breath stiffen.

Gabby stood examining the doors. Sand-coloured blockwork,

cut with precision, surrounded the sturdy entranceway. Frank followed the track of her gaze but stopped and stared at the image carved in relief in the masonry at the centre point. His subconscious gripped his hand and rubbed it against the side of his leg. He looked down at his palm. It was bare, just as it should be but, even so, he could still see it on his flesh; the image that their book had burned into him, the image that had placated Balal now stared back down at him from above the doorway: Kester's mark, that's what Balal had called it. The small castle was built by Kester? Surely not; that would make it centuries old even though it looked like it had been built yesterday.

Anya drew in a sudden breath and turned, Frank turned with her. A single masked figure, clad in black, stood before them. With the speed of a striking cobra, Anya took a step forward and, gripping the figure by the arm, pulled them towards her while delivering her palm into their throat. In a seamless movement she hurled them to the ground as four more masked figures appeared behind them as if they'd just sprung from the earth.

Each were dressed from head to toe in shimmering black. Their tight black sleeveless tunics, braided in silver and green clung to well-defined torsos like a second skin, the glint of a small black flame embroidered on the collar. Black masks covered their mouths and noses, hoods covered their heads leaving just their unflinching eyes trained on the four teenagers.

Each one shifted easily from one foot to the other, their hands still, poised an inch away from the deadly blades that hung close on each side, hugging their hips. The air filled with a thick hint of violence.

One stepped forward as the one Anya had thrown was quickly on their feet, retreating a step as the one at the front drew a rapier from its scabbard with the speed of the wind and pointed it straight at Anya.

'Declare yourselves.' A woman's sharp tone cut the air as if she'd deftly and expertly wielded her weapon across it. Frank noted an unusual accent. None of them spoke. The woman in black took a commanding step forward, the tip of her lethal blade making a small indent in the top of Anya's throat, forcing her to raise her chin. 'Declare yourselves,' she said again, slower, sharper. Frank didn't think she'd ask them a third time; nor did he want to find out.

'Don't hurt us,' he said.

She looked at him, slowly moving her sword across from Anya's throat to his chest, pressing the point just far enough into the material of his shirt for him to feel like the end of his life was but a flicker away, to understand she meant business, that she would run him through without a moment's hesitation. Frank raised his hands. The others followed suit.

'We don't have any weapons,' he said, feeling the quiver in his voice, his heart bashing his ribcage.

The woman didn't move, her hand on her weapon firm and steady, the muscles on her pale arms tensing. Her dark eyes pinned Frank. She flicked her head and her four companions moved quickly around the others, encircling them, hands ready to draw the sharp steel that clung to each thigh. Silent. Each one showing the sculpted muscle of their tanned arms, taut and toned. Any thoughts of the unspoiled fortress dispatched themselves from Frank's mind, the sounds of birdsong left his ears and all he could smell was the cold steel of the deadly blade pressed against his chest.

The woman slowly raised her other hand, palm upwards, and waited. Frank shrugged. He felt a firm push on the blade as she cocked her head, her hand calmly twisting so the point ruffled Frank's shirt. Her hand remained outstretched and her eyes shifted coldly to Frank's raised arms. Frank came to his senses as the penny dropped with a clatter. He held the small transparent time bead between his finger and thumb and lowered it, careful not to make any unexpected movements. He dropped it into her gloved palm and she quickly placed it into the pocket of her tunic.

'Please,' said Anya, her voice carrying a desperate edge. 'We didn't mean to...I mean we just found this by accident.'

135

The woman didn't take her eyes off Frank, narrowing them just enough for his anxiety to rise a notch. She nodded to her team, each one grabbing one of their captives, subjecting them to a cursory body search. They returned a shake of the head standing back behind them with a rigid confidence.

Gabby, Cas and Anya stood frozen to the spot. Frank sensed that any one of their muscled assailants could probably dispatch all of them with their bare hands if they wanted to. The woman nodded to one of her companions and then to Frank. Quickly he was frisked again, the guard relieving him of the map. She nodded again, then cast her steely eyes back to Frank, flicking her sword towards the door.

'Move,' she snapped with a flick of her head.

29

THE FEAR

Frank and the others followed her silent footsteps as she pushed open one of the doors and stepped into the shadows of the castle's entrance hall. The other black-clad captors swarmed invisibly around them, rattling their nerves as they were closed in, heavy iron bolts pushed across to secure their imprisonment. Frank's eyes adjusted to the relative gloom.

The hallway wasn't what he'd expected; it was less than grand. Though the threshold was wide, further inside the building the space seemed to diminish. Grey flagstones funnelled down a corridor into the depths of the building while a pair of mahogany staircases, one on each side, led up to another floor. The stone walls were bare and Frank felt their chill. A brass bell hung just inside the door.

The woman re-sheathed her sword and un-gloved her hand, extended a thumb and forefinger into her mouth and emitted a shrill whistle, piercing the thick blanket of silence that had descended on them. The sound of low, guttural barking and the thump of heavy paws on stone did nothing to ease their fear as, from down the corridor, sprinted three large dogs. Ferocious or murderous didn't quite do them justice. Looking like they'd been hewn from the rocks of the underworld, each came to a shuddering halt and sat obediently at their master's feet, eyes fastened purely on the strangers in the room, ready to rip out their throats. Frank was scared around Orpheus, but these maniacal beasts made Dagmar's dog look like a stuffed toy.

Gabby rocked on her heels and took a step back. Instantly the dogs started up; on their feet, violent barks punctuated with wild snarls, slobber escaping in great clumps as the animals lurched on all fours, feeding on the fear in the air. Frank pressed himself back, only to find the hand of one of their masked captors grip his shoulder firmly. The captain held up a finger and the noise instantly stopped, though its echoes still reverberated around the hallway. If the display of frothing beasts was their favoured method of gaining compliance, it was one hundred percent effective. Frank looked at the petrified faces of the others and knew they weren't going anywhere.

The leader turned to face them, pulling down her face covering and folding back her hood. Frank couldn't believe his eyes. She was barely older than him. With her mask off, her green eyes, flecked with gold, sparkled like the stars, even in the half-light of the entrance hall. Her pronounced cheekbones were sprayed with freckles and the long, dark braid of sunburst red that hung stiffly down her back had a length of scarlet material tied in at the end. Her face, pale as alabaster, was completely expressionless.

'State your business,' she demanded with her unfamiliar accent.

Her hands lingered over the hilts of the daggers and the muscles on her pale arms flexed. Frank looked at the others. The woman waited, her mouth tight, emerald eyes penetrating him. She grabbed his chin and pulled his face back to meet her commanding stare.

'We weren't trying to find you,' said Frank.

Quicker than a spark, she drew her hand back and sliced her palm across Frank's battered and bloodied face. He cried out, more in shock than in pain.

'He's right,' said Anya. 'We weren't sure what we were going to find. We certainly didn't mean to make anyone think we're some sort of threat.'

The woman took an imposing step over to her. The dog's ears pricked up and the room crackled with tension. One wrong word and they'd all be dead.

'Then state your business,' she said, again, her unbending words bouncing off the walls, to be met with the sound of slow, heavy steps from the same direction from whence the dogs had arrived. There was not the merest movement in her whole body at the sound. Neither did any of the others move at the footsteps, drilled in the confidence of someone familiar with their surroundings, unhurried, despite knowing that their hounds had signalled something unusual was occurring in the confines of the entrance hall. Frank didn't want to take his eyes off the leader of their group of captors, except his attention was drawn to movement behind her as a giant of a man marched into view.

Frank beheld the huge frame. Taut, rounded muscles coated his body, pushing and straining, held prisoner by his black uniform. Each of his limbs like they'd been stripped from the oaks in the forest. His gleaming dark hair was almost luminous in the half-light, like a thick oil slick hanging down to his shoulders, radiating power. His face was coated in a beard to match, with eyes like the night.

He moved with the ease of a person confident in his body's unfailing strength and stood in imposing silence, eyes wandering slowly over the gathering, regarding everything with frightening, unerring poise. There was much about the man that Frank could have been afraid of. But there was one thing that about him that quickened his breathing, had him reaching deep into his mind as it began to unravel. The orange streak in the man's hair.

Frank's feet filled with lead. The man just fixed his eyes on Cas and waited; he might just as well have grabbed him by the throat or set the dogs on him, quickly having the desired effect as Cas paled.

'We're looking for something to do with the Simbrian,' said Cas, his eyes finding the floor as the woman snapped her head round. She acknowledged with a slight nod of her head, no movement from the rock of a man; imposing and statuesque, like he'd been hewn from a granite mountainside.

'I'll take them to Zachery,' he said in an unbending voice. The woman moved to one side as the man stepped to the bottom of the staircase and snapped his fingers. A dog moved obediently over and sat, alert. With a twitch of his head he indicated they should follow and Gabby led the four of them up in the wake of the man's impressive physique. Two of the guards fell in step behind them, cutting them off from the outside world. Frank looked back as they were led away; the young woman opened the front door and disappeared through into the afternoon without so much as a glance in their direction.

30

Zachery

They followed in anxious silence to the top of the stairs and into a long corridor. Warm light spilled through the line of square windows that overlooked the front of the castle. The gleaming cherrywood floor welcomed their footsteps, oozing the warm, honeyed scent of polish. Pictures and large candle holders hung at regular intervals along the silver stone of the walls. Like the outside, the stonework looked like it had been laid only the day before. Warm and welcoming were words that would do it justice.

The stairs continued up to the next level but they were ushered down the corridor, passing a slightly open door through which the sweet sound of someone playing a lyre eased itself though the soft, fluid music had no effect of soothing the edge of Frank's frayed nerves. Who or what the black guards were emptied from Frank's mind as he stared at the broad back of the huge, warrior-like man, at his slick mane of back hair, wondering to where they were being led.

Their silent escort quickly arrived outside a smart, wooden door at the end of the passageway. As he gave it a brisk rap, a voice from the other side gave them permission to enter and they were led through into a large, brightly lit, office with a large desk at which sat a grey, stone-faced old man wearing a white shirt under an unusually cut sleeveless purple tunic embroidered with fine gold thread. His pronounced jowls gave a naturally miserable lilt to his features.

He looked up as they entered and dropped his swan-feather quill, the bored expression deepening as a glint of the sun lit his bald head. He leaned on the desk and pushed himself up on his knuckles, his arms shaking with the effort.

'What in Kester's name is this?' His gravel-filled voice low, gruff and unwelcoming. He studied them, dull eyes gazing at each of their faces in turn, his expression cold but filled with curiosity.

'They managed to disrupt the shield,' said the huge guard, a sentence that did nothing to improve the man's temper.

'Disrupt the shield?' His eyes widened. 'Has Esryn seen to it?' The guard nodded and Zachery exhaled, closing his eyes momentarily. 'Very well, thank you Morrin. If you could fetch Larrimus and Qaas, please.' Morrin gave a sharp nod. His fearsome gaze went from one frightened face to the next before ducking under the doorframe and closing the door behind him.

Zachery stared at the door for a moment, then down to the papers on his desk, shuffling them into a pile. The four teenagers glanced at each other as the quiet of the room pressed in on them. Zachery sat and sniffed, ignoring them, not bothered by the silence, pushing his rolled-up sleeves higher on his arms and picking up his quill. He went back to his papers and muttered under his breath.

Frank was about to say something when the door opened again and in walked a tall, elegant but plain-looking woman in a straight, colourless dress and a younger man who was dressed in a tunic similar to the one Zachery wore, which flared at the bottom, upon which Kester's brand was embroidered. His thick, dark hair was short and bowl-cut.

The man immediately pinned his stare on all of them before addressing Zachery in a language Frank didn't understand, his eyes fierce and his arms animated. He kept looking over, fixing them with his glaring ice-blue eyes. The woman rolled her eyes.

'Yes, Larrimus,' replied Zachery, glancing over in Frank's direction. 'I understand. Do you think I'm stupid or something?' Larrimus cooled but continued to mutter in his foreign tongue when the woman interjected.

'You were lucky,' she said. Her ice-pale eyes, circled in tired shadows, flicked across their faces. 'Very lucky. Esryn doesn't usually allow any trespassers to live.'

'Esryn?' said Gabby, her dry voice struggling to relax.

Qaas said nothing.

'The Order of the Sandulum Assassins,' said Zachery, looked at their enquiring faces, 'or the Black Flame, are without equal and she is the most skilled among them. Many a throat has she cut before the victim had a chance to blink.'

Cas took a deep breath and a sideways glance at Frank.

'Like I said,' said Qaas. You were lucky.'

'But she's only—'

'Nineteen, yes. Perhaps your youth saved you. Just.'

She walked gently in front of them and stopped across the room from Zachery and Larrimus. There was something about her, the way she spoke and the shift in her walk that wasn't quite right. Zachery cleared his throat.

'Why are you here?' he said.

There was nothing menacing about the way he spoke, but his voice carried a weight of authority reserved for the likes of Jackson. Larrimus looked on with a stare of cold steel.

'We didn't think we'd find...this,' said Frank.

'That's an answer to a different question,' shot Larrimus, clenching his jaw, a strange accent on his tongue. 'Why are you here?'

'Okay Larrimus, calm yourself,' said Zachery with a huff, his face tightening and his eyebrows knitting in Larrimus's direction.

'Yes Larrimus,' said Qaas. 'Perhaps if your temper was a little cooler, our guests might relax and, who knows, maybe they might be willing to elaborate if we were a little more welcoming.'

'Guests. Huh,' said Larrimus with a snort of contempt. 'We don't do guests. Not anymore. Why don't you get Esryn to get it out of them?' He narrowed his eyes at the youngsters and folded his arms. Zachery looked at Frank.

'Your name?'

Frank hesitated, quickly thumbing through the options in his mind. The others shifted uncomfortably as the room hushed.

'I'm Frank,' he said, his voice uncertain and feeling a hint of regret at giving himself away, not that he had much choice. Zachery's silence was meant to elicit more. 'Frank Penny.'

Zachery stopped and leant back in his chair. He arched his old fingers at his lips, pressing his palms together, letting out a long, tired breath. His eyes travelled to Qaas and then to Larrimus; Frank detected something in his look, as if something unspoken had passed between them.

Zachery opened a drawer in his desk. He reached in, ducking to peer inside then pulled out a few papers, placing them on the table in front of him. He licked the tip of his index finger and slowly flicked through the leaves as the rest of the room looked on in silence. He stopped, pulling out a short piece of parchment which rolled up at the edges as he placed it on the table. Straightening it down with the flat of his hand he cleared his throat and looked up. He paused, his face still looking like it had been slapped. He looked straight at Cas, back to the paper and then back to Cas once more.

'So you must be Hardcastle Jones.' Cas nearly choked as the words left Zachery's lips. Zachery focused on Gabby and Anya. 'And which one of you is Anya Wilde?' Anya nodded and flicked her hand up, Zachery nodded. 'Miss Asaro,' he said to Gabby before looking back down at the parchment. He looked at Gabby again, his eyes lingering, hard, before a glance and a slight nod towards Qaas and Larrimus.

'How—' began Frank, but Zachery raised his hand, demanding silence. His lips moved as he silently read the words on the paper.

'It looks like you've already come to our attention,' said Qaas. 'Nice of you to join us.'

'Nice,' muttered Larrimus, giving her a look, sarcasm on his lips. His cynical eyes leaped back to Frank. 'I hope, for your sake, it's for the right reasons.'

'The Simbrian is something not many people are aware of,' said Zachery. 'But you've been busy.' He laced his fingers on the desk. 'What I'd like to know is, how busy?'

He leaned forward and waited. Like Spargo, his eyes and

silence drew on Frank's willpower and he felt the sideways glances of the others.

'How do you know,' said Gabby, who appeared to have had enough of just standing in silence while their three hosts began to dance rings around them. Larrimus screwed his nose up.

'Why don't you just answer—'

'We don't have to answer your stupid questions.' Gabby already seemed determined to get on the wrong side of their captors.

'We have people on the outside, Gabby,' Qaas interjected, her calm tone quelling the rising tension. She turned to Zachery. 'Perhaps our guests might like something to eat and rest a while before we chat? And Frank should get that cut seen to.'

Zachery sniffed.

'Guests,' muttered Larrimus, pithy with barely concealed hostility. Qaas's expression didn't change.

'Yes, Larrimus, surely you wouldn't want me to refer to them as prisoners?' Larrimus twitched as Qaas looked back to Zachery for a response.

'Very well,' He picked up the bell on his desk and rang it. The impressive figure of Morrin opened the door immediately. 'Show our young guests to the Aldas room and see they are fed.' He looked Frank up and down. 'And get them cleaned up.'

'We're not a pack of hounds,' said Gabby, her temper stirring on her tongue. She turned to Frank. 'I think we should just leave.'

'Leave,' said Zachery, a jolt of amusement in his voice. 'Oh, I'm sorry but I'm afraid you can't leave.'

31

ESRYN

Morrin, accompanied by one of his hounds and another of his shadowy guards, led them from Zachery's office and back down the sweet-smelling corridor. Frank took in his surroundings, carefully trying to judge the layout of the building, the windows, any exits; committing as much as he could to memory.

Up another polished wooden staircase they were led until Morrin stopped outside one of the many varnished wooden doors that stretched along the length of the landing. His beast of a hand turned the doorknob and he pushed the door with a flick of his wrist. It swung silently open. Morrin stood aside, folding his immense arms across his chest and looking down on the four vexed faces. A flick of his head and eyes indicated they should enter. Frank hesitated. He looked at Morrin's hair, the orange streak, the emotionless face. Darkness; unflinching darkness poured from the eyes looking back at him, a carbon copy of Dagmar. A petulant breath later and he was following the others into a large sitting room.

Lavish didn't quite do it justice. Three sofas, quilted in red velvet sat in a square in front of an open, unlit fire. A large, fine rug adorned the floor and sumptuous plum drapes hung at the large, rectangular windows that allowed the late summer light to enter unchecked. A large chandelier pulled at the ceiling, a silent peek into the wealth that had created the whole place. Gilded cherrywood furniture was placed carefully in and around the room and two doors hung squarely in the left-hand wall.

They all stopped in the middle of the room, taking in their new, opulent accommodation, then turned to Morrin.

'There are two bedchambers through there,' he said, jerking his chin towards the doors, his voice low and harsh. 'And a bathing room.'

With that, he turned and left with his guards, closing the door behind him, silence spreading over the room, rigid faces on all of them as Frank started to think that, whatever they had stumbled into, their ordeal had only just begun.

No one spoke for a few minutes. Anya dropped herself into one of the sofas and wiped a few strands of loose hair from her face. Frank followed, the pain in his face drawing his touch, his ribs still burning. Gabby stood with her arms folded, deep in thought while Cas started a slow sweep of the room.

'What are we doing?' said Gabby. 'I'm not staying here.' She walked to a window. 'Let's just go.'

The door jolted open. Frank was on his feet as the young woman who had led their capture strode in, her young face the shade of thunderclouds. The black sleeveless tunic clung to her upper body, her deadly daggers laced tightly to the outside of her thighs, her bone-white arms taught and honed. Her flame-red braid with the length of red cloth hung down her back.

She stood before them, a small wooden box in her hand. Despite her slight physique, she looked every inch the killing machine they'd been led to believe she was. Cas took an involuntary step back. Esryn didn't appear to notice.

'I've been ordered to see to your wound,' she said, fixing her eyes on Frank, a slight glance to his battered face. Although Frank nodded, a glance at her hands hardly comforted him knowing she was going to play nurse-maid.

'You?' he said, sitting back down. 'Why you?'

She looked him up and down.

'Do you want it fixed, or shall I just leave you to it and come back when it's infected?'

Frank let out a breath, feeling her eyes wandering over him, sizing him up as if her natural instincts had kicked in. She approached in a slow casual gait, silent, completely ignoring the others and knelt in front of Frank who felt a rush of nerves. She placed the small box on the floor and opened it, producing a small bottle containing purple fluid and a small wad of cotton. She un-stoppered the bottle and tipped it onto the cotton. Frank watched the purple spread through the white swab, noticed the callouses on her knuckles, the white lattice of scars that ran down each finger and over the back of both hands.

Esryn pinched the cotton between her thumb and forefinger held it up, awaiting his silent consent which he gave with a slight turn of his head, allowing her access to the rip on his face. She reached out and swabbed it on to the cut on Frank's cheek. An intense pain immediately cleaved its way through his flesh, making him recoil. He pushed her hand away and let out a yelp.

She looked directly at him, her ice-green eyes glinting.

'Didn't I say it might sting a bit?'

He might have been wrong, but he thought he saw a faint smile tug at the corners of her lips. She lifted the cotton to his cheek once more. Even though he was prepared this time, he still sucked in through his teeth as she dabbed at his cut a second time. She discarded the pad and reached into the box again, producing a small round tin. She unscrewed the lid, wiped her fingers around the clear salve inside and reached up to Frank's cheek. Frank flinched; Esryn's face sparked in irritation.

'This won't sting,' she said.

Frank looked at her, unable to read anything on her face and nodded, letting himself relax a little. He felt her gentle fingers on his cheek, then another searing pain shot through his teeth and turned his head away. He let out another gasp as his skin burned. He looked at her.

'You said—'

'I lied. Don't be such a baby.'

Stifled laughs reached his ears from the corners of the room, adding to Frank's sudden sense-of-humour failure.

'Give me your sano stone any day,' said Frank, shifting his gaze to Gabby, barely able to bring himself to touch his burning face. Esryn snapped her head up and gave Gabby an unfettered look of hostility, her eyes lingering before she packed the medicine back in the box and stood.

'It'll be better by the morning,' she said, still humourless. 'Qaas will be sending up fresh clothes.'

She turned to leave but Frank's head was full of questions. He stood and reached out to stop her. Before he had a chance to blink, Esryn had dropped the box, drawn both her knives and turned, one long blade pointed horizontally at his neck at the end of her straight arm, the other down by her side. She looked ready to skin him. He hadn't even heard the smooth sound of steel on leather as she'd unsheathed them but their deadly glint had him taking two steps back, stumbling against the sofa, his arms up.

'W...w...wait. I didn't mean to...'

She fixed her formidable eyes on him. Where they had sparkled like meltwater in the entrance hall of the castle, now they flashed black as tar, depthless, like she faced the fiercest warriors from the Black Sands, focused and fearless. Her hands were tight on the hilts of her daggers, the muscles in her arms tense. She looked like she would cut them all down. She turned, looking at the others. A few moments passed in silence until, cautiously, she sheathed the blades. Anya had automatically sprung to her feet and looked balanced and poised, as well as completely out of her depth as her eyes widened like a cornered cat.

'No more sudden moves.' She looked at Gabby. 'Especially from you. Sorcerer.' She spat the word like it had filled her mouth with salt then looked at Anya. 'You.' Esryn jerked her chin. 'You look like you can handle yourself.'

Frank noticed Anya's body relax. She nodded, her face going from Esryn's face to her knives and back again.

'Can you show me how to use those?' she said, glancing down the sides of Esryn's legs.

'No.' She turned back to Frank, looking him up and down then shifting her eyes to the others, deliberately and slowly, taking them in. 'Zachery has requested your presence at dinner. He'll send a runner for you. You might want to get cleaned up.'

Esryn picked the box up once more and headed to the door, her braid swung lazily at her back, Frank watched the swing of her hips as she opened the door.

'Where are we?' he said. She turned to meet his gaze, a quizzical look on her face. 'This place?' Esryn looked at Gabby.

'I know what you're thinking,' she said. 'But once the shield is up, there is no way through it from this side.' Her eyes wandered over the four faces. 'You're not going anywhere. This is your new home. Get used to it.'

32

The Dinner

The door from their accommodation gaped in Esryn's wake. Not that any of them felt like venturing out. A cursory look through the adjoining doors revealed the bedrooms that Morrin had told them about, each containing two large beds, neatly dressed in exquisite flower-patterned quilts as if they'd been freshly made for their arrival. Off the larger bedroom, a small bathroom with a sunken marble bath called at them to get clean.

Gabby stood at one of the impressive windows, a vacant stare through the glass and into the woodland clouded her. Milky sunlight basked her face.

Frank joined her, keeping his distance as she wrapped her arms around herself as he approached, taking a step away. She looked tired. They all looked tired. Cas sat on one of the sofas while Anya decided to take a bath.

'I've got a bad feeling about this place,' said Gabby, keeping her eyes straight ahead.

Frank wasn't sure how to respond. Gabby seemed locked into herself, tensing her shoulders, squeezing herself.

'We'll find a way out,' said Frank. 'We just need to think of a plan. It can't be that difficult.'

Gabby gave nothing in return, just glanced at him. Eyes that accused him, told him she thought it was all his fault. She stepped past him and headed to the bedroom. No acknowledgment.

He watched her disappear through the bedroom door and felt himself flinch as she pulled it shut. He felt his shoulders drop, turning to Cas.

'We'll find a way out, right?' he said. Cas nodded, unconvincingly. They'd all heard what Esryn had said before she left.

'Sure,' he said, inspecting the rug.

But Frank also felt the ominous creep of doubt in his bones. They'd nearly been skinned, twice. Once by Balal and again by a group of deadly, black-clad killers. They had nothing in return and getting out meant having to get past Morrin, Esryn, the full group of assassins and then Balal and her murderous band of Sapirai. Guests they might be called, but prisoners felt like a better description. So Frank slumped himself down next to Cas and waited.

After an hour or so there was a light knock at the door. Frank was on his feet as in stepped a primly dressed woman with her hair tied into a neat bun, a pile of neatly pressed clothes stacked in her outstretched arms. Her grey eyes flicked from one face to the next. Her plain, pale face showing no sign of emotion. She placed the pile on the polished wooden table, gave a shallow nod and left.

Frank slumped back onto the sofa, immediately feeling the soft comfort of the expensive material and padding of the cushions that met his tired limbs.

'What are we even doing here?' said Cas.

Frank had no answers. He knew there had to be a reason, a reason why they'd nearly got themselves gutted in the woods by a ferocious band of wood folk and their monster of a leader. But he had nothing. No answers and no real clue what they were looking for. They were trapped in a small fortress that looked as new as the day it had been built with no idea why, or what the place actually was, but his mind wasn't in the right place to think of an escape plan. He knew they needed answers, quickly and the fact they'd been invited to dine with their hosts that evening felt like the ideal place to start asking questions.

Frank took his time to freshen up. Despite his new sense of incarceration, the softness of the warm bathwater and the quiet solitude of the bathroom, away from the others, had Frank closing his eyes and feeling his problems fall away. For the briefest of moments he imagined himself elsewhere, somewhere where nothing mattered and he was living the life of a normal teenaged boy, where the Simbrian never existed, where he could just walk away from all the problems that hung from him like leaden weights.

He submerged himself completely, blocking out everything around him, to extinguish his fresh surroundings and stop himself thinking about what the castle might mean for them. Being told twice that they couldn't leave meant only one thing to Frank – that he'd find a way out if it killed him.

The clothes they'd been brought were a good fit, if unconventional. The cut of the material, the lack of a collar on his shirt and the shapeless, saggy trousers looked as if they had been fashioned in a different time. Like they were from a travelling band of acrobats or, worse, an ancient version of the Jesters.

Following his bath, Frank had stayed in the bedroom, keeping a deliberate distance from the others, not wanting to invoke Gabby's look of contempt that had darkened his mood once more.

The bedroom mirror was tall and bordered in silver set with opals. He stood in front of it, buttoning up his shirt, when he was aware of Cas talking to an unfamiliar voice at the door. Anya opened the bedroom door with a light knock.

'Time for dinner,' she said with a raise of her eyebrows.

A young man, not much older than they were, escorted them down the same flight of stairs by which they'd come earlier in the day, down to the first floor. The corridors were still bright with sunlight, despite the onset of evening. They followed his shiny black hair that hung to his shoulders. He was dressed similarly to the woman that had brought them the fresh clothes – plain, clean and unusual. A few people, presumably servants or custodians of some sort, passed them, curious eyes on them each time as Frank began to understand that this wasn't just the secluded home of a few crazy fools, it appeared to contain an entire household; a small community running to its own rhythm.

They arrived at a pair of double doors. The young man pushed one open and went in without a look back. Frank, Gabby, Cas and Anya followed. Their escort bowed and left, a sideways glance as he went.

Zachery sat at the head of a long, polished dining table set with gold plates and sparkling silver cutlery, an exquisitely crafted golden goblet in his pale hand. He lifted it to his lips as they entered, stopping when he saw them.

'Ah, thank you for joining us,' he said. He indicated to the table with a swish of his arm. 'Please, take a seat.' Frank studied his surroundings as he and the others started across the parquet flooring. Once more, the room was beautifully appointed. The whitewashed walls were crisp and bright. Fresh lilies adorned the table and the air was heavy with their sweet scent. A large oil painting dominated one of the walls. A portrait of a handsome, seated, middle-aged man, dressed in the purples and golds of royalty, overlooked the room. Serene, yet commanding.

Zachery was flanked by Qaas and an empty chair. Larrimus skulked in his seat a couple of places down from Qaas and another woman with high cheekbones and flowing golden hair sat across from him. Morrin, Esryn and the group of killers were nowhere to be seen. Frank noticed the empty chairs were scattered amongst the assembled diners. A deliberate ploy to split them up.

They all hesitated, each of them weighing up where to sit. Frank wasn't that bothered and pulled back the seat opposite Qaas and sat.

'Nice of you to join us,' said Qaas as two smartly dressed men came in from the door at the far end carrying platters of sweet smelling meats, rice, spiced vegetables and sauces. 'You'll find our cooks here are extremely talented.' Another servant stepped forward and poured wine into intricately cast golden goblets in front of the four teenagers. Qaas raised her glass. 'Here's to our new residents,' she said, her eyes shining. 'I hope you all enjoy being part of our community.' She angled her glass towards the table and took a slow sip, her gaze lingering on Frank over the rim of her goblet. He thought how even the slightest of snakes could contain the most lethal venom.

Zachery helped himself to the various dishes that had been laid before them.

'You've met Larrimus,' he said. 'This is Al-Fajr.' He nodded to the slight woman who looked nervously at the four unfamiliar faces. 'I'm afraid Bakran and Morrin won't be joining us.' He smiled. 'Now, eat.'

'Thanks for the welcome,' said Gabby, 'But we're not planning on staying very long.' She picked up her drink and downed a large mouthful, slamming the goblet back down on the table. 'In fact, we'll be out of your faces tomorrow, if that's okay.'

Qaas loosed a low laugh under her breath, her indifferent eyes on Gabby, but it was Larrimus who spoke.

'What didn't you understand when Zachery said you couldn't leave, hm?' His pale face creased up. His words slow and bitter.

'I thought he was joking,' said Gabby, meeting his stare. 'You can't keep us here.' She turned her angry face to Zachery. 'You can't.' Zachery cut into the simmering lamb, loading his fork up with the saffron rice he'd heaped onto his golden plate, but said nothing. Gabby turned back to Larrimus. 'Anyway, you said you didn't like guests.' Larrimus screwed his nose up.

'Where are we?' said Cas. Zachery chewed carefully and swallowed, then pointed his fork at Cas.

'You mean you came here, at great risk to yourselves, found us here, but you don't know what you've found?' he said.

'So it would seem,' said Anya. Larrimus snorted out a laugh.

'Dumb kids,' he muttered under his breath, drawing a look from Qaas.

'Watch your tongue, Larrimus,' said Zachery, a glint of a warning on his words and in his eyes. Larrimus narrowed his eyes, a retort on his lips, but said nothing. Zachery's face relaxed. 'Let's eat,' he said. 'We'll talk in a while.'

The meal passed in awkward silence. They filled themselves with pan-fried fish, crusty bread, roasted tomatoes with mild cheese and tarragon, then light, flaky pastry dripping with honey and crusted with nuts. The blonde-haired Al-Fajr said nothing and barely looked up from the table but Frank couldn't fault the quality of the dishes that were served as plate after plate were brought in by a trail of servants, all of whom cast attentive looks at the strangers in their midst, as if word of their arrival had spread quickly throughout the castle.

Zachery dabbed the edges of his mouth with his bright white napkin and set it down. His bored eyes, red with thin, scattered veins studied them.

'Now then.' He placed his palms flat on the table, bracing his weight on them. 'Shall we talk about what you know of the Simbrian?'

An unconvincing smile nudged at his jowls and Frank noticed Al-Fajr, who had yet to utter a word during their uncomfortable meal, raise her head. She looked first to Zachery, then to each of them in turn, then to the portrait that presided over them.

'About time,' muttered Larrimus. Frank, glanced down at the table, fixing his stare on an invisible point ahead of him.

'What's it got to do with you,' shot Gabby.

She drummed the palm of her hand on the table. Cas and Anya glanced at Frank, their faces tight but they remained quiet. Qaas smiled disarmingly. Like a rattlesnake, thought Frank, while Larrimus fidgeted on his seat. Silence shifted through the room, wrapping itself around them, trying to draw their secrets out. It didn't, they wouldn't let it. They'd learned the hard way about revealing too much. Frank hadn't even breathed anything to Libby so he was never going to talk to this collection of oddly-dressed strangers. Zachery didn't wait long.

'Very well,' he said.

'I thought you knew?' said Gabby, her face still. 'So why don't *you* tell *us* what we know?'

Zachery ground his teeth, a narrow look of irritation at Gabby, then turned his old head to the portrait on the wall to his right.

'You know your king wouldn't have been so benevolent.'

33

THE KING

Zachery gave a proud nod. 'No, not as understanding. Not in his most secret hideaway.'

'King?' said Cas. 'What king?' Gabby looked up but Frank spoke.

'Kester.'

He let the words escape from under his breath, turning his head to Zachery. Zachery's face broke into a broad smile at the mention of the name as all eyes turned to the huge painting. Zachery, Qaas and Larrimus all raised their goblets. The quiet woman followed their lead. Frank looked up at the face of the man in the picture. Despite his time at Excelsus and their quest, he'd never seen the face who set the whole Simbrian disaster in motion. He was certainly handsome. His flowing golden locks hung around broad shoulders and his serene face bore a steady look of authority. His left hand, adorned with rings ripe with precious gemstones, rested on the jewelled pommel of his sword while the palm of the other was held facing forward. A short rod of blackened iron hung from his neck.

'Well done, Frank,' said Zachery, his eyes still on the portrait. 'Quite a man.'

'You mean you knew him?' said Anya.

'Anya, he lived zillions of years ago,' said Cas with a roll of his eyes. 'No one alive could have known him.' But Zachery placed his goblet down and looked at Anya with a soft smile, reminiscence in his eyes.

'Oh yes,' he said. 'I was his most trusted servant.'

Frank nearly choked on his wine, as did Gabby. Zachery had to be kidding, although he looked as likely to crack a joke as Millington Johns. He noticed how Zachery's eyes wandered over all of them, waiting for them to ask him more.

Larrimus jerked his chin to the servant at the door, who disappeared, returning a minute later with a hookah, which he placed on the table. He took the pipe in his mouth and drew in a long lungful of scented mist, still looking at them through narrow eyes.

'You're telling me you've been here for, what, a thousand years or something?' said Frank, sensing the amused tone of disbelief in his voice. Qaas answered:

'We don't count,' she said.

She wasn't joking. Her voice told them what they needed, as did the look in Zachery's eyes. He let her comment sink in but Frank was struggling to grasp what it meant.

'You've been here since the time of Kester?' said Cas, his voice revealing the doubt they all felt. 'But you're no older than my grandad.'

Zachery chuckled.

'I would have thought you'd have known more about time beads,' he said. 'Seeing as you managed to bring down the shield. Here, we don't age like you do outside.'

Frank looked at Gabby, who widened her eyes back at him, his mind instantly back in her kitchen at Crossways. Keeping a cube of ice under the tiny time shield that Helen had just about managed to create was one thing – but this, this stretched his brain in a way he couldn't comprehend. Dozens of people assembled in a centuries-old castle, kept suspended in time. It was too much to take in. Too much. Zachery appeared to notice.

'All of you?' said Frank, wondering what festering pit of power they'd stumbled upon. Zachery shook his head.

'Not all, Frank, but most. A few have joined us over the years, most earlier on.' He looked at Al-Fajr. 'Some more recent but, as you might imagine, we can't just let people leave. For security.' His repeated words hung in the air. 'Once people are here, they must be committed to our cause.'

'You said you had people on the outside,' said Anya.

'Information,' said Qaas. 'They bring us information.' She ran her eyes slowly over each face, sipping her wine. A look that told Frank they'd been watched or, at the very least, had someone pass on details of their quest. Someone on the outside. Someone they must know. 'So we know you've been very diligent in tracking the Simbrian guardians.' She looked at Zachery. 'Five so far, isn't it?' Zachery just raised his brows. 'And now this map has lead you to us.' She produced the map from under the table and slid it across to Frank. 'I don't expect you'll tell us how you came by it, so you can have it back. It's of no use to you now you're here.' Frank picked up the piece of paper.

'Who?' he said. 'Who's been passing you information about us?'

Larrimus stopped his long draw from the hookah and thumped the flat of his palm on the table.

'Enough questions,' he said, snapping at Frank. 'We know enough, so why don't you fill in the blanks?' Zachery raised a palm to Larrimus's irritation, earning him a stiff look which he ignored. But Frank knew from what Larrimus had said that they hadn't the whole story. He glanced at the others, determined to keep it that way, until they could figure a way out of this.

'What does Irundi mean?' said Anya, her soothing voice aimed at Qaas.

'It's old Rossian,' she said. 'It means tower of the king.' Well at least that made sense. 'We keep our Rossian names here, too, as a mark of respect to Kester, and although the old language fell into disuse some time ago a few of us still remember it.'

'It's getting late,' said Zachery. He raised his eyes to the window, where the early autumn sun still burned bright, then got to his feet. Immediately, one of the servants dashed over to pull his chair back, before stepping back into the shadows of the wall. Zachery pulled his tunic straight, brushing himself down. 'If you can assign them their duties in the morning please, Larrimus.' Larrimus tensed. Zachery turned to Frank. 'I'm sure we'll talk some more. After all, time is the one thing we all have.' He walked towards the double doors, the heads of the four students turning after him. 'I hope your quarters are comfortable enough. Now, if you'll excuse me.'

'Are you sure we shouldn't have them housed in more...secure quarters?' said Larrimus to Zachery's back. The old man turned his head and Frank noticed the hidden shake of the head in Zachery's eyes before he left the room.

'Have you learned nothing,' said Qaas, a quiet authority in her voice.

'I've learned that we don't trust strangers,' he said. He looked deliberately at Gabby. 'And we trust some strangers less than others.'

34

The Duties

The sheets he slept in were crisp and silken, the pillows plush, the mattress impossibly soft. Exhaustion had coated his bones and pain still splintered his face and side, although it had dulled from the previous day. A glance in the gold-framed mirror in the sitting area confirmed a significant healing of his cheek, more than was naturally possible, except for Gabby's stone. The small assassin with the face like bone china appeared to possess more than just a natural ability to rip her adversaries apart, but he was still stacked with unease at the relaxed and friendly reception they'd had over dinner.

They'd been the essence of polite, apart from Larrimus who just wanted them thrown into the dungeons, assuming they existed. A prison within a prison. Frank hadn't the energy to try and figure it out. Perhaps they were all naturally gracious. They certainly came from an age when, he assumed, particular company, including Kester's court, would have run to the rules of good breeding and sophistication, but it was difficult to swallow. A polite jailer was still a jailer.

The heavy velvet drapes were pulled shut. Frank, opened them a few inches, noticing the light from outside hadn't changed since they'd first entered the room and had undoubtedly shone relentlessly throughout the night.

They'd been led to Kester's hidden fortress in the forest, the tired and bored head of which appeared content to let them be. He knew by now that there had to be a reason, everything in their book was there for a reason, he also knew there had to be a way of getting out. Perhaps he'd missed that amongst its pages.

The next hour had them all stirring and dressing for whatever the day held. Despite their unusual surroundings, each of them was grateful for the warm bath, soft bed and new clothes. Still, escape was never far from Frank's mind. He'd put the map into the possessor, the small magical pouch he'd been given by his gran for their venture into Kzarlac, not that its unusual powers worked in the confines of the castle but it still gave him the feeling of safekeeping, away from the eyes of their hosts.

'What's our plan?' said Cas as they sat on the plump cushions of the sofas, easing themselves into the morning, refreshed from the battering they'd received the previous day.

'I'll check out the shield,' said Gabby, stretching out her feet and resting them on the low table that sat in front of the fireplace. 'There must be a way through. They said they have people on the outside.'

Frank nodded, but was unconvinced. He'd been running the same thought through his head before the others had got up and came to the conclusion that there must be a well-drilled and long-established routine that allowed what must be limited access to the clearing, one undoubtedly controlled by Zachery or, more likely, Morrin but he didn't think Gabby would take too kindly to him pushing her idea back.

'We should look for the time bead,' said Frank. 'I'll go back to the top of the tower and have a look. If we can get that down...'

'You won't.' The snide tones of Larrimus brought their conversation to an abrupt halt. Frank returned his spiteful look with a grind of his teeth and felt his breath quicken.

'Who asked you?' he said. Larrimus huffed.

'Mind your tongue,' he said, slow and purposeful. Laying the words out as a veiled threat.

'Or what,' said Frank. 'You'll have us chucked out.'

Frank's retort had them all chuckling, leaving Larrimus steaming in the doorway. Frank had developed an instant dislike for the sour man with the odd bowl-cut and couldn't hide the grin that he hoped had crept further under Larrimus's skin.

'Joker in the pack, eh?' he said, taking a step into the room. 'Well let me tell you, it isn't possible to take the head bead down from the inside.' He surveyed their faces as their expressions started to drop. 'But at least you'll have as much time as you want to try it.'

His dry chuckle had Frank wanting to grab him by the throat. They were in his territory. Larrimus held all the good cards and he wanted them to know it.

'Perhaps we should discuss it with Zachery,' said Gabby.

'Yeah,' said Frank. 'We should discuss it with the guy in charge, not their pet chimp.'

'I run the castle,' said Larrimus, snapping back. Frank sensed he'd pinched a nerve. 'And don't think you can just turn up and assume who's in charge.' He stood rubbing his palms together, hanging in the door like an unwanted smell.

'Have you come to give us a guided tour?' said Anya, melting the spiked atmosphere. Again, Larrimus huffed.

'No,' he said. 'As Zachery mentioned last night, I'm here to assign you your duties.' Larrimus could hardly hide his delicious look, pausing to let his words sink in. He certainly quietened the room. He looked at Frank. 'You and Mr Jones will become part of Wen's team in the kitchen. She's been short-handed for some time.' He jerked his head back. 'Cati here will show you the way.' He motioned to a young girl standing in the passageway, then turned to Anya. 'I've an interesting proposition for you, Miss Wilde.' Anya straightened. 'You're welcome to join the Black Flame in their practice area over in the western edge of the estate. Esryn's request.' Anya's eyes widened.

'Seriously?'

Larrimus gave a slight nod, then looked at Gabby. 'You're coming with me.'

35

The Questions

The young servant girl led Frank and Cas along the corridor to other end of the castle to a stone, spiral staircase.

'The kitchens,' said Cas to her back. 'What are we meant to do there?'

Cati spoke, not looking back.

'Don't worry,' she said. 'We'll make sure you understand the routine.' She turned, giving them a slight smile through the gaps in her yellow teeth. 'Wen'll have you making bread before the day is out.' She continued down the stairs, heading down two levels. 'We start at seven in the morning,' she said. 'Unless you're on dinner duty, then it's two in the afternoon.' As if anyone could actually tell what the time was, thought Frank.

The spiral ended as they entered the castle kitchen, the sort of space that Frank had always imagined was the bustling hub of a castle. An enormous oak table ran down the middle of the room. Three large ovens were set against one of the walls, while a line of store cupboards ran down the other side. Frank was immediately hit with a heady mix of the bitter aroma of freshly ground coffee, the sweetness of baking bread and an abundance of unusual, sharp spices that filled his senses and had him drawing in long, satisfying breaths.

In amongst the half-dozen, primly dressed cooks a short rotund woman was barking instructions, her small eyes checking and overseeing the bustle of food preparation. Cati led them over, weaving unnoticed through the industry of the kitchen.

The head cook looked up, and jerked her chin at the two boys, rubbing her hands on her apron. Strong, brisk movements.

'You can get started on the potatoes,' she said to Frank before looking at Cas. 'There's scraps to put out on the compost heap. You'll find it out the door at the end of the long passage and past the poultry sheds. Collect the eggs after that.' No smile, no hello, just instructions. 'Lunch is served at one o'clock. We're never late.' She looked at them as if they were an unfortunate smell, giving them their cue to get out of her way.

'We've not had any breakfast,' said Frank, feeling the rising smell of cooking pulling at his stomach. Wen sniffed.

'Then help yourself to some morka and jam.' She indicated to one of the larder cupboards with a nod of her head, still stern, but an empathetic note in her voice. 'Be quick.'

'Morka?' said Cas.

'Bread,' said Wen, before turning to bark more instructions at her charges.

'You'll have to excuse her,' said Cati. 'She still uses the occasional Russian word. Can't help herself sometimes.'

Frank had never worked so hard and, once the shift had finished, never wanted to see another potato in his life. The kitchen catered not just for Zachery, Qaas and Larrimus, but for the entire troupe of assassins, the household staff and others that worked in the castle. To the side of the kitchen were a number of enormous store rooms, cooled by the thick stone of the castle walls, stacked with fresh fruit and vegetables, none of which showed any signs of rotting. A stone staircase led down to a well-stocked wine cellar.

They worked through the clearing of breakfast and right up to the serving of lunch, with a short break for refreshment. Throughout, Frank wanted to know what they knew but it hadn't been the place to ask questions, not that they had had time to talk and the kitchen ran entirely to the military precision of Wen's command.

***

Frank and Cas lay on Frank's bed, Frank inspecting his fingertips, one of which he'd caught in the peeler, drawing a thin line of blood from the skin. He picked at it, sucking through his teeth at the soreness.

'I can't go through that every day,' said Cas.

'Perhaps this is your destiny calling,' said Frank. 'The first Excelsus graduate to open his own restaurant. Makes all those cunning and dexterity lessons really worthwhile.'

He felt his attempt at humour fall flat.

They both looked up as Anya walked in. Her forehead was lacquered in a thin coat of sweat and her hair was swept back behind her ears and tied in a short ponytail. The same sheen covered the olive skin of her arms. She threw herself on the bed and let out a long breath, a slow smile spreading over her face. Frank and Cas exchanged looks.

'Have fun?' said Frank.

'Amazing,' she said. 'You won't believe how skilled they are. Quick. Deadly.'

'I think we already know that,' said Cas.

'Yes, but when you're learning with them, you can see how dedicated they are.' She turned on her side and propped her head up on her hand. 'They were practising with long-staffs. Honestly, when Esryn was in the ring it was like watching a ballerina.'

'Long-staffs,' said Frank.

'Yeah.'

'No potatoes, then?' He and Cas descended into laughter as Anya's brow creased, acting as their cue to tell her about their day in the kitchens.

'Well the shepherd's pie was awesome,' said Anya. 'Thanks boys.'

'Don't mention it,' said Cas with a roll of his eyes.

'Can't wait for tomorrow's session,' said Anya. Frank felt himself growl inwardly at her enthusiasm. Their focus should be wholly on escape, not planning the next acrobatic combat training session in a place that seemed determined to hold them hostage.

'You mean you're going back?'

'Sure.'

'Are you sure they don't just want to use you for target practice,' said Cas. Anya grabbed a pillow and bashed him with it.

'You better watch out, Cas. A few months with this lot and I'll be ten times as good as I am now. Excelsus can take a hike. Do you know there's an assassins' guild in Sandulum? They're all graduates.'

Frank was about to ask what the point of being a world class killer was if you spent your entire life incarcerated in a relatively small clearing in the middle of a blackened forest when heavy footsteps outside the door had them looking up.

In walked Gabby, a look on her face that would freeze the sun. She stomped into the boy's bedroom like a child denied their favourite treat and threw herself down next to Anya. Asking if she'd had a bad day seemed like the move of a fool, so Frank waited for her to thaw.

'Well?' said Cas.

'Well what?' Gabby's tone dared him to ask again. Cas didn't try.

'It can't have been worse than peeling potatoes and taking out the rubbish all day,' said Frank, but Gabby looked like she was burning on the inside.

'I've spent the whole morning with Qaas.'

'Qaas?' said Frank. He'd thought she looked like she'd had a bellyful of something less palatable, with a bowl-cut. Gabby nodded.

'And don't say she seemed nice,' Gabby said to Anya. 'She's... odd.'

'What did she want with you?' said Frank.

'It would be quicker if I told you what she didn't want with me.' Gabby shook her head. 'She spent the morning being really sickly sweet, asking me to help her file some papers – although everything seems to be written in a different language – but you'd have to be a fool not to see what she was doing and I could see right through her.' Gabby's voice possessed nothing but contempt. 'All her questions were about my abilities and those of my mum and grandmother. She wouldn't let it go. I thought she'd ask me to take her back through the generations, right back to when the castle was built. Like some sort of not-fun quiz.' She puffed out her cheeks and shook her head. 'For some reason she wanted to know everything about being a sorcerer. Stupid woman.'

'Why would she be so interested in your family history?' said Anya.

Gabby shrugged.

'Search me. I was as vague as possible. I'm not having some smiley willowy wraith feigning interest about me, and my family's business is nothing to do with her.' Gabby ran her hand over her face and pinched the bridge of her nose. 'But that's not the worst of it.' She looked up. 'I've got to work in the laundry.'

In any other circumstances Frank would have been highly amused, but Gabby's telling of her hours spent with Qaas unsettled him and had done nothing to lift his dark mood.

Although escape was on his mind, he also wanted to know what was going on within the sparkling stone walls and why they had been led here. He could sense it in the others. Perhaps they'd have to stay for a while to find out but, for now, they were all too tried to think about a plan.

'I'm not sticking around,' said Gabby, shuffling to the side of the bed and getting to her feet. She looked at Frank, a demanding look Frank knew all too well.

'Okay,' he said with a thin slice of resignation. 'I'll come with you.'

36

THE SHIELD

Frank followed on Gabby's heels. He knew exactly what Gabby was planning as they headed down the stairs and out into the monotonous sunshine, checking for prying eyes.

Gabby was wordless, walking three steps ahead of him, not looking back. He couldn't shake the feeling that she was angry with him, that she thought this was still all his doing. She made her way quickly over to the edge of the clearing, near the spot where they had entered the day before, and stood staring out into the forest, her hands planted firmly on her hips.

Frank stepped up beside her, giving her a sideways glance before following her gaze into the trees. What he saw wasn't the bare, soulless bones of the blackened vegetation through which Balal had lead them. That was all gone, replaced by a tree-scape full of colour and life. The leaves danced to the melody of the sunlight which beamed through the canopy and onto the soft soil of the forest floor. It called to them, inviting them to cross the threshold at the edge of the clearing and enter.

Gabby drew in a breath, held up her hand and took a step forward. Immediately the air rippled around her outstretched arm as she tried to push through. As she attempted to move forward an invisible barrier between them and the safety of the forest held her gently but firmly, not allowing her to pass beyond the boundary. Frank watched as Gabby pushed, the shield hindering any sort of progress until she stepped back, her face bearing the realisation of someone defeated and confirming to Frank that their situation had just become more hopeless. What lay beyond was all just an illusion.

'You can't get through.' Morrin's voice grabbed them from behind. Frank and Gabby turned, greeted by his stone face and corded muscles. He stood squeezing his fingers to a fist, his huge forearms flexing, arms that could crush Frank's skull. Gabby folded her arms but Morrin's appearance had Frank's temper rising.

'Why don't you piss off, Morrin,' he said, his own words catching him by surprise, his bravado quickly fading at the snarl that spread across Morrin's face. The orange streak in his hair glowed in the sunlight. He took a step forward. Frank felt himself back off, the shield at his back.

'Why don't I just pick you up and chuck you through it?' said Morrin, looking like he wanted to do the military two-step down the nape of Frank's neck. 'See what happens.'

'Do you treat all your guests like this?' said Frank.

'You wouldn't like to know what I'd do with any new guests,' said Morrin, his hand going to his neck. Every muscle in his face tightened. Gabby, arms still folded, had no words. She took a step forward, making for the castle entrance, but Morrin slid effortlessly into her path, blocking her progress. He dipped his head right into Gabby's face and in a low, snarling voice through gritted teeth he said, 'You might think you can fool Zachery but, believe me, you can't fool me.'

Gabby pushed past him, her quick footsteps inviting Frank to follow, heading away from Morrin and his spiteful words. Frank could feel his eyes on his back as they headed back to the castle. Surely Morrin could see that they were here by accident, that they'd just stumbled on his assassins' lair without a clue what they were doing there. In no way were they trying to fool anyone.

'Gabby, wait,' he said. Gabby, still a few paces ahead, stopped.

'What is it, Frank.' There was an edge of bitterness in her words which he wasn't sure were aimed at him or just at their worsening situation.

'What's wrong?' he said. She scowled. He knew it was a lame question.

'Apart from the obvious? Apart from being trapped here with no way out with the prospect of washing sheets all day long until I never die?' Her emotion was deep, she looked at him, a pleading of sorts in her eyes. He took a consoling step toward her, but she backed away, creating her own invisible barrier between them.

'We'll get out of this,' he said. Another lame attempt at reassurance which crashed to the ground in front of him as Gabby turned and walked off.

They headed back up to their room in silence where Cas and Anya sat chatting on the sofas. Gabby headed straight to the girl's bedroom, shutting the door hard. Cas looked at Frank, a question on his face, while Anya got up and headed after Gabby.

'We just had a minor run in with Morrin,' he said. Cas nodded. 'Not something to be recommended.'

'But there's something not quite right,' said Frank. Cas leaned forward, his attention drawn. 'The way Gabby was taken off and questioned by Qaas this morning, then Morrin seemed to think she, or we, had some sort of agenda. He said she couldn't fool him.'

'Why would we be trying to fool anyone?' said Cas.

'That's my point,' said Frank. 'Anyone who knows us knows we're as clueless as a blind detective, so why the big deal. I'm not going to argue with him, but there was something in his face.'

'Perhaps it's because you were trying to find a way out?'

'No, it wasn't that.' He knew he wouldn't get there, not without asking Morrin, who looked like he'd rather take on two lions than talk to him. Whatever it was, Frank knew there was more to this place than just a group of immortals playing at castles.

37

The Errand

The next few days passed no differently. Anya spent as much time as she could developing her already formidable skills, converting what she could always do with her hands into the wielding of any of the array of deadly weapons the assassins used. Some days she'd come back from the ring exhausted, sometimes injured, even though she said Esryn had made it clear that they were going easy on her, but always bursting with exhilaration, as if she'd found her calling.

For the other three, however, the passage of time felt very different. Although the work in the kitchen was varied, there was nothing in it that interested either Frank or Cas and they just concentrated in getting though the day, each moment filled with a mixture of Wen's barking voice and thoughts of how to get out.

Gabby seemed to be having the worst of it. The skin on her hands had already started to dry out and callouses had started to form on one of her fingers. She'd managed to burn herself while ironing and had the feeling that the chief laundress was forever keeping watch over her.

It was obvious that the castle ran to a regular and well-worn beat, where nothing ever happened, nothing ever changed and nothing grew any older. Despite having the illusion of easiness, he knew it was a growing nightmare, one that the current occupants had accepted long, long ago. One that he would never come to terms with and he wondered how anyone could tolerate the humdrum existence that blighted their days. And everyone was tight-lipped about Irundi's purpose. Even their direct questions were met with silence or demands to get on with the tasks they'd been assigned.

It was difficult for them to keep track of time, but they were all given a day's break, meaning Frank and the others didn't have to haul their unwilling teenage bodies up at some ghastly hour. Even so, Frank found himself unable to sleep in.

The worries he'd had before their unfortunate jaunt through the silent forest, of his dad, Dagmar, Libby and Moonhunter had faded little, although they had been lessened by their inability to hatch any sort of plan to escape. Fleeing from the clutches of Etamin Dahke had been a two-piece jigsaw compared to what they faced here.

But underneath the veneer of its weird normality, there was something that still troubled him. The castle had some sort of connection to the Simbrian. How it was connected was currently out of his grasp. No one was going to tell them, even though the risk of them absconding was, apparently, non-existent.

**

He sat alone by the fireplace. Silence filled the room, no sounds from out in the corridor or from the window. It must be early, but he couldn't tell. Frank stretched, staring at his hands. His fingers ached from kneading dough the previous day so he flexed them, relishing the tightness as he extended them as far as he could. He couldn't accept that this first week would be the start of a new life in the confines of the pristine walls of the castle and knew he had to start at least a hint of a plan to undo what the map had got them into. He wished he'd never looked inside the back cover but was still convinced there was a reason they were here, finding what it was was a different matter altogether. Perhaps he'd missed something on the map.

Frank went back into the bedroom where Cas was stirring. He took out the possessor, reaching in and retrieving the torn page.

'What's the time,' said Cas through a cat-like yawn. Frank shook his head.

'No idea.'

'What's up?' Cas sat up as Frank sat on the bed.

'I just thought there might be something on the map that showed us the way out,' said Frank. He thought it was a sound idea. If the book had led them here, surely it would give them the way of getting back to their own world. He laid the map on the bed, with the intention of searching the detailed sketch carefully for any hidden pathways or signs that pointed to an escape route.

Cas leaned in, tucking the bedcovers around himself as both boys stared at the image on the page. It was different. The detailed drawing of the forest, the dark line running through the middle towards the cliffs had gone. In its place the image now showed a close-up of the clearing, the castle and the outbuildings clearly marked, the assassins' ring clear, the turret was now darker, inked in.

Frank flipped the page over, expecting to find the original picture, thought his eyes must be playing tricks but he was met with something else something that had him and Cas sitting up, not quite understanding what they were looking at.

Writing, in small lettering across the middle of the page – *seek the well of darkness.*

It was followed by a few words in a foreign language, indecipherable. *Beware the queen of the forest* remained.

Cas pressed his long index finger into the faint script. Frank's eyes were immediately on them, digesting them; he was sure they hadn't been there before but, given his incessant black mood and fatigue, he began to doubt himself.

'That doesn't sound particularly cheery,' said Cas, although Frank could tell his attention had been grasped.

'I can't believe it,' he said, looking at his friend, recognising the script for what it was. 'It's brought us here to find whatever this is.'

'Great,' said Cas with a hint of defeat. 'Then what?'

'I don't know,' Frank felt the heat in his voice. 'For goodness sake, Cas, at least try and be a bit more positive.' He felt Cas's look and sensed him quieten. Frank drew in a breath. 'Sorry,' he said, not sure he really meant it.

They waited for the girls to emerge, showing them the changed image as soon as they came through into the sitting room. Gabby was particularly animated about the unusual change, recognising that it was something important, something that might shorten their confinement and they both confirmed what Frank already knew, that the words hadn't been there before, that they had only appeared now that they were inside the four walls of the castle. He also knew that the map was doused with something special, that it defied the silent forest, Irundi and their aversion to anything enchanted.

'So there's a well here?' said Gabby. She looked at Anya. 'Have you seen anything like that around the grounds?' Anya shook her head.

'But they must get fresh water from somewhere,' said Cas.

'Although nothing ever goes off or gets stale in this place,' said Frank. Wen had told them that in their first days in the kitchen when Frank had asked as many questions as he dared about how the castle was run, hoping to gain an insight into the real function of the place, but whenever he strayed from the anything kitchen related, he was either met with silence or steered off the subject.

Gabby opened her mouth to speak as the writing melted back into the paper at the sound of slow footsteps approaching from outside the door. Quickly, Frank folded the map up and stuck it down the back of his trousers, he and the others trying to look as though nothing much was going on as Zachery appeared in the doorway.

'Good morning,' he said through a slouch of a smile. 'I trust you all slept well.' Shrugs and slight nods. Frank put his hands in his pockets as a short, uncomfortable silence settled itself between them. Zachery flexed his lips and looked around the room.

'Where's Larrimus?' More shrugs and silence. 'I thought he'd be here. He mentioned he was going to come and check on how you're finding your duties.'

'Do you do that with all your servants?' shot Gabby. Zachery appeared not to mind the spiked response and ignored her.

'Oh well,' he said. 'When he turns up, let him know I'm looking for him.' Gabby folded her arms, a deep frown pointed in Zachery's direction which he duly ignored again.

'Maybe he's forgotten about us,' said Anya.

'Let's hope,' said Gabby, flashing a mocking smile at Zachery.

'Can we help?' said Anya. Zachery dipped his eyebrows in Gabby's direction.

'Well, he is a busy man. Running Irundi keeps him on his toes, when he's not over at Morrin's shelter enjoying a glass of whiskey.' He let out a muted laugh. 'Perhaps you could make yourselves useful and take these to Bakran for me.' He held out his hand, fanning three envelopes before them. 'You'll find her in the Predek room on the top floor. Purple door. That's where the important work gets done.' Another smile on his otherwise cheerless face.

Gabby slumped back on the sofa.

'Why don't you do it yourself?'

Zachery twitched his nose at her. 'Very well,' he said with the faintest shrug, his tone clear he didn't care if they did or not and turned to go.

'I'll go,' said Cas. Zachery turned back and raised his eyebrows, nodded and handed the envelopes to Cas.

'Thank you, Cas.' He turned to Gabby, his face blank. 'Please don't think your bad manners are, for one minute, a sign of strength,' he said. Gabby took a long intake of breath, but thought better than to say anything. Zachery turned back to Cas. 'The Predek room. Top floor, purple door,' he repeated. Zachery pivoted on his heels and left without a look back. Gabby huffed.

'Should have just told him to get stuffed,' she said. 'Let him deliver his own stupid letters rather than swan in here and order everyone around'

'I thought he was really polite,' said Anya.

'I thought we needed to try and find anything to do with the well of darkness as soon as we could,' said Cas. He flapped the envelopes in the air. 'Gotta start somewhere.' He turned to Anya. 'Do you want to come with me,' doing an obvious job of ignoring Frank, but Anya shook her head.

'Sorry, I've asked to do some extra practice.'

'You're kidding, Anya,' said Gabby. 'It's your day off.'

'Yes, but I'm really enjoying it, even the bits where I get hurt. I'm learning things no one would be able to teach me at the academy and if we do get out of here, I might never get another chance.'

Despite their irrational surroundings, what she said made complete sense to Frank. His entire upbringing had been about doing things when he wanted for as long as he wanted. Not constrained to a school timetable or rigid, meaningless curriculum and, as Anya spoke, his mind wandered back to his carefree existence at Tresparrick farm, bringing an unexpected tightness to his throat and a feeling of confusion to his mind.

'Wish me luck,' said Anya before taking a deep breath and heading out of the room. Cas went to the door, letters in hand.

'Hang on a sec,' said Frank. 'I'll come and keep you company.'

An uncertain look carried across the room from Cas, but he nodded.

'What, you're leaving me here?' said Gabby. Frank turned.

'Say hi to Larrimus for us,' he said, before following Cas out.

38

THE PREDEK ROOM

The third floor of the castle had a different feel to the lower levels. The central wooden staircase reached a mezzanine which led neatly around the castle in one continuous landing off which were a number of doors and the now familiar latticed windows, allowing broad splinters of recognisable light to spread on to the wide ceiling. There was no silent shuffle of the servants or sign of any residential quarters or smell from the kitchens. The floors were warm, unlike the cold stone of the ground floor and the kitchen, like the level was set apart from the rest of the castle and Frank wished he'd taken the time to explore up here before.

A black-clad guard prowled the landing, a familiar, murderous dog at his heels, and stopped at the top of the stairs when he saw Frank and Cas approaching, holding up his hand and looking at them through half-shut eyes.

'State your business,' he said with a lift of his chin, voice firm and growling, his muscled frame struggling to keep itself contained inside his too-small tunic.

'We've been asked to give these to Bakran,' said Cas, showing him the letters.

Frank eyed him with disinterest, grinding a sole of his shoe into the stair carpet. The guard beckoned with his fingers and Cas handed the letters to him. He turned them over in his hand and ran his fingers firmly over the surface.

'Who are they from?' said the guard, dropping his hand to his dog who gave them a thorough well-trained sniff. Cas explained that Zachery had asked them to run an errand, the guard maintaining a naturally suspicious look in his eyes throughout, making Cas shift on his heels. He looked at Frank and handed the papers back to Cas, clenching his hand into a huge fist. Without another word he nodded to the far side of the mezzanine and stood to the side, keeping a firm hold on his dog's leash as Frank and Cas made their way past. Frank ran his hand along the top of the shining wooden balustrade on his way to the purple door to which the guard had indicated, silently checking his surroundings, checking for anything that might reveal a clue to whatever the well of darkness was. It might not be here, but he knew in his bones that it was hiding somewhere.

Frank didn't bother knocking. He turned the door knob and pushed, the door opening gracefully without a sound. The room was bright and he was immediately hit with the scent of rose-water as he entered. At the top of the building the sun found its way in easily and it flared on the hues of purple and gold that punctuated the sweet smell.

A floor-to-ceiling bookcase covered the far wall and the room was dominated by yet another large map of Byeland and Kzarlac, splashed across from the window. A dark-skinned woman was standing at a long, long table, her hands palms down on the polished wooden surface. She muttered to herself, turning her head slightly as her eyes shifted across a number of pieces of paper spread out before her. She shook her head and picked up what looked like a letter and began to read it, her lips moving wordlessly as she shook her head again and placed it back down, picking up another, repeating the same silent routine.

At the far end of the room, at the head of the table, sat a thick roll of what looked like tawny coloured material, although it was difficult to see.

Frank cleared his throat. The woman snapped her head round and peered at him over her glasses as he and Cas stood in the doorway. She looked at them for a moment.

'Out,' she snapped, quickly turning the papers face down on the table.

'We —'

'You must be the new kids.'

She said 'kids' like she wanted to wipe the word off her shoes.

'Yeah, we —'

'What do you want? No one's allowed in here.'

She wasn't rude, just straight to the point. Frank went to enter the room, but she stopped him with a straight arm, palm raised, raising his hackles. Her face hardened as she strode towards him, placing the flat of her hand on his chest, pushing him back.

'Which part of that didn't you understand? Out!'

Cas and Frank backed out into the corridor, although the woman more or less pushed them out on their heels.

'I know you're new here, but someone needs to tell you the rules, and one of the rules is that no unauthorised person is allowed in this room. Do you understand?'

'Sorry,' said Cas. 'But no one said anything about not coming in.' The woman looked at the envelopes in Cas's hand. She extended her palm.

'Are those for me?'

'Only if you're Bakran,' said Cas.

She nodded and snatched them from Cas's hand, no smile, no thank-you as she backed into the room and closed the door, the faint click of the lock turning echoing faintly in the corridor.

Cas let out a slight laugh.

'I'm sure if we stay long enough we'll come across someone who looks like they're happy to be here,' he said, looking at the closed door. Frank scowled. Despite the deliberate gaze from the guard, he felt like kicking his irritation out on the wall but Cas took the edge off his resentment with a hand on his shoulder. Frank resisted the urge to shrug him off. 'Let's leave her to it,' said Cas. 'Fancy a wander?'

Frank nodded.

'Sure,' he replied. 'Then you can tell me why you only gave her two envelopes.'

39

THE BLANK PAGE

They stopped once they'd reached the ground floor, having taken the stairs two at a time from the top of the castle. The same bare grey flagstones that met them when they'd been dragged in like criminals were cold underfoot. Cas stared down the corridor from where the dogs had been summoned, his eyes fixed on the darkness beyond as Frank opened the front door. Grey light and the scent of green grass spilled into the dim entranceway. They headed out and across the front lawn to the mature rose garden, away from people and out of earshot.

Once they'd found a secluded bench, surrounded by apricot and pale cream blooms, none of which showed signs of browning or wilting, they sat, expectant.

Cas took the envelope out of his pocket and rapped it twice on his thigh. It was addressed simply to Zachery Samuels. No address. It was sealed with a thick blob of red wax with no discernible markings. He looked at Frank, who nodded as Cas slipped his finger under the seal and opened the envelope with a hint of a click. He pulled the contents – a single sheet of paper – out.

Eagerness was quickly replaced with disappointment as they looked at the blank sheet. Cas flicked it over a couple of times to make sure they hadn't missed anything but for all the anticipation there was nothing. Whatever they were expecting, Frank was completely underwhelmed and immediately felt a sharp spike in his temper shoot up his throat. He grabbed the sheet and envelope from Cas's hand, balled it in his fist and threw it as far as his fuming arm could manage. He leaned forward, elbows on his knees and raked his hands through his hair. He loosed a long breath.

'Why is nothing ever simple?' he growled through gritted teeth.

'You know,' said Cas. 'We can all tell you're not quite yourself, mate.'

The comment hung there, pushing Frank for a response. He looked at Cas who just gave him an impish smile, soothing Frank on the spot. It was typical of his best friend; he never asked anything of Frank or assumed he knew better or what to do. It was a quality in Cas that Frank had always appreciated. What he left unsaid spoke more than the words he'd used. He knew Cas cared, knew they all did, but he was finding it difficult to reach out.

'It's not something you can help with,' said Frank, sensing an ease in his voice that he hadn't been able to find since he found out about his parentage. Cas just nodded, he didn't need to say anything else and in his face Frank could see his offer of talking whenever he felt he was ready and, for that, he was in his friend's debt. 'Thanks,' said Frank in a near whisper.

'I'm guessing you weren't going to hand this over?' Esryn's voice had them looking up as she appeared on the path, the screwed up piece of paper in her hand. She stood, feet apart, arms crossed, her face demanding. Frank couldn't think of anything to say as Esryn unravelled the discarded piece of paper. She held it out between her thumb and forefinger, the pale, thin scars tensing on her hand. 'Surely you would guess that all messages are masked,' she said, disappointment on her tongue.' Even then, they're coded.' She shook her head slowly. Frank and Cas looked at each other. Frank shrugged.

'Why aren't you out killing Anya?' he said with a huff, unable to bring himself to look at her.

'You should worry,' said Esryn. 'At least keep on her right side. She's good.'

'I guess you've had twenty lifetimes to know.' He could taste the barb in his voice. Esryn narrowed her eyes at him and flexed her hand.

'I have my duties to attend to,' she said.

'You should get out more,' said Frank. 'Oh, sorry, you can't, or don't want to, or aren't allowed.' She fixed him with a black stare. 'Which one is it?'

'You should mind yourself, Frank Penny.'

She cast her eyes behind her, then back. There was something in her look, just for a mere second, but he saw it. Some doubt. Something in his words that flicked a switch.

'We just want to know what's going on here,' said Frank. He jerked his head to the forest, beyond. 'There's something going on out in the world, something that involves this castle and you can't just hide yourself away shuffling papers and sharpening your knives.' Esryn looked like she didn't know what to say which made Frank's temper flare. 'Look, if you don't want to help us then get lost.'

Esryn's face blazed. She screwed the piece of paper back up, threw it at his feet and walked off.

Defeated before they'd even begun, Frank and Cas went back to the room where Gabby confirmed that Larrimus had showed up, but had looked at her like she was some sort of filth and not bothered asking where the others had gone. Cas explained about their short encounter with Bakran and the lack of any progress on what they were looking for.

'No sign of a well, then?' she said. Frank shook his head.

'Not on the third floor, but we need to take a look in that room,' he said. 'She basically chucked us out like I was about to rob the place of all its secrets.' He turned to Cas. 'You noticed?'

Cas nodded. 'Definitely hiding something in there. Looks like a good place to start.'

40

THE LINEAGE

It was the first time they'd ventured into the castle during the night. There was no curfew and they hadn't been told or warned to stay in their rooms. It was just none of them had felt like running the gauntlet of any of the guards and they were all feeling either too miserable or too tired to care.

They left the comfort and security of the second floor and moved carefully and silently through the castle to the shadows at the bottom of the staircase where Cas and Frank had found themselves earlier in the day. The top of the stairs still basked in the spectral glow of the sunlight but the landing was completely empty. No guard. No guard dog. It was eerily quiet, even the ghosts had disappeared, putting Frank on edge. He was sure Larrimus would have the place guarded around the clock but, then, why guard the place at all when no one would ever be able to get in and no one could get out. As burglar-proof places went, this would be top of the list by some distance.

Frank could feel their hesitation.

'Come on,' he said. 'The sooner we get in, the sooner we get out.'

'That's just what you said when we first stepped foot into the forest,' said Cas. 'Look where that got us.'

Frank wasn't sure if it was a mis-timed attempt at humour, or if Cas's comment was genuinely spiked, so he ignored him and headed out into the light and ran up the stairs, the others in his wake. He reached the top and followed the landing around to the purple door.

He put his hand on the doorknob and gave it a firm twist. As he expected, it didn't budge. He stepped to one side, allowing Cas room to spring the lock and push the door open.

Like all the rooms in the castle, heavy drapes adorned the windows. They were pulled across, a sliver of light passing unhindered through the room, cutting itself on the long table.

They moved swiftly and silently into the room, spreading out, checking for anything obvious. Frank moved to the back of the room, eyeing the books that crammed the shelves behind. Titles in foreign tongues. The map on the wall was marked with small purple flag pins, each one bearing a number, no discernible pattern to their distribution.

Ten minutes passed in which time, despite a thorough search, they'd found nothing of interest.

Frank turned to the long table, now empty, the weighty-looking roll of material had been placed on the floor at the end. He stepped over to it. Just by looking at it he could tell it was woven years ago and the fusty smell gave away just how old it was. He knelt at one side of the coiled cloth, running his hand over it, feeling the years groaning inside.

'Gabby, give me a hand with this.' Gabby knelt at the other end and together they managed to heave it on to the table where they dropped it with a dull thud.

Frank looked down on it, then, with a push of his hand slowly unrolled the long cloth down the entire length of the table, its width matching exactly so not an inch of wood was left uncovered. It looked ancient, the colour of autumn leaves, yet as though it had been made yesterday, bearing the spectre and craft of a master weaver. He wasn't sure what to expect but was surprised to see it was crammed from the start to just before the end with a web of lines that connected to thousands of what looked like names in small, calligraphic handwriting. Rossian names.

Frank's eyes wandered over its length, squinting against the darkness, absorbed as the strange picture drew him in. He walked slowly down the length of the table tracing the array of criss-cross patterns, noticing the bonds between one name and the next, linked by a fine strike of the quill. He could spend a week looking at it and still not see everything, every one of the secrets it held.

'It's a family tree,' said Anya, looking at the beginning of the roll.

She pressed her finger into the cloth. Frank walked back to the top of the table, his eyes focusing of the point of Anya's finger. He could just make out the name 'Kester' at the top, inked in precise script with a fine line leading over to Vega, his wife, then a perpendicular line leading down to Joleyon and Lashka. The names cascaded down the entire length of the cloth, like an intricate tapestry bursting with the life of people long forgotten, hundreds of people. Every name noted, its story branching out, covering every inch of the cloth. Each one connected to another, showing the parentage of the next line and so on until the incalculable array of names carried down the material to the other end of the table where Cas and Gabby stood. Just first names, no family names as though to preserve an element of anonymity.

Frank tried to follow the lines from top to bottom, but his eyes kept blurring, such was the intricacy of the image. He blinked to regain his focus, but the bad light and his tired eyes were unable to follow any of the links with any ease or surety. The whole thing was in danger of giving him a headache and, beyond that, he was struggling to understand why the castle was keeping it so secure.

'Look here,' said Gabby. Frank walked down to join them, glancing at the table, noting how the material suddenly became blank as he approached. The end of the line, the end of those descended from Kester. Gabby had her finger pressed into the fabric, denting the names – but there was nothing, just a smudge, like someone had written the last name but it had been wiped away. Frank followed the black swipe of ink that led to it, his eyes stopping at the name, the name that indicated the missing person's parentage. Frank felt his skin crawl. Etamin.

Images flared in his head, a picture of him standing before her, a puppet to her darkest urges. He could feel her breath on him, the seductive touch of the ultramancer, the tug of her exotic spell. Gabby looked him up and down as he shivered at the memory but he kept his eyes fixed on the cloth, knowing that this wasn't just an ordinary family tree. It showed everyone descended from Kester, the track of time that ran from when the Simbrian was created, the intricate assembling of his lineage from over a thousand years ago to the present day.

'They're looking for the Simbrian heir,' said Gabby. Her words just fell out like she'd cast stones from her hand. 'That's what they're doing.' Frank looked at the faces of the others as Anya joined them, standing in silence as they contemplated what it meant. Gabby went on. 'They've been tracking Kester's whole lineage, right from the start so they can identify the heir,' she said.

Frank's eyes dwelt again on Etamin's name, the line that led from it to an empty space. Her secret child, just like Menetti had said. Just like Everbleed's prophesy had foretold. Those at the castle knew exactly what they were doing.

'A child from the dark and the light,' said Frank, digging into his mind for the words that had been uttered to them when they had used Gabby's speak sand to learn something of what the Kzarlac Spy had been sent for. He traced the line back to Etamin. There was no other connection to the missing name, no father; but they knew who the missing child was – Valaine De Villiers. Whoever was searching for the final piece of the jigsaw, out in their world, their old world, hadn't been able to make the connection. Etamin had done a good job of keeping that concealed.

Cas ran his finger over the empty space.

'It looks like someone's been tampering with this,' he said before running his finger sideways along the material, stopping before he reached the edge. 'And here's something we didn't know.' He looked up, keeping his finger pressed to the surface. Frank looked, a flush of hollowness ran through him. Dagmar.

'Dagmar's descended from Kester?' said Gabby. Frank was stuck in silence. His eyes roved beneath Dagmar's name, checking to see if his own was inked in. It wasn't. Relief spread through him, his identity kept under his own shroud of secrecy, away from his friends, from everyone.

'I'm not sure it matters,' said Cas. 'Not only a complete nightmare, but a complete royal nightmare.'

Frank kept his silence. Cas was right; it didn't matter, shouldn't matter – except that it did. It mattered to him. Because Cas didn't know that he was looking at his own ancestry, his own blood. He felt himself blocking out the world at the realisation he was descended from the last king of Rossia, sat right at the bottom of the line – a long long line. But no one was ever going to know and seeing Dagmar's name in black ink just heaped more misery on him, bringing back the moment he'd stared into the jar containing Blackburn's identification formula, changing his life forever.

'Explain yourselves.' The sharp voice of Bakran rattled the room, turning their heads. She walked in, not in the least bit phased by encountering four teenagers in the middle of the night. 'Well?' She waited. Frank had no excuses prepared other than they were curious, which now seemed like a very poor one as she fixed her look of irritation and anger on them. Frank looked back to the long roll of material.

'We were just having a look —'

'Don't try and be clever with me,' she snapped. 'When I said no one was allowed in here without authorisation did you take that to mean no one except you?' Silence. 'In all my years I've never seen such disrespect.' She looked as if she was struggling to keep her temper leashed, one ill-placed response away from hitting one of them. 'Back to your quarters. Zachery will hear about this first thing.' She pushed them aside and started what looked like the long process of rolling the cloth back up.

'Can we give you a hand,' said Anya. Bakran looked like she was going to throttle her.

'Get. Out.' Her extended arm and pointed finger was their cue to leave, which they did without hesitation or a look back as they headed down the stairs, a single thought in Frank's head. Why were the castle tracking the Simbrian heir?

There was nothing he could think of that made sense. So what if the castle was tracking the appearance of the Simbrian heir? They already knew who that was and although they understood that the control of the Simbrian was in some way connected to the heir, tracking it in a small castle, completely forgotten in time, standing in the midst of a soulless forest and protected in a way that defied logic was simply unfathomable.

'Maybe they needed to protect the castle when it was first built, to protect the information, and it's stayed that way ever since,' said Anya. 'Like they've never known any different or fallen into the habit. You know what people are like.'

Frank thought she made sense. If, in the early years of the Simbrian's creation and splitting, there was a risk of certain knowledge getting into the wrong hands, it followed that Kester might have tasked his most trusted aid, in the form of Zachery, to keep certain secrets.

'Then there might be more here,' said Cas. 'If you think about it, why build a dirty great castle, make it invisible to the whole world except for a select few?' Frank felt the same; knew there had to be more, knew the well of darkness was here to be discovered. 'Perhaps Zachery might be more willing to tell us when he's giving us a bollocking tomorrow, now he knows we know a bit more.'

'Probably not,' said Frank. 'He'll just tell us that they don't like guests. As if anyone ever comes here.'

'Whoever put together our book was here,' said Gabby.

'Not necessarily,' said Cas. Gabby tightened her shoulders. Cas appeared to notice. 'I mean, they drew a map, but there's nothing to say they were actually here.'

'What, like someone draws a random map of a castle whose whereabouts is completely unknown to everyone except those that live here. Dummy.'

'If they were here,' said Anya. 'Actually in the castle, then they must have got back out again.' Anya's words hit him like a falling rock. He stopped trying to think and looked at her. She was right. He couldn't quite get it straight in his mind, but she was right and he cursed why he hadn't thought about it before. Someone had been here. They'd got themselves in somehow and, more importantly, had got themselves back out, otherwise the map would never have been drawn and the book would never have found its way into their hands.

'Then they'd know who it is,' said Cas. 'The person who put together our book.' Another useful nugget of information that Frank, through his inability to concentrate, had failed to recognise. 'We've never had a clue who it was. Just imagine if we could find out.'

From days of being downbeat without any sort of plan to free themselves, Frank had a sudden feeling they might be on to something, something that could lead to them getting themselves away. He also remembered what Larrimus had made clear during their first evening – that they didn't welcome any visitors. Perhaps there was a good reason why not.

'Who do we ask?' said Cas.

'That waste of space Zachery won't tell us,' said Gabby.

'I don't think anyone would,' said Frank. He knew they could try, but they'd been met with stony silence so far but he knew if you pushed adults just a little too far, some had the tendency of knocking down their own defences with shocking ease. It was a high stakes idea, but he knew exactly who he wanted to speak to.

41

The Orange Streak

They were ready for the runner, knowing they'd be sent for a soon as the castle woke.

'Zachery requests that one of you come and see him immediately,' said the young man who had knocked politely before entering their room.

Frank didn't think they had time to draw straws so volunteered himself on the basis that Gabby would probably tell him where to stick his lecture, Cas wouldn't want to go anywhere near a telling-off and Anya was anxious to get to the training ring to continue on her pathway to becoming a trained killer.

With silent wishes of luck from the others, Frank followed the runner along the landing and down the flight of stairs to Zachery's office door, the taut sound of a melody from a lyre echoing in the corridor. The young man knocked and pushed the door open without any signal from within, telling Frank to enter with a raise of his eyebrows and a twitch of the head. Frank signalled his thanks with a nod, took a deep breath and stepped in.

He knew he could handle any sort of berating for their actions. His general low mood was the perfect setting for confrontation, although he'd given himself a silent order to keep it calm, the intention to try and draw out some information. But he wasn't prepared for the tall, elegant figure of Qaas sitting to the side of Zachery's desk while Zachery made a show of making sure the papers in front of him were turned face down.

Qaas disarmed him with a smile, the way the Moonhunter sometimes did, as Zachery's open palm told him to sit on the empty chair they'd prepared for him.

'Tea?' he said, opening his palm to the teapot on his desk. Frank shook his head. Zachery poured two cups and handed one to Qaas. 'Thank you for coming so early,' said Zachery, polite as ever. Frank thought it was probably part of his breeding and keeping company with Kester that made him both approachable but undoubtedly ruthless.

'It beats peeling potatoes,' said Frank, eliciting a smile from the old man.

'You'll know I've spoken to Bakran.' A raise of the eyebrows to which Frank tried to keep himself neutral. 'Is it true you were in the Predek room without permission?' Frank nodded. There was no point denying it. 'Would you be so kind as to explain yourself?'

Frank glanced at Qaas, who continued to regard him over her cup.

'We're all just a bit curious,' he said.

'So I understand from the reports about you all,' said Zachery. He leaned back in his chair, pressing his palms together. 'Look, it's difficult for us to have new people join us, but there are certain rules and boundaries that I need you all to respect.' Frank nodded, knowing that whatever brand of advice or agreement Zachery was about to dispense he and his friends would completely ignore it. 'So you can consider the top floor of Irundi out of bounds. Am I clear?' Frank shrugged and nodded. If that was all that was being asked of him, then fine.

'We appreciate you need time to settle in,' said Qaas. 'Al-Fajr was the same when she arrived although she arrived willingly.'

A knock at the door had them looking up as Morrin entered the room, his huge frame faltering slightly at the sight of Frank.

'Just my usual morning report,' he said, his fingertips going to the side of his head, caressing the strands of orange, igniting a fear in Frank, conjuring an image of Dagmar's name on the Kester lineage.

'Thank you, Morrin,' said Zachery. 'If you could leave it for now and report back after lunch, please.'

Morrin gave a jolt of his head and left. Zachery went to speak but caught the look on Frank's face.

'Don't mind Morrin,' he said. 'He's not as bad as he seems.'

Qaas gave a slight nod.

'I've met someone else who has the same mark,' said Frank, brushing the side of his head. He wondered if they knew. Silence. 'I wondered what it meant.'

Zachery's mouth hung open like a fish, as if Frank had done a good job of veering him off the castle ground-rules. Zachery looked at Qaas.

'Perhaps it might help Frank understand that we're not here to make his life difficult,' she purred.

Zachery appeared to turn something over in his mind before leaning forward onto his desk, inspecting his fingernails.

'Very well,' he said. He paused, as if thinking where to start. 'I remember the whole episode with Morrin's grandfather, Drow,' he said with a look that Frank couldn't decipher. 'Such a glory hunter. Fiercely loyal though, except loyal to the wrong people.' The opening lines of Zachery's telling had Frank leaning forward in his chair. 'You see, it was widely known that Rossia would be split at some point and as Kester got older and his time was getting near, people started their posturing, to show their allegiance to either Joleyon or Lashka. The Council at the time proved to be a breeding ground of lies and mistrust. It was the worst of times.' He shook his head and closed his eyes momentarily before continuing, fixing his gaze on Frank.

'Remember, the Simbrian had already been created and dispersed among the seven guardians. Kester's greatest secret, but secrets have a habit of seeping out, especially when you have no idea who to trust. Apparently the idea of the Simbrian became known but the identity of the guardians couldn't be prised from anyone. I think that only Kester and Mildred Everbleed actually knew, with the others involved kept separate so they might have known parts but were completely unaware of the whole and no one really knew what knowledge anyone else had, or whether it could be relied upon.

But Drow worked out that Everbleed was the key. She went back to Prismia and he followed close behind.'

'Why?' said Frank.

'For obvious reasons,' said Qaas. 'The wretched piece of lowlife that he was. Drow would swear loyalty to Kester on one hand, but kept a broken bottle behind his back in the other.' Qaas's nostrils flared. 'He tracked Everbleed down and kidnapped her. Well, tried to kidnap her. Most well-informed sources think it was on the orders of Lashka, an early attempt to seize power, maybe, but that was never proved. Lashka always had a reputation for remaining as clean as the meltwater from the Longshadow mountains while those around her took the fall, much like the current incumbent in Alsha Kar. But, despite appearances, Everbleed was as sharp as one of Esryn's blades. She set a trap and her would-be abductors were captured as they tried to seize her and paraded in front of the Prismian people. Drow was forced to make a public apology and denounce his future ruler, that snake, Lashka, something that would have lingered long and hateful inside him.'

'Which still burns in the Dag line to this day,' said Zachery with a solemn shake of his head. 'And cemented their life-long hatred of the Prismian nation.' He rubbed his eyes. 'Then, as a final and lasting gift to remember her by and, as an eternal warning to anyone else who might be lured by the might of the Simbrian, she placed a curse on Drow and his descendants.' Frank hadn't seen it coming, but knew what Zachery was about to say. The hair, the brand of her curse. 'She took her staff and set it flaming, and ran it down the side of his head, burning the hair to the skin.' Frank winced. 'In its place grew orange, the Rossian colour of treachery, to be laid on all of his descendants. So, each generation will have a streak of fire running through them as a reminder of their family's duplicity and betrayal.'

So there it was. A succinct explanation of the mark the Dags carried, fashioned by an old seer centuries ago as a reminder not to cross the Everbleed line and Zachery's description had him making an involuntary motion to his right temple.

Frank had always thought of Everbleed as more of a lamb, a gentle soul using her abilities to help those in power and keep them from the wayward paths they inevitably crossed, but Zachery's description was brutal, like she'd branded Drow just for his misplaced loyalty. No messing, total authority. There was nothing soft and soothing about that. Zachery continued:

'But the effect seemed to backfire.' Zachery's eyebrows lifted. 'Drow ended up marrying Lashka's daughter and rather than learning from the experience with Everbleed, the Dag family appear to have adopted their new-found colours as some kind of badge of honour and have made it their business ever since to try and track down the Simbrian. Century after century, although there was an attempt at some sort of family reconciliation with Byeland when one of the Dags married into Joleyon's bloodline, but that only seemed to make the situation worse and the family have been treated with suspicion ever since.'

'Such a blatant attempt at sedition,' said Qaas. 'And to think that some of Joleyon's blood now flows in part of the Dag line.' She clenched her jaw. 'I understand you have made the acquaintance of the current Dag?' Not exactly a question, but a well-positioned fact to reveal about what they knew of him. Frank nodded.

'But you have Morrin here,' said Frank. 'From what you're saying he's related to Lashka, to the Dags?'

'Morrin agreed to come here, once he found out about his ancestry,' said Zachery. 'To head the security here at Irundi to prove his allegiance to Byeland.' That's what he told you, thought Frank as Zachery's eyes searched his.

Following the story he'd just been told, it felt like lunacy to have one of your marked enemies heading the safety of the castle and whatever secrets of the Simbrian it held. Zachery appeared to read his thoughts, turned his mouth up and shrugged.

'Not all the family are bad, Frank,' he said. 'Not all.'

As Frank left Zachery and Qaas to whatever they did during the day, there was one question alone that devoured his mind. He mounted the staircase and headed up to the second floor, the kitchen could wait, the well of darkness could wait. He checked their room, making sure Cas and Gabby had left, then shut the door and faced the antique mirror that hung on the wall. He looked at the young man looking back at him. The circles under his eyes seemed darker than they should, the bruising had disappeared, but he looked nothing like fresh.

He let his eyes become unfocused, not wanting to begin the journey that would discover the tell-tale signs of his parentage. He felt his eyes close. He knew he must, but his courage, normally the thing that propelled him forward, sat back in his head and wouldn't move. He told himself it didn't matter, that he wasn't like Dagmar, that all he was came from his mother, the woman he'd never known. All he had to do was look, to confirm what he already knew.

A deep breath, then another.

Why was this so difficult?

He opened his eyes, focused on the right side of his head, on his unkempt blond hair. Nothing. He pushed his fingers through the golden strands, searching, raking down to his scalp, wanting to find some trace of the fire that he knew was in his blood. But there was nothing. No hint of orange or anything that marked him out as part of the Dag line.

He looked at himself once more. Took in the presence of his unfolding life on his tired face, his sagged body. The breath he let out was long, and quivered with emotion. Nothing ever made sense. Perhaps the curse only appeared when he was a certain age, perhaps he'd wake up on his sixteenth birthday, in a couple of months, to a sunburst quiff that revealed to his family and friends what he really was. All of this, all he had found out, he knew he would have to keep it to himself. No one, especially his friends, would want anything to do with him once they discovered. If they ever discovered.

But as he stared at himself, looked deep within himself, something began to stir in him. This wasn't what he was like. He could feel himself beginning to lose the sense of what he was, what he'd always stood for. The lessons his dad, despite his lies, had taught him. He'd been taught to stand up for what he believed in, whatever the cost, to be his own person, to find the answers, to keep going until his desire for the truth had been satisfied. This shouldn't be any different. He swore to himself that he'd find out exactly what had happened, what and who had brought him to this point, even if the truth might be hard to bear. He owed it to himself. Now all he had to do was to find a way of getting out of the castle.

42

The Threat

Frank decided the kitchen could wait a while longer. He'd nearly forgotten about the conversation he and the others had had before he was marched to Zachery's office, of the person he felt might get careless if his temper was tugged hard enough, give away who had come to the castle before. The guest they didn't want.

He stalked the grounds, through the gardens and to the outbuildings at the far edge of the clearing, on the edge of the circle of trees and the few small, scattered buildings that marked the assassins' training area. He'd not ventured over there before and the thought of encountering the black-clad guards of Irundi didn't exactly fill him with confidence.

It was quiet; neither Anya nor Esryn were there. He ignored the grunts from the two guards sparring bare-handed in the dust and they didn't seem to notice him as made has way around the edge.

'Morrin?' he said as one of them caught his eye. A flick of the head toward the largest of the stone structures nearby had Frank heading to the door.

Voices from within. Laughter.

Frank resisted the urge to barge his way in, knowing he'd likely end up at the point of at least one dagger. He knocked gently and the voices inside ceased immediately. Frank took the silence as his invitation to enter and pushed the door open.

Morrin sat at a shabby table, his huge frame squashed into a wooden armchair, one of his hell-hounds at his side. Larrimus sat on a stool opposite, any cheeriness on his face immediately wiped by Frank's appearance. Both held wooden goblets, an open bottle of wine on the table next to a jewelled dagger. A quick glance around told Frank the room served as an armoury.

Weapons dripped from the walls. Heavy swords, sabres, rapiers, all polished to a shimmering glow. Long pikes hung from the ceiling by sturdy loops of rope. An arsenal as deadly and uncompromising as the man who presided over it. Larrimus lifted his chin and looked at Frank through the bottom of his eyes. A bad taste on his face.

'What?' Morrin's words kicked him. His monstrous dog stiffened.

'Shouldn't you be ... elsewhere?' said Larrimus, drawing a mouthful from his goblet. 'I mean – not here.' Morrin huffed a laugh under his breath, the pack of two had already begun to encircle Frank. The two men looked at him, pinning him with cold silence. Looks determined to make Frank's interruption as brief as possible, but Frank wasn't put off.

'Someone was here,' he said, not taking his eyes off Morrin. Not even the slightest reaction, but something in Morrin's stillness sent a message. Frank took a testing step forward, nearing the table, feeling Morrin broaden his chest, filling the space in front of him, creating an invisible barrier between himself and Frank. Intimidating. Larrimus's eyes followed Frank's move, the corners of his thin lips tugging upwards.

'Someone was where?' His words were slow and deliberate, his nostrils flared at Frank. It was Larrimus's turn to laugh under his breath. But Frank detected the touch of a nerve.

'Don't play games with me, Morrin.'

Morrin's face darkened, his hand reaching for the dagger on the table. A calculated move. He pressed it into the wood with the flat of his palm, then spun it around with a practiced flick of his giant fingers. The rumble of the hard steel on the wooden surface filled the room as the dagger rotated. Morrin sniffed.

'You wouldn't like the sort of games I play,' he said, a large dose of malice on his strange Rossian accent.

He raked his fingers through the orange streak in his hair,

exactly like Dagmar. His penetrating scowl had Frank unnerved as he watched the dagger slow to a stop, the tip of the shining blade pointing directly at his midriff. Morrin dipped his eyes to the dagger, then to Frank, daring him to utter another word. Frank hesitated. He could sense Larrimus's amusement and threw him a glance, his mouth tight.

'It seems our young guest understands you perfectly, Morrin,' said Larrimus through his serpent's smile as Frank looked at the weapon, then at the slight smile that lifted Morrin's mouth. Frank's mouth opened and shut. No words came out. Morrin's smile thickened. Frank drew in a breath.

'Who was it?' A hot spike of anxiety shot up his spine as he felt the room tense.

Morrin clenched his fist, then flexed his fingers. Frank noticed his hand go to his throat, touching an invisible point, some kind of reflex.

'What is it I don't like about you?' he said, his cool mask slipping in a few blinks.

Larrimus put an arrogant foot up on the stool in front of him and dragged from his goblet, savouring every second of Frank's discomfort. Larrimus lowered his hand.

'What you have to realise is that things work here nice and smoothly and we don't need anyone else coming here and creating difficulties,' he said. 'Not you and your friends, not anybody.'

Frank was caught in two minds. The sensible option was to just leave what had quickly become an uncomfortable situation. Staying, asking more about a subject on which they obviously weren't going to co-operate seemed plain ridiculous and the less intelligent option, given the look that had spread across Morrin's face. He took a step back. The two men watched him like interested cats. But there was something unsaid in Larrimus's words, something given up.

'Just tell me who it was?' said Frank, a raise in his voice.

Nothing from Morrin. The atmosphere in the room thickened. Frank began to suspect Morrin's veneer of calm was straining under his words. He wondered how far to push, although he really didn't care if the big man rose to the bait. Morrin would flatten him with one hook from his mighty fist and gambling that he'd restrain himself was the strategy of a fool. Morrin sniffed and folded his arms in some kind of silent challenge. His whole look – his eyes, his jaw, his physique – roared dominance. Control. But Frank noticed the flush on Morrin's neck.

'Perhaps you should get back to your duties,' said Larrimus. 'Before you say something that brings you some trouble.' Not a warning but a clearly put piece of advice, but Frank felt the rise of his boiling anger, of his fogged mind.

'Who?' he demanded. 'Who was it?'

Morrin shifted in his chair, his hound loosed a growl. Frank felt the thin ice starting to crack under his feet and backed away again as Morrin eased himself slowly to his feet, pushing his knuckles into the table-top. Before Frank had time to move, Morrin had picked up the dagger and hurled it at him. It embedded itself into the door behind him with an impressive thud. He'd missed, deliberately – that was for sure, but Frank felt his breath quicken. Morrin's thunderous eyes bore into him.

'The next one will find itself in your throat,' he said. 'Now piss off and if I hear you as much as breathe again I'll rip your head off.'

Frank, until now, had not been scared of Morrin despite his size and brutishness. But that changed in an instant as he beheld the rage in the man's eyes and witnessed something of his true character, as if the briefest of outbursts had opened a window to something he hid behind his rough but polished façade. Larrimus hadn't so much as flinched, but Frank decided he needed to be out of the room and quickly. His eyes flicked to Morrin's hands, then he turned and opened the door, nearly knocking into Esryn who stood on the other side. She locked her eyes onto Frank's as he stepped past her, acknowledging the look on his face before stepping into the building and shutting the door.

His instinct was to belt it back to the kitchens and immerse himself in something routine, ordinary, but he waited across the training area. He stood scuffing the soles of his boots on the dry earth, thumbing through his mind for his next move when Esryn emerged from the armoury and made her way quickly across the ring to where he stood, her face stiff, expressionless.

Frank approached, making a grab for her arm, understanding what the consequences might be but Esryn simply dodged his attempt and stopped. Her questioning silence acted as Frank's cue.

'You heard,' he said. 'Inside there.' He jerked his head to the building. She looked him up and down.

'You should be careful with your questions,' she said.

'Why?' said Frank. She didn't respond. 'What are you all hiding?'

He couldn't read her, but thought there was something she wanted to say, felt that if he waited long enough he might draw it out of her. She looked back at the entrance to the armoury. Morrin stood at the open door. Despite being fifty yards away, he could feel his burning eyes.

'Just be careful, Frank Penny,' she said, backing away a few steps before turning and heading away. Frank noticed Morrin's head turn and follow her as she left.

43

THE WATER

Frank's walk back to the castle, to the kitchens, turned into a run. He daren't look behind him as he crossed the clipped lawns towards the sparkling stone of the castle. Whatever he'd thought he might learn from Morrin had been thrown to the dust in the training circle but there was one thing he was now completely sure of. He'd been sure of it even before he'd pressed himself into the nerve that had Morrin and Larrimus wanting to cut his throat. Someone had definitely been here and it was an experience they had no intention of retelling.

The brief encounter had left his nerves on fire, so he tried to settle himself before heading back into the entrance, leaning into the wall, finding himself turning and sitting, his face warmed by the sun, rough stone at his back. He pressed the heels of his hands into his eyes, thinking that he might just give food preparation and washing up a miss when he was aware of movement to his left.

Zachery emerged from the main doorway, head down, and headed round the side of the castle. He wasn't sure what possessed him to get up and follow on his heels but, although his senses had been dulled, his instincts remained sharp.

He stepped quickly to the corner, peering around the wall to see Zachery lingering by the door to the turret, clasping an envelope. Frank pressed himself back in an attempt to make himself as grey as possible, merging with the stone of the wall. He stilled, his mind willing Zachery inside. Zachery obliged, Frank heading after him as quickly as he dare, silent on the grass, keeping his footsteps light.

He reached the door, and carefully pushed it, grateful that, like all the doors in the castle, the hinges were well lubricated. The door swung slowly open, revealing the small entranceway by which Frank and Gabby had left the turret previously. Stone steps led up to the right, turning anti-clockwise. Frank stopped, the nagging feeling that he'd already lost Zachery crept in. He looked up and was about to head up the stairs when his attention was drawn by the sound of a door shutting then footsteps, footsteps coming his way.

A second to adjust to the direction of the echoing feet found Frank looking left, noticing that the staircase continued down, leading below ground level. He made the split-second decision to head up the stairs as a shadow appeared at the corner followed by Zachery himself who left the turret without a look back, sparing Frank the indignation of being caught loitering on the stairs.

Frank waited until he was sure Zachery wasn't coming back, then made his way down, turning the corner of the stairs. A set of worn brown stone steps led down, curving to the right and into darkness. Frank sniffed at the cool air before continuing. Down.

The stairway darkened quickly. Quick steps slowed to careful, carefully placed ones. Although underground, the air around him still smelled clean and clear. Unnaturally so. Down. Slowly. One foot finding the next step. Then the next. Frank could barely see the step in front of him, the darkness eventually bringing him to a reluctant halt. Silence. Then Frank heard it, not believing what filled his ears in the cold, dark, quiet. Water. The unmistakeable living breathing sparkle of running water. Water, down here.

44

SORCERER

His absence in the kitchen that morning didn't go unnoticed and as soon as he turned up, Wen told him he'd have to stay for the afternoon through to dinner, meaning he wouldn't be able to tell Cas about what he'd discovered, not that there was ever any quiet moments, especially as Frank arrived right in the middle of lunch. She barked a reprimand as well as instructions at him which he swallowed, before heading to the large sinks to commence a long bout of washing up, where he could plan his next move and invent strategies for avoiding Morrin.

He was exhausted by the time he arrived back at the room but when he told the others about the water under the tower he felt strangely invigorated, they all did. At last, they had something to hang on to, something that might help them understand why they were there and, hopefully, would show them the way out. Water. A well?

'And you said it was dark?' said Cas, who looked like he was doing his best to look pleased about venturing below the castle. Gabby gave him a tight look. Cas shrugged. 'What? Just saying.'

'The sooner we get down there, the better,' said Gabby, inspecting her dry hands. 'And you can lead the way.' Cas's shoulders tightened.

'I don't think we should go tonight,' said Anya. 'Not after last time.'

Frank nodded in agreement, although he suspected the castle had eyes everywhere which meant he wasn't convinced they wouldn't get caught whenever they decided to venture down the winding staircase from where Zachery had appeared.

'Why don't we try during lunch, tomorrow?' said Frank. 'You two will be on a break and Cas and I will have finished up. Everyone in the castle will be occupied with eating. There's never anyone around then. How about it?'

They all agreed. Tomorrow, they'd find out what their disastrous trek into the silent forest had all been about.

***

Frank woke with a sense of purpose for the first time in weeks. His bland existence in the castle kitchens made him feel lethargic. There was nothing amongst the cooking pots or wooden spoons for him to look forward to and when he looked at his fellow kitchen workers, he wondered how they even got through the same day, day after day, but no one seemed to mind. It was like they'd all been there so long that they just didn't know any other way, any other life, but he didn't feel sorry for them. They were there by choice, unlike him and the others, and they had to change that.

As lunch service started Wen excused Frank and Cas who quickly left the kitchen. They agreed to go different ways, split up in case the eyes of the castle were on them. Cas would head back to the room, then down through the front doors, while Frank would head down the long corridor that led to a side entrance and out to the composters. He'd join Cas and the girls at the tower.

He wiped his hands on his trousers and took a look around before heading away from the kitchen and down the passage. The cool stone, away from the heat of the kitchen and from the glare of the constant sun was a welcome relief, making him pause and take a deep breath in the dark. Before his next step he froze, his senses immediately aflame. A feeling that he wasn't alone had his skin chilling. He turned, face-to-face with the black-clad figure of Esryn, her face cast in shadow. He could feel her warm breath on his cheek. She'd managed to get within a foot of him before he realised she was there, a short lesson in the dexterity and shadow-dancing she'd honed like a viper over centuries.

Esryn's eyes searched his, then an uneasy glance over her shoulder, her eyes alert. Turning back to Frank, she placed an index finger against her lips. Frank felt himself go hot but, by the way she stood and the second glance behind her, he knew she wasn't there to cause him any trouble.

'You were right,' she said, her voice a near whisper. 'I heard you and Morrin the other day.' Frank felt the pin-pricks of irritation. Surely she hadn't come up here to remind him what a fool he'd been to try and unpick information from the surly head of the castle guard.

'What about it?' said Frank, noticing the caution on her face. In the harsh shadow of the passageway he could see fresh bruising around her eye socket and the dried blood on her nose and lip which she licked in an attempt to clear it. She glanced over her shoulder again, eyes darting around the semi-dark.

'Look, you haven't heard this from me.' She lowered her voice further, slightly rushing her words, looking for agreement on Frank's face. He felt himself nod slightly and Esryn went on. 'You were asking about the sorcerer.' She searched Frank's face, noticing the crease in the brow on his confused face.

'Sorcerer?'

Esryn chewed her lip. 'She was the one...'

Heavy footsteps had Esryn looking behind her once more. She looked back to Frank and headed quickly into the shadows and away as, at the end of the passage, the mammoth figure of Morrin appeared. Frank took one look at his face and headed after Esryn.

She'd vanished. He followed down the passage and out of the door, scanning the grounds, but she wasn't anywhere to be seen. He asked two passing orderlies if they'd seen where she went, but was met with blank looks and shakes of the head. She'd done what she was trained to do, to become part of the shadows. Away from the prying eyes of Morrin, of him, of everyone.

He felt the tightness of frustration anchor him to the ground. She'd been on the verge of telling him something, but that had been snatched from his grasp. He stood in the now everyday early-autumn sun, the milky shades of orange on the unshifting landscape that held them all captive, that had him yearning for cold, driving rain hurting his face, to see the fresh harsh carpet of frost on the grass and laying temporary siege to the limbs of trees before giving way to the bright winter sun. How anyone could bear being caught in the nowhere land of this time-trapped hollow in the forest he couldn't fathom. He'd find a way out, for him and the others, even if it killed him in the process.

He stalked the grounds once more. No sign of the pale killer. No sign of the monster in charge. Then headed to the tower.

'Sorcerer?' said Gabby. 'Are you sure that's what she said?' Frank nodded.

'It was the way she said it.' He recalled the hiss in her voice. 'Like she was talking about her worst enemy.'

'Explains why she's been wary of you,' said Cas. Gabby stiffened.

'Shut up, Cas.' She shot him a hefty glance. 'Just because she says there was a sorcerer here, it doesn't mean they did anything wrong.' She turned to Anya. 'Has she said anything to you?'

Anya shook her head.

'I've not heard her mention it. Not to me.' She paused. 'I don't know if it's connected, but Morrin was really unkind to her today. He was there at the clearing, which is unusual. He's never there at the start, he normally comes to see what's going on nearer the end of the morning. Anyway, he told me to sit out the training session we had planned, but told me to stay and watch, said I'd learn something important. Then he set Esryn against four of the others. Four.'

Frank puffed out his cheeks. He knew Esryn was skilled, but all of the Black Flame were hand-picked for their ability and, regardless of being their most proficient, four against one was no contest. Even Frank could tell that and it didn't take a genius to understand that Morrin clearly knew what the outcome would be.

'What happened?' he said.

'She got whipped, battered.' Anya winced. Frank recalled the blood and dark bruising and the tight humiliation on Esryn's face.

'She's the best by a mile, but Morrin stacked the odds against her deliberately, like he was trying to teach her a lesson.' Or dish out a punishment, thought Frank. 'She didn't complain, but I could tell she wanted to rip his throat out. She fought them to a standstill but he was having none of it. Once they'd all exhausted themselves, Morrin insisted she fight him, but she refused. The state she was in, he would have torn her to pieces. Then he started to call her all sorts of names, telling her she had much to learn about loyalty and how she should always remember where she'd come from. I couldn't bring myself to look at him, or her. It was so degrading.'

'Why?' said Cas. 'Why would he do that to the best member of his team?'

'I don't know.' Anya's face was flush with emotion. 'She spat at him, turned her back and walked off and he followed her. I must say he looked like he knew he'd overstepped the mark.'

Frank's fear of Morrin raised a notch. The similarity to Dagmar was even more evident, firing his determination to get away from the stranglehold of this weird place and its people.

'Come on,' he said. 'Let's find ourselves the well of darkness.'

45

THE PROPHESIES

Anya led the way down, darkness slowly enveloping them like tendrils of smoke before they came to a door. The smell of damp and earth pressed in on them, confirming they were well below ground level. She pushed to find it locked but the sound of water from within had a sense of anticipation gripping them. Anya turned and beckoned Cas, who sprang the lock and pushed at the door, reluctance slowing his feet but Anya pressed a firm palm into the small of his back as they crossed the threshold and into a large cavern-like room, hewn into the rock underneath Irundi.

The spherical subterranean chamber was lit from above by a circular hole at the apex, reminding Frank of the room in Alsha Kar where Etamin had shown him the nearly complete Simbrian. The thought shot a shiver down his back. The floor was smooth but uneven, lit by cinnamon colours that warmed the room from the beam of light.

A large crack ran across the entire width, drawing Frank's eye as he looked left and right to where it disappeared at the base of the wall. Around the edge, shelves covered the walls. But where Frank expected to see books, like some kind of library, he saw they were stacked with envelopes and sheets of paper. Hundreds and hundreds of letters, all neatly arranged around the entire circumference of the cavern.

The sound of running water drew Frank's attention, drawing his eye away from the unusual array of papers. He wasn't bothered about them, it was the water he was here for. He stepped forward, looking down into the narrow fissure in the floor. Water flowed beneath his gaze. Fast, clear water, so clear he could see the bottom of the gutter, knee deep, chilled. A stream. Not a well.

He looked left and right, checking he hadn't missed anything but the gulley just ran in from one side and out the other. Disappointment bound him; the familiar feeling of instant irritation kicking him. He carefully scanned the room. No sign of anything resembling a well.

Gabby wandered to the edge of the room, gently running the flat of her hand across the shelves, rippling the envelopes so they whispered in the shadows, whispered their secrets.

'What *are* these?' said Gabby, hushed as if she didn't want to wake the mysterious spirits that dwelt down here. Anya dared to pull one out, the sound of shifting paper on paper turning Frank's head. They gathered at Anya's shoulder as she opened it out.

'It's old,' she said. 'And it's written in some old language by the looks of it.' There were four lines of strange lettering that had Frank pursing his lips and his temper rising. He scratched at the back of his neck as Cas took another one. He opened it, revealing the same handwriting – this time a whole page covered in neat lines of indecipherable words.

'Shame Meredith's not with us,' he said.

'Right,' said Frank. 'I'm sure she'd be thrilled to be stuck in this never-ending nightmare with nothing to do but read a million stupid letters from a thousand years ago.'

He knew he'd spoken too quickly, an immediate reaction of the burning irritation in his throat that had raised the tone of his voice. He knew Cas hadn't deserved to feel his sharp tongue, Still, the look in Cas's eyes that told him he'd been bitten by Frank's words. Instant regret filled Frank, but he couldn't utter an apology

'Don't you dare,' said Gabby, the flame in her eyes a sign.

The room stilled and Frank felt its edges pushing in as the others looked at him with growing disappointment.

Frank pushed out a long breath, pushing back in his mind, feeling their frustration in him. They hadn't found a well, but he couldn't bring himself to say it, to admit they were still standing on the starting line.

The whole array of papers was baffling, even though they knew that Zachery had received some sort of communication very recently. From where and from whom was a mystery. Even though he could feel his usual sense of intrigue pulling at him, he could also feel the now familiar companion of irritation in his blood. All they seemed to do was stumble upon things beyond their grasp and he knew it wasn't anyone's fault but his.

He hurdled the water, the thud of his boots echoing around the cavern, and stood, hands on hips, looking at the endless lines of papers on the shelves. This was impossible. How were they supposed to find anything of use amongst all of this?

'This looks interesting,' said Anya. She'd followed Frank across the division and stood to his left. She looked at him. 'Don't you think?'

Frank pushed down the urge to tell her exactly how interesting he thought the whole thing was, but her usual pacifying tone was a welcome oasis for his low mood while he could feel Cas and Gabby ignoring him. He looked at her, a smile tugged at her lips as she waved him over. He took a few steps towards her. Anya nodded at the wall where a small pair of glass doors were sunk into the tawny stone. Behind them, recessed further, was a single shelf upon which sat three envelopes, held upright by two silver bookends, each one cast in the shape of an eagle, the symbol of Byeland.

Frank stared into the cabinet, the shine from the skylight casting his reflection back at him. He couldn't look at himself as he sensed Cas and Gabby at his back. Anya was right. It was interesting, and strange.

Anya lightly gripped the wooden handle on one of the cabinet doors and gave it a tug. Locked.

'Here,' said Cas, stepping between Anya and Frank, springing the lock in half a heartbeat. Frank felt his shoulders sag. Cas stepped back, allowing Anya to pull the doors of the cabinet open. 'Careful there are no traps or curses or anything,' said Cas, causing Anya to pause.

Frank reached in and took all three envelopes with a single grasp. He lifted the flap on the first one and drew out the piece of paper from within, taking in the stale smell of ancient paper as it rose up. He opened it, anticipation etched on the other's faces which promptly turned to disappointment as the open paper revealed two lines of writing in a language Frank couldn't decipher. Without looking, he knew the other two would only reveal the same.

He pushed away the desire to screw it up and throw it into the fast-flowing water. He looked at Cas with a slight nod. They really could do with Meredith. But he could tell they were all thinking the same thing, the questioning look in their eyes as to why? Among the thousands of papers ordered neatly around the room, why had these three, whatever they were, been separated from the rest?

'Perhaps you should put those back?'

The calm tones sent a shiver through Frank as he turned. The slender figure of Qaas stood in the doorway, but it was the large feline that stood at her side that took his attention. Thigh high, sleek and black as midnight and perfectly still. The panther blinked at him, had them locked in the crosshairs of its jade eyes. Qaas watched them, the whole castle was constantly watching them.

'It's an interesting room, the Bemara, I can see you think so, but you shouldn't really be down here,' she said, not moving from the doorway.

'We were just exploring,' said Gabby. 'It's kind of boring sweating yourself to death in the laundry every day, you know.'

Qaas smiled. The panther bared its teeth.

'I'm sure it must be but, like I said, you shouldn't be down here. As you all already know, there are certain parts of the castle that are out of bounds. How did you get in?'

Cas fidgeted as Qaas's eyes landed on him. Knowing.

'Like I just said,' said Gabby, not looking too impressed. 'We were just exploring and found the door.'

Frank could sense the attitude beginning to brew under Gabby's breath.

'Where are we?' he said. 'And what are all these?' he gave a short sweep with his hand toward the walls and the contents of the shelves. Qaas's eyes followed the arc of his arm. She stepped forward, her large cat following at her side, making Cas move behind Frank, his wary eyes following the panther's every languid step.

'Oh don't mind Burra, Cas. He's completely harmless.' Frank looked at the enormous canines protruding down from the cat's jaw and knew she was lying. 'All of the written notes you can see in here are the work of a single person. Letters, scribblings, prophesies...'

'Prophesies?' said Anya, more in a whisper than to the others. She took the envelopes from Frank. 'Everbleed's prophesies.' A statement rather than a question. A nod from Qaas.

'That's right Anya. Mildred Everbleed's life's work is contained in this room.'

'All of it?'

'All of it.'

'But...' Gabby elbowed Cas in the ribs.

Frank knew why. They all knew there was one prophesy that had found its way into the hands of Dagmar. The foretelling of the Simbrian heir, the one thing the castle appeared to be tracking in the Predek room.

'She was quite productive, then,' said Anya. A mastery of understatement.

'Quite so.' Qaas paused. 'She had some interesting abilities, some of which I witnessed first-hand and, I believe, anyone in her bloodline is equally blessed.' She ran the calm fingertips of her hand through the short black fur on Burra's head. 'Look, I wouldn't want you to get into any more trouble with Zachery,' she said. 'He can be quite...protective of his little collection.' Frank felt himself relax a little at the hint of amusement in her voice. 'I suggest we leave,' She angled her head back to the door. 'If you would put those back, please.' She nodded to the three envelopes in Frank's hand. Frank handed them to Cas who placed them back behind the glass doors and locked it under Qaas's watchful gaze, counting the envelopes with her eyes.

'Why are these kept in there?' said Frank. Qaas twitched her nose and gave a slight shrug. She stepped to one side, her sign for them to leave.

'I'm sure Zachery has his reasons. Now, it must be time for you to get back to your duties,' said Qaas. She looked at Gabby with a wide grin. 'Those sheets won't launder themselves.'

Gabby ground her teeth, looking at Qaas like she wanted to punch the smile off of her face, then led the four of them past and to the stairs. As Cas brought up the rear, he was stopped by Qaas's palm on his chest.

'Burra,' she said. Measured, unruffled. She snapped her fingers at Cas. The large cat was on its feet, prowling around Cas who stood, looking like he was preparing to be eaten. The panther sniffed him, a slow, deliberate action, before turning away with an indifferent look. 'Just making sure you're leaving empty handed,' she said. 'Which is probably the cleverest thing you've done today.'

Frank glanced back, seeing the relief on Cas's face, glancing at Burra who sat obediently by Qaas's side, the image of a jet black statue that would rip his head off.

46

THE TRANSLATION

The colourless day passed into an even more dreary evening. They met up back in their rooms, wearied by the hours spent in the custody of the castle. Only Anya appeared relaxed as she updated them on her progress that afternoon with the group of trained killers, of her new ways to strike with a blade. A different way of thinking, of killing, of defending. Their different language of death.

They'd been showing her a new disarming technique which she couldn't quite master and had led to a painfully pulled bicep and twisted elbow. Esryn had been notably absent. Frank resisted the urge to tell her the whole thing was completely pointless if they were to spend the rest of eternity hemmed into the few acres of ground the assassins called home.

Gabby sat picking at the dry, blistered skin on her fingers, her eyes fixed on her hands, keeping her thoughts to herself.

They'd learned about the legends surrounding various anti-ageing stories such as the youth tree of Aryth from Markowitz, when she was their myths and legends master, before she had made off with the prophesy about the Simbrian heir, and although she'd painted the stories with colours so vivid they'd stayed bright in Frank's imagination, made the secrets of eternal youth seem worth paying a hefty price for, he was certain it was nothing but a curse if you ended up incarcerated like this.

'Why would Qaas be so sure about Zachery having Everbleed's entire archive down there?' he said, breaking the silence that had set hard between them. Gabby raised her eyes at his question, but he saw nothing but distance in them.

'Maybe he likes collecting things,' said Cas, 'And he's had a while to read them all. Anyway, he's not quite got the entire archive anymore.' He lifted his eyebrows at Frank. Gabby and Anya looked at him with interest. 'Has he?' Cas shook his head. 'I saw you.' Frank let a smile drift over his face. Dipping his hand into his pocket he drew out an old piece of paper.

'Qaas was too distracted making sure the thief among us wasn't up to his old tricks,' said Frank. 'So I gave you the envelopes, but managed to keep this.' He flapped the small sheet in the air, immediately grasping the attention of the others. 'Good job you didn't try, mate,' he said to Cas. 'The panther looked kind of hungry.'

'Very impressive,' said Cas. 'Perhaps you have some sort of ability after all.'

Frank opened up the paper and showed it to the expectant faces. Two lines of writing in a foreign language – thirteen words. That was it.

'I suspect it's in old Rossian,' said Cas. He looked at Frank. 'That's what Meredith would tell us, I'm sure.' He raised his eyebrows and Frank felt the prickle of irritation. 'We all know that's when they were written.'

'So now we have it,' said Anya. 'Who do we get to translate?'

'I'm not asking any of the sour-faced jobsworths in the laundry,' said Gabby. 'And it's not like we can ask Zachery or Qaas or that miserable git Larrimus. We know they've been here from the start but they'd lock us up if they knew we'd taken it.' Not like we're locked up here as it is, thought Frank.

'Well, we know that Wen speaks a bit. I suppose I could ask her,' said Frank. A slight attempt to redeem himself.

'Good idea,' said Cas. 'She kind of likes you, Frank.'

At least someone did.

Frank was in the kitchen early the next morning. He'd left Cas sleeping peacefully, taking the envelope with him. He'd tried to memorise the words but found they left his head as soon as he read them. He didn't think it sounded right just to blurt out some random old Rossian to Wen. He already thought she saw him as a bit odd, a stranger in her even stranger world and to attempt to speak to her in her old language, without making any sense, would only serve to confirm what she probably already thought.

As he suspected, he'd not beaten Wen to it. In fact, he wondered if she even slept, or if the constant light from outside kept her awake. Whatever, she never appeared lacking in energy or her appetite for doing a thorough and robust job which, in some ways, pulled on his admiration. She stood at the large table kneading dough, her impressive forearms flexing with each push to the mammoth amount of mixture. She glanced at him as he entered acknowledging him with a smile and a twitch of her head.

She always whistled and hummed her way through preparing breakfast for the castle in a way that reminded him of his gran, a thought that filled him with both joy and sadness, together with a fear that the outside world might be further away than he hoped. But, luckily, she was in a good mood and he knew he had to ask her before the kitchen filled with its usual collection of cooks.

He joined her at the table and spent a few minutes helping with the bread making, pushing the dough into large baking tins before Wen set about peeling the day's potatoes.

'You still speak old Rossian, don't you?' he said.

'Not so much, the odd word here and there as you know. No one here bothers anymore, but I like to keep my hand in. Reminds me of the old days.'

'I think Zachery does, too.'

A nod.

'*Mr* Zachery certainly doesn't let go of the old ways,' she said with a puff of her chest. Frank sniffed at her loyalty.

He pulled the letter out of his pocket. Fingerprints of flour now coated the outside of the old brown paper. Wen eyes widened.

'Wherever did you get that?'

'Larrimus gave it to me,' he lied. 'Said I should try and learn some while I was here, he thought you'd be a good person to ask.'

'Did he now?' She muttered a curse. Frank nodded.

'Can you tell me what this says, please?'

He unfolded it, showing her the two lines. She lifted her hand and held the corner of the sheet. Her eyes shifted across the page her lips moved as she read, her mouth emitting a low mumble.

'Well that's a load of old nonsense,' she said with the usual sharp edge on her tongue, looking at Frank then back to the writing. 'And Larrimus gave this to you, you say?'

Frank just shrugged.

'What does it say?' She looked back at the letter as if checking she hadn't made a mistake.

'It says "the hand of the king holds the key and the key fits all".'

'What, but that doesn't—'

'Exactly. Now you can tell that useless man to stop wasting your time. And mine.'

She turned back to the bucket of potatoes. Frank stood at her back, he could feel the lines on his brow getting deeper and deeper. He felt like asking her if she'd misread the letter or whatever rubbish Everbleed was meant to have written. He repeated the words in his head, over and over. A circular chant that made less and less sense the more he silently recounted it until he was brought back to his senses by Wen's brusque tone.

'Well don't just stand there. That bread won't bake itself.'

The more Frank thought Everbleed's odd offering would tell him something he wanted to know, the more ridiculous her scribblings became. What on earth was that supposed to mean? The hand of the king? Wen was right, it was a load of old nonsense and when he told the others they looked just as perplexed as the old cook. With a shake of the head, Frank put the folded paper into the possessor along with the map, which he checked again for any changes. There were none.

Under his gaze the words 'seek the well of darkness' still taunted him, the riddle that they needed to solve, that had to hold the key to their escape but as Frank read and re-read the faint letters, he knew they were no nearer to getting back home. But then something caught his attention. He'd noticed the few words written underneath but not paid them any attention due to his inability to translate. He counted them. Carefully and Methodically. And again, to be sure.

Thirteen; there were thirteen words in the foreign script. He pulled Everbleed's note back out and unfolded it. His eager eyes flicked from the map to the letter. Checking, rechecking then confirming. The words on the map were exactly the same words as those written on the piece of paper they'd taken from Everbleed's archive.

47

THE UNWELCOME GUEST

Frank couldn't fathom the connection. The well of darkness, the words Everbleed had written, the hand of the king — it just didn't make any sense. None of them could fit any of it together but there was a rising feeling that they'd moved an inch closer to the reason they'd been brought to Irundi. Still they didn't feel they could ask anyone about the well of darkness. It was too obvious, information that would have them watched closer, or locked up which was something they couldn't risk. Seeking the well of darkness was something they had to do for themselves.

The following day, he and Cas decided to search as much of the clearing as they could, just in case they'd overlooked something obvious. Perhaps there was a well of sorts hidden among the carefully cultivated landscape that surrounded them. It was there, somewhere. Of that he was certain, he was beginning to sense it, picking at the small crumbs of hope they'd found so far. They agreed they needed to re-check, leave nothing to chance.

'I'll head over to the far side, around the buildings,' said Cas. 'Hopefully I won't run into Morrin.'

He gave Frank a nod and headed off. Frank watched him, the dip of his head, the hands in his pockets, looking tired and cheerless, just like he felt, before wandering towards the rose garden.

Gabby sat on one of the benches that hid themselves between the array of soft blooms and delicate scent. She sat with her legs curled under her, picking at her hands in the now too-familiar ritual that didn't appear to stem the irritation on her skin. The faraway look in her eyes told him not to speak.

She looked up at him, a slight smile at the corners of her mouth, then unwound her legs, creating a silent space on the bench next to her. Frank sat. Both of them looked wordlessly out across the garden, towards the castle and the trees beyond.

'You okay?' he said, knowing she didn't look it.

He dipped into his pocket and brought out a square of chocolate he'd salvaged from the kitchen, breaking it in two and offering her a piece. Her sad eyes looked down, brightening slightly as she took it and popped it into her mouth. She didn't answer, but took in a breath and continued to look across the emptiness.

'Everywhere I go people hate me,' she said. 'Either because I'm Prismian, or a girl who can handle herself or because of the way I look or, now, because I'm a sorcerer.'

He noticed the tears well in her eyes.

'I don't hate you,' said Frank at which she shut her eyes and gritted her teeth, drawing in a long breath. He knew it was the lamest possible response, that all the prejudice she'd faced throughout her life couldn't be distilled and rectified just because he was her friend. He should have understood that. He thought she'd want him to say something but he immediately realised that some things don't need an answer; that silent understanding spoke at a greater level than the rubbish, ill thought-out few words he'd chosen in its place.

'I miss my Mum.' A single tear travelled down her soft cheek. She didn't bother to wipe it away. 'I need to get back,' she said. 'Perhaps I should harvest some thorns to line Larrimus's pillow cases?' She managed a smile as she got up. 'Thanks for the chocolate. See you later.'

He nodded as she turned and headed back to the castle. He watched her, thinking how miserable both she and Cas looked, a reflection of what he felt inside. He had his troubles, but so did she and there was no reason for anyone to pick on her just because of what she was. He'd been brought up to fight against any sort of injustice, any sort of discrimination and, whatever issue the castle inhabitants had with her being a sorcerer, their attitude was unacceptable.

He got up, determined to find even the fragments of some answers.

He started a circuit of the castle. No sign of anything resembling a well had him kicking the ground and bashing a frustrated sole of his boot against the stonework.

Round the building he continued, turning the corner to see Esryn sitting in the glow of the sun against the smooth wall of the castle, the grey stone continually warmed by the never-ending daylight. Even spending so long in the sunlight hadn't tinted her ivory skin. Looking loose and relaxed, her red braid hung down the front of her black tunic, the blaze of scarlet flaring on the material.

She bore a breastplate of leather armour on her lap, her feet together, knees splayed to take its weight while she dabbed a cloth into a bowl of oil and applied it gently to the hard hide. Not a twitch as he approached, but she knew he was there even before she could see him. Of that he was convinced. He stopped in front of her, casting a partial shadow over her, watching as she moved her skilled, broken hands over the surface. Still she didn't acknowledge him, her breathing silent and steady. Something about her always had him on edge.

'Don't you miss the night?' he said.

She just raised her head to the sky in answer.

'There are many things I miss, Frank Penny,' she said. 'Some much more than others.'

'What did you mean the other day?' he said.

Esryn continued the ritual of applying the bright greenish-yellow oil to her tough leather breastplate. He watched the battle-scarred fingers work in concentric circles across the hide. There was fresh bruising to her neck and the cuts to the backs of her hands had barely begun to scab. Different wounds from their encounter in the castle corridor.

'Morrin have it in for you?' he said with a jerk of his chin. Her long eyelashes flicked a beat. She didn't look up. Just a barely audible frictionless sound of the gentle rubbing of her cloth filled

223

the air. He noticed her eyes roam the area around them. She looked up and around, her eyes sharp. Frank felt the edge of nerves, his eyes following hers, realising she was checking for any windows that might overlook them. There were none. No one watching from the shadows. No prying eyes. As if she'd found this particular spot for that very reason. Esryn returned to her oiling.

'Apparently, uttering a syllable about a particular previous visitor isn't to be encouraged,' she said.

'About who?' Esryn shook her head but Frank continued. 'Tell me about the sorcerer.'

A muscle in her jaw flexed. She looked around again. Eyes clear, alert, wary.

'It's not...' She finally met his gaze. 'Not something we talk about. So I'm told.'

Her words were laced with bitterness. She dipped her eyes once more and continued her oiling. Frank sat beside her, bracing his back against the heat of the stone, dipping his head against the brightness of the sky. What he wouldn't give to have the sky bathed in dark and starlight. How he never knew he'd miss something so simple so much.

'Why not?'

'What did I say that you didn't understand?' said Esryn, her voice flat and unyielding.

Frank leaned forward, steadying his arms on his knees.

'Look, Esryn. I understand that you might be wary of outsiders but, whatever you think, we were led here for a reason and I'm sure it has something to do with the person you can't talk about. The sorcerer.' He was sure she flinched, just slightly. Her face tightened, just slightly. Frank pushed his frustration down. Now wasn't the time, especially in the face of a trained killer. Still Esryn stayed silent. Frank scratched his head in irritation. 'I don't want this all to be for nothing,' he said.

Esryn let out a breath, heavy and audible, then put her cloth to one side. She ran her scarred fingertips gently across the surface of the armour, tracing its contours.

'She did the same as you,' she said. 'She brought the shield down.'

Her voice was steady, but weighty. Frank let her words sink in. She, a woman. Again. The woman whose shadow they'd been stalking for more than two years. The one who had visited the guardians they'd uncovered – Edwina Chetto, Sapphire Hark. The one who'd served them with warnings, whose fingerprints were all over their quest and the Simbrian. It had to be the same person. She'd been here, left her mark and Frank felt a spike of excitement in his bones.

He left the silence between them as a prompt for Esryn to continue, but she stood, adjusted her trousers and cast a careful look around the open space and up to the walls again. She hauled up the leather breastplate and slung it over her shoulder with the dexterity of a magician. Frank jumped up, careful not to have her reaching for her blades.

'Hang on,' he said. 'What about her?'

Esryn stopped and turned, her face unreadable.

'I told you, she brought the shield down. That's all you need to know.'

An authoritative step away, towards the assassins' area to the west. Against any sane judgement, Frank grabbed her arm. She swivelled round, her green eyes meeting his, but didn't look to savage him.

'What do you want, Frank?' Her pale cheeks tightened, showing no emotion.

'I want to understand what brought us here. And why you're all so wary.'

'I have no idea what brought you, but you should fear what you followed. She brought nothing but sorrow...and treachery.' A flicker of something deep in the pools of her eyes. 'Sorrow and treachery,' she repeated. 'And loss.' Darkness in her voice, the tell-tale signs of a storm brewing. 'I hope you and your friends don't leave a similar taste.' She looked right into him. 'It wouldn't end well if you did.' Then she stalked off.

48

THE WORD

Esryn's heavy words clung to him for the next few days. He kept a look out for her. He didn't think the castle and its grounds were big enough for her not to cross his path but she had become a ghost in the wind, deliberately avoiding him. Even Anya was kept occupied doing training that didn't involve Esryn which made him suspect Morrin's dominant presence kept her concentrated on other things.

He'd told the others about her evasiveness but how she'd showed him a little light, just enough to heighten his interest, before shutting the door in his face. But there was something under the skin of all of this. He was sure. And their unexpected presence in the castle had set the fox running.

It was difficult for them to keep track of time, though the rhythm of the castle seemed to run to a gentle tune. Everyone seemed to understand when to eat and sleep, despite the unchanging light of the outside. He and Cas were in step with the routine of the kitchen and they'd all agreed to keep their heads down for now. No need for Wen to remind them or bark orders at their backs. Even Gabby agreed, despite the ruin that being in the laundry was bringing to her hands.

She'd remind them how the chief laundress would keep her busy all day, without much consideration for breaks and kept a close eye on her. Then Qaas would make the occasional appearance, ushering Gabby's boss to the door where they'd engage in hushed conversations, delivering a look in Gabby's direction before leaving.

'No one wants to talk about their previous visitor,' said Frank. 'You'd think Esryn would feel safe doing anything she pleased, but even she was guarded.' He turned to Gabby. 'And the way they treat you. They're spooked by the mere thought of a sorcerer.'

'I'm glad they're all running scared,' said Gabby. 'And they can keep running.'

She chewed at the end of her finger. The castle had remained tight lipped, no one would utter a word to them about their unwanted guest. Not even Wen, who brushed off Frank's veiled interest. Even though they were becoming more accepted, they knew they were being watched closely, any sign of dissent or curiosity reported back to Zachery.

'They probably talk about us all in old Rossian,' said Anya. 'Perhaps we should try and learn some, catch them at it.'

'Maybe the other sorcerer knew a bit,' said Cas. 'So she could either know what Zachery and Qaas were talking about, or could read Everbleed's notes.'

'Or just to spook them even more,' said Gabby.

But Frank was suddenly gripped with an odd notion.

'Hang on Cas.' The merest thought had leapt into his mind. A connection he'd not even considered, one he was surprised to hear knocking inside his head. The others looked at him. 'I wonder...I just wonder if our sorcerer is being clever with us.' Without a word he was on his feet and heading out of the room.

He still couldn't fathom from where the idea had sprung. Maybe it was the lack of anything resembling a well anywhere in the castle grounds, maybe it was his waning appetite for the riddles the Simbrian continually threw at him or the absence of any clues to help them get out of this mess but as he rushed down the stone staircase and flung open the door to the kitchen he had a growing feeling that he must be right.

The cooks were in the middle of the preparations for the evening meal. The room was alive with the scent of roasting lamb and the sweetness of rosemary and cranberries. A large pan of beer-scented gravy bubbled away next to pans of simmering carrots and cabbage, his grumbling stomach nearly diverting him away from the reason he'd run all the way down to the bottommost layer of the castle. His eyes shifted quickly. No sign of Wen.

Cati was knelt at one of the large cupboards, retrieving a number of ornate silver platters that looked like they'd easily furnish a table fit for Kester. She gave Frank a deferential nod.

'Where's Wen?' he said through quick breaths.

Cati twitched her head towards the door to the cellar.

'Getting the wine,' she said, adjusting the salvers awkwardly in her hands before turning to the long, central table. The same routine, day after day, year after year, century after century. How she could endure the monotony for so long? How could anyone? Frank nodded his thanks and headed quickly to the narrow entrance that led down the slender spiral stone steps to the cool and dark of the wine cellar.

He'd only managed half a dozen quick steps when a stout figure appeared from the shadows below. On seeing Frank she loosed her grip on the bottle before wresting it once again, clasping it to her chest.

'My goodness, Frank,' she said, a sharp note filled her accent. 'Have you any idea how old this wine is?' Frank held his palms up. 'And it's Larrimus's favourite.'

Frank suddenly wished she'd dropped it, but resisted the urge to smile.

'Sorry,' he said. She just gave him a tight-lipped look and took another step towards him. Frank pressed himself against the cold curve of the wall to allow her space to pass. She huffed as she headed back up to the kitchen, Frank following in her wake.

'It's not your shift,' she said.

Frank shook his head at her back.

'Can you tell me something?' he said as she strode through the kitchen to a cabinet that contained the beautiful, jewelled wine goblets that were their hosts' constant meal-time companions. She didn't stop or acknowledge him. 'Does the word "well" have a different meaning in Rossian?' She placed the bottle of wine down on the dresser and flipped open the glass doors with simple efficiency, quickly plucking four goblets out before flicking the doors shut.

'Can't you see I'm busy?'

'Can you just tell me? Please.'

'Tell you what?'

Frank drew in a breath.

'The word "well". Does it have a different meaning in Rossian?' Frank waited, silent pleading that his idea held water. Wen must have seen impatience spreading across his face and nodded.

'Of course,' she said. "It means "key".'

49

THE THEFT

He ran back to their rooms, not breaking stride nor drawing breath. There was no well, no hole in the ground, no place that masked an ancient spring or a clue to help them in their quest. It was a key, a damned key. That's what brought them here. He was so annoyed with himself. So annoyed. Ever since this whole thing had begun, since the moment they'd tried to break the curse that had been so tightly bound in their book, they'd all known there was no simple way to the Simbrian and so it had proved once more. No, the road they'd chosen to tread was next to impossible.

The well of darkness. The key of darkness. That is what they sought, what they needed, another small piece of the puzzle to complete. To finish what they'd set themselves on this impossible path to achieve. And now his head thundered with all the force of a tribal drum, reciting the word over and over. Key.

He flung the door open. Gabby, Cas and Anya looked up from the sofas. Gabby glared at him; he knew he should have told them where he was going, what had struck him from nowhere rather than just sprinting out and leaving them to guess, knew he would be met with cold stares when he returned.

'It's a key,' he blurted out. 'That's what we're looking for.'

The ice started to melt as he explained what Wen had told him, barely able to contain the thrill on his tongue.

'Does that help us?' said Gabby. 'I mean, the key of darkness. How are we meant to find that?'

'What do you mean? Of course it helps,' said Frank, unable to keep the annoyance from showing in his eyes. 'There's no well, we need to find a key.'

'I get it,' she said, irritation on her tongue. 'The key of darkness. There's probably a thousand keys in this place, held by each of the bores that live here. Know where to start?' Frank looked back at her, deflated, their eyes locked. '*That's* what I mean.' She folded her arms.

'Or we could try and look on the bright side,' said Cas.

Gabby looked at him.

'What bright side.' Gabby rose, shoved her hands into her pockets and walked to the bedroom. 'There is no bright side,' she said.

Frank, Cas and Anya sat watching the closed bedroom door, Gabby's bleakness infecting them, despite Frank's hope of a breakthrough.

'She's right,' he said. 'They might as well have a hundred haystacks out in the grounds. We're never going to get out of here.'

He dropped himself onto a sofa next to Cas, lead weights on his mood. Silence. He noticed the look on Anya's face, a hard resolve that had her on her feet and leaving the room.

Frank tried to think of what he could possibly do next. To try and figure out what the key of darkness meant. He could sense that Gabby had all but given up, her world of ill-treatment and distrust becoming more difficult to bear by the day and, by the look on Cas's face, he could tell he was headed down the same path.

There was something he wasn't getting, something he couldn't grasp. There seemed little point of building a castle in the middle of a thick, toxic forest and hide it from the world just to spend your time tracing the descendants of Kester. There appeared to be no practical reason to create something so specific – unless you were hiding something valuable. Hiding a key.

He sat staring into the empty fireplace, the minutes ticked by and yet they didn't, not in this castle until he'd had enough and was about to get up when Anya reappeared, her face firm and resolute. She stepped into the room and Frank's eyebrows raised as she was followed by the honed figure of Esryn.

Frank got to his feet, noticing her hands flex by her thighs. A stubborn reflex. He looked at Anya who closed and locked the door.

'I thought Esryn might help us,' she said. She looked at Esryn, who nodded, the bond between assassins plain. Esryn stared at Frank who shifted on his feet.

'How do we know you won't —'

'Report you?' she said. Frank blinked, his silence answering her question. 'I won't. I gave Anya my word.' Frank looked at Anya again.

'We don't have anything else, Frank,' she said with a shrug.

Frank knew she was right, they desperately needed inside help and Esryn was the only one who appeared to show even the slightest hint of rebellion, the only one who had tried to help them try and make sense of their prison.

'Anya keeps saying how you all just want to go home,' said Esryn, her face still, emotionless. The mention of home had Frank closing his eyes and throwing out a long breath. He looked at Cas, who nodded. 'What do you want to know?'

'Have you ever heard the phrase "the hand of the king holds the key and the —'

'— key fits all.' Esryn's expressionless face looked at him. 'Of course.' She paused. 'It's one of Everbleed's ramblings.'

'Do you know what it means?'

'Exactly what it says.'

Frank thought it was a stupid answer, but thought better than to be that direct with a moody assassin but she seemed to catch his annoyance.

'If you don't want my help, then you'll have to work it out for yourself, Frank.'

Frank bit down on his irritation, feeling his teeth clench.

'The key of darkness.' He threw the line at her, wondering if she'd bite, if he'd be able to reel her in.

She stilled, as if he'd thrown a bucket of freezing water over her. She glanced at Anya, uncertainty in her eyes. She looked behind her at the shut door, her eyes sharp, then turned back to Frank.

'You know about the key?' Her eyes searched him.

'No,' said Anya. 'We know it's important, but we don't know what it is.' Esryn stepped further into the room. She rubbed her thumbs across her fingertips. 'Can you tell us?'

If it was possible, Frank thought Esryn's face turned even paler. She paced to the wall by the windows, a glance at the outside, then stopped and turned to the three students, her arms folded, gripping her biceps.

'You think someone as astute as Kester would have left it to chance that the seven guardians would somehow be discovered or reunited and by a throw of the dice bring the Simbrian back into being?' She let the comment hang for a moment. 'Some might have split it and left it at that, but not our king.' None of them spoke, knowing Esryn was on the pathway to revealing something they needed to know. 'The key is exactly that – the key. The Simbrian cannot be fully complete without it. You can have all the parts, but it needs the key to ignite its soul.'

'You speak about it like it's a living thing,' said Frank.

Esryn looked at him and nodded.

'That was the main reason Kester had this castle built and cast it aside from time. No one could find us here. No one could find the key. Except...' Her voice trailed off. The bedroom door opened and Gabby entered, stopping when she saw Esryn, her eyes flicking to Anya.

'She found you and took the key,' said Anya. 'The woman.'

Esryn's nod was slow and filled with loathing.

'She was a cunning little rat, the sorcerer who came.' Esryn could barely get the words past her lips, a tightening of her mouth at the appearance of Gabby. 'She charmed all of us, especially Zachery.' Her tone chilled Frank. 'But it was Morrin who fell hardest for her beauty. She wore her tight clothes, her teasing smile and her luscious blonde hair like the assassins wear their daggers. But she was so much more deadly.' A glance at Gabby. Distrust on her white face.

'Zachery had entrusted Morrin with one of the keys. He wore it on a chain around his neck and never took it off. Morrin would be the last line if danger called.' Esryn turned to the window and looked out. 'But danger comes in a variety of disguises. She knew, like a wolf senses the weak prey. It didn't take long for her to get close to him, into his bed and, one night, when they were alone together, using her beauty as her spell, she took his key and disappeared into dark of the forest. She used the key to break through the shield and was gone.'

'So she took all of you in, including Zachery,' said Frank.

'You shouldn't talk about Zachery like that,' said Esryn. 'He's been here the longest and deserves your respect.'

Frank huffed, he could see it on the others – respect was something to be earned, not wielded by right.

'Morrin's been here just as long,' said Frank. 'And he doesn't appear to have an ounce of your respect.'

Her glare, full of frost, had him on his guard.

'That's different,' she snarled, showing her teeth. 'What lies between me and him.'

'Of course it is,' said Frank. 'Because you all seem to play by your own rules.'

Esryn clenched her teeth.

'You think you understand, but you don't.' She kept her sharp eyes on him. 'Carelessness is trained out of us.' A glance at Anya. 'But Morrin forgot, in his bed chamber with his desire for that woman he forgot, and his careless stupidity cost me more than you could possibly imagine.' Her face, its look of stone, sent a shiver through Frank. The words were the first she'd uttered that were hollowed out with emotion and she wielded them like her fists. 'So, what do you want, Frank Penny?'

'I want to go home. Isn't that what everyone wants?'

She shook her head.

'There are many others who would disagree with you. That protecting our secrets is more important, more important than anything, than people's happiness.' Frank didn't respond, but there was something in her words that didn't fit with her expression, like she didn't believe what she was saying. He kept his silence, remembering Spargo's deft tactic of drawing people out by keeping his mouth shut. He watched her as she played with the torn piece of red material tied in the end of her braid. 'You'll never get past Balal,' said Esryn. She looked around, the same primed look she wore like a second skin. 'You'd need me to help you out of the forest.' There it was. He immediately realised the reveal in her words. Words that told him she would help them; consider it, at least. Esryn silenced. She appeared to realise what she'd said, a slight slip of that carefully placed veil.

'Then —'

A shake of the head.

'There's nothing for me in your world.'

In your world. Such a strange choice of words, yet that was how she saw them, as travellers from a different time. But there was something Frank wasn't getting, something that the momentary distant look behind her eyes told him, something he didn't quite understand.

'There must be something for you, I know it. Come with us, Esryn. Please. Come with us.' He looked to the others for support, sensing that if he could just convince her to help them they'd be on their way.

Esryn froze, as if Frank's words had knocked the wind out of her. Her eyes gleamed lime and she chewed at the inside of her mouth. Then, to his surprise, her eyes watered and a faraway look again filled her porcelain face. She pinned Frank with a tearful stare and when Frank looked back he saw nothing but unbound sadness in the depths of her expression as a single tear ran slowly down her pale cheek. There was something there, something she wanted to say but she couldn't get the words past her lips.

'Come with us,' he said again, quieter, a hint of pleading in his voice. She inspected her boots, grinding the ends of her toes into the floor. She lifted her chin, her face hard, a young woman not used to voicing her feelings, her hope, her hurts and said:

'You can't help me. I'm beyond help.' Before walking across the room, opening the door and away.

50

The Portrait

Anya puffed her cheeks out. 'What was all that about?'

'No love for the sorcerer, that's for sure' said Cas.

Gabby's face darkened at him.

'Shut up, Cas,' she said. 'And it looks like what we need has already been taken from the castle.'

Frank had thought the same thing. The woman who had visited had made off with the key, that much was clear and it explained why everyone was so jittery around Gabby. It was also clear that the unknown sorcerer had sought out Irundi, goodness knows how, with the sole intention of stealing that one thing in particular.

'I don't understand why our book would lead us here if what it wants us to find has already been taken,' he said. 'Assuming the book was written by the same person who took it.'

'You didn't hear what she said,' said Cas. Everyone looked at him, blank expressions. 'She said that Morrin's key was taken. That he was given *one* of the keys'

'I think we all heard that,' said Frank.

'She said "his" key. Not "the" key.' Frank sifted the conversation with Esryn, knowing he'd missed her misplaced word. But Cas hadn't. 'So, there must be another one, at least one, somewhere here.'

'You think they had a copy made?' said Anya.

'Why not?' said Cas. 'It's logical if you think about it. Keeping just one carries all sorts of risks; including having it nicked when you've got your pants down.'

'If I was them I'd be more worried about having a master thief around than a sorcerer,' said Gabby.

'It could be anywhere,' said Frank.

'No,' said Cas. 'It can't. Something that valuable. Remember Morrin had it round his neck, like you have with your locket, Frank.' Frank made an involuntary move with his hand. 'He kept it on him at all times. It's not the sort of thing that you'd be careless with.'

'Maybe – remember Culpepper?'

'Yes, but he was an arrogant twonk. These people here are die-hards. They've been here for a thousand years to keep and protect their king's secrets and to track his line. Nothing's getting through here, just look at the ridiculous precautions Kester put in place.'

'Until *she* came,' said Gabby. 'Perhaps they got complacent. No wonder they were so pissed off when someone pulled a stunt like that. And she used it to get through the shield.'

Gabby's words halted them. Find the key. Get through the shield. Escape.

'The hand of the king holds the key,' said Anya. Her eyes darted to the floor, trying to fit the puzzle together. She looked up. 'Everbleed was never wrong.'

'So the key is buried with Kester. In his tomb. In his hand. It makes sense when you think about it,' said Cas.

'Which is where, exactly?' Frank tried to keep the irritation from his voice but could tell by the looks on the other's faces that he'd failed. Cas just shrugged.

'Well maybe you're so clever you could get that giant portrait of him to talk,' he said, tossing Frank's testiness back with sarcastic ease.

But Frank felt an idea being dredged up through his brain, something in Cas's words. He stared into nothing, trying to think.

'You've got that look on your face again,' said Gabby.

Frank looked up, his focus on her face.

'Cas is right,' he said.

'I am?' said Cas. Frank nodded.

'The portrait's the only image of Kester here. Well, the only one I've seen.' He could feel himself getting closer, close to the answer, even though it remained annoyingly beyond his fingers. 'It must have something to do with it. It must have.' He cursed and felt his body spasm. What wasn't he getting?

'Sounds like an idea,' said Gabby. 'Let's go and have a look, shall we?'

51

THE KEY OF DARKNESS

They had no idea what the consequences of getting caught out at night again would be, but what could those that kept the castle actually do to them? Working in the kitchen or the laundry was punishment enough, unless there was a dungeon, in which they would never age, spending the next thousand years not rotting. Now, that was a scary thought.

But the prospect of finding a key that would provide them an exit route from the castle was too much to resist. Esryn had told them the sorcerer had used the key to break through the shield. If they could somehow find it, somehow, Gabby, with her ability, might be able to do the same, open the shield then they'd run, run like the winds of death were after them and they wouldn't be caught.

They bided their time, resisting the urge to emerge too soon from their room, waiting until they thought the castle would be asleep and the only issue they might face would be the possibility of one or more of the Black Flame patrolling, although Anya had told them they rarely did.

Frank thought any patrol would be outside in the light of the night looking for anyone trying to get in; they hadn't seen anyone around when they made it to the Predek room weeks earlier and had no reason to think the castle, with its centuries of doing things the same way, would alter its routine. Anya kept giving them reassurances that, with what she had learned, she would be able to keep one of them at bay long enough for the others to escape but that wasn't good enough. It was all of them or none of them. One shot, that's all they had. One shot.

They retraced the route they'd taken on their very first night when they'd had dinner with Zachery, Qaas, Larrimus and the absent Al-Fajr, keeping away from the windows, the passageways well lit from outside.

They entered the dining hall and hurried over to the large portrait. Kester looked down on them, daring them to approach, his sharp eyes questioning their next move.

Frank's eyes scoured the picture. Just paint, nothing unusual. Kester's royal colours hung elegantly from his broad shoulders, his angular face bearing the look of authority, the palm of his hand facing towards them, halting them. Some kind of sign for Frank to mis-read.

'Perhaps there's something behind it,' said Cas. Frank nodded, he'd thought the same thing. A safe or an alcove, hiding the key, concealing their freedom. He and Cas lifted the bottom of the weighty portrait away from the wall, careful not to set it loose from its hanging, as Anya and Gabby checked the wall behind.

'Here,' said Gabby, taking the strain from Cas. 'You'd better check for any hidden compartments, I can't see anything.' Cas checked, twice, only to meet them with a slight shake of his head. Frank and Gabby slowly placed the portrait back in position and stood back.

A thick blanket of utter disappointment descended over them. They were sure they'd find something. Weeks of incarceration, of boredom, of the never-ending glare of the sun had put a razor-sharp edge on their hope, only to have it blunted before they'd got anywhere. Irundi was doing an excellent job of kicking them hard in the teeth. Frank cursed under his breath, drawing looks from the others. Red rage erupted from inside him, sending him kicking one of the high-backed chairs, then grabbing it and throwing it over with a terrific clatter that had them all looking at the door, then back to him.

Frank stared, unfocused, at the floor, rubbing the back of his neck, drawing in deep breaths to keep himself from tearing the place apart.

'Why don't you just go and knock on Zachery's door and let him know what we're doing,' said Gabby.

Frank glanced up, seeing the storm brewing under her skin, only a slight regret that he'd lost his cool.

'This is just stupid,' he said. 'I just want to get out and all we have to help us is a stupid riddle from Everbleed.' He could feel the heat in his blood. Frank looked at the portrait once more.

'There's no key in his hand, even a blind beggar could tell you that.'

Anya took a step forward, running her eyes over Kester.

'I guess her problem was that she wasn't that literal.' She turned to Frank. 'They were difficult times, so rather than just writing things plainly, sometimes she spoke in riddles.'

'*Sometimes?*' said Cas. 'So "the key is in the hand of the king" means it isn't in the hand of the king? I don't get it. His hand looks very empty to me. It's like he's waving goodbye to us or wants me to high-five him. He might as well be thumbing his nose.'

As Cas spoke Frank's mind stuck on his words. *The key is in the hand of the king.* A wave of realisation crashed over him.

'You're right,' said Frank.

'Right about what? The nose thumbing?'

Frank shook his head and stepped forward, nudging Anya aside. He ran his right index finger over the surface of the painting, over to Kester's extended palm. Nothing. He turned his left palm over, inspecting it for any sign of the mark that had inflicted him in the forest, that had saved him when Balal was about to decapitate him. There was nothing there. He ran the fingertips of his left hand over the king's palm.

There it was.

A faint prickling sensation ran through his wrist and up his arm. He did it again. The same sensation. He looked at his palm again. The faint outline of Kester's mark, the Qine, looked back at him, pulsing slightly, giving him the permission he needed. He held his palm up, holding it just a few inches from Kester's extended

243

palm, fingers splayed, aware of the others watching him. He could feel them holding their breath as his own quickened. He saw the surface of Kester's painted palm glow, inviting him on, daring him to make the connection.

Then he pressed his palm to the king's.

Pain pierced him like the cold steel of an assassin's dagger, pain like nothing he could have imagined. Unhindered white hot agony ripped into him, coursing up his arm and into his chest, welding him to Kester, binding them as one. The whole picture glowed, radiating hot jets of unforgiving white light. All sound was blotted from him. An agonising cry escaped his dry mouth, echoing around the room as Frank's knees buckled. He felt someone grip him under the armpits to stop him falling, still the hand held him captive, searing deep into his bones, tearing his soul, sending him spinning. He thought it was never going to stop, that it would turn him to ash. In between the screaming in his head, the sound of something metal landing with a muffled clank.

Then, with no warning, the pain stopped.

Frank collapsed to the floor, the heat inside him balled and fled as he vomited until he thought he'd dry himself out.

Cas was by him in an instant, sitting him up, kneeling behind him as a prop as Frank fought to recover his senses.

'Blimey, you okay mate?'

Frank exhaled long and loud, looking up as Anya bent down and went to pick up an object a few feet in front of him. She recoiled, sucking in air through her teeth before taking a napkin from the table, folding it over as many times as she could manage, then picked it up again.

'That's hot,' she said, holding it aloft. She looked at the object, a small straight rod of blackened iron. As innocent as it was fascinating. She looked back at Kester's portrait, Frank's eyes following hers. 'It's gone,' she said with a nod of her head.

Frank saw it straight away. The non-descript length of metalwork that once hung around his neck, that had been part of the picture, had disappeared, had become manifest and was now in Anya's hand. 'This must be it. Here,' she said, holding it out to Gabby, who took it. 'You'll need this.'

Gabby gave the end the scarcest of touches, checking it for heat, before dropping the napkin and giving it a close inspection. They all stopped, spellbound.

'There's an arrow etched into the metal,' she said, running her thumb over one of the tips. 'But I can feel there's something about it, like it wants us to take it.' She looked up. 'The key of darkness. We were right, this is what we came for. And this is our ticket out of here.'

Frank pulled himself to his feet, for a moment not knowing which way was up. He stared at the object in Gabby's hand, a thin length of iron that had nearly got them killed, that had led to their miserable existence in the eternal fortress of Irundi. It looked like nothing and certainly nothing like important, but they all knew, knew it was the life-force of something beyond powerful. The key that would ignite the Simbrian.

Gabby pocketed the key as Frank brushed himself down and pinched the bridge of his nose. He knew the noise he'd made would attract attention and wasn't going to wait around to see just how much.

'Come on,' he said. 'Let's go.'

52

THE ESCAPE

Quickly they ran, as silently as their hot breath would allow, down the stairs, two at a time towards the door through which they had been led when they first arrived. Towards their freedom.

Frank prayed it would work, that the key that had fried him beyond his pain threshold, together with Gabby's talent as a sorcerer, would open a silent window in the shield and they would be away before anyone realised. They reached the bottom of the staircase, a step away from the door when out of the shadows stepped Esryn, her eyes as hard as the steel of the scimitar on which she had her hand, ready to draw it out.

Frank knew she would cut them all to confetti before they had time to put their hands up, but he also sensed her hesitation and took a step towards her, hoping he hadn't misread the signs. Her hand shifted on the guard.

'Don't,' he pleaded, his palms up and facing towards her, glancing to the weapon and back to her. He could tell the others had stilled. His eyes silently pleaded with her not to signal for the dogs or alert the castle. Her mouth twitched, her eyes shifted to the others then back to Frank.

'I can't let you go,' she said.

He noticed her hand wrap slowly around the hilt. The tightening skin on the back of her hand emphasising the paleness of her scars.

'Yes you can.' Her grip tightened. Frank felt the hot spike of panic as he saw the glint of the first inch of the blade as she began to unsheathe it. She'd shred them all. Anya stepped forward.

'Come with us,' she said. Esryn hesitated. 'Please, Esryn, come with us.' Esryn paused, closing her eyes.

'I can't.' Said in a near whisper.

'Yes, you can. Whatever it is you're afraid you'll find, you can.'
Her eyes clouded.

'It's not what I might find. It's what I might not.'

He wasn't sure he knew what she meant, but he could hear the
emotion in her voice, could see it in the paleness of her face. They
waited, the door, their freedom, but a few feet away. Frank could feel
his breath tightening. Knew the more time that dripped by the less
chance their one shot at getting away had of success. Then Esryn's
hand flexed, her grip on the hilt of her scimitar tightened. She looked
at him, her eyes dark, sad, but at that moment he couldn't tell if she
was about to cut his throat or shed a thousand tears.

'We need to get going,' said Gabby, drawing a barbed look.

'Perhaps it's better that the sorcerer were gone,' said Esryn.
She looked back to Frank. 'You think you can get past the shield?'
Frank nodded. 'If you do, stay low, keep as quiet as possible and just
keep moving. Balal cannot cover the whole forest. You'll need your
wits and even more luck. Now, get going. The watch will be alerted as
soon as the shield is breached. I'll stall them as long as I can.'

Frank felt his insides calm, resisting the urge to give Esryn the
tightest hug. His eyes locked on to hers and they shared the briefest
of unspoken moments before he turned and led the others through
the front door and out into the glare of the interminable sun, across
the neatly clipped grass that ran around the front of the castle and
across to the spot where they had entered the clearing weeks earlier.
No one looked back.

They stopped at the edge of the clearing, gathering at Gabby's
back as she grabbed the key from her pocket. Frank just hoped their
logic would play out, otherwise he couldn't be certain what might
happen to them if they were caught. He knew that would be it, that
they would have to stay here forever and no one would ever, ever
find them.

He watched as Gabby held the key to the trees and stepped

forward. She pushed her hand into the shield, creating a ripple on the surface that spread out as if she'd thrown a stone into a pond. Frank's eyes followed the circles until they faded and were lost.

For a second, nothing happened, then, as he felt himself hold his breath, a flap peeled its way downwards, revealing a dark patch of woodland beyond. The silent forest, the window to their freedom. The oppressive darkness flooded in along with the strong odour of rotting vegetation, heightening Frank's senses and breathing a new fear into him and the others. The fear of what lay between the relative safety of the castle and the long black split in the earth that served as a divide between their world and the world of centuries past.

Gabby looked at the strained faces of the others then, without a word, stepped through the opening and into the night.

53

RUN

The black of the woods swallowed them, only the quick cracking of the dry woodland floor gave away the speed of their exit. Frank knew they needed to be light on their feet, to quell any thoughts of what lay ahead in the darkness, heeding Esryn's last words to them. They were deep in the jaws of the forest, jammed right down its evil throat. Nature didn't scare him, but this did; it scared the living shit out of him. He could feel its evil wiping itself on his bones as he led the others away, the unnatural menace that spread out around them, the dark he tried to push to one side of his mind and concentrate on getting to safety.

From the never-ending light under the time bead shield, they were thrust into darkness, Irundi at their backs. They had only guessed at the time and the sun had yet to hoist itself from its slumber and they were instantly disoriented. He only had a rough recollection of the direction out to the Black Feather, tried to drag it up through his memory, how they'd stumbled on Balal and how long it had taken her to lead them to Irundi.

Everyone around them knew the forest, from the strangers in the castle to the Sapirai. They didn't. He wished he'd done a better job of trying to convince Esryn to come with them, sure she would be their guide, as well as a lethal weapon against anything that watched and preyed on them. He hoped they wouldn't need her, but it was too late anyway, too late for her to unleash her own brand of hell in their defence.

He hadn't given any thought to what they'd do once they were out, not given anything much thought beyond running as fast as they could, wondering if their fragile relationship with Balal and her Sapirai was still intact. He hoped it was.

Frank willed the sun to start showing itself. He could only guess the general direction from which they'd entered the woodland all those weeks ago. Not a reliable marker but he had to trust his instincts, the others had to, had to put their faith in him.

So they ran.

Twenty minutes in he stopped to check his bearings, breath clouding in the pale of the waking sun. Splayed columns of grey sunlight started to leach through, the dark of the forest trying its best to swat it back. The others paused with him, shedding deep lung-fulls of air, checking him for signs that he knew what he was doing as he looked up through the mass of thick branches, the twisted web of something malign, pushing them down against their will.

Their breathing stilled. Tense quiet surrounded them, everyone's eyes wide and alert like a pack of hunted deer, watching, listening, wondering if death was waiting unseen in the shadows. Each face, made dark and ashen amidst the trees, bore unspoken dread. Without a word, Frank headed off again, thoughts of safety hauling him on, knowing that their journey into the forest had seemed like hours, knowing the return would feel longer, endless.

No one dared to break the silence of the forest. Frank's mind had room for only one thought — keep going.

On. Quick. Quicker.

There was no room for words, each stride took them a few yards further to the edge of the forest, to the narrow fissure that would breathe fresh life into the landscape, that would mark their salvation when they crossed it. Frank silently begged the woodland to be forgiving.

The undergrowth thickened, huge splinters of rock, gnarled old branches grasped at them like the living breathing arms of evil woodland wraiths. The trees loomed over them, preparing to smite them into dust, shedding anger at their attempt to outrun the rising sunlight. Closer, the trees grew closer, tighter. Huge, wasted trunks and knotted undergrowth held them up but they leaped and ducked, swerved and dodged as the unseen demons in the forest were left behind. Frank could sense their target getting closer as they headed further and further from the clearing that had been their prison for weeks, leaving it far behind.

Then there was a crack of wood and a thud behind him. He came to a breathless standstill and looked behind him to see Gabby coming to a wild, tumbling halt against a rotted, moss-coated tree-stump. She let out a grunt and stayed down.

Frank stepped back and grabbed her quickly under the arm, hauling her clumsily to her feet. She pushed him off, spitting and sneering from her soul as she stepped back and cursed, gripping her shoulder and wincing as pain flooded into her face. She opened her mouth but all that they heard was the familiar, bone-chilling sound of a shrill whistle from deep in the trees.

54

THE TERROR

Hot, wild panic thrust its way up Frank's throat. The signal had them all staring with wide-eyed terror into the endless dark of their surroundings. Their faces paled, alert like fretting rabbits.

He didn't need to say it. None of them wanted to die.

Frank legged it with the others close behind. He already felt wasted. His energy spent from running flat out since the beginning of dawn. His legs had begun to feel like the woodland floor was pulling him in tight and only the raw adrenaline coursing like fire through his veins pushed him on; that and the complete certainty that they had a cat in hell's chance of getting out of their oppressive surroundings. He could sense the untamed terror of the others, barely leashed within their frightened breaths.

Any sense of quiet had instantly evaporated in the thick shadows of the trees. The crack and snap of rotten wood splintering filled the previously silent void, signalling their location to everything within earshot.

On they pressed, feeling the trees pushing in, blocking their attempts at the quick progress he craved, echoes of their escape battering the stillness of the forest. Still the way ahead was heavy with vegetation; still it was nearly impossible to detect any discernible path that signposted the way to safety, still they ran.

They knew the Sapirai knew where they were, tracking their every anxious movement. Frank daren't look to either side. He forged on, the forest still and silent but for the swift and fragile movement of four teenagers being hunted by a group of cunning and deadly woodland creatures with nothing but bloodlust on their leader's blackened tongue.

Frank's lungs were busting. He sensed Gabby on his back of his shirt but that the others were dropping behind. He decided to slow to a halt, allowing them the briefest respite to ease their aching lungs. Cas doubled over, his hands on his knees, barking in deeps gulps, a thick strand of saliva dripping unchecked from his open mouth. Anya stood, hands on hips, her expression neutral. A blanket of silence shrouded them. No one could find the right words when, with no sound of rustling bushes to serve as a warning, two figures came barrelling out of the trees and took Anya and Cas down.

The small but lean and muscular Sapirai forced them both down into the rotting forest floor, a flash of deadly steel pressed to their throats as, out of the shadows shimmered a dozen more, barely discernible against the patchwork of woodland shades around them, some with their bows readied, arrows nocked, others carrying blades, the carved muscles on their forearms taught with anticipation.

Then Frank sensed her.

He could feel the stolid stench of death on her breath, standing mere feet behind him having appeared from nowhere as if she had just spawned from the trees.

'Greetings, whiteskin.'

Frank turned at the gut-wrenching growl, his eyes coming level with the broad feral chest of the woodland warrior. 'Balal is surprised to see you once more.' A wide grin, the black tongue snaking over her bark-skin lips, on her sharp, deadly teeth.

Frank took a terrified step back.

'Let them go.' He could hear the trembling on his words. Balal took a step forwards, backing Frank up further towards Gabby who grabbed him by the waist, her tense fingers digging in as he shielded her from the wild beast that consumed their attention. Balal loosed a chuckle under her breath. She jerked her chin at the two Sapirai pinning Anya and Cas who slowly got to their feet and backed away, silent as mist, at their leader's unspoken command. Cas grabbed Anya as they got to their feet and pulled her close, blood seeping from a wound on his forehead, barely able to conceal his shivering horror at the sight of Balal.

'You have bored of Irundi, hm?' She started a slow walk around the four teenagers, circling them, her black eyes pinning them one by one. 'Balal thought you would.' She chuckled. 'Better here in the woods with the Sapirai.'

She turned her head and looked in the direction from whence they had run. The serpent's smile vanished, replaced by a cautious loathsome look. She sniffed the air, drawing in a deep lungful before letting out a low, throaty growl. She turned back to Frank.

'Can you lead us out of here,' said Frank, surprised at the note of confidence in his voice. His head spun and he bargained on their brittle pact, the invisible symbol on his hand, keeping them all from a bloodbath.

Balal sniffed, her eyes roaming hungrily on their anxious faces before narrowing them at Frank.

'He who bears the mark of Kester thinks Balal is his servant?' Her voice low and brushed thick with threat.

'No...I...I...'

Frank felt his throat tighten like a hunter's trap under Balal's ogreish gaze. The huge muscles on her arms and chest flexing with each breath. She let out a near silent chuckle.

'I am indeed commanded, whiteskin' she said, looking around. 'But the pact demands payment.'

'What?'

'Payment must be made for safe passage out. The pact demands it.'

Frank was paralysed under her soulless eyes. A silence fell as Balal waited. Frank looked around at the others, none of whom looked capable of offering a response.

'You're just making it up,' shot Gabby.

Balal gradually unsheathed her sword, her gaze shifted slowly and intimidatingly to Gabby.

'I address the whiteskin. The sorcerer would do well to keep to herself.' She bored her eyes into Gabby, who flinched uncomfortably, before turning her attention back to Frank. 'Well?'

'How much do you want?'

Balal laughed. A low, evil drawl that made Frank's bones go cold. She tapped the tip of her weapon against her calf.

'How much?' Her voice low and grinning. 'What would you give for safe passage out, hm?' Frank couldn't move. 'What would Balal and her Sapirai want, hm?' His eyes looked beyond the muscular bulk to the woods beyond. If Balal noticed, she ignored it. The Sapirai murmured between themselves, a blur of unknown words as Frank's mind raced. Balal sniffed as she, too, looked beyond him. 'Balal will let the whiteskin choose, hm.' A smile to chill his worst nightmares spread across her face.

'I don't understand. Choose what?' said Frank.

Balal lifted her sword to his chin, the smile turning to a look of petrifying, endless dark.

'Choose which of you we take.' Words lightly thrown.

'What?'

Balal jerked her chin to the captive students behind him as Gabby's grip tightened on Frank's waist.

'You choose which of your friends the Sapirai can have. The rest of you will be escorted out of the woods, your freedom assured. That is the word of Balal.' She looked back at Frank, face creasing into a scowl. Frank offered nothing to her silence. Her stare pressed on him. 'Well?' The challenge in her voice plain.

'You have to be kidding?'

Her evil smile gave Frank the answer. He turned to the others, mirroring the shock in their eyes. Time stood still as Frank searched his tired brain for a plan.

'I can't do that,' was all he offered, feeling more pressure on the point of Balal's blade.

As if it were possible, Balal's face darkened, her eyes, like pits of thick tar, demanding a different answer.

'You will choose, whiteskin. Or Balal will take them all and only spare he who bears the mark.'

Frank's whole body was cold and leaden, but still a trickle of sweat ran down his spine. The eyes of the others on him, their fear at the nape of his neck, watching his movement, for his next words but Frank just shook his head.

'No,' he said. 'These are my friends. You have no right to make such a demand of me.'

The blow that came was hard, unseen and had Frank on the floor before he knew what had happened. He could feel the skin on his cheek tightening instantly. His head rang with the impact and, through blurred eyes, he could just make out the carved and muscular legs of Balal as she said:

'If the whiteskin will not choose, then Balal will do it for him.' Frank turned his aching neck up, looking into the fierce and dispassionate face that turned to the others standing behind Frank. 'And I choose all of them,' she roared, shuddering with the weight of her words.

She took a giant step over Frank's prone body and grabbed hold of Gabby, dragging her away. Frank turned onto his back as Gabby wrestled against Balal's impossible strength, muscles that had been earned the hard way. She clutched Balal's wrist with both hands, fighting with the futility of a mouse as it tries to bite the cat. 'Starting with the sorcerer.' She quickly re-sheathed her sword, a razor-sharp hunting knife appearing in its place.

She turned Gabby around in one bone-chilling move and pushed her hard onto her knees, latching onto her long, midnight hair, twisting it tightly around her huge fist and pulling her head back with ruthless barbarity, exposing her neck. Gabby's squeal of pain matched the untold anguish on her face as Balal's knife went to her throat. Balal looked deep into Frank's eyes, into his soul, and gave him a triumphant sneer.

'The whiteskin thinks he's so clever,' she snarled. 'Let's see how clever you are as you watch me cut your girlfriend's throat.'

The muscles on Balal's forearms tensed and Frank's mouth fell open in abject horror, Gabby's life but a swift flick of the monster's wrist from ending. Tears sprang in Gabby's pleading eyes as they locked onto his, knowing this would be the last time he'd see the spark of life within. Not here. Not like this.

Frank found he couldn't look away but Balal's expression suddenly changed in a frantic beat of his heart. She sniffed the air twice, three times, a deep pull on the scent of her home; her black eyes darting between her collective brethren, searching the familiarity of the dense forest, her kingdom. Her gnarled hand released Gabby's hair, pushing her forward in one swift movement, sending her face down into rotting stench of the forest floor with a barely audible whimper.

Quickly, Gabby struggled out of reach, grabbing hold of Frank's arm, anchoring herself to him as Anya tried to shrug off her assailants but they held her fast, despite a flicker of uncertainty in their eyes and that of their leader.

Balal took a tentative step forward, her tongue sliding over her lips, tasting whatever foul spirit she could sense in the air. There was a faint rustling from beyond the trees. Then she went completely still.

55

THE QUEEN OF THE FOREST

'Burra.'

Balal backed up as out of the trees sprang the lithe and muscled panther, an unleashed streak of black. The large cat bared its enormous canines, poised in front of Balal whose hand tensed on the hilt of her dagger.

Burra was followed by the imposing figure of Morrin, followed by Esryn and two further other assassins. Frank felt the Sapirai bristle. A nod from Balal had them reaching for their bows, but the calm tone from the trees had them all looking round as, out of Morrin's shadow, stepped the grinning figure of Qaas.

'Step your stinking midgets down, Balal,' she said, pinning the monster with her delicate stare.

Burra gave a silent snarl. Morrin heaved in a long breath, his tight, sculpted chest heaving against the black of his oiled, leather armour. Balal narrowed her eyes and tilted her head at her followers who twitched with aggression but stood still, alert, their shadows merging with those of the trees.

Qaas stepped forward into the centre of the gathering, a sleek, flowing movement of someone sure of their ground, Burra followed in the same, smooth style. Balal flinched as she passed, only the slightest movement, but Frank noticed.

Balal's nostrils flared and she watched Qaas's every step. Anya and Cas backed up as Qaas turned, hands on hips, an unreadable grin on her face, Esryn fell into place a step back from Morrin, her hands brushing the hilt of the daggers sheathed tightly to her thighs, knuckles white. The other two never shifting their eyes from the

Sapirai.

'What can Balal do for the queen of the forest?' hissed Balal.

Qaas's harsh eyes went from one student to the next, coming to rest on Gabby.

'This one's coming back with me,' she said. Gabby screwed up her face.

Frank looked at Esryn who didn't, couldn't, meet his eyes.

'I...' Gabby couldn't find the words.

'You what?'

'I don't...'

'You don't have a choice.' Qaas twitched her head at Morrin who strode over to Gabby, grabbing her roughly by the arm and stood, awaiting instruction. 'One sorcerer has evaded us. A second will not.' Words of solid authority. Gabby offered no resistance. Balal let out a low grunt.

'You intend to leave me with nothing?' she said, a hint of simmering on her tongue. Qaas's face flared.

'Keep that crow's tongue of yours to itself,' she said. 'Or shall I have Esryn skin you?'

'*You're* the queen of the forest?' said Frank, aware of the doubt in his voice.

He looked at Balal, the question hung in his eyes.

'These are ancient royal woodlands,' said Qaas, stepping silently over to him. 'The whole of Byeland and Rossia before that were for the people, but Kester claimed these for himself.'

'So what?'

'Mind your impudent tongue,' she barked. Her look, her tone reminded him of Etamin. 'Balal might think she has a claim —'

'My people were here centuries before yours,' snarled Balal. 'Thieves.' Qaas snapped her head to the woodland monster.

'And you mind yours.' A low, throaty growl spilled from Balal. 'My brother was no thief and he allowed you to roam the forest and live unfettered. And let's face it, you're hardly the welcoming talisman our visitors might expect.'

Brother. Frank looked at the others as the muted confrontation between Qaas and Balal unfolded. Qaas was Kester's sister.

'Yes, Frank,' said Qaas, catching the look on his face. 'My brother entrusted me to keep his secrets safe.' She looked at Gabby, revulsion on her face. 'He was always wary of sorcerers. Always.' She stepped towards her, to within a foot. A move of authority, of smooth control, her face inches from Gabby's. Gabby twisted in Morrin's grip in an attempt to broaden the space between her and Qaas but Qaas lifted her hand and gripped Gabby's chin tightly. 'He saw his daughter in all of them. Lashka bore their mark and harboured all the dark elements of sorcery. He knew what she was like, what you're *all* like.' Untamed hatred filled the air around her.

'Gabby's not like that,' said Anya.

Qaas's eyes stayed fixed on Gabby's.

'You're *all* like that,' she said through her teeth. Slow, stabbing words, her fingertips pressing further into Gabby's face. 'And natural sorcerers are a very rare breed.' She let go and turned to the others, Gabby's hand immediately went to her chin, rubbing Qaas's humiliating touch off her skin. 'And she just confirmed what my brother knew. The one that came.' Morrin's grip on Gabby tightened. 'Centuries of keeping hidden. Helping to keep the world safe, just as it was meant to be, just as he had asked and in she waltzes and ruins everything.' She paced. 'Everyone was spellbound by her beauty, her charisma. Even me. But betrayal is the stealthiest of creatures.' The bitterness in her voice was manifest. She looked at Morrin. 'Whatever the spell that got her into your bed, she betrayed us. Then she was gone.' She stepped back to Gabby. 'And I swore on my brother's grave that if another one crossed my path, I would keep them at the castle for eternity.'

'But I have no powers within the silent forest,' said Gabby.

'Precisely.' Qaas spoke the words with triumph. 'The world needs to be rid of your sort, of what you can conjure, of what that demon of a niece of mine was so happy to wield without pity. If only my brother had been brave enough to do the same to his daughter, the world would have been a much safer place but now we have our people at each other's throats.' She grabbed Gabby by the front of her shirt. 'Sorcerers.' She jerked her chin at Morrin. 'If you would escort this girl back to Irundi.' She looked at Esryn. 'And the others.'

'Don't you dare,' said Frank, taking a step towards Qaas, making a grab for her. The panther was on him before he knew it, knocking him onto his back, its heavy paws pinning him into the soft soil. Qaas stepped over, fury on her face.

'Don't you *touch* me.'

Frank daren't move. The huge cat's jaw mere inches from his face, its growl penetrating his skull, the tips of its rapier-like claws buried in his shirt and pushing painfully into his skin. Qaas stood over him, her face unreadable. She looked up and over to Balal.

'You can have this one,' she said, looking back at Frank, a twisted smile on her face.

'But the whiteskin bears the Qine mark,' said Balal. 'I am sworn to protect him. He is of no use to me.' Qaas's expression changed and she peered back down at Frank, deep suspicion on her curious brow. 'Like her,' said Balal. 'The one who came before.'

Frank's heart skipped a beat. The look on Qaas's face told him everything he needed to know about how she saw him and his unknown association with the thief who had robbed Morrin of his key, the sorcerer, object of her deep loathing.

'Then,' she said, her eyes burning into him. 'I will release you from your bond.' Balal's long black tongue wiped her teeth, a delicious grin spread across her face. Qaas looked up. 'I'll take these three back to Irundi. You do what you like with him.'

56

The Butchering Block

Frank was hauled along a barely discernible pathway. If he'd been able to look, he would have seen the lightly trodden track, just inches wide, showing one of the many intersecting channels along which the Sapirai moved silently through the forest. However, with his hands firmly bound with long vines of ivy, more of which had been wound round his neck like a manacled collar and held by two of Balal's sentinels, he could only focus ahead.

They led him like a condemned man towards what he could only assume was their butchering blocks deep in the forest, away from the safety of the outside world, away from his friends, away from the remainder of his life.

Balal had ordered him tied, her followers grinding him into the dirt with a ruthlessness reserved for their worst enemies as Qaas and Morrin looked on.

The bindings were so tight he immediately began to lose the feeling in his hands. He'd not had the chance to say anything to the others, knowing for certain that the timely intervention from Qaas would be the last he would see of them. Nor had he had time to plead for his life. Gabby's pitiful screams as he was dragged off still sounded in his ears.

The Sapirai didn't hurry. There was no need. The fight had left him the moment they'd trussed him up, he knew it was futile and as they led him further into the woods his head began to swim with thoughts of how few minutes he might have left. Then he tripped, landing heavily on his side, unable to hold his hands out to break his fall. A sad whimper left his lungs as pain pierced his side.

Her huge feet stepped into view. He didn't look up. He didn't want to see that evil, satisfied face and its silver fangs.

'Don't worry, whiteskin. A few more minutes and your suffering will end.'

She turned and Frank looked at her heels as he was dragged upright by his captors, his terrified breath coming in short bursts. He was going to die. Just a few more minutes. His last moments in bending humiliation among a band of bloodthirsty woodland creatures. He was going to die, of that he was certain.

He wasn't sure exactly what happened next, but as the cord around his neck tightened and he prepared to take his final steps he saw the captor in front of him drop like a chunk of lead, an arc of deep red spraying from its neck. The second guard followed a second later, the rope slackening.

Frank, free of his tether, spun round to see the fluid but mechanical movements of a hooded figure, cloaked in the midnight robes of the Black Flame, draw two blades and in a single elegant motion threw them both, felling two more of the small woodland creatures who shuddered as they hit the floor. They didn't get back up.

Balal turned, panic flared in her eyes which darted across the trees, processing what was happening. Too slow. Another blade slammed into her shoulder, deliberately aimed, designed to wound and warn. Strong hands grabbed Frank, shredding the bindings on his wrists and hauling him back. Balal hissed, but backed away, her huge hand pushing on the fresh wound. Red spilled between her fingers and down her torso as she yanked the dagger out.

The figure backed up, facing Balal and the Sapirai, pushing Frank firmly away, away into the dark of the surrounding trees, urging him to run. Two Sapirai rushed them, not quick enough to avoid the deadly edge of the rapier his saviour had silently and smoothly drawn and wielded with such precision that both woodland creatures were shredded before Frank's eyes. But he didn't hang about. Shielded by his unknown rescuer, he headed into the forest and back along the slender pathway, shouts from the Sapirai whirling around the trees, followed by the hollow bellow of Balal as they made their escape.

He ran. Faster than he could remember running at any time in his life, feeling death itself close on his heels. Balal would not let him get away. Back down the track he fled, pulling in great chunks of stale air from the silent forest as it closed around him, his desperate instinct to live kicking him with renewed energy.

Keep going. Don't look back. The urge for pure survival drove him on, his thighs burning with the effort of escape. No time to think of how he'd managed an impossible getaway and the person who had appeared from the trees like a woodland ghost. All he could think about was staying alive.

He felt the sweat on his neck before he felt something at his back, flaring every hair on his body. Something so close he could smell it. A frightened gasp escaped his lips at the thought of Balal dragging him to the ground but where he thought he was about to have his throat ripped out, he heard a low, muffled voice.

'Don't stop.'

On he went, conscious of the man at his back and as the trees began to open up, the cloaked figure overtook him, hurrying swiftly and surely ahead, Frank following on the tail of his black cloak. Frank was fast, but still struggled to keep pace with the broad frame that kicked and stamped the dense undergrowth as if it were made of dust and dodged the muzzled tree stumps and dead branches like a ballet dancer.

For what seemed like an eternity they sped, further away from Balal and her murderous tribe, further away from his friends who he'd left to the devices of Qaas. His sides ached, his throat burned with the effort of the escape until the stranger reached a small clearing, across from a shallow rock face into which a cave disappeared into darkness.

Frank stopped, watching as the man walked silently across and, stooping slightly, entered. Frank threw aside any hesitation and followed him in, unconcerned if it was safe or not, knowing that this person had saved him from the nightmare clutches of Balal and wasn't likely to harm him.

He felt the cool dark of the cave wrap around him like a comforting shawl. As he stilled his knees buckled. He placed a hand on the cave wall, feeling the cold, slick rock, heaving in the tang of moss and mineral as he fought to regain his breath, to stop himself falling to the floor, then vomited hard, choking up his emotion, his guts and his relief.

He collapsed his frayed body to the floor and turned, his back against the cool of the rough stone, burying his head in his hands, trying to compose himself, trying to wrest the last thirty minutes from his mind.

He let the minutes tick by, looking down the front of his shirt, trying not to let his terrifying experience break him into little pieces, feeling the tears rising in his throat.

Eventually, he lifted his head. The sweet silence of the cave making him draw in a long breath. A slow sweep of his eyes around the inside showed a large, deep cavern. The ceiling curved up twenty feet, with a small opening to the shifting autumn light beyond. Two bed rolls stretched out in the centre of the cave, neatly aligned, and a small array of dead wildlife – rabbits and game birds – hung from a makeshift rail on a frame of stripped hazel to the side.

His saviour was bent down on one knee, facing away, hunched over a pyramid of dried twigs and sticks, lighting a small fire in the pit that nestled in the centre of the cave. Flames spat into life. The figure got up, turned to Frank and pushed back his hood. For a split second, Frank thought it might be Spargo or that he'd be staring down the blackened gaze of Dagmar but was even more surprised to find himself looking upon the familiar face of Millington Johns.

57

THE ASSASSIN

Johns's sallow features showed no emotion, no evidence of the kamikaze rescue he'd just pulled off like he did it every day. He didn't approach. Whether it was the natural caution they'd encountered back in Crossways, or him simply giving Frank his own space and time to reassemble his scattered nerves, Frank couldn't be sure. Not that he cared. He owed this man his life. A debt he would never be able to repay. Johns eyed him.

'You okay?' he said. Still he didn't move any closer. He just looked Frank over as if checking for any physical injury. Frank nodded. No words. Then dipped his head back between his knees, grabbing his hair with his quivering fingers. 'You take your time. I'll get some food on.'

They sat in silence across the fire from each other, both feasting on the pheasant that Johns had butchered and cooked like he was a professional chef, his knives finding a different use. He took off his cloak at the warmth of the fire, showing a blood-red shirt with a rip along the bottom, a black flame sewn at the collar.

The adrenaline surge Frank had suffered that morning had subsided, leaving him hungry and exhausted, both physically and mentally. The autumn sun had reached its peak but provided little warmth in the cave, its delicate rays drained by the black of the forest and what Frank knew lay beyond.

'Eat some more,' said Johns, slicing more flesh off the bird and tossing it to Frank. 'You must have had all your wits scared out of you by that shit-fest of a monster.' Frank took it and ate, then drank clumsily from the water bottle Johns offered him, soothed by his calm, unafraid tone. Frank couldn't help glancing to the cave entrance, wondering what had become of his friends, knowing he would never see them again. 'Don't worry about them,' said Johns without a look up. 'They'll be fine.'

'Why was she so scared of you?'

'Balal isn't scared of anything, except the Black Flame. Anyone else unlucky enough to stumble into her and her bunch of savages won't live. Quite handy for Irundi. But she quivers at the sight of us. She knows what we're capable of and gives us as much respect as something without any morals can.' He looked at Frank. Frank looked blank – Johns, an assassin. 'How did you manage to get past her on the way in? There's nothing that escapes the Sapirai's attention in the silent forest.'

Frank just shrugged. Johns didn't push it.

'How did you know we'd be here?' This time Johns shrugged.

'Instinct. I know the young Asaro girl's a bit of an adventurer, so is that friend of hers. Seems like you all are. Once you'd all headed back, I checked with a pal in Rhaeder who found out none of you were around. So I hauled my way over here and waited.' He dipped his eyes to his hands. 'I should have warned her.'

'About what?'

'About how sorcerers wouldn't be welcomed.' Frank let his words settle. 'We learned that the hard way.' Johns noticed the question in Frank's expression and looked into the flames. 'I was there when it happened.'

Frank's jaw fell open.

'You mean you were at the castle.' Johns shot him a sideways glance.

'What else would I mean?' His testiness rose to the surface, making Frank feel foolish although why he wouldn't understand Frank's surprise was odd. Frank looked at his cloak, his shirt.

'So you were an assassin?' Johns glanced at the back of his hands. 'At the castle?'

'Was. Is. Still am, I suppose.' He sucked the remaining flesh off a bone and threw it into the fire, grabbing a cloth and wiping his mouth. 'It never leaves you.' He twitched his nose and stared into the lithe amber flames that danced before them. 'I was at the castle for years. Served my time. Some might say I was the best.' He spoke quietly and deliberately. 'But I got tired of the place. A few contacts used to come in regularly and they'd tell me about the outside world. I'd see them getting older, greyer, their eyes rich with the colour of their lives and even though I'd sworn the blood oath to the assassins' guild, I could feel myself getting a bit restless.' Frank watched his hands, the array of white scars glowed in the firelight as Johns flexed his fingers and clenched his fists as he spoke.

'Then we got this new contact. Young guy. Turns out he'd trained as an assassin, ex-Excelsus graduate, and was going to join us at the castle, but he'd met a girl and wanted to stay with her rather than devote his life – what would be his long long life – to the cause, so the guild struck a deal with him to allow him to live on the outside and gather information about the Simbrian and send it back to Qaas and Zachery. Him and I became friends.' Frank noticed Johns glance at the two bed rolls. 'I asked if I could be granted the same privilege and they point-blank refused.' Johns sighed. 'So life went on as usual for a few months.' He paused. A deliberate break in his tale as a distant look flushed his face. He lowered his voice. 'Then *she* came.'

58

THE CHOICE

Frank couldn't tear his eyes away, Johns continued to stare ahead as he took up one of his blades and began to run his fingers gently up and down its deadly edge. Frank's silence acted as his cue to continue.

'She brought the shield down.' His lips tensed. 'Right in the middle of a thunderstorm, as if that was an omen.' He loosed a laugh under his breath. 'We reset it straight away but it just rained and rained. Had to wait a week for a sunny day to set it again. She told us she was fleeing from Kzarlac, from Etamin Dahke the darkest of sorcerers, that she needed protection, something Qaas was happy to believe, but she never revealed how she knew about us, let alone how she found us and how she evaded Balal.'

Frank absent-mindedly rubbed his left palm.

'What was she like?'

'I hate to say it, but she was lovely. Spellbinding. Everyone loved her. I remember she had this shimmering golden hair and a smile to make the fireflies dance. But there was something else about her, calculating, brazen. Or perhaps that's me looking back on it. She made herself at home and became one of us in no time. We were all taken in. Morrin most of all.' He caught the question in Frank's face. 'The stupid man let his heart, or something in his pants, rule his head. He was trusted with the safety of...' Johns stopped himself. 'Anyway, she stole something, something Morrin was entrusted with, something beyond valuable, and disappeared into the night.'

Johns spoke with the bland monotone that Frank had come to expect but the subtle inflection told him something of the episode remained with him.

'So what happened?' Johns turned his neck from side to side, stretching the sinews and popping his joints.

'Morrin selected our best to go after her.' He turned and looked into Frank's enquiring eyes. 'Me. To get back what she took. I was to find her.' He paused. 'And ensure she never had the opportunity to seek us out again.' Spoken with ice-cold numbness.

To hear Johns, the odd-ball recluse, talk of his pathway to the murder of a woman sent a shiver through Frank's veins. He knew it was wrapped inside an assassin's soul but, still, he found it chilling that the man who sat before him would end a life without a second thought.

'But you didn't go back,' said Frank. Johns shook his head and Frank detected a barely audible sigh. The assassin reached for his cup and took a small mouthful.

'No.' Johns closed his eyes. Frank waited for him to elaborate. He didn't.

'Why not?' A reluctant look filled Johns's face.

'I already knew,' he said. 'Knew I'd not be going back.' He looked back to Frank. 'I wanted my life back. *A* life. So I deserted.' A thoughtful look. 'Two years before I started noticing things like the rain on my face, the taste of the food – started enjoying them again.'

'Not the most difficult of decisions,' said Frank, feeling the range of emotions about his short, suffocating stay at the castle.

But Johns just stared into the flames. A distant look descended on his grouchy features. Frank watched as his eyes glassed. Johns chewed the inside of his mouth.

'The hardest,' he said. 'It was the hardest thing I've ever had to do.' He looked at Frank. 'To leave behind something so special.' His words were laced with sadness. Johns got up and walked to the mouth of the cavern, propping his hand up on the arc of stone, and stared into the knotted black of the trees. 'That was over twenty years ago,' he said. 'And I'm still not sure I made the right choice.'

59

THE WAIT

After a while, Johns re-joined Frank by the fire. He took another two birds from the frame and started the process of preparing them for cooking. Frank watched him caress his blade like it was a living part of his gnarled hand. But he wasn't hungry. He couldn't shake off how badly their escape had gone. He'd nearly got himself skinned and gutted while the others had now vanished back to the soulless woodland fortress where, he assumed, they would be kept under much tighter security to spend their endless lives working for Qaas and her tiny puppet regime.

He couldn't leave them, nor could he face going back or running the gauntlet of the Sapirai.

Johns didn't strike up any sort of conversation. Happy with the quiet and the embodiment of someone used to spending their time alone.

'What are we going to do?' said Frank. Johns didn't look up.

'Wait a while,' he said. 'We'll just wait a while.'

'Wait for what?' said Frank. The rise in his voice not disturbing Johns one bit. 'We can't just leave them.'

Johns didn't stir.

'Just wait a while,' he repeated.

Frank let out an audible huff without response. Despite his new found admiration for his reclusive cave-mate, the move to inaction grated. His friends were out there and, after all they'd experienced he was determined not to stand idly by and allow them to be held captive. But he needed Johns's help.

He got up and dumped himself against the cave wall, looking

271

out. Frank watched the trees, watched Johns as the afternoon began to drift by in helpless silence. His body ached. The bindings on his wrists had left tender bruises and his legs and arms were flecked with a patchwork of cuts, the lashes from the harsh woodland as they'd made their escape from the monster that lurked somewhere out there in the darkness.

He paced the cave, pausing at the entrance each time. Johns looked like he'd nodded off, although Frank suspected a calm alertness permanently ran in his veins.

Something changed in the wind. Noises behind the tree line. At first he thought he'd imagined it, but the heavy silence of the forest just amplified any sound within. He took a step back, pressing himself into the shadows. There it was again, closer. He snapped his head to Johns, who hadn't moved.

Noises once more. Footsteps approaching from outside. Frank retreated in to the cave, beyond the fire, beyond Johns. Many footsteps. And there was just the two of them. Two, against the whole might of Balal's bloodthirsty woodland legion. Johns didn't move. He sat staring into the charring timber as it glowed like a sunset at his feet. He was the picture of studied calm, blinking slowly despite the rustle in the twilight outside. Johns's unruffled quiet did nothing to diminish the pictures in Frank's mind. Sharp desperate images of running from the feral beast. But there was nowhere to run, they'd end up being skewered on the end of Balal's double-pronged spear. Still Johns didn't stir.

Movement. Movement at the mouth of the cave had Frank taking further a step back, ensuring Johns was between him and the advancing strangers. His breath quickened, drying his throat, but he felt himself sag with relief as the unlikely faces of Gabby, Anya and Cas appeared in the failing light. Despite his fatigue, because of it, he felt tears well in his eyes and he fought to keep them from falling. They all ran to hug each other, even Johns looked up, allowing himself a look of mild elation. Frank looked at their faces, taut and grey.

'How...?' Gabby's voice trailed off as she spotted Johns. A question on her face as she turned back to Frank.

'He saved my life.' Frank glanced back. 'Turns out he's got quite a story to tell.' He looked back to the three tired but relieved faces. 'But how did you make it back?'

Gabby looked back to the cave entrance as more hushed footsteps drew near. Frank's ease at seeing his friends left him as fear seeped its way back into his veins. A figure appeared, closely followed by another, their cloaks and hoods silhouetted in the cave entrance.

Johns was immediately on his feet, blade drawn with a faint rush of steel on leather as the two approached. The smaller figure, dagger in hand, pushed their hood down, revealing the flushed face of Esryn who stood with her usual poise as the flickering light from the fire revealed her to Johns.

Johns froze. Completely froze.

Frank immediately saw a look of absolute shock sweep over his face as his mouth opened slightly. Something passed between him and the pale, honed assassin. More than recognition. The cavern shuddered at the sound of Esryn's blade as it fell from her hand and clattered to the floor. Her hand went to her mouth and, for the first time, Frank saw her smile.

'Millington?' she gasped.

The other stranger strode in, past Esryn and the four teenagers and towards where Johns was standing.

'It's okay Millington, she's with me,' he said from beneath his black mask.

Normally, Frank would have wanted to understand what had just passed between the young killer and his old, reclusive saviour but something else grasped him. The voice from behind the mask made Frank's blood spike. He turned as the masked man stopped next to Johns, his mind all of a sudden a web of confusion. He must have misheard, must have been mistaken. There was no way...but the man spoke again to Johns:

'Balal give you any trouble?' Johns gave the slightest shake of his head, his eyes soft. He didn't, couldn't, break his eyes from Esryn.

The eyes behind the mask met Frank's. Familiar eyes. He recognised them immediately, as he'd recognised the voice, yet knew he must be wrong. Must be. They couldn't be the hissing and unwelcome tones of his uncle Simeon.

60

THE REUNION

Simeon pushed his mask down. Frank could see the sweat gleaming on his top lip, wet hair flat against his forehead. A glance, a mere glance in his direction. Frank felt his teeth grind and his face tense at the man who had robbed his dad of his secret, who had made his world less safe, less safe for his friends.

He resisted the urge to throw himself at the miserable stick of a man and twist his snivelling head from his neck and stood frozen by the fact that he couldn't understand what he was doing there, in the middle of the evil woodland, talking to Millington Johns like he was his oldest buddy.

Johns still eyed Esryn. He appeared stuck with indecision until Esryn ran to him and threw her arms around him.

Johns grabbed at her, balling his fists into the material of her cloak and, to Frank's surprise, Johns started to weep, pressing his face into Esryn's red hair.

Simeon retreated into the cave as Frank glanced at his friends, unsure what to make of what appeared to be a reunion of some sort.

'How did you get away?' he said, drawing them over, away from Johns and Esryn, away from his loathsome uncle.

'Once they got us back to the castle, Morrin locked us in our room,' said Anya. 'I don't think they knew what to do with us, so we just waited. We all thought they'd thrown into a dungeon.'

'But then,' said Cas. 'Esryn came and got us, along with him.' He twitched his head toward Simeon, who'd sat himself on one of the bed rolls. 'Before we knew it, they'd got us out. No questions. No messing.'

'Did they take the key?'

Cas shook his head.

'Gabby still has it. I don't think they even know we've got it.'

'But Esryn,' said Frank. 'What persuaded her to come?'

But he knew, just by looking at how she clung to Johns like she would never let go, that Simeon must have told her. Johns had said leaving Irundi was the most difficult of decisions, now he knew why. Esryn took a step back, running the flat of her hand over Johns's face with a tenderness reserved only for lovers.

'You look...older,' she said, wiping her tears.

'And you still look as lovely as the day I left.' His voice quavered. 'I'm so sorry,' he said.

Esryn touched a gentle finger to his lips.

'I know you had to go,' she said. 'But now I have you back.'

'You're not going back?'

She shook her head.

'Never.'

'But you'll – '

'Grow old and die?' Johns nodded. 'I'd rather die a thousand times then spend another day without you.' She hugged him again. Frank noticed the sway of the knotted red material in her braid. An exact match for the shirt Johns wore.

His three friends looked beyond exhausted. Frank knew the dash through the forest would have been utterly relentless and, having related the story of his rescue in the hands of Johns to them, they now sat in silence by the fire, edging away from the nightmare from which they'd only just escaped, each lost in their own thoughts.

Johns and Esryn were slowly sharpening their blades on whetstones, a well-honed ritual. Frank noticed how their legs were touching, a comfortable bond that looked on its way to mending. She'd not taken her eyes off him as Frank told them how Johns had grabbed him just moments from his death. The slow, fond look of something with much greater depth than just friendship.

Simeon lingered further into the cave before shuffling towards the silent gathering and positioning himself as far away from Frank as he could. Frank glowered into the fire, forcing himself not to look across and through the amber glow. Only the methodical shift of stone on steel broke the air. Gabby sat next to Frank, tugging at her sleeves to keep in the warmth, pressing herself against him. Johns held up his knife, inspecting the edge closely.

'Are you sure we're safe here,' said Cas.

Gabby shook her head at him, looking at the deadly cut-throats woven between them. Johns gave a slight nod.

'Don't worry,' he said. 'Balal is afraid of nothing, except those from the Sandulum guild. She knows to stay well clear.'

'And Morrin?'

The assassins exchanged looks. Esryn continued to sharpen her scimitar in silence, Simeon stared into the fire.

'He won't come,' said Johns.

Frank caught the edge of his unconvincing tone. The ambitious head of the guard at the castle, leave them alone? Like hell he would.

61

UNFRIENDED

As the day darkened, Johns brewed some tea using nettles from the small store of supplies and started cooking the brace of pheasants he'd prepared earlier as sharp appetites took over from the day's trials. They all looked gaunt and hungry and in need of a month's rest but still managed some quiet conversation.

Simeon had moved away from the fire and was crouched against the far cavern wall cleaning his boots. It was difficult to know if he just wanted to give Johns and Esryn some space, or whether he was deliberately avoiding being near Frank and although Frank was beyond grateful that he and the others had escaped, his thoughts festered on the man who had betrayed his family, who was in bed with Dagmar, certain that Johns and Esryn, life-long protectors of Kester's secrets, wouldn't know.

He was obviously close to Johns, but that didn't mean that Johns knew about Simeon's duplicity and as the heady smell of roasting game filled the cave, Frank felt his anger tugging hard at him and he kept throwing blackened looks in his uncle's direction as he went about his slow, calm cleaning.

'You okay?' said Cas, who followed Frank's eyes across the cave. Frank didn't answer, but got up and stalked over to Simeon who glanced up through his dark eyebrows as he heard Frank approach. Frank stood a pace away from him, daring him to look him in the eye. Simeon ignored him.

'I know all about what you did, Simeon.'

Frank could feel the spite in his mouth, the flash of his barely leashed anger. He sensed the pause in the conversation around the fire and five pairs of eyes on his back. Simeon glanced in their direction, a slight twist of his gaunt face, covered with disinterest. With the merest look up at Frank he went back to scraping the dirt off his boots.

The red mist in Frank rose. He stepped toward his uncle, standing over him and shoved him on the shoulder, making him take a step sideways to keep his balance. Frank took a quick look over his shoulder as Johns shifted in his seat. Esryn looked on with sharp concentration.

'Did you hear what I said?'

Simeon stopped what he was doing, but looked straight ahead, taking in a long breath, then started scraping his boots again. Not a glance at Frank.

'Why don't you look at me, you coward,' spat Frank, grabbing Simeon's arm.

Before Frank had a chance to think, Simeon was on his feet, boots dropped, his fist instantly balled into Frank's shirt front. Frank felt himself being turned around and in half a heartbeat Simeon had him pinned against the cave wall. He was shoved hard. Blunt, cold rock pressing into his back. Despite his scrawny frame, Frank was shocked at how strong he was, like a wiry prize-fighter.

Now Simeon's sunken eyes met his; not the look of someone wanting to do him any harm, not the killer look that Esryn wore like a trophy, just the face of concern, a look to quell the anger that flushed on Frank's face. Simeon held Frank there for few a moments, letting the wrath eke out, then let go and stepped back, a look of discomfort barely hidden in the shadows. He held his hands up, palms facing Frank.

'Apologies, Frank. I didn't mean to...' He inspected the ground between them. 'Sometimes my instincts and training get the better of me.'

Frank stepped away from the rock, feeling the bruising beginning on his back. Thoughts of dishing out any physical retribution on his uncle quickly vanished like the rising smoke from the fire. The clothes, the mask and cloak told him one thing. His gutless weasel and poor excuse for an uncle was one of them. One of the Sandulum assassins. Trained in the cold art of killing, even though he surely couldn't be.

Frank looked him up and down.

'And what, exactly, do you think you know about me, Frank?' His fingers fidgeted and his angular shoulders twitched.

'That you're just going to turn us all over to Dagmar.'

A laugh escaped from under Simeon's breath.

'Believe me, Frank. That's the last thing I'd ever do.'

'But I know you're on his side. You were helping him and Markowitz get the prophesy.' Frank's words came fast. Simeon closed his eyes and shook his head like a disappointed schoolmaster.

'You know, Frank, for a smart kid you can be so stupid.'

Frank recoiled and burned.

'But my Dad can't stand you.'

'I know,' said Simeon, matter-of-factly, his voice sounding so underwhelmed it was obvious he didn't care.

'You knew my Dad was a guardian. And you stole his fragment of the Simbrian and gave it to Dagmar.' More shuffling and silence from the fire. Where Frank thought he was playing his ace, that his little nugget of truth would send Simeon flapping, his uncle just shook his head and shrugged.

'Yet here I am rescuing you and your friends from goodness knows what sort of end.'

Frank clenched his teeth. In his haste to get right down Simeon's throat, he hadn't stopped to think how the whole situation was playing out, his fatigue, the fog in his head muddling his thoughts. All of a sudden he had no words. 'Things aren't always what they seem, Frank.'

But Frank could sense the whole mood had changed in the cave. He glanced over Simeon's shoulder to the fire, his eyes flicking from Cas to Anya before locking on to Gabby's. They had all stopped what they were doing at the rising note in Frank's voice as he'd stepped away from the cave wall. Frank turned back to Simeon, resisting the temptation to punch him, knowing it would be met with more precision combat of the type Anya had been honing for the past weeks. Simeon now looked at him, waiting. Frank thought through his next move when he was aware of someone closing behind him. He turned.

'And when were you going to tell us?' Gabby's harsh tone cut into him. She stopped as he felt her daggers land, scoring painful hits through her rising anger. He opened his mouth but no words came out. Cas and Anya stood. All three of his friends looked at him through disbelieving eyes. 'Well?'

'Well what?' He attempted a half-smile to try and buy himself some time, to think of a plausible excuse but Gabby closed in on him, determined to rob him of any escape route.

'Don't you *dare*, Frank.' Again, he had no words. 'Don't you *dare* try and fob this off like it doesn't matter.'

He noticed her fists clench, sensed the darkest tempest brewing beneath her skin, could hear it in the quiver of her voice.

'Your dad's a guardian,' said Cas from across the cavern, his echoing words written with deep disappointment. 'I can't believe you didn't tell us.'

'Everything we've been through,' said Gabby through her teeth, the muscle in her jaw tensing, the intensity in her voice like a living thing. '*Everything*. And you *chose* not to tell us.'

He could sense she was on the verge of tears, her usually bold adolescent features turned hard and threatening, her temper primed to break free of its tether.

'I didn't think it was...'

'What didn't you think it was? Any of our business?' she spat, a deep loathing pulling itself from her lungs and into her throat. Raw emotion manifested itself on her skin as she took a step towards him. He flinched. 'Like none of this has anything to do with us? Like we're all just three dumb bystanders while you try and sort all of this out in your own stupid world? Without us? Aren't we in this together, or is this the Frank Penny show and we're just his stupid, useless friends?' She didn't take her burning eyes off him. 'Do we all mean *so* little to you that you felt you couldn't tell us? Thought you'd just keep it from us?' Her words boiled. 'I thought you were my friend, but you're not.' He felt her words knock the wind out of him. 'You *bastard*. You selfish, selfish *bastard*.'

Frank glanced at Anya, missing the split second when Gabby decided to deliver a full-bodied slap that bit his face and sent him sideways, her fingernail ripping a chunk of skin from his cheek, pain searing up into his eye socket. She piled into him, unleashing her temper like a malevolent spirit, throwing well-aimed blows like a seasoned bare-knuckle fighter as Frank closed his eyes and held up his hands to protect himself, pain and guilt on his skin. The only sound he could hear was the thumping frenzied beating of her fists on his face and head and Gabby's wild breath as she expended all her energy in her punches.

She stopped only when Simeon stepped between them, probably when he felt Frank had taken enough punishment, a gentle hand on Gabby's shoulder and a silent look quelling her fury. But something deep inside Frank wanted it to continue. More, he needed her to inflict more; the suffering, the hurt, it wasn't enough, not enough for him. He wanted more; more punishment. More cleansing. More of what he deserved. He needed someone to out him for exactly what he was. A coward. A spoilt, selfish coward. Someone who deserved no pity, no understanding from those he considered his friends. He'd let them all down.

Everything went quiet. Only the depth of Gabby's boiling breaths around the cavern telling the story of the effort she had expended. Frank peered through his fingers, Gabby's black expression, fierce as a cornered bear, staring back at him. The soul of their friendship ripped out and thrown on the floor between them. He'd been pulling it to pieces since he'd learned about his dad but Gabby was the one who had decided to put it out of its misery. For good.

As Simeon lowered his hand and stepped aside Gabby stepped

forward and released a swift, hard kick to his groin with all the energy of an angry barbarian, sending Frank to the floor with a throaty howl, before she turned and headed across the cave to re-join the others, leaving Frank in a crumpled heap of wretched writhing. Unforgiven. Unfriended. Alone. He stared at the receding heels of Simeon's boots through his clouded eyes, gasping quietly as the dull ache churned his guts.

He deserved it, every last sharp cut of pain. He deserved all of it, the whole heap of wrath and misery that any one of them cared to hand to him. She was right. He knew it. He knew he should have told them, knew they would find out sooner or later and knew this was how things would end up because he had kept it to himself. Because he thought he knew best. He winced at his arrogance, at the behaviour that showed himself truly to be the son of Dagmar Dag. Of all the bad decisions he'd made since the whole quest for the Simbrian started, this had to be the worst by many, many miles.

So he lay on the cold, unforgiving floor of the cave and curled himself into a ball, waiting for the fire in his groin to extinguish itself. He knew it would dull, but that would be the easy part. Even when it had gone, he had no idea what he'd do next, couldn't see beyond the next minute.

Through narrow eyes he watched the others around the fire, picking the succulent flesh off the birds that Johns had cooked up. He could hear the murmuring of quiet speech, the occasional chuckle from Johns, Simeon and Esryn. He could see how his three friends huddled together, talking quietly, relaxed. Without him.

He let the time tick by. Even the pull of hunger wasn't enough to get him to his feet and join the group around the fire. Occasionally he'd notice eyes looking in his direction, then more hushed voices. Johns even looked round and said something to make the others laugh as he turned back, reminding Frank of Spargo's jeering in the cells back in Rhaeder. What he'd give to be back there, away from this, away from the wreckage he'd created. As the day darkened, the demon within him darkened with it, convincing himself there was no way back.

62

THE MORNING AFTER

The spat with Gabby brought him a sleepless night. The callous floor of hard rock an unrelenting thorn in his side throughout the black hours in the silent cave. Even though the fire still flickered throughout the night, cold seeped through him, mocking him as he lay where Gabby had kicked him. All that occupied his mind was the damage he'd done to his friendship with Gabby, Cas and Anya.

Not even the thought of Morrin attacking them in the silence of the moonlight entered his thoughts, even though Johns, Simeon and Esryn took turns on watch. Only the acid sting of his own disappointment in himself kept him restless. As each hour passed he felt the rising urge to talk to Gabby, to tell her it had been a mistake but she made an obvious show of settling herself as far away from him as their confined space would allow. He also knew he could never reveal the real reason for his distant and moody behaviour.

Dawn finally broke, stirring the cave into wakefulness. A milky, grey mist had enveloped the forest, the sun unable to cleave its way through, adding to Frank's misery. He kept himself wrapped up, thinking no one would want to speak to him after the previous night but, in the muffled voices of the three assassins, Cas came and sat beside him, pulling his knees to his chin.

'You alright?' he asked.

Frank propped himself up, his mind fogged from lack of sleep and the unforgiving conversations in his head. He nodded, pinching his eyes in an attempt to clear the blur. Anya chatted with Esryn, glancing over occasionally while the beautiful assassin showed her some simple moves with her deadly weaponry, nodding when Anya repeated them with unspoken ease.

Gabby sat poking the fire with a charred stick, listening to Esryn and Anya, sometimes engaging with Johns whose soft smile wrinkled his ageing face as he spoke. Not once did she so much as raise her head in his direction. It was as if he wasn't there.

'Explains why you've been so moody lately,' said Cas. 'You should have told us, you know.' He stared blankly ahead as he spoke. 'Anya said you probably had your reasons and we shouldn't be too hard on you, but a friend should know when he needs to ask for help.' Cas looked at him, a gentle smile on his lips. More than Frank deserved. More grateful he'd never been. 'I know a bit what it must feel like, remember when I thought my Dad was the Kzarlac spy? I didn't know what to think, or what you'd all think of me.'

Frank nodded and immediately realised, once again, just how wrong he'd been all along. Cas hadn't kept it to himself when they were convinced Xavier Jones was working for Kzarlac. He'd told them all straight away, despite what they all might have thought or said and the problems it might bring for their friendship. Even though Cas had been run through with shame and disbelief, he'd trusted that his friends wouldn't judge him, would help him make sense of it and, above all, would be there for him. That's what friends did. And here was Cas, throwing understanding Frank's way where he deserved none.

More bitter disappointment rose in Frank's throat; Cas had made him feel worse by trying to make him feel better, but Frank couldn't blame him for it. He knew it was a mess of his own making and his friend had instantly found room in his heart to forgive him. That's what friends did, too.

'I think I've made a real hash of things, mate,' he said. Cas put his arm around him as he slumped forward, bracing his elbows on his knees, his palms wrapped around his chin. 'A right hash.'

Johns stood and walked over to Frank and Cas. Frank's eyes followed his slow, easy gait. He stood before the two boys, scratching at the extra day's growth on his chin.

'Breakfast?' he said with a smile and a twitch of his head back to the fire. Frank shrugged. He looked over to Gabby, who chatted with Esryn, as if the shadow of their collective ordeal had created a spark of friendship between them.

Frank drew in a long breath. He was starving and whatever Johns had been cooking up set his stomach growling. Johns descended onto his haunches, rubbing his knuckles.

'We all bear our scars,' he said, his voice low. His gaze lingered on Frank's beaten face. 'It's how we deal with them that makes us who we are.' A flicker of sympathy crossed his face. 'Come on,' he said, holding out his hand to Frank. 'Things mend. If you want them to.'

Frank grasped Johns's hand and hauled himself to his feet, slowly stretching the cramp in his bones, exiting the cold of the night and the dense feeling in his head. He brushed his fingertips at the deep gouge on his face, wincing at his own touch and looked back at Gabby who didn't break her conversation with Esryn, ignoring him; something heavy still grabbed at his insides, something he knew would take a long time to rid himself of, something that might never repair.

63

Out

The mist that straddled the trees outside gradually cleared, unlike the dense fog in Frank's head.

The three assassins stood in the small clearing at the mouth of the cave, shrouded in conversation. Esryn held Johns by the arm, leaning into him as Simeon said something that made them both laugh. A picture of easy friendship that had Frank looking at Gabby.

The four of them sat around the fire but no one offered any conversation. They should be elated. They'd prised the key of darkness from the jaws of the castle and engineered an escape. What it was all about was still a mystery, had to be important in the context of the Simbrian, but none of them looked like they gave a damn.

Frank picked at his nails, biting at the rough corners, looking up as Johns, Esryn and Simeon all walked back into the cave and set about packing up their belongings with industrial efficiency.

'Time to move out,' said Johns, swinging his pack onto his back with liquid ease. Gabby was immediately on her feet and walking towards the light, as if she'd been released from some kind of disgusting punishment in the form of sitting within six yards of Frank. Esryn sheathed her daggers, tying them so they held seamlessly to her hips and concealing others under her cloak. She unsheathed her scimitar, gave it a quick inspection and slid it back. She looked at Anya with a nod. Anya got up and followed her out to where Simeon was already packed and waiting.

Cas waited with Frank who could sense a little awkwardness. Frank just felt resigned, he could feel it on his face as Johns approached.

'Don't concern yourself, Frank,' said Johns. 'She'll come round. Feisty young thing, your girlfriend.'

Frank bristled.

'She's not my girlfriend.'

Johns shrugged.

'Just as well,' he said, kicking dust to extinguish the dying embers of the fire.

They gathered in the hollow light of the cave entrance. Simeon paced the perimeter of the small clearing and returned to the group.

'I don't think Balal will have the stomach to face three of us,' he said. 'But I can imagine revenge will be on her mind. Esryn will lead. Cas, you next then Anya.' He paused, reaching into his cloak and pulling out the longest dagger Frank had ever seen, death on its silvered blade. 'Take this. And don't hesitate if you need to use it.' Anya's face, normally fresh and unassuming became tense and humourless. She looked at Simeon and gave a single nod before taking the dagger and placing it carefully in her belt. 'Gabby, you'll be in the middle with Millington right behind, then Frank and I'll bring up the rear. All clear?'

No one spoke. Frank still couldn't make eye contact with his weasel of an uncle, still unsure of his place in all of this. Spyro had been clear that he'd stolen Lawrence's part of the Simbrian, so what was it Frank didn't understand? However, right at this moment, both Johns and Esryn were one hundred percent trusting of their fellow assassin, as were his friends. Simeon could wait. 'Let's go,' continued Simeon, looking at Johns, before turning to the students. 'Stay in line, stay close, keep moving. And if anything happens...' he scanned each of the student's faces. 'We fight, you run.'

Frank thought their ordeal would have taken much more out of them, so where they found the reserves of strength to race through the dark and twisted trees he wasn't sure. Except they all knew death was on their heels.

Esryn was like a gazelle, weaving seamlessly through the terrain. She never looked back but never got herself too far ahead, a sign she was in tune with those that followed, keeping the group tight.

With each step safety neared. Frank could hear its silent call from far up ahead. His ears were sharp, just waiting, waiting for the shrill whistle that he knew would sound. The whistle that would bring about a bloodbath. The thought shredded his nerves and wreaked havoc on his attempts to focus on the route ahead. Having Simeon at his back was strangely reassuring, kept him running, running for his life.

On they went. Frank guessed they'd been going for a little under an hour, with just a few stops to rest their aching lungs, when he saw Esryn take a shallow leap into the air and stop. For a ghastly moment, Frank thought she'd been surprised from the undergrowth until Gabby did the same. Then Frank saw it. The deep, unearthly chasm that they'd crossed goodness knows how long ago. The divide that separated the silent forest from the outside world. Frank felt a final burst of strength in his thighs as he sprinted and jumped over the evil scar and landed on the other side. Safety. They'd made it. Alive.

Suddenly the woodland erupted into birdsong, the trees had the wonder of life breathed into them and the yellowing leaves of autumn were falling around them. Frank never knew he'd miss something so simple, so much.

They all stopped, Johns and Simeon reaching into their packs for water. Cas sat on the woodland floor and doused himself from Simeon's water bottle but Gabby seemed to be struggling. She covered her face with her hands and started to cry. Her slight cries quickly becoming big, choking sobs that had them all quiet. Johns stepped forward and pulled her in. Gabby let him. Johns held her, casting a look at Esryn whose expression was of unspoken pity.

Frank resisted the urge to console her. He wanted to be the one to help, to tell her everything was going to be alright, to be the one she sought in her sorrow but, as he watched her press her head into Johns's chest he realised that ship had disappeared over the horizon.

'It's okay,' said Johns. 'It's over. No one's going to hurt you now.'

Gabby put her arms around him, her weeping showing no signs of stopping, Simeon's receding footsteps signalling the others to walk on, to give her the space her emotions needed.

They followed and waited at the edge of the woods, looking across at the Black Feather, shuffling their feet and looking anywhere but at each other. Minutes passed before Gabby and Johns appeared, Gabby making no attempt to hide her tear-stained face. No look at Frank.

Johns gave Esryn a deep hug, then looked over to the inn.

'I don't know about anyone else,' he said. 'But I could do with a beer.'

64

AL-FAJR

It was a sign of their ordeal that Frank found the sight of the Black Feather as welcoming as ice-cold limewater on a burning summer's day. Where there had been nothing to redeem it on their way into the forest, now that they all sat around a large table, each with a full pint of watery ale and sharp looks from the locals, they felt the weight of the past twenty four hours shed itself from their tired but grateful skin.

It was mid-morning, but the inn was already starting to fill and, except when they first entered, no one paid them any attention and went about their conversations – hushed and loud – with a freedom Frank thought he'd never see again. It was a huge relief to be back in civilisation, relieved in knowing that he'd aged another day but feeling like his experience had aged him far more. Not just him, all of them.

All three assassins sat with their backs to the wall, looking out into the bar area. Gabby positioned herself at the other end of the table, preferring the company of Simeon to his. Another hard slap in the face. He felt the scab on his left cheekbone where Gabby had torn a chunk from his flesh, dabbed at the bruising. A trophy, of sorts.

Frank took several large gulps from his glass, drawing comfort from the cool feeling in his throat. Cas did the same while Esryn and Johns chatted to Anya about their time before Irundi and their training.

Esryn placed her hand inside her tunic, brought it back out and placed it, palm down, on the table. Her flaming green eyes pinned Anya before she slid a sheet of paper across to her. Anya took it and read the few words that Frank could see.

'Esryn says I can try and get into the guild,' said Anya.

Esryn looked up.

'Good people are hard to find,' she said. Her eyes smouldered at Frank. 'Anya's a natural. I'm sure they'd consider her.'

Johns gave the shallowest of nods.

'Doesn't matter what they teach you at the academy of yours,' he said. 'You can't deny if someone has a natural ability.' He looked at Esryn. 'And there are only a few of those. That letter of recommendation should be all you need.'

'Can't wait to hear what your mum and dad have to say about it,' said Cas, earning him a shove. He looked at Esryn. 'You know the Bemara room?' Esryn nodded, guarded. 'Why are three of Everbleed's writings kept separate in there?'

'You mean why are they so special?'

Cas nodded.

'Of all the letters, notes and prophesies Everbleed wrote, they are the only ones that centre on anything to do with the Simbrian.'

Frank looked up, as did Gabby and Anya. Mention of the Simbrian brought their quest back into focus, the whole reason why they'd ventured to Irundi in the first place. Frank hadn't thought about it for days, wrapped up in his own troubles and their plans to escape from the castle had moved his focus completely.

'How do you know that?' he said. 'I thought only Zachery and Qaas knew what was in the room.'

Esryn looked at Johns who raised his brows.

'After all these kids have been through, I don't think there's any harm,' he said. A nod from Simeon.

Esryn took a breath and drew a mouthful from her glass, draining its contents.

'I've been in there,' she said. 'Once, when I first came to Irundi.' Her assassin's eyes went from face to face. 'I brought one of the prophesies with me and Zachery wanted to show me that it would be kept safe, so he took me to the Bemara and let me see the cabinet.

He didn't have much of a collection back then, he's accumulated a lot more since.'

'What was it,' said Frank. 'The letter you brought?'

Esryn looked into her empty glass.

'Everbleed wrote a prophesy about the Simbrian heir,' she said, her words nearly knocking Frank from his stool. She looked up. 'That's what Bakran is there to track, so we can find out who it is, the one with the perfect bloodline. So they can be protected.'

An image of Valaine De Villiers entered Frank's head, her closeness to Dagmar, Etamin's secret child. Did Bakran know that? The family tree didn't appear complete when they'd looked.

'But Dagmar has it,' said Anya.

Esryn shook her head.

'There were copies made,' she said. 'The one I took to Irundi was the original.'

'How did you have it in the first place?' said Anya.

'My grandmother knew Everbleed,' said Esryn. 'When she knew I would be going to Irundi, she gave it to me for safekeeping.'

'Is that what the woman was after?' said Frank.

Both Esryn and Johns shook their heads.

'No,' said Esryn. 'I told you what she took.' A glance at Johns. 'The key - something beyond value. Something irreplaceable and dangerous.' Her face creased into a look of hostility.

'The key of darkness,' said Johns.

'It fires the Simbrian,' said Simeon, his hollow eyes staring at them over the pint glass that he held with both hands. 'The Simbrian can be re-created but it needs the heir and the key to operate it.'

He said it like he was talking about a new piece of farm machinery, but in a second Frank could feel the final pieces of the eternal jigsaw as they began to move themselves into place. The woman who had robbed the castle had used the key to destroy the first creation of the Simbrian, giving them the clues to find the second one.

Why it had led them to take it, when it was completely safe

where it was, would never have been found, was something he hadn't begun to work out. 'Irundi was meant to keep both the key and the identity of the heir from falling into the wrong hands.'

'Why is the prophesy so important?' said Frank.

'You don't know how important,' said Esryn, pausing. She ran the tip of her index finger in a small circle on the table. 'I will always remember it. *When the end of a summer comes, a child from the dark and the light, the one that completes the circle, will choose between a better future and eternal night. The secrets of countless generations will gather and a riddle that only exceptional talents can unravel. Hidden until great danger befalls them. There will be a reckoning. Beware — the red flame will be summoned and the power will pass if the heir is slain.*'

He knew the first part, had witnessed Everbleed's toothless face in the flames, but the rest of the message sent a chill through his bones as Esryn went on. 'It confirms something that no one knows. The Simbrian can only be controlled by the Simbrian heir.' She paused. 'But the heir's power can pass to the person who kills them, but only once the Simbrian is complete.'

Her words sent a shiver through Frank. He had no kind words for De Villiers, had never liked anything about her. She was offensive, angry and treated everyone like they were her worst enemy. But if Dagmar knew about her identity, then she was heading down a darkened, dead-end alleyway with nothing but his sword and her ultimate fate at the end of it.

'We live in troubled times,' muttered Simeon.

'We know Dagmar only needs one more part of the Simbrian,' said Gabby, turning the heads of everyone at the table. None of the assassins showed any emotion, as if they were used to receiving and processing the information of nightmares. Frank glowered at Simeon. Johns nodded.

'Troubled times indeed,' he said.

'Is there a guardian in the castle?' said Gabby. 'Qaas, or Zachery?'

Frank felt the squirm of his inside. He expected a sarcastic comment from Gabby about his secret-keeping, but she didn't even look at him, couldn't bring herself to, despite his pleading eyes.

'Don't tell me,' said Cas. 'It has to be Qaas.'

It could be any of them although she sounded an obvious candidate. Kester's sister, but Esryn shook her head.

'No, I think that would be too dangerous.' Not that keeping yourself hidden in the depths of the unforgiving forest made you an easy target, thought Frank. 'No, it's not Qaas.' The four teenagers stared in anticipation.

'It's the Al-Fajr woman.'

Frank nodded. Once, he might have been filled with excitement at the revealing of a guardian, to place another welcome piece into the puzzle but the gloss had been wiped away.

'How can you be sure?' said Anya. 'I don't think I've heard her speak.'

'She's never mentioned it, not to me, but I heard Zachery asking her about it once. She said that she hadn't been able to talk about it unless someone asked her. I can't think why not, given what she knew about us and how safe she must have felt.'

'So she's safe, then,' said Anya, looking around the table. 'I mean, it'll be impossible for Dagmar to discover where she is.'

It was as if Anya was about to bring their quest to protect the guardians to a sudden end, that they could be sure a guardian was finally out of Dagmar's reach.

But Frank knew.

As soon as Esryn spoke about Al-Fajr's discussion with Zachery, he knew. He thought back to his conversation in Spargo's office, when Spargo had spoken about the curse on the guardians. How they were unable even utter anything about their guardianship if they'd already been relieved of it. Not unless someone asked them first. He knew what it meant, that Al-Fajr didn't have it any more and he considered the likelihood that she'd found her way to Irundi simply for her own safety.

'But there's something else,' said Esryn. 'Something to do with

Excelsus.' Frank looked up, his interest caught by the question in her voice. Esryn turned her head to Anya. He noticed a shift in the others. 'I thought about it when you were telling me about the academy during our training. Something you said to me.' Anya turned her mouth up, 'Al-Fajr is the rough Rossian translation of her name.' Frank sat up. Johns's eyebrows dipped, as if he was working out something in his head. Even Simeon looked on with interest. Esryn's gold-flecked eyes travelled from face to face. 'It means "princess and hunter of moons".'

65

MORRIN

Hunter of moons. Surely not. *Surely not.*

Esryn just stared blankly at him. No words, but Frank was suddenly beyond listening. He looked at Gabby who, this time, met his eyes.

They'd all got the connection, even if Esryn had no idea what it meant for their quest. Frank could barely take it in; he knew Esryn wasn't wrong, he'd noticed how thorough and practiced she was with anything she did, cast from a careful, meticulous mould.

And how obvious did it appear right at that moment? Moonhunter's constant and enduring interest in Frank's progress; in the Simbrian, in everything they were doing, her attempts to elicit information from them but without ever mentioning or referring to it specifically. It had never been just idle curiosity, it was more intense than that but why not just ask. Others would. Spargo had. So why didn't she? Perhaps they brushed her too close; touched her and her secret and something bit her like the sharp edge of toothache.

Now things were different; now things had changed. Now he thought about it, it seemed mind-numbingly obvious – Moonhunter, his mother's adolescent lover, was a guardian of the Simbrian.

Frank drained the remainder of his beer, attempting to process the information Esryn had just laid before them. He couldn't and, judging by their faces, neither could the others, but he was the only one who knew Al-Fajr wasn't who they were looking for. It was the unassuming head of Excelsus. He caught Simeon looking at him, certain that Esryn's revelation would stir something from his academy days, his time spent in the secret society inhabited by

Spargo, Dagmar and his dad. Knowledge gleaned about the curse that inflicted anyone who spoke about the secret they once held.

His mouth was suddenly dry and he found himself looking around the tavern to signal for another beer when he was aware of heads turning and chairs scraping further down, towards the door. A wave of hush spread through the inn, heading gradually in their direction. A glance down the table confirmed that all three of their assassin companions had already noticed, two steps ahead of him. Frank noticed the sharp eyes, the hands going under the table, the utter concentration blotting everything else out. He looked back, feeling the pinpricks of nerves on his skin. Looking back to the bar his breath stalled at the sight of the orange streak as the sea of people parted and up to the table strode the massive figure of Morrin.

Morrin stared down at them, his chest straining in his black shirt, ice dripping from his dark eyes. The whole tavern watched him, the strange figure from an even stranger time, before gradually going back to their conversations, cautious glances on his broad back. He sifted the faces in front of him, coming to rest on Johns.

'Well, well,' he said. 'Millington Johns. Desertion seems to have aged you.'

Johns dipped his head.

'Morrin,' said Johns. A mere acknowledgement. 'You're a long way from your small empire.'

Morrin snorted and looked a Simeon.

'I never trusted you, Peth.'

'Likewise,' said Simeon, his eyes narrow, unyielding.

'You know why I'm here.' Morrin jerked his chin at Esryn. 'You need to come back with me.'

Straight to the point. Silence. Morrin's features stayed stone-still, as grey as clouds at the head of a rain-storm. Esryn's eyes couldn't bring themselves to meet his. She picked at an imaginary spot on the oak table and tightened her lips.

'She doesn't need to listen to you, Morrin,' said Johns, his eyes feeling for Esryn's. Morrin shifted his gaze.

'And why should anyone listen to a traitor like you, Millington.'

Movement from behind Morrin had the bar emptying rapidly. The inn filled with the sound of scraping chairs and rushing feet as three more figures, clad in black, showed themselves, their weapons already gripped firmly. Johns stilled, hunched over his drink, still eyeing Esryn as a sinister smile broke over Morrin's face, reminding Frank of Dagmar. Esryn pushed herself back on her chair.

'I have all bases covered, Esryn,' said Morrin. 'You know the drill.' His other assassins fanned themselves out, drawing the eyes of the three at the table. Esryn was their best killer but Frank wasn't sure of Simeon's ability or whether time might have rusted Johns a little. 'Time's knocked the edge off you, Millington,' said Morrin. 'I can see it. You don't train every day, like we do, so think before you do anything that might end your short life and those at this table.'

'Come, now, Morrin. You know it's against the code to harm fellow guild members.' Calm tones from Johns.

'Since when has the code bothered a run-away like you?'

'Why does she have to go back with you?' said Anya, a fierce look that Frank had rarely seen before.

'The castle needs her.' He looked at Gabby, a nod of his head. 'And her. I have my orders.'

Johns drummed his fingers on the table. A casual gesture.

'Let them be, Morrin,' he said. 'Just let them be.' He lifted his head, meeting Morrin's wild eyes. 'You go back to your small world, your immortal prison if you wish, but let these youngsters go.'

'And why should I do that.'

'Too long, Morrin,' said Johns with a slight shake of his head. 'You've been there too long. Too long for your own good. So long that you've forgotten.' Morrin curled his lip and growled.

'You stopped having any say over me the moment you left the castle, you deserter.' He looked at Johns like he was about to wipe him off his boot. He flicked his head at Esryn again. 'Let's get going.' He looked back to Gabby. 'And bring that girl.'

Esryn looked at Johns, then to Morrin, indecision on her brow.

Frank could only imagine the pull of the life bond she'd made with her role in Morrin's band of lethal weapons set against an uncertain and foreign existence in the outside world with the man she loved. He watched as the strong and confident woman he'd encountered these last few weeks fought the battle in her mind.

'I'm going nowhere,' said Gabby. 'And Esryn's staying with us.'

Morrin snarled.

'Shut it, sorcerer.'

Johns let out a chuckle under his breath.

'Glad to see you're okay pushing young girls around,' he said.

Simeon didn't try to hide the wide smirk across his face as Morrin's temperature rose.

'I think Millington has a point,' said Simeon. 'You should try someone your own size, if you can find someone as freakishly large as you.'

'Give me a reason why I shouldn't wipe that grin off your face, Peth,' barked Morrin, his hands flexing on the hilt of his dagger.

None of the assassins looked particularly bothered, although Frank felt they were stalling, mentally weighing the situation, their options.

'Two reasons,' said Johns. Morrin lifted his chin. 'First, there's a big old world out there, Morrin. A world that you used to inhabit before you got all high and mighty, wanting to rule your own sweet little kingdom. Don't you remember what it was like to dream, to have something to aim for, to want to grip the world by the scruff of its neck and explore every dark corner it has to offer? Have you forgotten what it's like to see a different sunrise and not the same old sky day after day after long, lonely day?' Morrin's lips twitched. 'Immortality has a very high price indeed, Morrin. Look at me; I'm many years older than when I left the castle, but my life is richer for it, even if I had to make the greatest sacrifice.' He glanced at Esryn who had fixed her eyes on him. He held her stare and a tear came to his eye. She reached across the table and took his hand gently in hers. 'The greatest sacrifice,' he repeated. He turned back to Morrin.

'It's the life in your days that really matter. Not the days in your life.' He pulled his hand from Esryn's. 'But you know I gave up Esryn to live my life how I wanted. Something I regret.' He glanced at Esryn, the shades of something unspoken between them. Both of their faces bore the invisible scars of something that once was, that had withered and trembled on the ground, but the fresh green of life was still there, barely, but it was still there. 'Life is full of choices, Morrin, some good, some bad, but some are completely impossible. But we all do what we think is right at the time. So let them be, let them live their lives.'

Silence had spread across the table, broken only by Morrin's shuffling feet. Frank found he couldn't take his eyes off of Johns as he stared across the table top, pity written in large letters across his rutted brow. Frank glanced at Gabby, caught her eye and they both looked away.

Morrin let out a huff.

'Very sentimental, Millington,' he said, although without the edge that had tainted his voice so far. 'And your other reason?'

'Oh, that.' Johns looked around the room at the faces of the other three assassins. 'If you don't leave us alone, we're going to whip your sorry arses right back to Irundi.'

66

THE FIGHT

Before Frank could even start a breath he was propelled back as Johns, Simeon and Esryn lifted the table and shoved it, top-first, towards Morrin. The dull thunk of daggers hitting bare wood followed, then the almighty grunt of Morrin being floored as the table connected with his large frame, knocking him back, off balance.

In the time it took Morrin's accomplices to throw their weapons, Esryn had her scimitar drawn. She was up and across to one of them in half a heartbeat, her feet gracefully brushing the seats of three chairs en-route, her blade wielded like a poet utters a verse. She dropped one of them – not fatally, but enough to disarm, her adversary immediately putting their arms in the air.

Simeon sprang at another, throwing a hefty glass which caught his opponent on the temple, smashing and sending them sideways. Simeon was on them blade in hand as his opponent went to draw their sword, wrestling them to the ground. Frank and Cas cowered behind the upturned table as chairs and beer glasses tumbled around them.

Anya stood as the third assassin readied to strike at Esryn's back while she disarmed her opponent. Esryn turned, aware of the danger, ready to dodge as the blow whistled in. She twisted her lithe body back, avoiding the tip of the blade by a matter of inches before raining in a combination of hard punches, flooring the assassin in an instant.

Johns had leaped across to pin Morrin down, bearing all his weight on the big man's chest, his dagger held at Morrin's ear.

'I said you should leave them, Morrin,' he said amidst the

crashing of furniture around them. 'What is it about good advice that you don't get?'

Morrin snorted derision, pushing Johns off, his immense weight tossing him like a doll. Johns crashed through a chair, splintering it into pieces and rolled over, up on his feet like a veteran acrobat, placing two yards between him and Morrin whose blackened stare bore into him. Morrin leapt at him, connecting with his huge fists, bloodying Johns's nose as he delivered a fist to Morrin's temple, jerking his head sideways. More adeptly aimed blows connected before Morrin stepped back, a look of surprise on his face, one that showed he thought he would walk all over Johns but Johns just wiped his nose and gave a smile, a smile that showed he wasn't afraid, that he relished the fight.

Simeon still wrestled on the floor, his opponent delivering a knee to his exposed flank, knocking the wind out of him, gaining the upper hand as they drew a small knife from their boot. As Simeon attempted to recover, Frank saw the assassin's grip tighten on the handle, ready to thrust it into Simeon's gut. On instinct, he threw himself across the floor and grabbed the wrist of Simeon's assailant as he prepared for a killer blow.

The assassin rolled over, his back pinning Frank to the floor, pressing down, delivering a solid elbow into Frank's ribs. Frank let go, but Simeon was already weighing in, fists flying, not letting up until the assassin went limp.

Neither Johns nor Morrin made a move, eyes on each other, assessing, considering their next moves.

'Come on, Morrin,' said Johns. 'I'm an old man compared to you, what are you waiting for?' Morrin's fists clenched. 'Or is it still that I practise three times a day that's got you worried.' Morrin flexed his hands, anger staining his face. 'What, scared of death, or scared of life?' Johns's mocking words had Morrin stilled. 'Come on big man, let's have your best shot. I'm not scared of death.'

Morrin heaved in a long breath.

'Oh, really?'

A slight smile tugged at his mouth as he reached his hand behind his neck and pulled out a deadly throwing knife. In a blink, he'd drawn back his hand and flicked his powerful wrist. Johns watched as the blade spun across the bar and embedded itself in Esryn's neck as she knelt over one of her opponents. Morrin watched as Johns's face went hollow. His mouth opened but no words came out as Esryn fell to the floor, her eyes wide, blood brimming from the fatal wound. Johns was over to her in an instant, cradling her head as a crimson pool appeared beneath her and started its spread across the beer-stained floor.

'Scared of death, now?' said Morrin, triumph on his tongue, a brutal stare fixing on Johns's back as he held his hand over the fresh wound, looking desperately for a way to stem the flow of blood that would soon rob him of his beloved Esryn.

'No!' Anya's voice raged out of nowhere. The whistle of steel cutting the air filled the room as she threw the dagger she'd been given. Morrin's look of victory turned to alarm, as if he'd completely forgotten about his latest trainee and as the blade sliced through his throat. He looked at Anya, surprise in his eyes as they dulled before his huge frame collapsed to the floor with a shuddering thud.

The fighting stopped, the remaining assassins, though disarmed, looked like they'd lost the appetite. Frank was on his feet, his eyes on Johns as his desperate voice fractured the air.

'Help, please. Help.'

Esryn's eyes were closed, her face grey, the last drops of the long but short life on her shallow breath. Gabby was immediately by Esryn's side, Johns's pleading eyes on her as she held her healing stone over the gaping wound in Esryn's neck, her face a picture of studied concentration. Slowly, she uttered an incantation, longer and more complicated than Frank had heard before. Her controlled, calm words of comfort a barrier against the red tide that flowed out of the assassin's neck as, by her practised sorcerer's hand, the wound gradually closed and the bleeding stopped.

Esryn's eyes remained shut, some colour returning to her

cheeks. Gabby waited, eyes on the pale-faced assassin as if checking for signs of life.

'She'll be okay,' she said. 'Another minute and —'

'Don't,' said Johns with a raise of his hand. He looked at Gabby, tears on his cheeks, gratitude etched on his face. 'Thank you.'

Gabby just gave a shallow nod.

'She should drink something sweet when she comes round,' she said, looking up at the deserted bar, littered with upturned tables and chairs and splintered timber. 'I'll see if there's some juice.' She got up, leaving Johns leaning over Esryn.

Gabby quickly returned with a large glass containing red liquid as Esryn's heavy eyelids lifted. Johns propped her head up, holding the glass to her lips before gently tipping it, allowing the contents to slowly empty into her mouth. She looked at Johns, reading the look on his face.

'Don't worry,' she said, her voice dry. 'Now I've found you again, it'll take more than a scratch to keep me from you.' Johns leaned down and kissed her forehead and Esryn sat up, looking at Gabby. 'I take back anything bad I ever said about sorcerers,' she said.

67

GONE

Frank had never felt so grateful to be back in his room at Polly's. Irundi and the silent forest had torn a big chunk out of him, making him realise what he had and what he had to lose. He lay, curled up on his bed, understanding that he'd shattered his friendship with Gabby and shoved the pointed end of a large pick-axe into the cleft that had opened up between him and his friends. Still he retained a distant hope that he'd be able to stitch it back together, but finding all the pieces seemed an impossible task.

They'd left the wreckage of the Black Feather, compensating the inn keeper for the damage the fight had inflicted on the place. Morrin's party took his body back into the forest while Frank, his friends and the three assassins made their way back to Rhaeder where Johns and Esryn said their heartfelt goodbyes and headed back to Crossways to begin what, Frank hoped, would be a new, happy chapter in their lives. The episode in the forest and the inn had touched them all, created an unspoken bond that would be difficult to break.

Simeon had just melted away into the afternoon. There one minute, vanished the next, leaving Frank with Gabby, Cas and Anya to decide what they should do with what they had discovered. What the possession of the key might mean.

They agreed to meet at Laskie's late the next morning, giving themselves time to rest and heal, so Frank returned to Polly's where, as usual, Polly fussed over him without any question about where he'd been, despite the gouge on his face.

His interest in the Simbrian hadn't been reignited, but he was still disturbed by what Esryn had told them.

Al-Fajr.

Princess and hunter of moons.

Moonhunter.

He burned at how she'd played them all along, but still didn't quite understand the relationship between the woman in the castle and the head of the academy. Were they related? It was a visit he knew he'd have to make, a conversation he knew he had to have, wanted to have.

He sighed inwardly, wondering about Moonhunter's dynasty, wondering if their book might have revealed something else in his absence.

He sat on the edge of his bed. The autumn sun, low in the morning sky glowed bright and orange through his window, balm to his aching limbs, his aching emotions. He looked at the drawer in his bedside table where he'd thrown the book after it had bitten him on his discovery of the map and the outline of the hand. It had saved them all – just. He knew it would; the book had a reason, a purpose for which he was yet unaware.

Whoever had woven the pages together knew they would need protecting, knew about Balal, her heinous tribe and the oath she and her ancestors had sworn to Kester and had warned him about the queen of the forest, not that it made him feel any more comfortable about the whole episode.

He loosed a long breath and shook his head in an attempt to flush any remaining thoughts about their excursion into the silent forest from his mind. He reached across and flicked the drawer open and looked inside.

Nothing.

The book wasn't there. Frank shrugged to himself and, through curious eyes, pulled the drawer out further. It was empty. In a ridiculous attempt to convince himself he was wrong he pulled it right out and turned it over in his hands, inspecting it like a carpenter checks for quality. He threw it onto the bed with a flick of his wrist and knelt down on the floor to look into the void created by the drawer. He thrust his hand in, wondering if he'd thrown the book with such force that it had somehow got stuck behind, but the space was also empty. The book, their secret, enchanted and undecipherable book, the one thing that had led them on in their crazy quest to keep their world safe, was gone.

Frank had lurched from interest to indifference during their hunt for the guardians, since they'd first met Wordsworth Hums under the academy, and there had been more than one occasion where he'd wearied and been tempted to throw the thing on the fire, to stop what it was trying to tell them. But now it was gone, he was immediately consumed with an odd feeling of loss. So, despite knowing it was a stupid idea, he started to conduct a thorough, fruitless search of his room. He even patted his pockets several times, just in case but there was no doubt. It was gone.

***

'What do you mean "gone"?' said Cas. Frank cocked his head to the side and flexed his eyes at him. Cas shrugged and went back to his rhubarb shake.

'I'm sure it's in the house, somewhere,' said Anya. 'Are you sure you didn't take it with you to the forest?'

Frank shook his head.

'Like I said, I couldn't be doing with the thing after it nearly burned my hand off.' He looked at his palm. 'I know exactly where I chucked it.'

'So where is it?' said Cas.

A long note of exasperation carried as Frank let out a breath.

'We can't lose it, Frank,' said Anya.

'*I know.*' Frank bit, his temper unleashed. Anya just stared blankly at him, silent. Heads in Laskie's turned their way. Frank grabbed at his hair. 'Sorry,' he said, eyes closed. 'Sorry for everything.' He slumped down into a chair.

'Perhaps Frank does know where it is, but is choosing not to tell us,' said Gabby. Her eyebrows flicked up, but she wasn't smiling.

'Don't be so childish,' said Frank, instantly regretting his arrogance. He deserved every slight Gabby threw his way, he knew it, knew he should agree, find it amusing even, but his tongue was ahead of his brain. Even so, Gabby didn't respond.

The jingle of the bell at Laskie's door had Frank looking up. In walked Libby with two of her friends and went to the counter where Mr Laskie greeted them with his brown-toothed smile. As they ordered she looked round, scanning the room for an empty table. She noticed him, her steamy smile capturing Frank in an instant. Frank felt his head go light.

'Think, Frank,' said Anya. Gabby looked up and followed Frank's gaze.

'I wouldn't bother, Anya,' she said under a barely concealed scowl. 'I'm afraid Frank can't think properly when his brains are in his underpants.'

Cas and Anya chuckled at Frank's expense. Frank ignored them and stood, buoyed by the sight of Libby winding her way through the tables towards him. He daren't look back to the table where the others sat. He could already picture the look on their faces and heard Gabby tut under her breath as Libby neared.

Despite his uncertainty about the older boy he'd seen her with he felt the now familiar surge of adolescent heat in his blood. She entwined him in her arms and stood on her toes, kissing him on the cheek. She looked at Gabby then back to Frank.

'Where have you been?' she said with a smile. 'I was getting worried, term started a couple of weeks ago.'

'It's a long story,' said Frank, feeling the events in Irundi falling around him.

Libby smiled at the others, her eyes resting on Gabby.

'Don't worry, Gabby, I'm going to sit with my friends.'

She shot a fake smile in Gabby's direction, who returned the gesture, not looking the least bit concerned. Libby unwound herself from Frank, scratching the ends of her fingers with her thumbnail, a faint yellow rash on her fingertips and down the back of her hand.

'Why don't I come to Polly's in the morning?' she said. 'You can tell me all about it then and I'll see if I can find something for us to do?'

She widened her eyes and ran the end of her fingertip across the underside of Frank's chin, teasing the point of her tongue across her lips then looked back at Gabby whose expression had turned the shade of thunderclouds.

'Okay,' said Frank. 'See you about ten?'

'Ten?' said Cas, 'You're getting up late.'

'Who said anything about getting up?' said Libby, a wayward grin drawn right across her face, turning Cas's face a light shade of pink.

She planted a quick kiss on Frank's lips and made her way back to her friends without a glance back. Frank watched the sway of her hips as she walked across the café to the window seat where her friends looked on.

Gabby pushed her plate hard across the table.

'I've kind of lost my appetite,' she said.

Anya looked at Frank, turning the subject back to their book.

'So where do you think it is?' Frank felt his shoulders drop as he thrust his hands into his pockets. He drew in a long breath.

'I'll ask Norris when he gets home. Or perhaps Maddy's been into my room; maybe she got a bit curious and forgot to put it back.' He didn't think Maddy even went up to the top floor unless Polly sent her to get Frank for tea. 'I don't know, but it has to be somewhere.' He scanned the glum faces. 'Let's meet up back here tomorrow after lunch and I'll let you know what they say, okay?'

'Are you sure you'll have the time,' said Gabby. 'Or any energy left?' The others could barely contain themselves as Frank shook his head and headed back to Polly's.

But both Norris and Maddy had nothing to offer. Norris looked blanker than an empty page and shrugged.

'Are you sure, Norris?' said Polly, hands on hips, sounding like she was about to pronounce him guilty.

'Can't think of the last time I went up there,' said Norris. 'What about you Maddy?'

Maddy gave a nervous shake of her head, her cheeks turning to cherries under Frank's gaze. It was her usual reaction and in the years Frank had been staying with the Quigleys she'd always been the same, but Frank couldn't shake the feeling that the book's disappearance was no coincidence.

68

The Thief

He didn't bother to get dressed the following morning. Polly served up a cooked breakfast before she and Maddy prepared the shop for the day. Frank just went back to his room and lay on the bed. He closed his eyes and allowed sweet thoughts of him and Libby to enter his weary mind until the clock struck ten. Polly's voice climbed the stairs from the landing below.

'Frank, visitor.'

Frank swung himself round, stood and went to his door, anticipation raising the hairs on his neck as the footsteps on the staircase neared. He held out his hands to the approaching sound but a bewildered look cut across his face as Gabby appeared.

'Ah, didn't know you cared,' she said, holding her arms out to him.

'Very funny.' There was something about her warm tone that knotted his stomach and he couldn't cast aside that he loved it when they were getting along. He'd been awful to her, but he'd missed her. 'What are you doing here?'

'Pleased to see me, then?' She cocked her head to one side. He'd really missed her.

'You know what I mean. I was expecting...'

'The lovely Libby.'

'Yeah, so why are you —?'

'Frank.' Gabby's snapped interruption swiped the air like Esryn's rapier. Her smiling face turned serious, she had his attention.

'What?'

He wasn't sure what to think, he couldn't recall Gabby coming up to his room on her own in all the time they'd known one another. She drew in a breath, but hesitated, glancing back down the stairs. She pushed her way past and stepped into his bedroom, turning to face him, silhouetted against the morning sun. She glanced around, looking like she was checking if they were alone. She stood wringing her hands, looking back at Frank who could feel a familiar uneasy feeling brewing in his guts. He stepped into the room after her. She opened her mouth but her hesitation appeared to get the better of her and no words came out. She took a deep breath.

'Look, Frank,' she said. 'I really don't know how to tell you this.'

'Tell me what? I thought we could tell each other anything.'

He immediately regretted his words as Gabby raised her eyebrows at him.

'It's about...'

She looked at the bedroom door as the sound of approaching feet on the stairs filled the small room. Gabby swallowed as, into the doorway, stepped a sweetly smiling Libby.

Libby stopped, her face quickly dropping, turning to ice as she looked Gabby up and down, the cheeriness that she drank like a milkshake all but evaporating. Frank noticed Gabby's lips tighten and her breath shorten as the two girls embarked on a silent showdown.

'What's *she* doing here?' said Libby with a flick of her chin.

Frank suddenly felt trapped in his own bedroom, the atmosphere blanketed in tension. He shook his head.

'I don't know. What *are* you doing here, Gabby?'

Gabby's expression had changed from unpleasant to growing fury.

'Why don't you ask her?'

She kept her voice slow and steady, flicking her index finger at Libby. She folded her arms and raised her eyebrows at Libby, her usual tactic to elicit an answer. Frank looked back to Libby.

'Ask you what?'

Libby shrugged, but didn't answer. Her expression hardened.

'Are you going to tell him, or shall I?' said Gabby.

Libby's jade eyes narrowed, her unspoken animosity towards Gabby plain. Silence the weight of an anvil filled the space between them.

'I don't know what you're talking about,' said Libby. She looked at Frank. 'You know she just wants to cause trouble between you and me.' Gabby let out a derisory huff under her breath. 'Honestly, Gabby -'

'Honest isn't a word you should use, Libby.'

Gabby placed undue emphasis on her opposite's name. Frank wasn't sure what was going down before his eyes, but he could sense that Gabby felt she held the aces as she turned to him.

'I only found out yesterday, Frank.'

'Found out?' He looked at Libby. 'Found out what? What's going on, Gabby?'

Libby was still fixed on Gabby, a look that dared her to go any further.

'Why don't you just leave us alone and go and get some more metal stuck into your head,' said Libby.

Gabby just cocked her head.

'Ask her what she's got on her hands.'

'What?' said Frank.

'Her hands? Go on, ask her.'

Libby clamped her hands under her armpits as Gabby spoke. Both Frank and Gabby fixed their eyes on her.

'What?' said Libby. 'Look, Frank. You know she's never liked me. Wonder why? Because she fancies you, that's why she's here causing trouble.'

Frank winced at the venomous look she threw Gabby's way. Still Gabby remained still, assured.

'Don't be stupid,' said Gabby. 'Frank's my friend, that's all.' She glanced at him. A brief, timid look.

'Huh, like we all believe that,' shot Libby. 'Why don't you just leave? No one invited you here.'

Frank had no idea where all of this was going, the two girls looked like they were set in for a morning of trading adolescent insults with each other and he really had better things to be doing.

Without warning, Gabby took two steps toward Libby; heat flushed through Frank as, for a moment, he thought Gabby was about to punch her but she made a grab for Libby's right wrist. Libby batted Gabby's hand away, and again as Gabby tried a second time, latching on to her and, despite Libby's protests, yanked her arm and held her hand out towards Frank.

Libby struggled to break herself free but Gabby, stronger and determined, held her firmly as she showed Frank the fading marks on Libby's fingertips. Libby shoved Gabby hard, releasing her hand which she shoved back into her armpit as Gabby steadied herself, nearly losing her balance against Libby's weighty and venomous push.

'Get off me,' she said. 'What's your problem, you gypsy.'

'You see, Frank?' Frank didn't. 'The rash, those marks.'

'What about them?' said Libby. 'It's just a stupid rash.' She looked at her fingertips, then at Frank. 'I caught something from my little sister last week. That's all.' She scowled at Gabby, looking like she wanted to rip her throat out. 'What the hell are you taking about? You walk in here, knowing Frank and me were meeting up and go on about a stupid skin infection. You must be desperate.'

'Thief's spite,' said Gabby. Calm. A moment's pause. Frank's brow creased. 'It's thief's spite. After we talked about it at my house —'

'*Your* house,' said Libby with a disbelieving look at Frank. 'When were you at her house?' but her raised voice and hint of rising anger didn't throw Gabby off her stride.

'I asked Mum about it and she told me that the first few people to touch an object that's stolen will get a rash in the shape of a spiral. That it will last a few weeks before it clears up and that the rash will be the colour of whatever flower was used to make the mix.'

'What?' snarled Libby. 'Do people like you always talk such pathetic nonsense?'

But Gabby ignored her.

'I used it on our book when I first took it home for the winter holidays, just after I met you, remember?' Frank nodded. 'There's not much that flowers in the winter, but it was mild and the gorse flower was out early. There's plenty of it growing on the common land and foothills around the village, mum uses it for some of her stuff.' She calmed her tone. 'They're yellow.' She fixed a black stare on Libby. 'The flowers are yellow, and so will the rash be. I saw it on your hand yesterday.' Libby sucked in a breath and looked like she was resisting the urge to claw the triumph off Gabby's face. 'You stole our book. Go on, deny it.'

Libby took a guilty look down at her fingertips, at the fading accomplice of pale yellow lines that twisted down her fingers as tears welled in her eyes. She looked at Frank as one released itself and ran down her cheek.

'It's just a book,' she said.

She bit her lip. No one spoke. Frank's head pounded with confusion. Moments ago he was preparing himself for a sensual morning with the auburn-haired girl he thought he knew and, now, he stared into her emerald eyes not knowing what to think. Gabby took a step back, allowing Frank's trust in Libby to break, to shatter in front of her.

'How...?'

'I'm sorry, Frank. I didn't realise it was so important.' There was pleading in her glassy eyes as Frank started to shake his head, the distance between them growing quickly. 'I'm sorry,' she repeated, placing her hand over her mouth to stifle a rising sob before she turned and hurried down the stairs.

69

THE RECONCILIATION

Frank stared at the empty doorway, his stomach churning as his emotions began to rip him apart. He wished she was still there, that he hadn't just heard her admit she'd stolen from him, stolen something so valuable. He knew she wouldn't have given up the secret unless she'd been caught red-handed or, in her case, yellow-handed. He didn't want to believe it, didn't want the girl that made his troubles disappear to be something he didn't want her to be but, in an instant, her actions had changed everything and the one good thing in his life had just disappeared, receding like the wind through his bedroom door in tears.

Trust was everything. Difficult to build, so easy to destroy. He had come to realise this with every fragment of deceit he'd unfolded about his dad, his past and from his own inexcusable actions in keeping things from his friends. His ears rang with Libby's last apologetic cry but he knew, deep down, that she had betrayed him, that the loose, casual feel of their relationship, the carefree spirit had been irreparably damaged. It could never be the same again.

Frank felt his throat tighten. He slumped down on his bed, bent his head forward and clasped it in both hands, digging his fingernails into his scalp, raking them through his hair. He squeezed his eyes shut and puffed out his cheeks, his mind racing, filled with images of Libby, her simple loveliness, her smouldering smile; images that pleaded with him to see her again but wondering if he would. Of all the things he'd gone through, of all the trials and tests of the last few years with the academy, the Simbrian, his dad – this was undoubtedly the worst he'd ever felt.

He sat there, heart still splintering into tiny shards, wondering if he'd ever get back up, whether he'd ever want to, when he remembered he wasn't alone. In his instant retreat into his frayed emotions he'd forgotten Gabby was there, a witness to everything. Counsel for the prosecution. He looked up and where he expected to see triumph and smug justification written across her pierced face there was none. Just unedited concern, concern for him, concern for the miserable wretch of a teenage boy who had let her down but who now looked upon him like she cared, was there for him, like she would always be there for him.

'I'm sorry, Frank,' she said. Her tone carried a true depth of sincerity but still he couldn't find any words. 'Really,' she said. She sat next to him, curling her tanned legs underneath her. Frank held his head in his hands again, staring down at his knees, his mind fogged. 'Look, it's no secret that I didn't really like her but when I saw her fingers at Laskie's, yesterday I knew straight away what it was.'

He couldn't bring himself to look at her. Couldn't make sense of his emotions. Anger, embarrassment, sadness – they all burned bright inside him. He took a few deep breaths as Gabby gave him the space to calm himself.

'Why didn't you say anything to me in Laskie's?' he said.

'Because I didn't want to make her, or you, look foolish in front of everyone.' She clasped her hands together and placed them gently in her lap. 'And I hardly slept last night because I've been fretting about telling you because...because I knew how much it would hurt you.' Frank stared at the wall. 'I'm sorry. I know you really liked her.'

A genuine concern carried in her voice and he could see it written across her face as he glanced at her. Despite her antipathy towards Libby, she'd struggled to find the words that she knew would hurt, even though he knew she'd had to tell him. It was the right thing to do and hadn't been easy.

'It's not your fault,' said Frank.

'No, it's not. But I know how you feel about her and...' He sensed Gabby's throat tighten as her soft voice trailed off.

'And what?'

'I didn't know how you'd react. You might have thought I was just being awkward and I didn't want you to think I was deliberately trying break you up.' Frank didn't respond. 'And breaking up is hard to do,' she continued. 'Especially as she's your first girlfriend.'

'What makes you think she's my first?' He looked at her, a glint of a smile in her eyes tugging at the lost cheeriness buried somewhere beneath his misery. He let out an unexpected laugh. 'Okay, she is... was...whatever. And how do you know about breaking up.'

'There's a lot you don't know about me, Frank Penny.'

The cheeky grin on her face lit up the room. Lit *him* up.

A calm spread between them and Frank felt his mood lift a little as he and Gabby sat there in slightly uncomfortable silence. Neither of them appeared to want to talk, both of them understanding that the other needed the quiet, a balm to begin the healing of the deep rift that Frank had cleaved in their relationship. But Gabby hadn't been afraid to come and tell him, to do the right thing, however painful it was for her or for him.

'What are you going to do?' she said after a while.

Frank sighed.

'I don't know.' He looked at Gabby, taking in her sympathetic face. Her gaze lingered on his tired eyes and he felt the pinpricks of something on his skin. She went to speak but he stopped her. 'Gabby,' he said. She offered silence, not looking away, drawing his words from him. 'I'm so sorry.'

He couldn't help himself as his voice broke and tears streamed down his face. She moved in and put her arms around him, gentle in her movements, caring in her warmth, in a way he didn't deserve. He felt her closeness, felt the warmth of her breath in his hair. She let him cry, healing tears that began to mend the bond between them. No words were needed.

Frank pulled himself away, wiping the tears from his cheeks. He felt no sense of shame, of embarrassment, letting her see him like this.

He pushed himself back on the bed and sat against the wall, looking at her, the smile on her face. A smile to make the fireflies dance. He knew his tears weren't just for the way he'd treated her and the others. He had to tell her, tell her the whole truth about himself. To purge himself of his inner demons with her help. It was a big risk but, taking a deep breath he said:

'I need to tell you something.' He noticed her go still, perhaps weighing up what he was about to say, realising she might not like it, or him, again. She waited. 'I found out something about myself that...that...' What was he to say – that he couldn't live with the knowledge or stigma that he was Dagmar's son? That he was the first-born of the individual responsible for tearing apart her country in a bloody invasion? That he was related to the man who had made her and her precious family flee their homeland, to be treated like second-class citizens in a country that barely understood what it was to be a refugee? Still she waited. Frank needed to tell her this, to get the words out. To get beyond the barrier he'd put up between himself and his friends. He felt himself grind his teeth, felt his chest tighten – then he opened the gate. 'I found out that Dagmar is my real father.'

There. He'd said what he thought he'd never have to say. Gabby just stared at him as he explained how he'd discovered his true parentage, about how it had consumed him by the hour until his head felt like it would explode and how he couldn't face telling anyone, not even his friends, let alone admit it to himself.

The whole story took just a minute in the telling, yet it felt like another miserable day but he could feel the shackles of his own emotions being shed as he spoke, as if sharing his burden had started to set him free. He said it and waited for her to launch a full out verbal and physical assault, or get up and leave him to his own misery.

He stared at his hands. He couldn't look at her. She shifted, making him flinch, but she just put her hand on his. A touch from inside her heart.

'I'm so sorry, Gabby,' he said, his eyes meeting hers. 'I'm so terribly, terribly sorry.' The strain in his voice was clear.

'I don't know what to say,' she said, squeezing his hand tenderly. Frank shook his head.

'Me neither,' he said. 'But you were right. Back in the cave. I am a selfish bastard.'

He felt her squeeze again.

'I guess it's easy for me to say you should have told us.'

'I was just so worried that you'd see me...differently. Like someone who robbed you of your home.'

He felt the knot in his throat tighten.

'I thought you knew me better than that, Frank.' Her voice was mild, lacking any form of judgement. 'I was more annoyed with you because you were keeping it all in all this time.'

Frank knew she was right, that he should have said something rather than sulk around like a broody teenager, getting under everyone's skin, letting them guess what was eating him. He could see the extent of his selfishness and how unforgivable it was. He let out a long breath and shook his head.

'My Dad had always taught me to talk about things that were troubling me...' He broke off and tilted his head back. 'My Dad. What does that even mean?'

Small silences interrupted their conversation.

'It's a lot for you to take in, Frank,' said Gabby. 'I'm not surprised you've been acting like you have, now that I know.'

'You mean you don't hate me?'

He'd been so sure she would.

'Hate you? Far from it, Frank.'

Her chestnut eyes met his. Something unspoken lay behind them, something soft and kind, the way she could be, disguised and hidden behind her hard exterior and he felt his life, until now slipping from view, turn a little warmer. She reached for his cheek, running her thumb over the scar she'd left on him. He closed his eyes at the gentleness of her touch.

'Sorry about that,' she said.

Frank shook his head.

'Don't be. It'll be something to remind me never to be such a jerk again.'

She broke off her gaze and pulled her knees up to her chest.

'You need to tell Cas and Anya.'

'I know.' Frank let out a long sigh. 'I'll do it later, once I've got our book back.' He noticed the look on her face change. 'Please don't say you told me so.'

That smile again.

'I'll come with you if you like.'

That spark. Frank laughed.

'Thanks for the offer. I'll go, then I'll go and see Moonhunter.'

'Are you sure. Perhaps we should all go.'

'No. I think I need to do my penance. Anyway, just to clear the slate, I also found out she knew my Mum when she was younger.' Gabby shook her head.

'You're kidding.' Frank's look told her he wasn't. She puffed out her cheeks. 'Wow. Any more surprises?'

'No. I think that's me all done and surely that's enough for one day.'

She reached for his hand again, clasping his palm and rubbing her thumb across the back. He watched as she made small, delicate circles on his skin. Their eyes met and she pulled away, leaning back against the wall, her shoulder nestling against Frank's. Comfortable, casual.

'What I don't get is why? Why did she take it?' said Gabby.

'She might have seen us with it in Laskie's,' said Frank.

'But so what,' said Gabby. 'What would she do with it? She's just an air-head.'

She stopped herself as she caught Frank's look, but he let the comment go.

'And how?' said Frank. 'Polly never said anything about Libby coming in when I wasn't here. I'm sure she would have let me know.'

'But we do need it back, Frank.'

Frank let out another long sigh. Whatever was going to happen between him and Libby, he knew he'd have to retrieve their book, which meant even more discomfort sooner than he felt he was ready for.

70

THE BREAK-UP

The residential area in the north of Rhaeder seemed deserted. The street on which Libby lived appeared longer than he remembered. Frank stood at the slick, black door of Libby's house and stared at the knocker. He had to do this, however much his mind told him it was a bad idea to see Libby so soon after what had gone down in his bedroom earlier that day.

He lifted his hand, dropping it back down, looking up and down the street, wondering if he should just leave. Come back later when everyone had cooled a bit. He felt a twist in his gut, thinking of all the times he'd been to her house, sneaking in when her mother wasn't around, the excitement and wild passion of being with her, the idyllic afternoons spent in her room with nothing to think about but being a normal teenager.

But he could feel the difference in him already. The disappointment. The betrayal. She'd stolen from him then lied about it and he wasn't in the mood to forgive. Maybe that was a good thing.

Grabbing his reserves of courage, he knocked. Immediately he hoped no one was at home but heard footsteps from within. He held his breath as the door opened. Libby stood across the threshold, her eyes red and puffed. As soon as she saw him she adjusted her frame, more upright and confident, sweeping her hair back over her shoulders. His heart fell like a stone. For a moment the silence gripped him, unable to think what to say while thinking of a hundred things he wanted to say.

'I've come to get my book back.'

It sounded lame, wrong. Libby's eyes searched his.

'I'm so sorry, Frank,' she said. He nodded. He felt she was, but it didn't make any difference. Still he couldn't think what else to say, unable to navigate these unchartered and tricky relationship waters. 'I just thought it was a joke, but Ralph asked me if he could get to see it. You're always so secretive so I thought it would be a bit of fun. And I was annoyed with you because I hadn't heard from you.'

'Ralph?' Frank's insides burned with a newly ignited flame at the mention of the unfamiliar name. 'Who's Ralph?'

Libby's face froze.

'Just a boy I know.'

Her answer was too short, the words of hidden secrets.

But Frank couldn't make the connection. Why was some smug, arse of a boy after their book? He dug deeper into his memory's reserves. He knew it was in there, somewhere. He knew he was familiar, he'd known that when he'd first seen Libby with him but he'd not been able to place him, and the events of the past few weeks had erased it from his mind.

Then, as he stretched his recall to the limit, so far he thought he'd curse, he grasped it, his faded memory of the boy who he'd seen Libby with gradually began to give itself colour. Frank fit the piece of the jigsaw that he'd been unable to complete since Gabby had exposed Libby, but the immediate realisation had his wits prickling and his mind racing. He had a recollection of a boy who he'd briefly encountered on his very first day at Excelsus, standing with Professor Lanks in his intake's registration area.

'Ralph Jackson,' he said, the words passing his lips without thought.

'That's right,' said Libby. 'He was head boy at your academy.'

Frank stared through her, processing the information.

'Ralph Jackson.' He couldn't believe it. 'Governor Jackson's grandson.' A statement, not a question.

Libby nodded. Frank turned, his mind running quicker than he could fathom.

'What does he want with my book?'

'I don't know.' Libby shrugged and leaned on the doorframe. She sniffed. Frank's silence drew more from her. 'He was talking about you, asking if you had any secrets and I said I'd seen you with it. You lot had it in Laskie's when Gabby said you were talking about something that didn't involve me, remember?'

'Does he still have it?'

Libby nodded through doleful eyes. Frank turned and started to walk away but Libby grabbed his arm.

'Frank.' There was a hint of pleading in her voice. 'I'm sorry. Ralph can be...well...quite charming and...please give me another chance. Please.'

Her green eyes wetted as they searched his face, silently begging him not to leave. She still looked lovely, tempting. He stepped towards her and pulled her in close, her familiar embrace warming him as they wrapped their arms around each other, his face in her hair.

He wanted to say "yes". He nearly said it, but in the depths of his heart he could tell things wouldn't be the same between them. That he'd have to end up choosing between her and his friends. He knew Gabby, Cas and even Anya, with her inclination towards forgiveness, wouldn't want anything to do with her. As he breathed in her sweet scent he knew there was no contest. They held each other for a few moments before Frank let go. For the last time.

'I'm sorry, Libby,' he said, a slight quiver in his voice. 'It's over.'

Her hand went to her mouth. She stifled a sob as hot tears sprang from her eyes. Then, with his heart hurting more than her could have imagined, he turned and walked away.

71

RALPH JACKSON

He knew he should have asked Libby more. Asked her more about why Ralph Jackson had asked her to steal the book although the answer was already grabbing him by the throat. Long angry strides seized him as he made his way back along the lane that led from Libby's house and into the town. He could feel the hacking of his boots on the pavement shedding his anger and frustration. His emotional wick had burned right down and he fought to keep his tears leashed. Seeing Libby had reminded him of how he felt about her, how he used to feel, how he could still feel, how he might feel in the future.

No. It was over. He was sure. The gut-wrenching pain was all too new, too raw, an enormous knot of razor-sharp turmoil that he couldn't begin to untwist. He wished he'd never embarked on a summer of heady passion with such a lovely but wayward girl. He vowed he would never make himself feel like this again and love, however it hunted him, whatever plans it had to make a mockery of his young life, could go straight to hell with his spit on it.

He felt his anger start to boil as he walked, consumed by his thoughts but was awakened from his fog with the sight of someone walking up the road towards him, heading in the direction of Libby's house.

The long, elegant, confident strides of Ralph Jackson, hands tucked into his trouser pockets, a distant, untroubled look on his face. He didn't as much as glance at Frank, who hunched his shoulders and angled his head down as he approached.

Frank's insides flared. How dare this imposter bring down

part of his life without the slightest thought. The selfish, self-serving charlatan. A younger version of his grandfather, cast from the Jackson mould and groomed to get what he wanted with slick ease and efficiency, not caring who was in the way.

Frank stepped into Jackson's path as he passed, shoving him hard in the shoulder, spinning him ninety degrees before he had time to think. Jackson's hands went up; a natural reflex to protect himself as his eyes tried to focus on Frank. He took a step back, but Frank moved with him, grabbing at Jackson's shirt, determined to get right into his face.

'What's your problem?'

Jackson was sharp-eyed, wary, but a slight smile tugged at his lips when he realised who had pushed him.

'You're my problem. You got Libby to steal my book.'

Jackson didn't look concerned in the slightest.

'Really?' His face broke into a wide grin, adding fuel to Frank's already raging fire. 'That's not all I got her to do.'

Frank's temper flashed.

'Shut up. Give it back, or I'll get you arrested for theft.'

Jackson loosed a short laugh from under his breath. He leaned forward.

'I didn't steal it, Frank.' The barely hidden amusement in his voice had Frank clenching his fists. 'Although learning that Libby's younger sister was Madelaine Quigley's new best friend was wonderfully coincidental for me.' He noticed the look in Frank's eyes. 'It was her that found it in your room, in case you were wondering. I got Libby to ask her to have a look, then I just had to convince your lovely girlfriend to twist her little sister's arm and let's say she was happy to do it.' He sniffed arrogance. 'With the right encouragement, of course.'

A salacious look spread over his face. Frank shoved him hard, sending him a step back.

'I don't care, just give it back or...'

'Or what?' Jackson's smug superior look had the inside of

Frank's head screaming. 'Or you'll tell my grandfather?' He feigned a look of concern. 'Oh, unfortunately I don't have it anymore, I wonder who has?'

There were no words Frank could conjure in response. He knew Jackson had him cornered, knew that his powerful grandfather had orchestrated the whole thing and, in doing so, had revealed a hand that Frank had long suspected he held. Information about the Simbrian was like gold-dust, a currency beyond any riches known to Byeland or Kzarlac and both Dagmar and Jackson coveted it like a junkie denied the fuel for their addiction. Now he'd used his grandson as a willing accomplice to find out what Frank and his friends knew.

'Don't worry Frank. Whatever secrets you thought you had are safe with me. Oh, and in case you were wondering.' Smugness on his face, 'Apparently your girlfriend really likes her men a little older...' he leaned into Frank's face, '...and more experienced.'

His arrogant smile widened, showing a perfect row of brilliant white teeth as Frank's temper erupted. He shoved Jackson hard and swung an uncontrolled fist towards his chiselled jaw. Jackson jerked his head back, dodging the wild blow with ease.

He gripped Frank's shirtfront in both hands and quickly pressed him against the wall, delivering a solid, painful punch to Frank's abdomen, following it up with a crunching fist across Frank's left cheek, rattling his teeth, producing pin-pricks of dazzling small lights before his eyes and sending him to the floor at Jackson's well-polished shoes. He doubled up, spluttering, head spinning.

Jackson placed the sole of his shoe on Frank's chest and pushed him over onto his back and into the gutter. Frank offered no resistance.

'You need to understand when you're beaten, Frank. Go home. And always try to remember who you're dealing with before you try to mix it up, right?' He took a step back. 'Now, I ought to see if young Libby's up for a bit of consoling, if you know what I mean.'

Frank didn't respond. He just stared down at the pavement,

his eyes bleary from Jackson's precision blow. Saliva drooled from his mouth, coloured red, the pounding under his eye worsening by the second.

He listened to the sound of Jackson's slow, sure footsteps receding up the road. He could just make him out through his blurred vision, heading towards Libby's, not a glance back to check if Frank was alright. Bastard.

Frank rolled himself to a sitting position, wiping the blood away across his cheek.

He squeezed his eyelids tight together and clenched his stomach muscles as much as he could bear, willing the wind that had been knocked from him to return. Jackson's blow had been practised, the consummate Excelsus graduate with a hidden talent for nicking other people's girlfriends.

Frank dabbed at his face, regret beginning to eke its way in. Regret that he had decided to tackle Jackson, taller and stronger than himself, regret that he'd neglected Libby to the extent that she'd been seduced by the charm of the governor's grandson. He had been determined not to feel bad about things but he couldn't help but feel it was of his own making. He didn't blame Libby, nor Jackson, nor his friends for being disappointed in him; he just blamed himself.

He screwed his face up, the pain still biting him as he pushed himself to his feet. A group of young children passed him, each of their curious, cautious faces watching him like he was the star attraction in a travelling company of curiosities. He was tempted to glower back at them, to scare them off, but he hadn't the energy or the heart. He brushed himself down, wincing, then headed in the direction of the academy, knowing his next confrontation was likely to be the most testing of them all.

72

THE GIFT

Frank found Meredith standing with Honeycomb Maddison at the doors to the academy as he mounted the polished marble steps at the entrance.

'Hi Frank.'

She took a long look at his battered face and raised her eyebrows at Honey.

'Have you been in some sort of accident,' said Honey, making a face.

'Nice to see you, too,' he offered.

Something inside him was glad of the interruption to his journey to Moonhunter's office, but after all he'd been through over the last few weeks, he had no idea what to say to them.

'What are you doing here?' said Meredith. 'Everyone's been talking like you and Cas have left, along with those girls you kick around with. Even Emerald seemed concerned. What's going on?'

Frank looked at her, then to Honey, whose expectant stare started to make him feel uncomfortable.

'You're not in some sort of trouble, are you?' she said.

'It's a long story,' he said. 'In fact, I'm on my way to see Moonhunter now.'

The girls looked at each other as if they'd suddenly become part of some great adventure.

'Good luck with that,' said Meredith. 'No one's seen her around the academy since the start of term.'

The comment made Frank pause.

'Has she left?'

'No, she just keeps to her office, apparently.'

Frank nodded.

'I'll see you around.'

Both girls nodded back as Frank strode off, trying to ignore the hushed voices at his back. No one knew what he'd been through. The cuts and bruises were just surface wounds of something much deeper. Johns was right, the scars on the inside told more of a story than anything anyone could see and he'd been cut and bruised enough to last a lifetime.

He could feel his chest begin to tighten as he made his way into the west wing, hoping that this would be the very last time he'd have to walk this way. Once he'd exposed Moonhunter for the deceitful and contemptable person she undoubtedly was, he'd vowed never to have anything to do with her or the place again.

The atrium unsettled his nerves, as did the eye on the door as he stepped across the small, enclosed space. He gripped his locket, feeling a strange kind of significance now he knew about his mum's association with the principal.

He waited for the door to disappear, but nothing happened. Unusual. Moonhunter always knew who was outside the door and had always let him in. Frank raised his fist and went to knock, but something made him hesitate, something in his mind told him to leave, told him now wasn't the right time, to come back when he was better prepared and not to enter into a discussion where she was bound to tie him up in intricate knots.

He lowered his hand, just the sound of his own breathing filling the air around him, and turned to go when he heard the door latch click and the door opened. Moonhunter fixed her eyes on him, alluring as ever, her rainbow hair tied loosely back. But there was something different in the way she looked at him, searching his face for something lost. She studied him for a moment.

'What do you want, Frank.'

She was different, emotionless at the sight of him. He felt the same.

He barged past into her office to the sound of the door closing behind him, as if she were barricading herself in. Turning, he saw something simmering on her face underneath the autumn storm that brewed on the ceiling of her strange corner of the academy.

'What do you want,' she repeated, the harsh tone telling him she would rather he wasn't there. Her crystal filled with strands of black and orange, slamming and sparking on the inside. Under the force of her stare Frank stalled, suddenly feeling the fist of intimidation at his throat. Moonhunter was calm, she was always calm, but she was clearly filled with something else at his arrival.

He looked back to the door, but Moonhunter blocked the way, her stony face looked ready to smite him to the depths of the earth but she'd walked between the raindrops for far too long and she needed to hear what he had to say

'I know,' he said, his voice as steady as his surroundings would allow. 'I know what you are.' She didn't respond, kicking anger back into him. 'Why didn't you tell me?'

'Tell you what, exactly?'

She knew what he meant. Behind her composed, cat-like expression, he could sense she knew. Still she was determined to skirt around the subject, to give him nothing. He felt his temper tugging hard at its tether.

'That you're a guardian; a guardian of the Simbrian, or your family are. You knew we were involved, yet you said nothing. You might have saved us all a lot of trouble. You could have told us and you didn't.'

Moonhunter closed her eyes and drew in a long, solitary breath, as if she was cleansing herself. And again.

'I couldn't tell you.'

Frank noticed the easing in her posture.

'Couldn't, or wouldn't?'

Frank just wanted to tear her to pieces. He'd never trusted her and now he knew why, why he couldn't put his finger on her eel-like posturing, her continual scouting around the subject of the

Simbrian. But he still sensed a shift in her, a relaxation.

'Sit down, Frank.'

Moonhunter jerked her chin to the seating area behind him, the broad smear of severity now washed away. Frank shook his head.

'Don't tell me what to do.'

The words hissed from his mouth. How dare she feel she could command him after all she'd kept hidden. He'd said his piece, revealed he knew her secret, he was done with her company and went for the door, pushing her aside.

'I said, *sit* down.'

The ferocity in Moonhunter's words grasped firmly on his tail as he headed away from her. He wasn't going to stop and listen to her lies but, as he reached the door, a strange feeling shivered through his body. A calm, ethereal scent surrounded him, sandalwood and jasmine. He felt himself relax and, before he could take in what was happening, he found himself turning and heading back towards the principal, who was now consumed with a concentrated stare.

Frank sat, knowing she'd bewitched him but unable to do anything to resist. Moonhunter sat opposite, crossing her long legs while he felt anchored to the chair. She slowly surveyed his face; nothing soft or serene about her expression now. He felt like he was sitting against his will but, at the same time, had no desire to get up and leave. She appeared to notice the question in his face.

'The Simbrian is something I can never talk about,' she said.

'But you're a guardian,' said Frank. 'I know that.'

'I could never speak its name because my family, or I, no longer have our piece of it.'

Frank just stared, gathering his thoughts as her words seeped in. He tried to dismiss the thought that she was making sense, but her words spoke more than she knew. He quickly began to fit together the pieces of the last two years, all the uncomfortable meetings and stilted conversations at the hands of Moonhunter, the continual tango around the subject, never once did she mention it, not once did he or his friends. It remained unsaid, and now he knew why.

'Then who has?' As the words left his lips he could only think of one thing, that Dagmar had already taken it which is why he froze to his seat when Moonhunter said:

'It was given to Becky; your mother.'

73

THE FRIENDSHIP

The words crushed the breath from him. Moonhunter's unwavering eyes told him she wasn't joking. She had no idea she'd just catapulted his world into the realms of the unbelievable, of the bizarre.

'It's a relief that you've asked me about it,' she said. 'The Simbrian curse is a terrible thing, I believe.'

Frank still had no words, nothing to give her in return except his stunned silence. Moonhunter's expression relaxed. 'Maybe I should tell you about it. About me and Becky?'

Frank felt himself nod, not completely sure he was ready to hear what Moonhunter had to say, but she took his silence as her cue to continue. She paused, collecting her thoughts, a soft expression returning to her face.

'When I was growing up, we moved from house to house, town to town, country to country. We never stopped in one place long enough for me to settle and I never knew why. It was just the way we lived our lives and I never made any friends because of it. Then we came here and took a house on the outskirts of Rhaeder.' She was serious as she spoke, her face tight. 'I used to go walking on my own, escape in my own daydreams as far away from the house as I could, as far away as my suffocating mother would let me. She just stayed in, playing the lyre.' She paused and her eyes glassed, a faraway look took her but Frank unexpectedly shivered – the lyre. 'The sound still haunts my dreams; the lonely spectre of my nomadic childhood, like she was playing only to welcome in misery, playing for death, even.' She looked back at Frank and a slight smile tugged at her mouth.

'Then I met her. Your mum. I discovered the lake where she

lived, where your grandmother still lives. One day I was walking around the edge and...there she was.' Moonhunter's face brightened as she looked to be conjuring memories in her head, memories from long ago. She smiled at Frank. 'She was sat cross-legged, throwing stones at small stone towers she'd built, trying to knock them down. I stood watching her from behind, willing each throw would find its target, but she kept missing and cursing.' She tossed her hair. 'Such bad language. Her dog was rolled out on the banks of the lake. "Why don't you come and try?" she said. She didn't even turn round, she just knew I was there. I didn't know how she knew, not then. So I joined her. Me, the shy lonely girl from out of town. The girl who'd never made any friends. I sat with her, took up a stone and knocked the furthest tower down with my first throw and she nearly died laughing. She laughed until I thought she would devour all the laughter in the world. Then she looked at me and that's when I saw it for the first time.'

'Saw what?'

'The fire in her eyes, Frank. Fire. Real, pure flame lighting her with vivid brightness from the inside. I'd never known such spirit could exist. Not in my world, not in the tepid life I led and I knew from the very first moment I saw that wildfire looking back at me, knew that I wanted to be like her. That I wanted her.'

Frank found himself drawn completely to Moonhunter's encounter as she brought his mum to life in front of him. He could see her, imagined he, too, was there at the lakeside, throwing stones and laughing. Moonhunter went on.

'So we quickly became best friends.'

'Lovers,' Frank corrected.

Moonhunter paused, looking on the verge of denying it.

'That came later but, yes, I loved her. I've never stopped.'

She retreated momentarily into her own thoughts.

'You're Jenny?' said Frank. He looked on her, recalling the many stories his gran had told him, about the wild couple of adolescents she harboured like the head of a criminal gang. His mum's best friend. It was Moonhunter that had kicked along with her carefree mother. Moonhunter nodded.

'Genevieve,' she said. 'After my grandmother. 'I've kept it as my middle name. That was us, Becky and Jenny. We were in constant trouble. She had no boundaries. None. And I was happy to follow her wherever she took us. It took me a while to get used to the untamed spark in her soul. The impudent and mouthy vixen that she was. She took no nonsense from or notice of anyone, except your grandmother, most of the time. Whenever we were caught up in the town stealing or being unruly, we'd be hauled back to her house. Becky would tell the authorities we were sisters and, for a time, they believed her, she was that brazen about everything. But your gran didn't seem to mind, she'd let us go anywhere and do anything. Even Governor Jackson came and told us to obey the rules, but Becky didn't live by their rules, by anyone's rules.' She lowered her eyes, locking them on Frank. 'Becky wasn't *like* wildfire, Becky *was* wildfire.'

Again, Moonhunter withdrew into her own thoughts. Frank could sense she was replaying each and every misdemeanour in her mind, a calm, reflective smile at the corners of her mouth. 'We had so much fun.'

'So what happened? Something must have changed,' said Frank.

Moonhunter's expression became more reflective.

'My mother became suspicious of what I was up to. I've no idea why she would care. She was usually too preoccupied with her own troubles to care what I was doing. For once in my life I had freedom, a freedom I never knew existed and in the shining light of my blossoming affair with your mother she decided it was time for us to move on. She knew what Becky meant to me and she only wanted to do one thing – break us apart. She'd never known such happiness and she couldn't stand seeing it in me.'

'What did you do?'

'I wished her dead. That's what I did. I wished her gone, gone so that we could be together. I told Becky, the girl with no boundaries, no rules and she said she'd do anything for me. Anything. Then she left me at your gran's house, told me to stay and she'd sort it all out.'

Frank's heart skipped a beat.

'My mum was going to kill your mum. For you?'

Moonhunter hung her head, then looked back up.

'That's right. I watched her go. Watched her as she walked away from the cottage to end my misery at home.' Frank felt the ice in his bones. Moonhunter watched him pale. 'You don't understand the bond that existed between us, the complete determination not to let the other come to harm.' She paused. 'I would have done the same for her, Frank. I'm sure, looking back, I would have killed someone for Becky.'

Frank's mind went blank. Hearing Moonhunter describe his mum in both the same then very different terms to how his grandmother had spoken about her was a complete revelation.

A pin-sharp picture of the track leading away from his gran's cottage fell into Frank's mind. Of a determined teenage girl, the rebellious beauty that was his mother, striding away towards Moonhunter's house to send her mother to an early grave. He stared through Moonhunter with disbelief.

Despite being sceptical about her over his time at Excelsus he had no doubt that the words on her lips were the truth. How did someone have it in them to even contemplate that? Doubtless he'd do whatever he could to protect his friends, that much had stayed with him from his encounter with Balal, but this was loyalty on a different level.

Moonhunter gave him a moment to digest her words. She scooped up Star and began to stroke her methodically and therapeutically, banishing the memories through her fingertips with each sweep of her palm.

'I know,' she said. 'I couldn't believe it myself at the time, but I'm ashamed to say that I wanted her to do it. My parents were going to leave, take me to goodness knows where and I wasn't old enough to stop them. At that moment I couldn't bear being parted from the one good thing in my life. We told each other we'd never be apart and we meant it. That's when we wrote our promise, the promise to each other that we'd always be together.' She reached to the table at her side and picked up a piece of paper, unfolding it on her lap, revealing the other half of the love letter Frank had shown her before. The same words, different writing. 'It sounds so silly and sentimental now I say it, but I'm sure you'll know about raw, young love.'

She cast him a deliberate look, her turquoise eyes dancing on his. He was sure he wouldn't have done the same for Libby.

Moonhunter got up, discarding her lithe cat onto the arm of the chair. She went to her desk and poured two glasses of water. Frank watched her, less wary than he had been in the past, noticing how calm and relaxed she appeared to be, her slender hands on the pitcher, aware he was looking at her, this woman who guarded a trove of secrets about his mother.

Not all of them, he imagined, were tales he would wish to hear, but he knew she hadn't finished her story, not given what he knew of their journey into the silent forest. She wandered back, handing a glass to Frank and returning to her seat, both hands clasped around her drink, peering into the clear contents, focused, summoning the next chapter from her mind. Frank waited, sensing he didn't need to ask her to continue. Without looking up, she said:

'But things didn't turn out the way I expected.'

74

THE CHANGE

Frank felt himself hold his breath and his skin flare. He couldn't take his eyes off her as, once more, his fascination with her re-ignited, her raw magnetism drawing him in. The look in his eyes told her to go on.

'I waited, went for a walk, waited some more. Your gran and I played cards until it got dark and I ended up sleeping in Becky's bed. Iris didn't seem at all concerned that she hadn't come back.' She made tiny back and forth movements with her hand on the glass, rotating it gently. 'I hardly slept, filled with regret for what I'd asked her to do, even though it was unspoken. Churning thought after thought about my mother; Becky with blood on her hands. Such hideous images haunted me all night and I spent the darkest hours taking it all back, even if I still didn't want to leave.'

'Did she come back?' said Frank.

Moonhunter looked at him, a gentle smile. She nodded.

'I heard her downstairs before the sun rose. I thought she'd come up and tell me what had happened but she didn't, so I got up and went downstairs.' She paused. 'I found her wandering by the lake. I could barely make her out in the dark and when I caught up with her we hugged forever and she told me I didn't need to leave, that I would be able to stay in Rhaeder for as long as I wanted. But there was something different about her. Something I couldn't put my finger on, not at the time, but I knew, instantly, that something had changed.'

Frank was still fixed on the principal, absorbing every syllable as the words tumbled from her mouth. Had his mum actually killed for her girlfriend, the way Moonhunter described the encounter, her felt she might, but his mind kept flicking to Irundi, to Al-Fajr and he knew she couldn't have.

'She told me she hadn't done anything to harm my mother. Even though she admitted she was going to; for me. But there was a look in her eye, not quite faraway, but you know when you have something on your mind and it distracts you, rubs and picks at you in a way that you find it difficult to concentrate on anything else.' Frank nodded, his recent experiences enough for him to totally understand what it was like to have something fill your head that just wouldn't go away. 'At first I thought it was something to do with me. Although I'd not actually asked her to do anything to hurt my mother, I couldn't help thinking she was angry with me, or blamed me in some way for getting her to do it. But it wasn't that at all.'

Moonhunter paused, like she'd run out of words, as if she was already weary from recounting the whole episode. She played with her glass again, lifting it to her lips and taking gentle, measured sips. She looked around the room and sucked on her lips.

'Go on,' said Frank, urging Moonhunter to finish what she'd started.

'I kept asking her, but she kept telling me nothing was the matter and she was just tired. She told me to go home and ask my mother about something called the Simbrian. I'd not heard the word before. So she went to bed and I went home, not knowing what I might find.'

'Was she alright, your mother?'

'I could barely open the front door, such was my fear of what I'd be walking into. I wondered if Becky was telling me everything was alright just to save me from the truth, that she had killed her. I wondered if I'd find the house empty but there she was, preparing breakfast and...and singing. I'd never heard her sing, not in all my years but there she was, singing.' Moonhunter let out a laugh, as if she was seeing the scene for the very first time. 'She had the voice of a lark and when she saw me she hugged me so tight she squeezed the

342

breath out of me and a light danced in her eyes, a light I'd never seen before. Then she cried. Just held me and sobbed so hard I thought she'd never stop but once she did we sat down. That's when I asked her and that's when she told me.' Moonhunter stared into her water, into a world she had all but forgotten.

'Told you what?' said Frank.

He realised he had perched himself right on the edge of his chair, all sound cut out except the unravelling story that Moonhunter spilled at his feet.

'The family curse she called it.' Her tone had changed, more serious, like a cold, dark hand from the past had gripped her by the shoulder and pulled her into its unsavoury embrace.

'The Simbrian?' Frank hadn't needed to ask as Moonhunter nodded back at him.

'She told me all about it, about her passionate desire to protect me from it and how it had totally ruined her life and that of her mother and those that had gone before. I didn't believe her at first; who would? It seemed so made up, so fanciful. You would know.'

Frank nodded, turning his mind over at how the conversation must have gone.

'But it explained everything,' said Moonhunter. 'In that moment, my entire existence made complete sense. My life on the wind, living in fear of something unknown, always running. The Simbrian, its power, its temptation. She lived in daily terror that those who had always sought it would one day knock on her door. A visit from death that would leave me without a mother. She loved me, her only child, and would do absolutely anything to protect me.'

'I don't understand,' said Frank. 'What has this got to do with my mum?' Moonhunter paused.

'She told all of this to Becky. The whole story of the Simbrian; of how our family were one of seven, how it came into being with Kester and how throughout the whole of its existence, ruthless and power-hungry individuals had wished to seek out each one and possess the power for themselves and how this had kept us running for all of our lives. And that the possession of it would one day pass to me.'

Frank still couldn't quite grasp the end of the delicate thread that she had spun. Moonhunter caught the confused look on his face.

'You see, Frank. After my mother had laid it all out Becky gave her a proposition, one that she knew she'd jump at.' Moonhunter's eyes widened. 'She offered to take on her part of the Simbrian.'

'She did *what?*' Frank just stared back at her, unable to blink.

'She said to my mother that she would become the guardian. That she should transfer the guardianship to her.' She swallowed. 'To set me free.'

Frank had no words. A cold shiver shot through his body. Nothing could have prepared him for this.

He got up but found he couldn't move his feet. He wrapped his arms around himself, searching for answers to questions he didn't even have yet. His dad *and* his mum; both guardians? How was that even possible? Moonhunter stood, but kept her distance.

'Perhaps you should sit back down, Frank,' she said. 'There's more.'

75

THE OBSESSION

Frank stared at her. More. What more? How much more? Whatever Moonhunter had to offer him, he wasn't sure his head was clear enough to absorb anything else. It felt like his brain was beyond full, yet he sat back down, feeling the soft cushions hold him down against his will, ready for Moonhunter's next revelation. He held her gaze, preparing himself.

'I said that she was different, after she came back that night,' Frank nodded as Moonhunter's tranquil, mellow tone started to soothe him. 'She was never the same again. She became increasingly distracted. I could tell there was something constantly on her mind. And our relationship changed. I think that I was different. I should have been grateful for what she'd done but in the days and months that followed I started to experience feelings of guilt, as if I'd made her do something I shouldn't have, even though I knew she'd done it of her own free will. For us.'

Moonhunter's eyes shifted, became momentarily sad, distant.

'There was something on her mind that she wouldn't tell me. We'd told each other everything up until then, had no secrets and I became so jealous of whatever she was hiding.' She flexed her hands and balled them into fists. 'My mother allowed me to spend as much time as I wanted at the cottage and when I stayed over I'd wait until Becky was asleep and read her mind.' Frank felt his eyes widen. Moonhunter appeared to notice. 'I know. I'm not proud, Frank. But it began to eat me up. It had been just the two of us for so long that it felt like she was being unfaithful, if only in her head.'

'You can read minds,' said Frank.

He said the words in a near whisper, as though he only meant to think them. His mind was immediately taken back to the hunt for the Kzarlac spy, the near-invisible marks that had appeared on his temples, marks that Moonhunter had recognised. He thought about it – of course she could do that. He cleared his throat to banish the memories. 'What did you find out?'

'Her head was completely full of the Simbrian. Clear thoughts, sharp images. Obsession. Thoughts that had started to consume her, took her to new places. She was wondering who the other guardians were, about Everbleed's prophesies. How to create it. I knew in a second that the Simbrian, its legend and its power, had seized her completely but that was as far as I got.'

She screwed up her nose and looked through Frank.

'What do you mean?'

From what he now knew of their relationship he thought that Moonhunter would have as much opportunity as she wanted to extract all the information she wanted from his mum.

'She knew I'd done it,' said Moonhunter. 'Knew I'd read her mind. She didn't say so, but when I tried again she'd already learned how to shield, to block her thoughts from me.' She lifted a finger towards Frank. 'That would explain how you were able to block whoever was trying to get inside your head, Frank. You seemed to have inherited that aspect of your mother's gifts. But it was a gift she learned overnight. One day she couldn't, the next day she could. No one does that. Certain skills take time to learn. Becky had no right to be able to do that.'

'Unless she already could.'

'You mean she let me in? Let me see what she was planning?'

'Planning? What was she planning?'

'I don't know. All I know is that she changed. She was the same wild, sweet thing I'd always known but it was as if a switch had been turned on inside her head.' Moonhunter hesitated, as if she was searching for the right words. 'Looking back, I can see that my mother was just the start. I think Becky wanted to find all the guardians. I think that's what she set out to do.'

Frank could feel himself shaking his head as he searched for a reason why anyone in their right mind would want to embark on such a ridiculous task, or know where to start.

'You don't realise what sort of person she was.' Moonhunter's voice broke slightly. 'I sometimes find her difficult to describe. Yes, she was so very gifted. She'd do silly little things. She's the one who changed the colour of my hair.' Moonhunter smiled as she sifted the blue and pink of her long locks through her fingers. An unwanted reflex had Frank touching the side of his own head. *No orange streak.* 'But...' She searched for the words. 'But she was...complex.'

She paused, like an artist stopping to regard the picture they'd created. 'Becky had some amazing abilities. I have, but they were nothing compared to what she wielded. She was both angel and demon. Light and dark. She could be ruthless and scheming one minute, warm and tender the next. There was this black, unholy side to her that she kept leashed, most of the time. I could tell she had a plan, could see it in the fire in her eyes. I asked her what she was doing, but she never told me, said she wanted to protect me and I wasn't to worry or come looking for her if she went away.'

Frank didn't think he could feel any worse than he already did, but Moonhunter's portrayal of his mother had him sinking to new depths. The stories about her from his gran had always been amusing and whimsical but now he was learning that she was also brushed with the breath of midnight, a black tempest beneath her untamed approach to life, a trait that might dwell in him. Moonhunter noticed the change on his face.

'But remember Frank. Remember who your mother was.' She leaned forward, gently grasped the locket that hung around Frank's neck and ran her fingers over the ornate metal fretwork casing. She pierced him with her hypnotic eyes. 'Around your neck is everything you are.' She recited the words like a mantra before letting go. Frank broke her stare. 'I don't know what it means, but if you have a tenth of the talent that Becky had, then there's something inside you.

Something powerful.' She reached out a slender hand and touched Frank's chest. 'You don't realise. It's in there, Frank. It sleeps. And there will come a time when you will awaken it.'

As she touched him he felt the wind leave him and a softly spoken word echoed in his head. A strange yet familiar word, uttered by an unfamiliar voice. Like he'd never heard it before but knew its deep and profound meaning. He'd heard something when he'd been touched by Edwina Chetto, and again by Sapphire Hark, but the clarity with which it resonated made him close his eyes and an image of his mum appeared in his head, felt her magic clasping at his shoulder.

Absolatum. She spoke the words to him clearly and precisely. *Absolatum.*

He opened his eyes, unsure what had just passed between them. Moonhunter looked at him, a question on her face, but Frank didn't answer. Her comment had made him uneasy, wondering what she meant, what might be lying dormant inside, ready to unleash its own brand of hell on the world. It wasn't something he wanted to think about right now, he knew he needed more from Moonhunter.

'So what happened,' he said. 'After you found out about her obsession with the Simbrian?'

Moonhunter drew in a long breath.

'We were still close, but things were never the same between us. Our relationship drifted, like most teenage romances. Then she met your dad and she moved on. I could see that she'd fallen for him and I couldn't bear it.' She picked at her fingernail. 'I wanted to leave but my parents stayed. Eventually, they split up. My mother left and I haven't seen her since. To be honest, I don't care where she is.' Frank's mind filled with an image of the quiet woman in solitude in Irundi, but he said nothing. 'I'm not sure what was worse, taking me away from Becky, or taking Becky away from me. Either way, I couldn't stand being in the same room as her, to keep me from harm she'd taken away the one thing I wanted and I still can't forgive her.'

'Did you and my Mum ever talk about it, the Simbrian? Or

what she was going to do?'

'No, never. I didn't feel I could talk to her about it, not after what she'd done. Done to save me. I felt too guilty. She kept me from the bitterness of one day being a guardian, but being without her was far worse. She'd laid a whole different curse on me without realising. Then, one day, Becky without saying goodbye, like I thought she would. Looking back I should have read the signs in the days leading up to it.' Moonhunter's palm opened and her fingertips ran gently over the writing on the page, as if the tender touch reminded her of something else. 'I never saw her again.' She paused, allowing the pain in her veins to leach out. 'I understand she went to Kzarlac and Dagmar somehow ended up with our part of the Simbrian but I don't know how or why. Becky was so determined to guard it with her life.' She stopped, biting her lip, looking like she had something she wanted to say, but didn't quite know how. Frank just looked at her, hoping his silence would be enough to draw it out. 'I think Dagmar might have had something to do with her death,' she said.

'My dad always told me she died in an accident.'

A shake of the head from Moonhunter. He burned at his dad. More lies. He burned at not knowing. Moonhunter appeared to sense his anger.

'Don't be hard on him, Frank. Your mum adored him. When she met him, they were inseparable. I was terribly jealous but she gradually became more absorbed in him, and the Simbrian. I didn't believe what we had was just an adolescent crush. It was more than that. She was my world, not that my world was ever very colourful or filled with excitement, but she was.' More sadness in her eyes. 'It took me a very very long time to get over her.' She looked at herself in the mirror. 'And it never really goes away.' A silent tear rolled down her cheek. She opened her mouth to speak, but her breath caught on her emotions. 'And I realise that if I'd never met her, if I hadn't wandered down to the lake that day she'd be alive today and you would have grown up with your mum, like every child deserves. Needs.' She could barely contain the raw, unfettered quavering in her voice. 'I don't expect you can ever forgive me.'

She dipped her eyes to Frank's chest and took his locket in her hand, once more. She let go, lifted her hand to her mouth and brushed her lips over her fingertips, her eyes closing at the feeling, breathing in the long lost, but not forgotten, scent of timeless love. Tears welled in her eyes, quelling all other thoughts in Frank's mind.

He felt his chest tighten at the sight of the strong, confident woman he'd experienced at Excelsus as her emotions frayed. She looked as if the last few minutes had knocked every ounce of joy from her and it was never going to return. As she gripped her own face in an attempt to hide her tears from Frank, he leaned forward and, without a thought, wrapped his arms around her and hugged her.

They shared something, shared a loss. For all his time being wary and guarded about the beautiful head of the academy, a different feeling washed through him. Compassion for the teenage girl who still stood gripped in the fist of the passionate tornado that was his mother, who had tried but failed to overcome the loss she felt and the feeling that it was all her fault. There was no anger, no ill-will, no judgement. Just understanding.

76

THE UNEXPECTED LINE

Cas, Gabby and Anya listened in complete silence on the walk over to his gran's cottage as Frank recounted every detail of his conversation with Moonhunter, careful to give them everything. No omissions. With Gabby's support he filled the others in on his relationship with Dagmar, not keeping count of the times he apologised for his behaviour and off-handedness over the past few weeks.

As he suspected, neither Cas nor Anya laid any judgement on him, they offered sympathetic words and easy silence, clearing away any last splinters in their fractured friendship that he'd caused earlier in the summer. Although he knew they could never fully understand the depth of the waves he'd been riding since he'd found the truth about his life, sharing his problems with those closest to him, with those he knew truly cared and would always be there for him, brought him some peace.

What they'd all been through over the last few weeks was enough to test the resolve of the most fiercely loyal of warriors. Yet here they were, all four of them. Together. Bruised. Marked by their experience. But together. Frank looked at their tired faces and felt the breeze of friendship swirl around him. He couldn't reconcile this with how stupid and selfish he'd been. How his moods and petulance had nearly driven an irreversible wedge between them, but they'd survived him and had accepted him for who he was, not what he was. It was too much to ask, but they were his friends and he now knew it would take far more than that to sever the bond they had forged since they had embarked on the quest to protect the Simbrian.

They'd identified six of the seven guardians. The six that

Dagmar already knew about, whose fragments of the unbreakable power he had already assembled in his secret chamber, unseen in Alsha Kar. Wordsworth Hums, Montrose Menetti, Edwina Chetto, Sapphire Hark, his dad and Moonhunter had all been stripped of their birthrighe in one way or another. All had been either caught, killed or betrayed to fuel Etamin and Dagmar's thirst to dominate the world.

They'd all paid some sort of price and, soon, the world would feel the weight of the price tag if Dagmar could finish the job he'd been so proficiently and effectively pursuing. There was only one more to find. One. They had to stop him. And at least they knew as much as Dagmar, maybe more. After all, they had the key of darkness.

Although there was no definite proof that Moonhunter's piece was now with Dagmar, Frank could feel it in his bones. His mum had gone from Moonhunter, to his dad, to Dagmar and on to goodness knows who or what else. Wildfire. That's how Moonhunter had described her. Wildfire.

She'd sought Dagmar out, had a sexual relationship with him, knowing what he pursued with venom, that he wreaked death and destruction across the border to find, and took a fragment of the Simbrian right into the hornet's nest. The question hung in front of him, but beyond arms-length, out of reach – why hadn't she run from him?

It was unfathomable how he was tied in to all of this. The creeping death that was the puzzle of the Simbrian was all over his skin. His dad, his mum. Why, when he had stumbled on this mystery completely by accident, was he beginning to think that might not be the case at all.

***

They arrived at the brow of the hill and stopped, looking down the shallow valley to the lake and the small, lonely cottage. Frank stopped, images of his mum and Moonhunter as teenagers, walking arm in arm by the cool, still water entered his mind. Moonhunter's words were still fresh. The emotion she'd shown, the absolute bond she'd had with his mum was still difficult for him to absorb but he found himself smiling as he imagined them both tearing up the neighbourhood and retuning to the lake like two young outlaws.

Iris greeted them with her customary gruffness, shooing them out the back to the shores of the lake. The soothing green landscape and the tranquil water brought back a welcome normality, washing away any lingering blemishes from the silent forest and bringing a brightness that had been absent during the past few weeks.

Cas stood skimming stones, while Anya sat slowly sharpening the dagger that had brought Morrin down. Iris joined them with a jug of limewater and five glasses, Ingozi panting at her side, and sat in silence as they listened to the plink-plink of stones on the water and the smooth sound of steel on the whetstone. Iris began to pour the drinks.

'I didn't know you knew Aurora Moonhunter,' said Frank. Iris gave him a sharp look.

'I don't.'

'Yes you do, and she knew Mum.'

Iris stopped pouring and turned her head.

'She what?' Her brow creased and her eyebrows met in the middle.

'She knew Mum.'

'I don't think so.'

'She was her best friend.'

'Jenny?'

Frank nodded.

'I only found out yesterday, but the G stands for Genevieve – Jenny.' Iris thought for a second and just shrugged.

'Who'd have thought it,' she said with a sniff, like she couldn't give a damn. 'She tell you much?'

'A bit. From what I'm beginning to learn, Mum was more than just clever, gran.' Iris hmphed and pulled her skirt up over her knees. Frank thought she might enlighten him but was met with silence.

'Moonhunter said there was no one else even close to her abilities.' Iris shrugged, took up a glass and a mouthful of limewater, her eyes looking out over the lake, distant. Frank wasn't about to ask about what she knew of his mum's Simbrian connections, or where she went after her obsession grabbed her, so he thought of a softer tack, one that might be a pathway to the bigger subject. 'So why didn't she get an invite to the academy?' It was a question that had crossed his mind in the aftermath of his meeting with Moonhunter. He could see that Moonhunter would have dodged an invitation due to her nomadic existence, but not his mum. 'You don't live that far away from the town and you know Governor Jackson.' Iris let out a grunt. Deep down Frank knew there was something he wasn't getting. Iris continued to stare stoically across the water. 'Gran?' She pursed her lips.

'I would have turned it down,' she said. 'Rebecca wouldn't have wanted to go.'

'That's not what I asked,' said Frank. He glanced at Gabby who looked on with interest. He sensed his gran turn unusually quiet. She looked down, eyes focused on the ground. 'So why didn't she get an invitation?'

She looked up at Frank then, without any further words, she rolled up the sleeves of her frayed and shabby old cardigan, the one she wore like a second skin. The piece of clothing that had been her constant companion ever since Frank had known her. She always wore one, always with the sleeves down, even on the fiercest summer's day.

It was as if the ink on her arms had jumped up and grabbed Frank by the throat. He was beyond words as he watched his aged grandmother run her fingers gently across her skin, tracing the contours of the familiar markings, the same marks that he'd seen a hundred times on Gabby's body, delicate stems of roses, bedecked with faded thorns and entwined with daisies. Prismian tattoos. Gabby gasped, drawing the attention of Cas and Anya who stopped what they were doing and looked over.

Iris looked at herself with unfocused eyes, absently tracing the lines.

'Red roses for the beauty and blood of the Prismian martyrs, thorns for the oppression and suffering of the ages, delicate daisies for the new life, the gift of the future and kindness of the people.'

She rolled her sleeves back down. Frank couldn't find the right words. She didn't look up for a moment, but when she did there was, for a mere breath, a fierce resolve in her eyes, a look of sharpened steel jutting from her old features on a level that Frank had not previously seen, despite her inherent brusqueness. She huffed, gathered her arthritic shoulders and stared in silence once again across the water.

That was why. Excelsus didn't invite Prismians, not until a few years ago.

Frank felt Gabby's eyes on him, but he just gawped at his gran, who seemed intent on ignoring him.

'Why did you never tell me?'

He didn't mean to raise his voice but she gave him a sharp look, sensing his trouble at keeping a lid on his temper. Iris gave a shrug and huffed loudly.

'You wouldn't understand,' she said, short as usual.

'Why don't you try us,' said Gabby, the hard edge to her voice catching Iris. 'Frank's had enough secrets to last him for the rest of his life, the least he deserves is for you to tell him.'

She cornered the old woman with her words. Gabby's look to Frank was of sweet camaraderie, of solidarity of someone who was there for him, who understood what had battered his emotions and who stood shoulder to shoulder with him in his attempt to claim his life back. His smile to her was filled with affection and admiration. She smiled the same sentiment right back at him.

Iris looked at the four faces. Anya and Cas were also unflinching in their silent demand. She drew in a breath, her face covered in reluctance.

'Very well,' she said, then looked deeply into Frank's eyes. 'No one understood the problems of being descended from her. To be her only living descendent created attention from all sorts in Prismia, so I decided to leave.' She screwed her face up and hunched her shoulders. 'All those bloomin' people thinking they own you, that you're something to be gawped at. Like I was some sort of freak in a travelling circus. Well, I told them where to put their big noses, and I wasn't going to let it affect Rebecca. When I came here, found this place in the middle of nowhere, it all went away and I could go about my business without anyone even looking in my direction.'

She nodded to herself, but there was a simple, unanswered question.

'From who, gran. Who are you descended from?'

Iris leaned forward, her face close to Frank's and whispered.

'Everbleed. We're descended from the greatest seer ever to have lived.'

There was no joy in her voice as she spoke, no sunshine or elegance in her words. Instead she spoke like it was a curse, like the way Sapphire Hark had talked about her family's guardianship of their fragment of the Simbrian, something that blighted their existence. All sound was cut from the lakeside.

'Are you absolutely kidding?' said Gabby.

The look of granite on Iris's face told them she wasn't.

'It's not something anyone ever needed to know,' she said. 'Not even now.'

'But...Everbleed,' said Anya. 'I learned so much about her at the academy.'

'Huh. Don't believe everything that bloomin' place tells you,' snapped Iris. 'Thinking they own me. Re-writing my history.'

Her stony face hardened even more and she pulled her cardigan tighter.

'Why didn't you tell me?' said Frank.

'What, and have you know you're the end of the line? What good would that have done you?' Her voice showed no signs of tempering. 'Everbleed's blood is complicated. I should know.'

'So Mum never got her tattoos done?' said Frank.

'That's right. Not here, not in Byeland. No one would have known where she was from just by looking at her, but Jackson knew.' She huffed. 'I would have told him where to stick his invitation, anyway.'

An image of the self-serving head of Byeland Council and his smug-faced grandson entered Frank's mind, raising the heat in his blood. He had their book, knew their secrets, *his* secrets and he flared at the thought of him knowing his family's heritage.

His life's roadmap had taken several wrong turns in the past few months but, even though he could have been annoyed by his gran's secret, there was something about her revelation that he was, in part, Prismian that made him feel better about himself.

He'd been carrying the curse of his Kzarlac parentage for months and it had torn into him like a pack of wild dogs and preyed on his teenage temper so much that he hadn't been able to control it. It had dominated his thoughts, clung to him like a parasite and made him difficult to be around. He also knew it and knew his friends hadn't deserved to continually walk the tightrope of his irritation but the revelation about his Prismian heritage brought some light to his shade.

Iris got up. She looked annoyed with herself, as if she'd given something away and regretted it or that baring something that she'd kept so close had unleased emotions she'd kept in check for such a long time.

'I've got things I need to be getting on with,' she said, an unconvincing air of an excuse to leave them in her voice. 'You kids go and have some fun. Don't let life get too serious and don't worry about where you've come from, just concentrate on where you're going.'

77

THE PERFECT BLOODLINE

They watched her retreat to the cottage and close the door behind her. Part of Frank was sorry that they'd made her tell them, but knowing about his Prismian connection provided a bit of balance to him. He hadn't yet got used to the idea of Dagmar's blood flowing in his veins and, if Zachery was to be believed, some of Joleyon's, but to have Mildred Everbleed dwelling within him made him feel slightly invincible. Okay, he didn't have any of her talents, but he was aware that just the feeling of something special could make you different. That the ghost of someone so significant and influential could give him wings.

'You should get your tattoos done,' said Anya. 'I'll come with you.'

'So will I,' said Cas. 'Just to see how much you squeal.'

Frank laughed with them but Gabby didn't. The look in her eyes detached, looking in on herself. The other three stopped laughing and Frank looked on as Gabby's face dropped, a jaded shadow like he'd never seen before. She stared at him, stared like he'd turned into something else, something he didn't want to be. Her chestnut eyes lay anchored to his, her soft lips slightly apart as if she couldn't get her words to form properly behind them.

'Frank. No,' she said, lifting her hand slowly and covering her mouth, like she didn't want any other words escaping from it.

Frank shook his head, laying a concerned look on her which she mirrored. An awkward silence, unseen but heavy, jammed itself between them. There was something she'd understood, something he hadn't, something she'd only needed a moment to work out.

Gabby got up and for a moment he swore she backed away from him, but checked herself. He looked at the agitation that swept her troubled face, afraid to ask her a question that he didn't want the answer to.

'A child from the dark and the light. The one that completes the circle,' she uttered in a near whisper, as if she'd only meant herself to hear the words. 'The one that completes the circle.'

She looked up, she opened her mouth but the words stalled in her throat as she looked at him through glassy eyes. Silence held them, none of them able to speak. Gabby's face was fixed on him, though he felt she was trying her best not to look elsewhere, that there was something on her lips she was about to say that would change everything.

She looked at Cas and Anya, as if trying to draw support for something, but they looked as perplexed as Frank. 'It's you Frank,' she said, eyes dancing on the floor, then back to him. The words bit him and he felt a bolt of cold travel from his head to his feet. Tears welled in his eyes as he breathed in her distress. Again Gabby looked at Cas and Anya 'Esryn said the prophesy referred to someone specific, someone with the perfect bloodline. From each of their foremost families – Joleyon, Lashka, Everbleed, your ancestors are from Byeland, Kzarlac – the dark and the light, and Prismia. Prismia completes the circle. From the first day of the Simbrian. The circle. It's you, Frank, the last in Everbleed's line. It can't possibly be anyone else. You're the Simbrian heir.'

Her words struck him hard. Irundi had it wrong. All this time and they had it wrong, they weren't tracking the whole picture. Three bloodlines, not two. The perfect bloodline.

Frank couldn't move. He didn't even try to contradict her, to tell her her reasoning was askew as her words sunk in and trapped him where he stood.

It couldn't be true. He was just Frank Penny, simple Frank Penny the farm boy from Smithwood; ordinary, nothing special, the boy who had mistakenly been invited to Excelsus academy who had no talent, no gift, nothing to offer. That wasn't the silhouette of someone destined to be the Simbrian heir.

All along they'd thought it was De Villiers, knowing she was Etamin's child. She was much more likely to fill the shoes of someone so unique. From the dark and the light. Those that had waited centuries to uncover the heir believed it was her. But all the signposts pointed to something more fundamental; the Simbrian heir wasn't something that could be engineered, couldn't be forced on the world or conjured by the loathsome ultramancer. It wasn't something that the vulgar abilities possessed by the exceptional and powerful Etamin Dahke could bend to her will. The heir couldn't just be created, its existence was celestial, otherworldly as if he had been summoned centuries before, like he had existed in all the lives of his ancestors within whom he lived and breathed until the day, this day, when his destiny came knocking at his reluctant door.

'You know I'm right, Frank.' He didn't answer. 'And you know what this means.'

All of a sudden it dawned on him that the remaining Simbrian guardian wasn't the person they needed to keep safe. It was him. They'd find out and come looking for him. He would have to evade Dagmar and Etamin. His life and the lives of everyone he'd ever met, and hadn't met, depended on him keeping out of the hands of his bitter adversaries.

'It means,' choked Gabby, fighting back tears. 'It means...it means...'

She couldn't make the words, couldn't cross the void. Frank held his hands up and nodded, an image of his real father pressed itself to the front of his mind. His real father, Dagmar Dag and himself, the son Dagmar didn't know existed. His only son. He stared into Gabby's eyes, his mind recalling the prophesy as the realisation hit home.

'Dagmar's going to have to kill me.'

The story concludes with ...

Frank Penny and the Rise of the Red Flame

Lightning Source UK Ltd.
Milton Keynes UK
UKHW020625190822
407545UK00009B/943

9 781739 661304